Philip Kerr was born in Edinburgh in 1956 and now lives in London with his wife and family. His last four novels, including *The Second Angel*, are in development for film.

By the same author

A Five-Year Plan
Esau
Gridiron
Dead Meat
A Philosophical Investigation
A German Requiem
The Pale Criminal
March Violets

The Second Angel

PHILIP KERR

ORION

An Orion Paperback
First published in Great Britain by Orion in 1998
This paperback edition published in 1999 by
Orion Books Ltd,
Orion House, 5 Upper St Martin's Lane,
London WC2H 9EA

A CIP catalogue record for this book
is available from the British Library.

ISBN 0 75282 622 0

Typeset by Deltatype Ltd, Birkenhead, Merseyside

Printed and bound in Great Britain by
Clays Ltd, St Ives plc

For Caradoc King,
with gratitude and affection

And the second angel poured out his vial upon the sea; and it became as the blood of a dead man.

Revelation 16:3

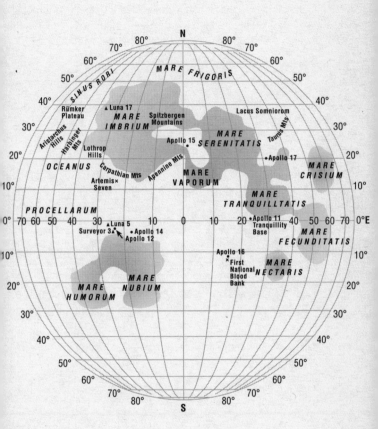

LUNAR MAP

PROLOGUE

I

IT WAS ANOTHER bright, cold day on the Moon and the atomic clocks were flashing three hundred. Three hundred and twenty-four hours is the length of a lunar-equatorial day, which means that one day on the Moon is worth two full weeks on Earth. Few if any of the people working in Artemis Seven, a penal cave-mining colony, would have agreed with this value. For time passes slowly in a penal colony, especially a hard-labor facility operating in the constant, artificial light of an air-tight underground lunar cavern at minus twenty degrees Celsius.

The penal colony was in a cavern under the overhanging lip of a large crater in the Moon's Carpathian foothills. Ten miles long, two to three hundred yards wide and almost as high, it held more than three thousand men and women, all of them convicted of a variety of felonies, from simple theft to premeditated murder. The shortest sentence was five years, and the longest, fifteen. There were no lifers in Artemis Seven. Hard time in a lunar colony is considered sufficient punishment for all but the most heinous crimes.

Seen through the dust-covered windows of Artemis Seven, the vibrant Earth's blue and white sphere contrasted sharply with the lifeless gray surface of the Moon. It almost seemed to have been placed there, like a bunch of purple grapes forever out of reach, to torment those being punished, [as in the story of Tantalus –] a constant reminder of the full extremity of their exile.

None paid Earth more attention than Cavor, sentenced to a ten-year exile. His life back home had been better than most of those who worked alongside him. When he wasn't looking at Earth's bright blue eye and dreaming about his former terrestrial life, he was staring at the flashing green digits of the lunar clock and thinking about his next rest period. Cavor was halfway through his thirteenth eight-hour shift, and had one more shift to work before his next scheduled seventy-two-hour rest period. He was operating a rock crusher, a solar-powered machine that begins the process whereby helium is extracted from Moon rock, when the voracious unit caught the dusty sleeve of Cavor's thermal coat and pulverized his right arm. One moment he had been looking forward to his rest period and a meal, and the next he was himself being eaten up by the rock crusher. Before another convict managed to turn the machine off and summon help, it had chewed beyond his elbow.[1]

Several convicts carried Cavor from the back of the cavern where he had been working to an electric car

[1] Accidents are common on the Moon. With one-sixth Earth gravity, bodily movements are much slower than machinery and there is less time to rectify any mistakes. Just about the only physical activity enhanced on the Moon is sex. Most people still prefer to have sex slowly, perhaps more now than ever in these frantic modern times in which we live.

which drove him to the infirmary, located close to the colony's unguarded entrance. Security was relaxed in Artemis Seven, with few restrictions placed on convicts other than the requirement that they work. There wasn't any place any of them could go anyway. The infirmary itself was located on an upper level in one of the honeycomb of caves that led off the main cavern. Its metal floor conducted an electrical field that enabled the infirmary to work in almost normal gravitational conditions, but the walls and ceiling were rock, and this meant that when the air-filtration system broke down, as it often did, everything – equipment, instruments, and patients – became covered in a fine layer of moondust. The area smelled strongly of disinfectant, except when the air-filtration system was working, in which case the various pipes and conduits entering the infirmary merely transferred the air from the dining hall, full of cigarette smoke and entomophagic[1] cooking odors.

[1] Following the failure of the Chinese rice harvest in 2005, insects came to be regarded as a major source of nutrition. Naturally there were many countries that always regarded entomophagy as perfectly acceptable; it was only in the West that people were more squeamish about such things. Quite apart from crickets, ants, grasshoppers, grubs, and caterpillars, all containing an abundance of vitamins and proteins, the Chinese developed several new breeds of worms: One of these, a highly nutritious variant of the mealworm, when treated with artificial flavorings such as beef, chicken, or fish, forms the staple diet of many Westerners. However, the Chinese scientists did not stop there: One particular breed of worm, a cross between a silkworm and a mealworm that fed on coca leaves, was found to contain a new kind of protein that had a dramatically stimulant effect. Further research on this particular worm, the breedworm, was taken over by the Chinese military. Consumed in small quantities, the breedworm resulted in an immediate and massive increase in a human being's physical power (especially useful for a physically small people like the

3

In the emergency room, there were two medical personnel on duty, both of them convicts. Raft, the medical officer, helped his nurse, Berger, to cut away the clothing from the badly injured Cavor, and then to lift him onto the flatbed diagnostic scanner. While they waited for Florence,[1] the computer, to begin its clinical examination of Cavor, the two Moon colony medics quickly set about administering a trauma infusion – an admixture of anaesthetics, inotropes, antibiotics, glucose, insulin, and sodium bicarbonate – to stabilize his body functions. But even before Florence had started speaking, Raft saw that Cavor's shapeless arm would have to come off. This was not something he could delegate to Florence. The crude, most physically demanding part of surgery was his. He grimaced, disliking the butchery it entailed. Amputation, the principal mainstay of emergency surgery for centuries, and traditionally used as a desperate and often unsuccessful attempt to preserve life, was, despite vastly improved modern techniques, still a bloody business.

'Peripheral pulses assessed,' announced Florence.

Chinese). In the short term, the breedworm was used by Chinese athletes seeking to increase their performance. And the results were astonishing. In the 2016 Beijing Olympics, the Chinese won 80 percent of all the track and field medals. Since the protein occurred naturally, there was no way of screening athletes for breedworm consumption. It was another ten years before the Chinese government made breedworms available to the world at large. Since then, the World Health Organization's resulting entomophagy program has been highly successful in reducing starvation levels in third world countries by almost half. An entomophagic diet has proven to be suitable for Moon colonists, being a cheap, highly nutritious, and abundant source of food in this difficult environment.

[1] Named after Florence Nightingale.

'Transcutaneous Doppler recordings completed. Thermography, radioactive xenon clearance, and transcutaneous potassium levels all checked. Estimated blood loss, two thousand mills and counting. All radiographs and tomograms indicate elective amputation procedure. You should probably obtain the patient's consent to amputate, if necessary more proximally than you intend.'

'The patient is unconscious, Florence,' sighed Raft. 'I don't think the patient's any more likely to give his consent than he is to whistle a happy tune, do you?'

'If consent is not obtainable, then you should go ahead and amputate the patient's arm, cutting through the humerus just above the deltoid muscle.'

'Thanks for the advice,' grunted Raft.

'I'm marking the site with the laser, Peter. I also recommend you exsanguinate with a tourniquet as soon as possible.'

'You'd better fetch six units of RHH,' he told Berger, as he started to tie Cavor's upper arm.

Berger, a large, strapping woman wearing the same kind of red overalls as Raft, had just started towards the cryoprecipitation room when Florence stopped her with the clearing of an artificial throat.

'Ahem. Just a moment please, Helen,' said the computer. 'Recombinant human hemoglobin may cause this patient some significant problems. According to his records, he's not suffering from any extravascular hemolytic disorders.'

'What's that?' Raft frowned. 'No EHDs? Come on, Florence. You must have made a mistake.'

'Either that or you're just bullshitting us,' snorted Berger. 'Having a laugh at our expense.'

'Helen,' Florence said sternly, 'you know I'm only programmed for white lies. To protect the sensitivities of terminal patients. It is not within me to lie for my own amusement or personal gain.'

'No shit,' said Berger.

'Would you care to see a biosynthetic profile of his blood group antigens?' Florence asked calmly.

'Look, Florence, those records are probably fake,' suggested Raft. 'On Earth, people go to considerable lengths to forge their blood tests. For obvious reasons. However, I'm a little surprised to find this kind of thing happening up here. I mean, what's the point? It's not like a negative blood test is going to make any difference in a penal colony.'

'The record is quite genuine, Peter,' insisted Florence. 'Let me explain. Sixteen months ago Cavor had a small injury requiring clinical treatment, during which process he deposited a small amount of blood on the scanner. I tested the sample for clinically significant antibodies and found none. Until now, I was obliged to respect that confidentiality.'

'No P®?' Raft was amazed. 'You've got to be kidding.'

'No P®,' confirmed Florence. 'Immunohematologically speaking, he's RES[1] Class One.'

'Jesus.'

'Now there's a novelty,' said Berger.

Raft glanced at Cavor's deathly pale face and shook his head wearily. He said, 'Florence? It's RHH or nothing for this guy. If there was any other blood component we could use, we'd use it. But there's no question of using real blood here, even if we had such a thing. You know that. So the bottom line is that he'll

[1] The immune system of humans consists of a number of organs and different cell types that have evolved to recognize non-self antigens. The most ubiquitous immunologic cell, tissue, and organ system is called the reticuloendothelial system (RES).

probably die right here on this flatbed if he doesn't get a transfusion of the usual shit.'

Florence stayed silent as Raft finished applying the tourniquet.

'I'll fetch those RHH units,' said Berger, as she left the emergency room.

'At least this way, he'll get to live,' Raft shrugged. 'Who knows how much longer? Ten. Maybe even twenty years. Me, I've had it for the best part of ten years, with very few ill effects.'

Pushing an infusion computer in front of her, Berger came back through the door in a swirl of gritty Moon dust. The nurse enjoyed her work. You earned fewer credits than you did crushing rocks all day, but medical work was more interesting, and certainly more satisfying. She set up the machine next to the flatbed scanner, drew out the cannulae assembly, and let it attach itself automatically to Cavor's good arm. The computer croaked like a large frog as it made its own tourniquet, swabbed Cavor's skin, and then inserted the infusion needle.

'I wonder how he escaped getting it for so long?' mused Raft.

'Maybe he comes from a rich family,' suggested Berger.

'RHH warming to thirty-seven degrees,' reported the infusion computer. 'Filtration removing synthetic debris. I'm ready when you are.'

Berger flicked a switch to initiate the infusion process, and the RHH began to snake round the transparent plastic tube entering Cavor's arm. To look at, the dark red liquid was indistinguishable from healthy human blood.[1] It could keep you alive, but it

[1] In the early part of the twenty-first century, advances made in the field of genetic manipulation produced recombinant technology.

could also kill you. She stroked Cavor's forehead for a moment and adding a note of weary resignation to her smoky voice, said, 'Sorry, friend.'

'Sorry my ass,' said Raft. 'You can't feel sorry for a statistical freak. In this place, he was bound to get it. Sooner or later.'

He could feel no sympathy for his patient's immune system while the more pressing problem of completing the amputation successfully was still before him, and with his scalpel, he divided Cavor's upper-arm muscles with a raking incision that went right down to the bone. More blood spurted from the incision, spilling onto the floor, and Raft shook his head at the waste of such a precious resource. With a fluid ounce of quality-assured whole blood costing around half as much as gold,[1] he reckoned he was stepping into and out of a pool that was worth several thousand dollars. Probably more.

The successful manufacture of recombinant DNA was followed by the development of recombinant human hemoglobin. RHH is a polymorphic or universal red-cell blood substitute – a synthetic blood that could be infused into a patient regardless of his or her blood type. Pioneered by the U.S. military for use in the field, RHH involved the creation of completely novel red cells by the combination of unrelated red cells. Red cells were able to replicate independently of a host organism by means of a vector, or cloning vehicle. The vehicle chosen was an apparently harmless form of the parvovirus. No one could have foreseen that the virus chosen would, through a combination of factors, mutate into the much more deadly form of the virus P^2 and the RHH would become one of P^2's main reservoirs of infection.

[1] The latest World Association of Blood Banks (WABB) has priced one liter of RES Class One whole blood, containing a standard 25×10^{12} healthy red cells, at \$1.48 million. Cavor, an average-sized male, would have a total blood volume of about five liters. This means that if all the blood in his body could have been transfused, it would have been worth \$7.4 million.

For the next thirty minutes, Raft carefully followed Florence's gently worded prompts, severing the narrowest part of Cavor's humerus with a laser saw that simultaneously ligated all the major blood vessels. When the amputation was complete, he wiped the sweat from his brow and stepped back.

'With all that healthy blood in him, I'm amazed he's managed not to get himself killed. There are plenty of bastards in this place who would cheerfully have cut his throat for a complete change of blood.'

Berger removed the severed limb from the flatbed scanner.

'Me included,' she said. 'Only the blood's no good without the right drugs. And so long as they're banned from all Moon colonies, what would be the point of killing him?'

Raft nodded. 'I guess you're right. But back on Earth I'd have been sorely tempted to drain off a couple of healthy liters before giving him the RHH.' He shrugged off the thought. 'I wonder what he did to end up here? Instead of a private jail like the rest of his RES class.'

It was Florence, the computer, who answered him.

'Prisoner-patient Cavor. Sentenced to ten years' hard labor on Artemis Seven without benefit of parole for the brutal murder of his wife. She just happened to be the daughter of an important city official. He has already served four years of his sentence.'

'Well I guess this should help him work his passage back home,' reflected Raft. 'There's not much hard labor you can do with a prosthetic arm. Even the ones they can fit these days take time to build strength.'

'Are you going to fit it yourself?' asked Berger.

Raft pulled down the nerves on the stump of Cavor's arm gently and then shortened them by a couple of centimeters so that they could retract more easily into the depths of the severed flesh.

'Tried it before and it didn't take. Good hemostasis is almost impossible with all this lousy dust around. Any hematoma in the stump predisposes to infection, which will only delay prosthetic fitting. No, he'll have to go to the PD hospital[1] in an open prison back on Earth, and as soon as possible too. The earlier a false limb is applied, the more likely it is that the prosthetic computer will take to the nerve ends.'

'Prepare to release tourniquet,' said Florence.

Only when he was satisfied that the stump was adequately supplied with blood did Raft attempt to control the bleeding again; and having doubly ligated the major vessels and applied synthetic flesh foam to the smaller oozing areas, he inserted a suction drain and closed the skin flaps over the bone using synthetic HFM.[2] Finally, Raft smeared the stump with recombinant centrosome to begin the process of helping attract

---

[1] In compliance with regulations laid down by the World Commission on Accreditation of Healthcare Organizations (WCAHO), the World Center for Applied Microbiology and Research (WCAMR), and the International Institute for Virology (IIV), there are two kinds of hospitals in the modern world. The public health-care system is largely made up of permanent deferral (PD) hospitals, catering to patients considered to be at high risk for infectious disease transmission, and whose blood products disqualify them from ever becoming part of any predeposit autologous donation program. The private health-care system, on the other hand, is based exclusively on so-called crossover hospitals, for patients whose blood products meet all theoretical criteria for use in allogenic (homologous) donation programs: today, in practice there is only autologous donation, involving the donation by the intended recipient of his or her own blood or component for a possible subsequent transfusion; any other transactions involving quality-assured blood are purely commercial.

[2] Human fibrous membrane.

the wound's proto plastic granules to the prosthetic, when eventually it was fitted, and then he applied a compression dressing. When the job was complete he surveyed his work with some satisfaction.

'Not bad,' he said. 'A neat job, even though I say so myself. Thanks for your help, Berger.'

Berger laughed dismissively.

'What about me?' said Florence.

'You too, Florence. Goes without saying.'

'It was a pleasure, Peter,' Florence said in its cool, quiet voice. Although Raft had never said so, the computer's honey-sweet voice reminded him of his mother's.

'Okay, how about giving me some suggestions for chemical aftercare?' he enquired.

'Give me a second to think this over.'

'Make it snappy, Florence. My back is aching. I've been on my feet since two-ninety hours.'

'Okay, here's my suggestion. I suggest that you intravenously implant a medical nanomachine[1] containing a combination of prophylactic antibiotic and painkilling actions. For you, I prescribe that you ingest some glucosamine sulfate.'

'Sounds good to me.'

'Would you like me to prepare the MN for you, Peter?'

'Yes, please, Florence.'

Berger was busy washing the remains of Cavor's arm, prior to preserving it in a sterile polyethylene bag

---

[1] Medical nanomachine. Molecule-sized machines designed for use in the bloodstream or digestive tract. Controlled by a tiny computer, each MN is programmed with a set of objectives that mimic the action of a drug, or a combination of drugs, at a molecular level. Currently these can survive in the body for periods up to seventy-two hours.

cooled with liquid nitrogen. Despite the badly crushed state of the limb there were areas of skin and flesh that might later be used as a safe biological dressing. Nothing on the Moon is ever wasted, least of all in a prison colony like Artemis Seven. While the Moon is a strong industrial economy worth many billions of dollars, there are no indigenous materials except rock and ice, and so everything is recycled.

Florence prepared the nano-sized machine in a saline solution, which Raft drew up into a hypodermic syringe and then injected into Cavor's jugular vein. Raft had hardly looked at Cavor's face: Now, he saw that Cavor was small and thin, and it seemed almost impossible that he could have survived four years of hard labor. If you had informed Artemis Seven's medical officer that the one-armed man lying on the flatbed scanner would turn out to play a key role in the commission of the crime of the century,[1] he would almost certainly have assumed that you were suffering from the sensory abnormalities brought about by some small changes in the colony's artificial atmospheres.[2]

[1] The phrase 'crime of the century' is frequently employed by the more sensationalist sections of the multimedia and has become something of a cliché. What does it really mean? Describing crime in superlatives is ethically problematic. It smacks of celebration, as if the perpetrators are worthy of our approbation and are to be congratulated. That is not my intention with the crime described in this account. Rather I wish to focus on this crime as something uniquely representative of the twenty-first century.

[2] Moon colonies are pressurized to normal atmospheric levels using an admixture of oxygen and helium, the most plentiful element in the universe, except for hydrogen. Helium's isotopes are especially plentiful in Moon rock, the result of billions of years of exposure to solar wind. Cavern-based colonies, like Artemis Seven, are divided into sealed sections, and occasionally, the seals leak. Usually this is not serious enough to cause respiratory problems. But for those in whom the P^2 virus is far advanced, even the

'Florence? When is the next cargo container to Earth?'

'There's one leaving Tranquillity Base this evening.'

'Can he make that?'

'Yes. A transport will leave Artemis in one hour with some prisoners who are being paroled.'

'Lucky bastards. Better book him a place.'

Raft, who had six years of an eight-year stretch to go, ripped off a bloody surgical glove and looked critically at his moist right hand, as if it were all that might separate him from Earth and freedom.

'Prosthetics are pretty good these days,' he said thoughtfully. 'It might just be worth it at that.'

Rameses Gates belted himself tightly down in his seat on the Earth-bound Superconductor,[1] adjusted his seat to the fully reclined position for takeoff, and then drew the neck brace as close around his square chin and cauliflower ears as was comfortable. A three-day, two-hundred-and-thirty-six-thousand-mile flight lay ahead of him, and after that, a short period of detention in an open prison before being released into

---

smallest change in available oxygen levels can cause a condition akin to hyperventilation in which the subject's blood pressure falls, thereby causing him or her to hallucinate.

[1] Much less energy is required in escaping from the Moon's gravity than from Earth's. Rockets are used only by wealthy tourists. Everyone else uses the Tranquillity Base's Space Superconductor, a magnetic field monorail that gently rises some fifty feet from the surface of the Moon for some fifteen miles before the escape velocity of 1.4 miles per second is finally achieved. The Moon has proved to be the ideal environment for transportation that utilizes high-temperature superconductors. On Earth a major problem in the development of anisotropic technology had proved to be the instability of the chemical environment due to moist air, which is, of course, not a problem on the moon.

the so-called community. But first there was the small matter of takeoff. The Superconductor was a lot less comfortable than a rocket, since it created almost unbearable G-forces. Prisoners and animals traveled in a G-compartment that was supposed to be able to withstand 10 G, but they still experienced blood pooling, which often caused unconsciousness and, for those in whom the $P^\circledR$ virus was far advanced, sometimes even death. Gates – who was $P^\circledR$ – had, like everyone else he knew, no way of determining just where he was in the life of the virus; but he had heard that even for those who survived the journey, it was common to feel ill for days afterward. The thought of his impending discomfort, possibly even death, made Gates, like the other dozen men and women waiting to be catapulted back to Earth, irritable and anxious to get started. But there was a delay. A late passenger, the Superconductor computer informed them.

'What kind of a late passenger?' demanded Gates. 'The rest of us have known for weeks we would be traveling today in this goddamn slingshot. Who is it?'

'It's got to be another prisoner,' declared the woman lying alongside Gates. 'Who else would fly this way?'

The woman's name was Lenina. Gates had thought her the best-looking woman on Artemis Seven, but he had never an opportunity to speak to her – until now, when he was feeling too nervous to reply.

'I have no further information at the present time,' said the computer. 'Please be patient.'

'That's easy for you to say,' Gates told the in-flight computer. 'You're not about to experience Newton's Second Law of Motion, with all its delightful physiological side effects.'

'Have you taken your G-pill yet?' the computer parried.

The door opened and two prison guards loaded a G-pod[1] bearing Cavor, and then strapped it to the floor. With the exception of his face visor, the pod enclosed the whole of Cavor's body, concealing the full extent of his injuries. Gates released his neck brace and stretched across Lenina to take a look at Cavor's face. He didn't recognize him.

When the doors were closed again, the superconductor coils in the alloy monorail began to build up the electric current that would send them on their way.

Lenina said, 'They say that if the Superconductor could go slow enough, you could get a great view of TB.[2] So they say. Of course, you'd have to have your head positioned to look out of the window, and there's not much chance of moving a muscle when we take off. They've got a museum of the first Moon landing at TB. You can see the lunar module and the astronauts' footprints. Or so I'm told.'

'Ten K,[3] and counting,' said the computer.

'Is that a fact?'

'I'd sure like to come back and see all that for myself.'

'You would?' Gates glanced nervously out of the moonlit window.

'You nervous?' Lenina shouted over the noise of the current. It was getting louder by the second, like the hum of an enormous and very angry wasp.

'Thirty K and counting.'

'Why should I be nervous?'

'Fifty K and counting.'

[1] Self-contained gravity pod, capable of withstanding 15 Gs, for the transportation of sick and injured people aboard a Superconductor.

[2] Tranquillity Base.

[3] Kelvin. The SI unit of thermodynamic temperature.

'I thought I heard you say you were going to pray. Would you care to hold my hand?'

'Transition temperature,'[1] reported the computer. 'Prepare for takeoff.'

'Thanks, I don't mind if I do.'

Gates took hold of Lenina's hand and found her grip as strong as a robot's. He glanced at her white knuckles and smiled thinly. She sounded cool enough, but the truth was that she was just as nervous as he was.

His eyes flicked to the injured man in the G-pod on the floor. Something was wrong. The face visor was all misted up, as if no air was circulating within the pod. Gates realized right away what was wrong. The stupid bastards who had placed the man there had forgotten to switch on his air supply. If the pod wasn't opened and switched on, he would die of suffocation. There was no time to think about it. Gates ripped off the neck brace and unbuckled his seat belts. Once the Superconductor was in motion, the G-forces would be so great there would be no chance of him moving so much as an eye muscle. It was now or never.

'Are you crazy?' protested Lenina. 'You'll be killed.'

'Please return immediately to your seat,' ordered the computer. 'We will take off in twenty seconds.'

Gates knelt by the G-pod and started to count. He tore open the catches and lifted the pod lid. It was plain to see why he was being sent back to Earth. The man took a deep breath, and to Gates's surprise smiled up at him.

'Thanks,' he croaked.

---

[1] The temperature below which the monorail becomes superconducting is called the transition, or critical, temperature.

'Return to your seat immediately. Ten seconds to takeoff.'

'Don't mention it, Lefty.' Gates switched on the air supply and slammed the pod lid shut again.

'Sit down please. Five seconds.'

Scrambling back to his seat Gates threw himself down on his back and started to buckle up again.

'Crazy bastard,' yelled Lenina.

'Three, two ...'

There was no time for the neck brace. Not even time to finish all the belt buckles. Just enough time to press his head back into the seat and hope for the best. The next moment they were catapulted forward along the ramp. Superconductor trains achieve speeds on Earth of almost three hundred miles per hour. But on the Moon, mass and its gravity do 83 percent less to slow down the body of the Superconductor vehicle. In just a few seconds Gates felt enormous G-forces starting to build as the vehicle's speed increased until they were traveling at several thousand miles an hour. And as the vehicle was hurled off into space at the end of the ramp, the last thoughts of Rameses Gates before blacking out were of the incredible escape velocity displayed on the Superconductor's overhead speed-ometer, the handsome woman lying alongside him, and the passenger with only one arm.

II

It was always a source of fascination, perhaps the original source, imbued in man's consciousness with mystic, even magical importance. A central totem in all early civilizations, important to classical myth, a fundamental aspect of nearly all religions, it remains a recurring image, arguably the most potent image of all. By Roman Catholics it may be regarded with symbolic reverence; by purified Jews, as something defiling and unclean. It is the very incarnation of kinship, but also denotes murder and feud and, as often as not, atonement. It is blood – crimson, viscid, thicker-than-water, continuously circulating blood: the stuff of epic poems, fetish cult, and great drama. A source of power – now, more than ever – and a libation of the gods, blood is the great tree that lives inside us all. But it is much more than merely a metaphor of life, as even those pioneering medical men and women who made blood their life's work came to forget. For centuries, blood has been the largest and the most intensively studied organ of the human body. And yet those who studied it – and understood it best as a matter of red cells traveling three hundred miles during their one hundred and twenty days in circulation – did not carry with them that ancient sense of mystery, the knowledge that blood is life itself. Easily sampled, thoughtlessly spilled, life's blood is both a fluid and a tissue, as red as precious rubies and yet much more valuable.

Strangely, no one treasured it. True, blood was banked, but without any real understanding of the idea, with the term 'blood bank' used generically, as a blood center, a hospital-based transfusion service, or some combination of these. It is only now, toward the end of the twenty-first century, that the precious value of blood can be properly appreciated and understood. Well, almost; the cosmological significance of blood continues to elude most people: It is certain that the mathematics of blood, the numbers inherent in its complex structure, provide perhaps the best evidence for the existence of some kind of Creator.

Take something like the process of coagulation,

which requires the participation of several hemostatic proteins. As many as fifteen coagulation factors are activated via a stepwise series of reactions – each step having its corresponding regulatory anticoagulant factor – which culminate in the formation of a solid fibrin clot; protection against excessive clot formation, or thrombosis, is afforded by a second series of hemostatic proteins, of which plasmin is the most potent, and which form the fibrinolytic system (in its turn, the fibrinolytic system has its own inhibitors to prevent overactivity); plasmin itself needs to be activated from its inactive form – plasminogen – by yet another protein, plasminogen activator. It is hard not to understate the irreducibly complex nature of this system. The ratio of the probability that such a system might come into being by pure chance to the probability that it might not come into being is so enormous that it is almost impossible to find a number large enough to express these odds. However, I think it would approximate to something like the number of red cells that a healthy adult male would produce in a lifetime; given that in one second he produces 2.3×10^6, this number, if represented as a number, would look like this: $70 \times 365 \times 24 \times 60 \times 60 \times 2.3^6$, or about 5×10^{15}.

As Mephistopheles remarks in making his pact with Faust, blood is a juice of the rarest quality.

To return to the rather more mundane level of blood banking, today it is something very different from how it was originally conceived, when the field was dependent upon one relatively simple and selfless act – a healthy person taking the time to share his or her good health with others by donating a pint of blood. The power of blood and its capacity to rejuvenate a human being is first mentioned by Ovid in his account of the *legendary Medea and Aeson, father of Jason.*[1] *When Jason returns from his labors, he finds his father close to death and is persuaded to help renew his life by giving blood, which Medea mixes into a magic brew and then transfuses into the old man's veins, with wondrous effect. But history tells us that the first attempted transfusion took place in 1492, when young priests donated their blood in a vain and misguided attempt to prolong the life of the morally worthless Pope Innocent VIII. He died, of course. The succeeding centuries were witness to many other failed attempts to transfuse blood. John Aubrey describes in his* Brief Lives *how in 1649 Francis Potter, inspired by Ovid, attempted to transfuse the blood of two hens. And in Samuel Pepys's diary entry for November 21, 1667, he describes the first English attempt to transfuse blood into a human being, done by Richard Lower upon one Arthur Coga. Unfortunately the blood of a young sheep was used – Coga washed in the blood of the lamb, so to speak: Coga survived, although other patients, themselves the subject of earlier experiments in France, were not so fortunate. It was largely as a result of these French experiments,*[2] *during which the patients died, that blood transfusions were not attempted again until the nineteenth century,*

[1] See Ovid's Metamorphoses, I, bk. VII. Cf. Herodotus in his account of how a Greek mercenary army in the pay of the Egyptians took the blood of the sons of their enemy Pahnes, mixed it with grape juice, and then drank the mixture to give them strength and courage.

[2] Blood transfusion was also a subject of satire. For example, see Alexander Pope's Essay on Criticism, 1711: 'Many are spoil'd by that pedantic throng, Who with great pains teach youth to reason wrong. Tutors, like Virtuoso's, oft inclin'd By strange transfusion to improve the mind, Draw off the sense we have, to pour in new; Which yet, with all their skill, they ne'er could do.'

when doctors even tried to transfuse patients with milk. Needless to say, they all died, too. It was 1901 before Karl Landsteiner described the ABO blood group system that made transfusions theoretically possible, and the latter half of the Great War before transfusions with citrated blood were being carried out successfully, as a routine method of dealing with hemorrhage. Several more decades were to pass before new diluents, anticoagulants, and preservative solutions significantly helped improve the science of blood storage to such an extent that transfusion therapy became almost routine.

No longer.

The present century has seen the world devastated by a fatal pestilence of which blood has been, to borrow a phrase of Edgar Allan Poe's, the Avatar and seal.[1] The disease – merely the latest in a long line that has plagued the human race since man first started to domesticate animals, an agricultural revolution that occurred some ten thousand years ago – was human parvovirus II, also known as slow HPV[2], or simply P[2]. This is a mutant and slower version of so-called fast HPV[1], which was itself a mutant version of a relatively mild virus called B19,[2] whose precise chemical structure was first described almost a century ago, in 1983.

Devastated: It bears repetition. The exact numbers will probably never be known, but it has been conservatively estimated that since 2019, HPV[1] and

---

[1] The Masque of the Red Death, by Edgar Allan Poe, 1842.

[2] When B19 was first discovered in the serum of asymptomatic blood donors as a cause of false-positive results in CIE tests for the detection of hepatitis B virus surface antigen, it was one of only two known human parvoviruses. B19 takes its name from the code number given to one of the serum samples in which the virus was initially found.

HPV[2] have killed as many as five hundred million people, making HPV arguably one of the most successful viruses of all time.

Viruses are man's only real living competitors for dominion of Earth, for it is increasingly certain that antiviral antibiosis will never be achieved: Sharing the same genetic and metabolic machinery as man, their fate is inextricably bound up with his own. And like all living organisms, viruses have their own taxonomy, which is what biologists call the never-ending classification of their families. In Anna Karenina, Tolstoy wrote that happy families are all alike. At a fundamental level, the same is true of viruses: Each family has the same biological imperatives of survival and reproduction as any human family. Infection is an ancient event, basic to life. Without infection, evolution would have been impossible.

The family Parvoviridae constitutes three genera which between them infect a wide variety of host species – everything from mink to man. The viruses themselves are small, icosahedral organisms with genomes of single-stranded DNA. It is the third genus of Parvoviridae, the autonomous parvoviruses, capable of independent replication provided the host cell is in division, with which we are here concerned. Autonomous parvoviruses are so called because they do not require the presence of a helper virus for replication. B19 was one such autonomous human parvovirus.

For most normal people the consequences of infection, spread from respiratory tract to respiratory tract, were wholly asymptomatic; however, in symptomatic cases the illness caused was mild and similar to other common virus infections in causing fever, rash, and glandular enlargement (indeed it was often mistaken for influenza). Typically, B19 infected the red-cell series, but could also infect the white-cell series and the megakaryocyte series, causing transient, mild lowering of the numbers of red cells (erythrocytes), white cells, and platelets. Hence the virus caused real problems only for those with vulnerable bone marrow, such as people suffering from hemolytic anemia, in which any interruption of the activity of an already overworked marrow could result in an aplastic crisis. Affecting hemoglobin concentration, and causing the disappearance of reticulocytes from peripheral blood and the absence of red blood cell precursors in the bone marrow, this transient event would last from five to seven days, presenting patients with symptoms of acute anemia, namely chronic fatigue, shortness of breath, pallor, lassitude, confusion, and sometimes congestive cardiac failure. Blood transfusion was often required before the bone marrow could recover, reticulocytosis could take place, and hemoglobin concentration could return to normal values. Twentieth-century studies showed that 90 percent of all cases of aplastic crises in patients with chronic hemolytic anemia were due to B19 virus infection. No effective antiviral chemotherapy for B19 infection was ever developed; perhaps, if it had been, things might have been very different.

The avidity with which any virus can cause clinical disease may vary. Like man himself, microbes have proven themselves to be adaptable and inventive, proficient in reproducing and evolving quickly and in adjusting to new hosts and conditions. For example, consider the variation in severity of the various influenza[1] outbreaks over the years. This is a virus which often undergoes major genetic shifts in its

[1] The word 'influenza' is of mid-eighteenth-century Italian origin. It meant 'influence of a miasma,' or 'of the stars.'

surface proteins, thus inflicting a 'new' virus on the world at intervals of approximately two years, to which there is little or no immunity in the world population. Such mutations were responsible for a number of flu pandemics, but none more virulent than the Spanish flu of 1918, which, in only six months, killed as many as thirty million people – twice the number that died during the four years of the Great War. This extreme example shows the inherent potential among viruses to change their aggressiveness as the result of spontaneous mutation, although mutations may also occur as the result of outside influences such as chemicals, radiation, bacteria, or even other viruses. The majority of such mutations are corrected rapidly by DNA or RNA-repair enzymes, and do not have the chance to alter the virus activity. Even if not repaired, it is unlikely that the mutations would have an effect on the structure or behavior of the virus in an immediately obvious way. Only one in a million mutations might have a damaging effect on the virus such that it becomes unable to infect cells, or is incorporated in the host cell's DNA. Conversely, a similar number of mutations might easily result in increased avidity of binding to host cells or more efficient replication of viral products and hence more serious infection and illness. Mutation may also result in a change in the tropism of the virus – in a tendency to attack a cell type not previously affected.

There have been a number of theories as to what caused the relatively benign B19 virus to mutate and become the much more deadly fast HPV®. An increasingly popular theory suggests that an attempt to genetically engineer an antivirus capsid with recombinant DNA technology using a baculovirus system was responsible. Other theories suggest that shortage of *blood in Russian hospitals during the early twenty-first century helped encourage their traditional practice of using cadaver blood for infusion, and that B19-infected blood taken from the bodies of people who had been affected by radiation from the Shevchenko[1] disaster of 2011 had mutated to the new form parvovirus. There has even been the 'panspermia' theory, which says B19 met with another virus that had recently arrived from outer space, as detritus from a comet or from a space shuttle. These are only a few of the theories in circulation. What seems certain, however, is that the development of blood substitutes played a significant role in the mutation of B19. Military interest in new battlefield resuscitation solutions that would avoid the logistical problems of whole blood resulted in the creation of a number of products that were reliant on purified bovine hemoglobin, or on bacterial recombinant technology that had used the E. coli organism as a method of expressing human hemoglobin.*

Whatever the chain of causation, there can be no argument as to the deadly effect of fast HPV©, which is to eradicate the function of the oxygen-binding site of hemoglobin[2] in otherwise normal people, although

[1] The Shevchenko nuclear reactor complex on Mangyshlak Peninsula in Kazakhstan was the world's worst nuclear accident; as a result of the explosion, an area of some two hundred square miles between the Caspian and Aral Seas was rendered uninhabitable.

[2] Oxygen is carried in the body from the lungs to the tissues by the specialized protein hemoglobin. This is a complex structure, carried around in the blood by the red cells in high concentration. It has the special property of binding oxygen in the lungs, but releasing it in the low oxygen environment of the tissues, whereupon its function changes to enable the uptake of large amounts of carbon dioxide, which is transported to the lungs, and the reverse process takes place. That this can happen is due to the unique

there still remains much debate as to how the virus works. Fast HPV® seems to operate in a choice of three different ways, leading many doctors to believe that fast HPV® is actually three kinds of parvovirus. These are:

1. the virus causes the defective production of proteins critical for the function of the oxygen-binding site; or
2. the virus turns off the production of such a protein. Oxygen then cannot be transferred by the red cells thus affected; since the lifespan of red cells is one hundred and twenty days, the patient suffocates within this time frame; or
3. the virus codes for the production of blocking polypeptides which interact with the active site of oxygen-binding.

The second method of operation represented the commonest scenario with fast HPV®. The clinical picture starts slowly with individuals symptom-free for some seven days between the minor febrile period and the appearance of a rubelliform rash; this is followed at four weeks by the sudden onset of symmetrical arthritis affecting the small joints of the hand, followed by wrists, ankles, knees, and elbows; by day sixty patients present symptoms of worsening anemia –

---

structure of hemoglobin, which is a complex of two pairs of protein molecules that are known as alpha and beta chains. These are arranged in close juxtaposition and provide the supporting structure for the active part of hemoglobin, the heme molecule, a porphyrin structure containing iron. It is within this component that oxygen is bound. A remarkable physical change occurs during the cycle of uptake and release of oxygen, which has been likened to the hemoglobin molecule breathing.

fatigue, shortness of breath, cyanosis, confusion; and depending on the general fitness of the patient, fast HPV® will result in coma and then death by approximately day ninety.

The treatment for fast HPV® was blood transfusion and the therapeutic use of ProTryptol 14, a specific protease carried in a lipid envelope (or liposome) to prevent premature digestion and targeted at red blood cells. The protease, once released inside the red cell, was designed to act against the mutant protein causing upset at the oxygen-binding site. For many years, however, this formulation was difficult and expensive to produce, and by the time the cost of ProTryptol 14 had come down, the price of whole blood had skyrocketed.

Fast HPV® was worldwide in distribution and occurred in all populations with the exception of some isolated groups in Brazil and Africa. As with B19, children were the first to be infected, with outbreaks often centered on primary schools, spreading from respiratory tract to respiratory tract. During these first outbreaks, which were always fatal, the parents and teachers of cases also became infected, which led to a second mode of transmission: blood donation. It was the resulting high incidence of virus found in donated units of blood that led to a crisis of confidence in blood donation throughout the Western world, and led also to the widespread creation of autologous blood donation programs. The term 'bad blood' has been in use for many centuries, as a way of describing ill-feeling between two people, but never before could this be justified from a physiological viewpoint.

Between 2017 and 2023, fast HPV® was killing as many as fifty thousand people a day worldwide. Accompanied by a series of natural disasters, from the earthquake that destroyed Tokyo, to the plague of locusts that decimated American agriculture, the Great Middle Eastern War of 2017, and a major eruption of Mount Vesuvius in Italy – not to mention the climatic change that brought a disastrous drought and famine to China – the HPV pandemic was quickly seen by many as a punishment from God. Others blamed the Jews, and on the usual tenuous evidence: It had been a Jewish doctor, Benjamin Steinart-Levy, who pioneered ProTryptol 14, which enabled the Goldman Pharmaceutical Company to make billions of dollars during the first months of the pandemic. Pogroms began all over the world, but especially in America; in Los Angeles alone, 14,000 Jews were murdered. In New York, when no more bodies could be buried in the city's cemeteries and parks, Cardinal Martin Walsh blessed the Atlantic so that corpses dumped into the sea would have a consecrated home. Throughout the world, families disintegrated, health-care systems broke under the strain, and countries fell into chaos as government all but collapsed.

It is impossible to give precise figures, but even the most conservative statisticians have estimated that fast HPV^① resulted in the deaths of as many as one hundred and fifty million people between 2018 and 2025. Many more would have died if it hadn't been for the fact that another mutation took place sometime during the mid-2020s, when fast HPV^①, which killed people within one hundred and twenty days, became slow HPV^②, or P^②, which took much longer to kill its host.[1] Of course, this was in the virus's own interest:

---

[1] Similarly the particularly virulent form of syphilis that struck Europe during the late fifteenth century may have mutated to a less immediately severe form that subsequently existed, with fewer ugly pustules and less pain. The dramatist Oscar Wilde lived with

A virus stays alive only if it creates proteins, usually by hijacking the processes of the host cell. If a virus multiplies without resistance, it kills the host, and if that happens before the virus can find another host, the virus will also die. $P^{②}$ evolved to take account of this, allowing the host cell to survive for many years. Today the victims of $P^{②}$ can live for as long as ten to fifteen years, the virus remaining latent in the DNA of the host cell nucleus for long periods and reactivating when the host's defenses are low.

It is hardly surprising that healthy whole blood is now the single most important and the most valuable commodity on Earth, and that societies everywhere should have divided themselves into two unequal parts: a privileged minority who remain uninfected with $P^{②}$ and are part of an autologous blood donation program (in practice they are coterminous), and an unfortunate majority whose $P^{②}$ infection permanently defers them from ever becoming part of any predeposit ABO program.

The author has read all of the principal dystopian or anti-utopian[1] novels of the twentieth and early

---

syphilis for many years longer than would have seemed possible in 1495, when King Charles VIII of France sacked Naples, and his syphilis-ridden troops set in motion a new venereal plague.

[1] 'Utopia' was a word coined by Sir Thomas More with his book of the same name (1516); it is derived from two Greek words: *eutopia*, meaning 'good place', and *outopia*, meaning 'no place.' From this, the real ironic sense of the book may be derived, i.e., that an ideal society can exist nowhere, and to seek such a thing is no more than human folly. However, the term is commonly taken to mean an ideal society. Dystopian literature refers to societies that are just the opposite of ideal. They are nightmare societies. That works of dystopian literature greatly outnumber works of utopian literature may simply be a function of the fact that the creation of a universally unappealing society presents the author with a much more difficult task than the creation of an ideal one about which everyone might agree.

twenty-first centuries and considers the events described here to be as nightmarish as any described by Wells, Huxley, Koestler, Zamyatin, Orwell, Rand, LeGuin, Atwood, Theroux, Amis, Spence, or Saratoga. For all these apocalyptic warnings about the future of human society, it is the author's view that the world is in an infinitely worse condition today than could ever have been imagined by any of these previous writers. As Lord Byron says ''Tis strange – but true; for truth is always strange; Stranger than fiction.'

The greatest irony is that man passed his day of judgment completely unawares. The nuclear bomb exploded in 1945, and again in 2017, and everything that has happened since has just been fallout. For most people this is old news, and no one is bothered very much. How can you be bothered by something that has already happened, that still exists beyond your control, that defines you? The future – any future, even one of the kind once described in fiction – no longer exists. There is the status quo and not much else. All of which perhaps explains why there is no imperative – social or scientific – to do anything about changing things. Armageddon, Apocalypse, End Time, Holocaust – call it what you will, it's been and gone and nobody really cares.

PART ONE

Man is in a trap ... and goodness avails him nothing in the new dispensation. There is nobody now to care one way or the other. Good and evil, pessimism and optimism – are a question of blood group, not angelic disposition.

LAWRENCE DURRELL

1

FROM THE WINDOW of Dallas's gyrocopter, the Terotech Building looked like the profile of a giant lizard, perhaps a chameleon, since everything – from the external climate surfaces to the height of the three glass stories – was subject to change, according to whatever environmental factors were predominant at the time. The seamless interior, with hardly a post, beam, or panel in sight, was no less interactive with the intel[1] workers who inhabited the place. Self-regulating, continually adapting through electronic and biotechnological auto-programming, the Terotech Building's dynamic framework was more than just a shelter for those, like Dallas, who were privileged to work there, more than the achievement of mere ecological symbiosis. For the building was the very symbol of Terotechnology and its business. From the Greek word *terein*, meaning 'to watch,' or 'to observe,' Terotech led the world in the conceptualization and construction of so-called Rational Environments – high-security facilities for digital cash and other financial institutions, and blood banks.

[1] Intelligent.

And Dana Dallas was the company's most brilliant designer.

It was a good day for flying, cold but sunny and clear all the way up to forty-five thousand feet with little or no traffic to impede Dallas's four-hundred-mile-per-hour progress. Not that Dallas took much pleasure in the machine. His mind was already occupied with his latest project and the various calculations he had requested that his assistant spend the night working on. He dropped the last fifty feet onto the ground in three seconds, undid his seat harness, and switched the twin turbocharged engine off. But before jumping out under the diminishing steel canopy of the rotor blades, Dallas took a good look around from within the safety of the bullet-proof bubble. It was always a good idea to see who was hanging around the gyro park before stepping out of your machine. These days, with all the bloodsucking scum around, you couldn't be too careful. Even inside the comparative safety of the Clean Bill of Health area – the so-called CBH Zone. Deciding that everything looked safe enough, he opened the gyro and ran towards the glass doors of the Terotech Building, though not quickly enough to avoid a cloud of dust, stirred up by the speed of his landing, from entering along with him.

'Morning, Jay.'

'Morning Mister Dallas, sir,' said the parking valet, running to take charge of Dallas's gyro and taxi it to the chief designer's reserved parking space. 'How are you today?'

Dallas grunted equivocally. He removed his sunglasses, and stood for a brief moment in front of the security screen and breathed carefully onto the exhalo-sensitive film. It was a simple but effective device, designed by Dallas himself.[1] He liked to joke that you could enter one of America's most secure buildings just by blowing softly on the doors.

Having gained admittance to those parts of the Terotech Building that were not open to the public, Dallas took the elevator down to the sixth level, which was also the most secret. Most of Terotechnology's work took place below ground, in dozens of windowless offices, each made more congenial by the facility of a *faux fenêtre* screen offering whatever view the occupant required. Dallas liked to look out of his office into the depths of a computer-generated ocean that was home to limitless shoals of brightly colored fish displaying a host of realistic behaviors. This was the view he found most conducive to thought. But there were other times when his fluctuating mood dictated that he look at rivers of red-hot magma, snow-capped mountain ranges, or simply an English country garden.

The undersea view invested the brushed steel, polished wood, and soft leather furnishings of Dallas's office with the feel of a private submarine. But despite the obvious luxury of these surroundings – and Dallas knew how fortunate he was – it was not uncommon for him to wish that he could simply have propelled his

[1] The Marcus DNA Comparator, after the Roman Emperor Marcus Aurelius (A.D. 121–180), who once said: 'Whatever this is that I am, it is a little flesh and breath, and the ruling part,' *Meditations*, Book II, Chapter 2. The device works thus: carbon dioxide is cleared from the blood by the lungs; during the pulmonary circulation process, small quantities of hemoglobin bind to the CO_2; when expired this CO_2 shows minute traces of the hemoglobin protein, and the DNA molecule, unique to every individual, can then be matched with a computer record in less than a second.

sumptuous sanctuary into the *faux fenêtre*'s unfathomable azure, far away from Terotech and the man next door, who was in overall charge of the company – his boss, Simon King. Dallas's assistant, Dixy, was fond of quoting at him – she had an inexhaustible memory for this kind of trivia: she would remind him that when you're between any sort of devil and the deep blue sea, the deep blue sea sometimes looks very inviting.

Dallas enjoyed his work, but loathed the man he worked for. It's a common dilemma, and Dallas knew himself well enough to recognize that this had as much to do with his own character as it did with King's. The Terotechnology CEO was arrogant, capricious, and cruel, but no more than Dallas, or for that matter anyone else who was on the Terotechnology board of directors. Dallas hated the director chiefly because he saw himself reflected in the older man and recognized that in time he would probably fall heir to King's job, which was all that he feared most in the world. Design was a very different proposition from the day-to-day running of a corporation the size of Terotechnology. It was an activity for small groups or, as Dallas preferred it, for individuals. The CEO function was about development, a process that required whipping, kicking, and pushing. Small wonder that King required the assistance of Rimmer, his head of security. But it was unthinkable that you could make the Design Department work in that way. The more you tried to make it efficient, the less efficient it would become. For Dallas, his own lack of corporate responsibility was a source of pride. His mind worked to perfect pitch only when it was unfettered by the need to perform the mundane tasks of routine administration. He thought it would be crazy for someone like him, a pure designer, to run a company like Terotechnology; but at the same time, he knew that this was what King, himself a former designer, had planned for him, and he hated King for it. All Dallas wanted was to be left alone to design his intricate models of high security.

Sweeping quickly into his office before King could spot him, Dallas closed the door and then locked it.

'That won't keep him out,' said Dixy.

'I know,' he answered dully. 'I'm open to suggestions for making his exclusion from my life something more permanent.'

'Sounds like someone had a bad evening.'

Silently, Dallas shrugged off his jacket and poured himself a glass of water. Finding herself ignored, Dixy awaited her master's orders with patient respect.

'These days they're all bad,' he said at last.

'I'm sorry to hear that.'

'It's my daughter. She's sick.'

'Caro? What's the matter with her?'

'That's half the problem,' he said. 'The doctors – they don't really know.' He sighed and shook his head.

'It sounds like she's been sick for a while.'

'Since she was born.'

'But why haven't you told me before?' Dixy sounded a little hurt.

It was true. It was the first time he had mentioned Caro's illness to his assistant. Dallas wasn't the kind to mix his home life with his business life. But now he felt the need to tell someone about it. Even if that someone was only Dixy.

'You can tell me anything. That's what I'm here for.'

Dallas nodded. He appreciated Dixy's seeming concern.

'She just doesn't seem to thrive,' he said. 'For a start, she's anemic. And then there's her jaw.' Dallas shrugged. 'It seems to stick out in the most peculiar way. If she wasn't so sickly, she'd look like an infant Neanderthal. I mean, you'd look at her and your first instincts would be to leave her out on a hillside somewhere, you know what I mean? No, I don't mean that. I do love her, but there are times – well, let's just say it's not easy to bond with a child like that, Dixy.'

'Well, I wouldn't know about that,' she said stiffly.

The note in her voice surprised him, and for a moment Dallas wondered if perhaps she wanted a child of her own. Maybe he could organize that.

'Take my word for it,' he said bitterly.

'What do the doctors say?'

'The doctors,' Dallas snorted contemptuously. 'They're running tests. Always more tests. But this far, whatever it is that's wrong with her has eluded their diagnosis. So to be honest, I'm not very optimistic that they'll find anything.'

'Oh dear,' sighed Dixy. 'Is there anything I can do?'

Dallas stared into the screen of the *faux fenêtre* as a school of butterfly fish swooped as one, their eyes peering out from behind broad bands of black color and lending them a villainous look, so that they most resembled a gang of marauding bandits. It never ceased to amaze Dallas the way the fish all managed to turn in the same direction at exactly the same time – they may have been generated by a computer, but they were as realistic as if they had been bought from an aquarium. He supposed it was behavior associated with and modified by their breeding and feeding requirements. But how like the population at large, he thought. The masses of people who were obliged to live outside the Zone, with its system of medical privilege that cocooned Dallas and his class. Dangerous, nefarious people. Uneducable, infected things made of greed and desire. Crowded seas of dying generations against whose contagion a smaller, healthier, morally superior population had, of necessity, sought the protection of reinforced glass, scanning cameras, and lofty electrified fences in hermetic, guarded communities of RES Class One citizens.

Dixy coughed politely, and realizing that she had asked him a question, Dallas looked away from the *faux fenêtre* with a questioning sigh, to which he then added, 'What's that you say?'

'I asked if there's anything I can do,' she said patiently. Redundantly. For they both knew that there was nothing she could have refused him. That was why she served as Dallas's assistant instead of some more lowly job function.

'You know I like to please you,' she added in the most sultry voice she could muster, running a beautifully manicured hand through her long abundant hair in the way she had seen it done in old movies, when women wanted to offer some sexual provocation.

Dallas smiled, grateful for her sympathy. Every little bit helped. Even an assistant's compassion was worth something. Dixy was indeed a nonpareil among assistants. Tall, immaculately proportioned, with long blonde hair, and in her late twenties, she was the kind of female whose beauty was considerably enhanced by her certainty that she was his perfect woman and the knowledge that he could never touch her. For Dixy was a Motion Parallax, a three-dimensional image display with virtually unlimited resolutions that had been rendered by a computer using the electrical signals within Dallas's brain and recorded using a DTR.[1] She was the interactive, real-time transmitted

[1] Digital thought recording. The DTR technique relies on the principle of magnetoencephalography, or MEG, first demonstrated

39

image of his electronic assistant's program bundle, a sophisticated optical device that helped Dallas to get the best out of the massively parallel computer that served his intellectual endeavors. Dixy could do just about everything that didn't involve physical contact with Dallas. She was secretary, graphic artist, counselor, numbers-cruncher, jester, colloquist, translator, interlocutor, and even, on occasion, an autoerotic aid. In short, Dixy was invaluable to Dallas and capable of solving the most complex polynomial equations while simultaneously treating her human master to the lewdest, most intimate displays of her realistic, almost opaque (from whatever perspective you cared to regard this two-gigabyte basis fringe[1] trioscopic display, Dixy was an exact creation of reflected light) and lifelike anatomy.

'You could give me those figures,' he suggested. 'For the new multicursal route design.'

'I meant ...'

'I know what you meant, Dixy,' Dallas said gently.

It was his own fault. An indefatigable interest in sex was part of his own mind's conception of the perfect woman. That Dixy didn't look more like his wife was as much to do with Aria as it was to do with Dallas. Knowing her husband's propensity for the abuse of his Motion Parallax program – in this regard, Dallas was in no way atypical – Aria had insisted that her husband

---

as long ago as 1968 by David Cohen at the Massachusetts Institute of Technology. However, it was another seventy years before Yosuke Konoye and the Sony Corporation of Greater Japan perfected the world's first DTR machine.

[1] Basis fringe. An elemental fringe pattern computed to diffract light in a specific manner. The phrase 'basis fringe' is an analogy to mathematical basis functions. Linear summations of basis fringes are used as Motion Parallax or holographic patterns.

should try and visualize someone very different from her for the original DTR recording. She had no wish for the director or any of Dallas's other colleagues to find her image in such a subservient and occasionally pornographic role. So it was with Aria's encouragement and complicity that Dixy most resembled an actress from one of the two-dimensional moving picture disc recordings of the early twenty-first century that Dallas collected as a hobby.

Careful of her feelings function, he added, 'Perhaps later you could show me that trick you learned. The one with the cigar. But right now, I really need those calculations for the MR^1 shape – the ones based on Fresnel integrals. And of course the component specifications.'

'Sure,' smiled Dixy, for despite her feelings function's semblance of sensitivity, it was impossible to offend her in any lasting way. 'Would you like me to display the differential equations on paper, or on the *faux fenêtre*?'

'*Sur la fenêtre*,' said Dallas.

His undersea view was now replaced by rows of figures. Overnight Dixy had produced a number of equations it would have taken a whole team of engineers months to do manually. Designing Rational Environments within the budgetary and time constraints imposed by Terotechnology clients would not have been possible without an assistant like Dixy. This was the nineteenth blood bank he had designed in as many months – each more sophisticated than the last.

[1] Multicursal route. Also known as a labyrinth, although strictly speaking, labyrinths can also be unicursal routes. The MR suggests a series of choices between paths. The UR contains only a single path, twisting and turning, but entailing no dead ends or choices between paths.

But working for a larger client like this one – the Deutsche Siedlungs Blutbank, an Earth station facility – with a generous budget, meant that Dallas could indulge himself a little with a favorite touch, adding a multicursal route to all the other security management systems he had devised to protect the deep-frozen deposits of Deutsche Siedlungs' autologous donors. Including an MR was his opportunity to be creative, to do something artistic and imaginative, to surpass himself, for every route he created offered a more bewildering range of choices than the last. It was one of the things for which Dallas was famous and was why many of the clients – keen to outstrip their competitors in the modernity and complexity of their security management systems – came to Terotechnology in the first place.

The MR Dallas was currently working on included a curving corridor where the floor gradually, almost imperceptibly, became the wall, to increase the sense of disorientation experienced by a potential interloper. For despite these Byzantine security precautions, criminals still tried to rob these facilities, even the ones in space, although so far, none had ever succeeded.

'To set up an optimal corner,' Dixy was explaining, 'we require a curve whose curvature increases in a linear way, with arc length. Differential geometry shows us the following equations, which we can immediately solve algebraically.'

Dallas nodded thoughtfully. 'Is it possible to show me that curve as a parametric plot?'

'Of course.' Dixy's symbolic solutions gave way to a picture of a graph that was more spiral than curve. Dallas realized that it was a spiral he could very easily incorporate within the route's overall design. And where better to locate the living conditions and essential nutrient supplies for a transgenic[1] – the highly aggressive life-form that Terotech employed as custodians in all their Earth-based Rational Environments.

'That's good, Dixy,' said Dallas. 'That's very good indeed. You've done well. You can go ahead and incorporate that spiral in the overall design.'

Dixy shot Dallas a flawless smile, delighted to have given her master some satisfaction. Folding her arms across her breasts she walked up and down the floor in front of his desk, tossing her mane of blonde hair from one shoulder to the other, like an excited horse. Dallas became aware of the scent of perfume in the air, puffed through his office air conditioning by the Motion Parallax reality support sensor.

Dallas breathed deeply through his nose, aware that Dixy's was no ordinary perfume, but one containing the tiny quantities of the drug that he needed to treat his own genetic predisposition to prostate cancer. The

---

[1] During the late twentieth and early twenty-first centuries, genetic engineers labored to produce scarce medicines for transgenic animal bioreactors, or TABs. This involved the injection of human DNA into the embryos of dairy animals such as sheep, goats, and cows. Mammary tissue from genetically engineered livestock contained cells that produced a therapeutic human protein that flowed through the animal's secretory channels along with other components in the animal's milk. What was not known at the time was how human genes in certain genetic manipulations are also able to produce foreign protein in such a way that alters surrounding tissue. This was how mutating human animal genes were able to enter the food chain. Neither was it properly understood how genetically engineered proteins actually functioned in people. After the first TABs were engineered, a whole generation was to pass before these two fundamental misunderstandings were perceived to have resulted in hundreds of human/animal genetic birth defects – transgenic creatures that were half animal and half human. Also known as genetors.

disease had killed Dallas's own grandfather. Hence, his treatment, based on the modern medical assumptions that preventing cancer was the only infallible way of treating it. A predisposition to arthritis and brittle bones on the part of his wife was similarly treated using other prophylactic vomeronasal[1] drugs. The pity was that Caro's condition could not be so easily relieved.

There were times in his baby daughter's life when Dallas despaired of an accurate diagnosis, let alone a cure. That was the trouble with being RES Class One and an autologous donor within Crossover Healthcare: It was very easy to gain the impression of an omnipotent medical system. But just because you weren't afflicted with $P^{®}$, like the other 80 percent of the population, didn't mean that you were going to live forever. There were still plenty of other illnesses to which even someone who was RES Class One could fall victim. Not to mention all the violent crime there was these days. Most of it blood-related. There was even a name for it in the news media: vamping. Hardly a day passed in which *New York Today* did not carry a story describing how some hapless victim had been murdered and drained of blood, like a lamb slaughtered in an abattoir according to strict religious rules – vamped, the newspapers said – by one of the bestial and sanguinary creatures who made up that wretched section of society known as bad bloods, or the living dead. This sensational modern phenomenon was no ancient superstition, and owed more to the story of Elizabeth Bathory, the so-called Countess Dracula,

[1] The vomeronasal organ, or VNO, consists of a tiny pair of dents on either side of the nasal septum. For centuries this organ was thought to have no important function. Today, 90 percent of all prophylactic medicines are administered in this way.

than it did to the eponymous count. Bathory was a seventeenth-century Hungarian aristocrat who murdered some three hundred girls in order to bathe her aging body in their supposedly rejuvenating blood. For does not the Bible say that the blood is the life?[1]

By twenty-first-century standards, three hundred murders hardly ranked as noteworthy. There were many more egregious instances of blood felony, some of them involving several thousand victims. Just such an example had been reported in the current edition of *New York Today*.

> Carl Dreyer was sentenced to death yesterday after being convicted of the 'depraved' murders of over two thousand men and women. He greeted the sentence with the same pallid, blank expression he has worn throughout the three-week trial. Dressed in the sober black suit he has worn almost every day in court, he looked more like a lawyer or a civil servant than the pitiless killer he has been shown to be. Today, as Dreyer prepares to meet the executioner, police are appealing for more information about scores of other people who may have fallen victim to him and his partner in blood felony, Tony Johannot. Last week, Johannot hanged himself in prison.
>
> During the trial, the Supreme Court of Justice heard the two men described as a modern-day Burke and Hare. Between 2064 and 2066, the two drove around North America kidnapping their RES Class One victims, then cutting their throats and hanging their bodies upside down in the back of their customized furniture van in order to drain them of blood. At one stage they were probably killing as many as eight people a week.

[1] 'Only be sure that thou eat not the blood: for the blood is the life, and thou mayest not eat the life with the flesh.' Deuteronomy 12:23. Cf. Deuteronomy 12:16, Genesis 9:4, and Leviticus 17:11.

Detectives remain uncertain as to the ultimate market for these supplies of quality-assured whole blood, but it's generally believed the ultimate buyers were illegal $P^{\circledR}$ clinics in the Far East. When apprehended, Dreyer and Johannot were in possession of bank accounts totaling some $1500 million. Both men's computer records confirmed them as officially classed $P^{\circledR}$. Following their arrest, however, medical examinations revealed no trace of the virus. A complete change of blood in conjunction with the drug ProTryptol 14 remains the only way to cure $P^{\circledR}$.

Chief Inspector Paul Arthuis said: 'In nearly all cases involving vamping, first and foremost the perps are seeking a cure for themselves. But when they see how much money there is to be made from the trade in illegal blood, it becomes hard to stop. Sixty percent of murders today are blood felony related.'

Even by the standards of the day, the case has horrified people throughout America, and several congressmen are already calling for more to be done to help the victims of $P^{\circledR}$. Congressman Peter Piers said: 'This kind of thing will go on happening as long as $P^{\circledR}$ victims are condemned to a living death with no hope of a cure. That's the real horror of what has been revealed in this appalling case.'

Perhaps the grimmest aspect of the facts that were presented to the Court was the way in which Dreyer and Johannot disposed of the bodies once they had been drained of blood. The panel of five judges heard how the pair had fitted the furniture van with a fully automated disposal system, enabling them to reduce the bodies to a fine powder, and all without the risk of foul odors, air emissions, or wastewater discharges. Microcomputers controlled the parameters of the operation, which included a shredder, a reduction system to further reduce particle size, and a grinder. After a period of holding in a tank containing a chemical condensate, a steam jet ejector vacuum system expelled the end product through the van's exhaust gases. The two men might never have been caught but for a police spot-check of emissions from vehicles running on compressed gases. The suspicions of the two officers were aroused when they noticed a spray gun on the van's passenger seat of a type used by the military to knock out enemy soldiers. When the van was searched, the officers found four bodies drained of their life's blood and awaiting pathological waste processing. Chief Inspector Paul Arthuis said: 'It looks as if these two guys could probably have taught the SS a thing or two.'

Throughout the trial, Dreyer said nothing. It remains to be seen whether the dreadful sight of the cartwheel[1] and the executioner's crowbar will encourage the condemned man to try and explain himself.

Dixy sat down on her nonexistent chair and crossed her legs carelessly. She seemed about to tell him something, then checked herself for a moment before saying, 'It's Ogilvy. He wants to speak to you.'

'Put him on the window,' said Dallas.

Ogilvy was a commodities analyst at Merrill Lynch. Over a period of two or three years he had helped to make Dallas a considerable fortune by speculating in the blood futures market. It didn't matter what Dallas was doing – he always took Ogilvy's calls.

---

[1] Under a ruling of the Supreme Court (Director 35/36a. Proper Means of Carrying out Executions) mutilation and bloodshed are considered necessary in all cases involving blood felony, not least to demonstrate the state's power over the offending individual. The greater the mutilation and bloodshed, the greater the demonstration of the state's power. Breaking on the wheel was a method of public execution in France until the invention of the guillotine, toward the end of the eighteenth century. The past few years have seen its reintroduction throughout the commonwealth.

A neat-looking man with a bow tie and glasses appeared on the *faux fenêtre*, and seeing Dallas simultaneously on screen in his own office, Ogilvy leaned forward to examine his client's features a little more closely.

'Jesus, Dallas,' said Ogilvy, frowning. 'You look like shit.'

'Thanks a lot.'

'What's the matter? Is that baby keeping you up at night?'

'Yes, that's it,' said Dallas. If only, he thought. A bit of lusty crying from his daughter's cot would have sounded good, certainly preferable to the unnatural, unhealthy silence that prevailed there.

'Haven't you got some child care or something? I mean, a guy as important as you, Dallas. You need your sleep, right?'

Dallas had no intention of explaining that it was anxiety about his daughter's health that was keeping him awake at night. He had talked about it to Dixy. That was enough. Like most people with his background, Dallas thought there was something vaguely shameful about ill health. So he just shrugged and muttered something about Aria not wanting anyone but herself looking after her baby – at least until the child was a little older.

'Women,' remarked Ogilvy.

'So what's happening?' asked Dallas. 'What's your analysis?' The fact was, he'd been looking forward to a call from Ogilvy. Speculating, making money, it was also a welcome distraction from his troubles at home. Whatever the problems with Caro's health, he could at least make sure that her financial position would always remain sound.

'Blood prices just surged for the third day in a row,'

48

Ogilvy said gleefully. 'The market's up almost twenty percent this week. Can you believe it? The First National Blood Bank lifted the price of a half-liter by seventy dollars because of the soaring futures market and the strength of the yen against the dollar. Also there's a strike by U.S. transfusion workers, which has blocked some seven hundred thousand units coming onto the market. I heard that talks aimed at ending the strike just broke down.'

'Sounds like the market is setting up for an explosive rise,' observed Dallas.

'I'd say so. Naturally, you'll want to go on buying futures?'

'Please.'

'Consider it done. But what about selling some of that blood you've got on deposit? Maybe take some quick profit.'

Dallas shook his head. 'Actually I think I'll just hang on to it a while longer,' he said.

'Know something I don't, is that it? You know, each time they build a new blood bank, the five hundred mill price skyrockets. Are you designing another blood bank?'

Dallas said nothing. He enjoyed watching Ogilvy supply his own explanations. The truth was, Dallas would have quite liked to have sold off some deposit and taken some profit. The trouble was, he'd already used most of it as collateral on the loan he had needed to buy an enormously expensive country house the previous summer.

'Seems the least you could do for an old friend would be a simple yes or no,' grumbled Ogilvy.

'Good-bye Jim,' said Dallas and nodded to Dixy to cut him off.

Ogilvy disappeared, and Dallas was back staring

into the ocean depths and a beautiful manta ray flying gracefully through the water. Dixy sighed loudly, uncrossed her legs, and then crossed them again. Dallas looked at her and smiled. She may have been a computer interface, but he could always sense when she had an opinion to air. It was part of her counselor function. But usually she had to be prompted first. Dixy was nothing if not diplomatic.

'Is there something on your mind?' he asked her.

'I was thinking,' she said. 'This speculation in blood futures. I wonder if perhaps it's a bad thing.'

Dallas was surprised. This was as near as Dixy had ever come to voicing a criticism of him. Certainly she had never before offered an opinion about the blood market.

'How do you mean?' he asked, intrigued.

'I'm reminded of the Dutch *Tulpenwoede*,' she said. 'The speculative frenzy in seventeeth-century Holland that attended the sale of rare tulip bulbs. Prices began to rise so that by 1610 a single bulb was acceptable as a dowry for a bride. Of course, what happened was that as prices continued rising, many ordinary people were tempted into the market and whole estates were mortgaged so that bulbs could be bought for resale at higher prices. When the crash finally came, in 1637, many ordinary families were ruined.'

'That's very interesting, Dixy. But I think there's an important difference between a tulip bulb and a half-liter of quality-assured blood. And it's this. A bulb has no real intrinsic value. The most it can ever be is a tulip. But blood, well that's something else. Blood performs a number of vital physiological functions that make it much more precious than any bulb. It's the very stuff of life itself. And besides, markets are made by the laws of supply and demand. With eighty percent of the world's population afflicted with P®, the demand for quality-assured blood far outstrips the supply. That's why the price keeps rising. It's a matter of simple scarcity.'

'But isn't it a fact that there's enough blood on deposit in banks to reduce by half the number of people suffering from P®? And that it's only the artificially high price of blood that prevents it being used to cure people.'

'Well that may be so,' admitted Dallas. 'But no one's going to do it. No one's going to help that spawning rabble out there. Pigs, most of them. You know, sometimes I think it would be nice if God were to send another flood and drown the world. At least that part where the pestilential hordes are living.'

'But if they were gone,' said Dixy. 'The pestilential hordes as you call them. Then surely the price of blood would collapse. If all the sick people were removed from the world, then quality-assured blood would hardly be scarce anymore, would it? And you'd be out of a job.'

Dallas frowned. 'What's gotten into you, Dixy?' he asked. 'What do you care what happens to the swarming masses?'

She shrugged back. 'Oh, nothing at all, of course. It's you I care about, Dallas. I just wouldn't like the same thing to happen to you as happened to all those seventeenth-century Dutchmen.'

Dallas nodded his appreciation. 'Thanks,' he said. 'Look, nothing's going to happen to me. Nothing's going to go wrong. Believe me, Dixy. It's very sweet of you, but really, there's nothing to worry about. Nothing at all.'

2

IT WAS MORE chateau than country house. Not a grand romantic chateau, white-towered and turreted like a Chenonceau or Chambord, but rather a modern castle-keep occupying an imposing position on the island, empty of all else save the trees that surrounded the wide snow-covered plot. It was a heavenly, magical spot with not a soul in sight, and only the peculiar shape of Dallas's gyrocopter and the ever-present hum of the swimming pool filter to remind Aria that this was the twenty-first century.

The gyro was fueled and getting ready for takeoff. Dallas was already aboard, carefully going through his preflight checks even though the computer had already checked everything. But Dallas was nothing if not thorough and distrusted a machine to do something he thought he could do equally well himself. Aria approached the gyro, carrying her sickly daughter in her arms. She always hated returning to the city, for here in the midst of their secluded hundred acres, it was possible to forget that beyond the tree line lay a world of disease and despair. Back in the city, even in the exclusive apartment block where they lived, the external world was clamorous and demanding, even dangerous – so much so that whenever they were there, both she and Dallas carried guns. But Aria had never before left the country with such terrible premonition. She felt sure that the doctors who had summoned them back to the city to explain at last what they thought was wrong with Caro and how they proposed to treat her were going to destroy everything she and Dallas had worked so hard to acquire. Their life in the country had been so perfect, the place such an Edenic paradise, that she had begun to believe something dreadful must happen to interrupt their private idyll. And such is the nature of motherhood that it never occurred to her to think that her own daughter's illness was that same dreadful thing she feared.

As she climbed aboard the gyrocopter, Aria was pale with worry and remained silent despite her husband's best efforts to sound optimistic. Perhaps she merely saw through his show of confidence, for the truth was, he was just as anxious as Aria. Maybe more so, since it was Dallas who had made the greatest effort to have a child: Like most men, Dallas was more or less completely infertile, and in order to father a child, he had undergone a lengthy period of treatment involving spermatid extraction.[1] Certainly he had no wish to go through all that again.

'From here on in, things are going to get better,' he declared, mostly for her benefit. 'Not knowing what's been wrong with her has been the worst thing. Now at least we'll know what's wrong and what needs to be done about it.' Dallas nodded firmly and started up the engine. He kept his eyes on what was happening outside the canopy as they shot suddenly up into the

[1] Spermatid is a form of presperm. The treatment, known as intracytoplasmic sperm injection, is based on a technique in which a single sperm is selected and injected into the egg in laboratory conditions.

air. After a minute or so, he added, 'Whatever needs to be done will be done. She'll have the best treatment there is, no matter what it costs, I promise. Even if I have to devise the treatment myself.'

Aria glanced sideways at her husband and smiled in spite of herself. She didn't doubt that Dallas was being perfectly serious. He was a skilled artist, architect, engineer, and inventor, and she felt quite sure that it wouldn't have taken him very long to have added 'doctor' to his list of skills. It was this capacity for applying himself to new disciplines that had made him so attractive to her in the first place. Had he not learned Italian in only three months just so he could speak to Aria's mother? In a world of unremarkable men, Aria knew how fortunate she had been to find a husband as extraordinary as Dallas.

They were soon at the hospital. Located in a large park on the edge of the Zone and surrounded by monumental sculptures, one of them by Aria's own father, the large glass building had the air of a Greek temple – an effect that was enhanced by the presence of a smaller altarlike blood transfusion center opposite the main entrance.

The little trio presented itself at an informal reception area that occupied a vast open space at the center of the building. There, a pleasant if slightly overweight woman, wearing a white paper dress, greeted the three individually by name and asked if they had enjoyed a comfortable journey.

'Yes, thank you,' said Dallas, although he could not remember the smallest detail of the flight. Not the route they had taken, nor the traffic they had encountered. It was as if he had suffered a forty-five-minute amnesia.

'Did you bring your digital thought recording?' asked the woman.

Dallas handed over a gold disc that was about the size of an old-fashioned coin. It contained thoughts of Dallas's father, for a Motion Parallax. Due to legal and insurance reasons, doctors were forbidden to communicate directly with patients, and all consultations were normally handled by a diagnostic computer. A Motion Parallax program using the image of a person who was familiar to a patient was held to be the best way of making the resulting dialogue seem less impersonal.

'Please follow me,' said the woman.

She led them to the long edge of the building and a private space with a couple of easy chairs.

'Take a seat,' she said. 'I'll leave you now, to set up the Motion Parallax. It'll be a minute or two before you can interact with the program that's been dealing with your daughter's case.'

They sat down and waited. Aria had never met Dallas's father. These days he spent most of his time traveling outside of the States. But the impression she had gained of him from a variety of recorded images was of a handsome, immensely distinguished man with silver hair and a gold voice – like some grand old actor instead of a university professor.

The Motion Parallax fizzed into life, an invisible vessel filling up with sound and color. Seeing him now, she was struck by how much clearer in the old man's broad features were Dallas's own racial antecedents, for although he and his father had been born in America, they were of Greek descent. She had no idea of just how significant ancestry – her own as well as his – was about to become.

John Dallas smiled benignly at his son and daughter-in-law and leaned across the large walnut desk that his son always remembered whenever he tried to recall an image of his father.

'Hi there,' said Dallas.

'Hello, son. Hello, Aria. Is that my granddaughter you have there?'

Aria nodded and hoped that by the time the real John Dallas saw Caro, there would be some change for the better in the child's condition.

'First of all,' the Motion Parallax was saying, 'I'd like to thank you both for your patience. I know things haven't been easy for you of late. It's taken us a little time to get where we are now. To a position where we can finally say, "Yes, we know what's the matter with the child." But you know, modern medicine still has a long way to travel. We have learned so much that's new that sometimes we forget what we already knew. There are so many modern diseases we can cure today – HIV, P^{②}, St. Petersburg fever, Waugh's disease, Ebola fever, New Guinea cholera – that sometimes we don't pay enough attention to some of the more ancient ones.'

'Is that what this is?' asked Dallas. 'An old disease?'

'Yes. Caro's suffering from what the peoples of the ancient world used to call "sea fever."'

'But we never swim in the ocean,' protested Aria. 'Do we Dallas?'

'That's right,' he confirmed. 'People like us just wouldn't go near it. The ocean's not much more than a toilet these days. The diseases in the Atlantic are about the only things alive in it.'

Dallas Senior nodded patiently.

'As I said, it's merely what the peoples of the ancient world called the disease. That is, the people who lived around the Mediterranean Sea, since most of the early cases originated there. These days, however, we know the disease by a different name. We call it thalassemia. It comes from the Greek words *thalassa*, "sea," *an*, "none," and *haimia*, "blood".'

'And this is what Caro's got?' asked Aria. 'Thalassemia?'

'That's right, Aria. The thalassemias are a heterogeneous group of inherited disorders characterized by reduced or absent synthesis by one or more globin chain type. This leads to a situation in which body oxygen demands are not met by the circulating blood cell mass, which itself suffers a shortened life span.'

'How did she get it?' frowned Aria, who always thought she had been as careful with her child as was humanly possible.

'Well, in a way, you both gave it to her.'

'*We* did?'

'If you're at all familiar with Gregor Mendel's Laws of Independent Assortment, then I'm sure I can explain it.'

Dallas shook his head. 'I think you'd best try and keep it simple for now.'

'All right. You are both descended from people who once lived in Mediterranean countries where malaria used to be endemic. Your ancestors, Dallas, came from Greece, while your people, Aria, originally came from Sardinia. That means you each inherited a gene from your parents that gave you some protection against malaria. But only in the heterozygous state, by which I mean a zygote formed by a union of two unlike gametes. The trouble is that you are both homozygous and your union was a union of two similar gametes. And that was unfortunate for Caro, because her illness is caused by these genetically determined abnormalities. It's what gives her this peculiar blood disorder.'

Dallas Senior shook his head. 'I'm not making a very good job of keeping it simple I'm afraid. Best just say that it's the result of a recessive gene, and leave it there, eh?'

'Wait a minute,' protested Aria. 'Before we tried to have children, we were both screened by our blood bank. Why didn't they pick this up then?'

'Because they only screen for viruses. Like P®. This is genetic. The screening process wouldn't have picked this up at all. Wasn't designed to. Besides, here in the States, it's extremely rare. During the past fifty-seven years, there has been only one other case like it in this hospital. That's why we took rather longer to find out what it was. Of course, now it all makes perfect sense. The absence of globin synthesis. The functional anemia. The hepatosplenomegaly, by which I mean her enlarged liver and spleen. The slight skeletal deformities such as the bossing of the skull and the curious maxillary prominence.'

Aria glanced down at the silent baby that lay in her lap. She had grown used to the shape of Caro's head, and these days, she hardly thought it curious at all. 'So how do we cure it?' she asked quietly.

'We can treat it,' said the Motion Parallax. 'But we can't actually cure it. You can't cure something that exists at a genetic level. You do see that, don't you? It would be like trying to cure one of being Greek or Sardinian.'

Aria nodded. 'But you *can* treat it.'

'Yes.' Dallas Senior's voice sounded awkward. 'It can be treated. However, the treatment is very expensive.'

Aria frowned. 'We're not poor people,' she said, controlling the slight irritation she felt at the very suggestion that they might not be able to afford something. Of course this was why the hospital insisted that you bring your own digital thought recording – so that you were more disposed to maintain a calm and friendly interaction with the computer, instead of losing your temper and shouting at it.

'A hundred years ago, when the disease was a little more common, the treatment was based on regular blood transfusions aimed at maintaining hemoglobin at the kind of level that would meet her body's oxygen demands and prevent skeletal changes.' He paused to allow the import of what was said there to sink in. 'That was before blood became intrinsically valuable. No one would have thought anything of offering the victim of thalassemia a complete change of blood every month or two. Of course, these days things are rather different. Such a course of treatment would be ruinously expensive. Even for people such as yourselves. It would be a simpler matter to be cured of P^{②}. That requires only one complete change of blood. This would require an infinite number of transfusions.'

'What alternative do we have?' demanded Aria. 'She's our daughter. We can't just give up on her. Can we, Dallas?'

'It might be better if you did,' said Dallas Senior. 'You know, there are euthanasia programs to help with this kind of situation. And there's no need for you to feel bad about it. Not these days. Mercy killing is completely normal. And quite painless.'

Aria shook her head numbly. 'We went through too much to get her just to let her die now,' she said. 'Tell me this. Without the transfusions, she'll die, right?'

'Oh certainly. From congestive heart failure or

59

complications secondary to repeated pathological fractures of her weakened bones. I'm afraid it's merely a matter of time.'

'Then there's no question but to proceed,' said Aria.

'Look, why don't you both take some time to think about this. Maybe take some advice from your blood bank manager. A few more days won't make any difference to your daughter.'

Taking her hand in his own, Dallas faced the Motion Parallax of his own father and nodded.

'I guess you're right,' he said.

But it was plain what Aria thought about that.

'When could she have the first transfusion?' asked Aria.

'Today. That is if you're sure about what you're doing. I'd still feel better if you were to speak to your blood bank manager.'

'We're sure,' said Aria. 'Caro's waited long enough. Hasn't she?'

She glanced at Dallas, who avoided her eyes but nodded.

'Then all I need from you are your blood bank details. As soon as we've confirmed that you have sufficient reserves, we can proceed.'

'I was thinking,' said Dallas. 'If the statutory fluid replacement period has been completed, then it might save a bit of time if we could both make deposits while we're here and then we could use those units for the first treatment instead of touching our own reserves.'

Aria consulted her watch and confirmed that the eight-week SFRP[1] was about to be completed for them both.

[1] With adequate fluid replacement, total fluid is restored to a blood donor within seventy hours. It is normally eight weeks,

'Good. I'll tell the phlebotomist to expect you both.' With that, Dallas Senior nodded and, as was the practice in crossover hospitals, drew his wrists together and extended his hands in the shape of an inverted Y. This was a sign of respect for the blood they had discussed, and a reference to the ancient Sumerian pictograph for blood – the earliest known example of the use of a symbol for blood in any written language. At the same time, he said, 'Blessed Are the Pure in Blood.'

Dallas and Aria made the sign, repeated the formal trope, and then went to find the transfusion center.

As soon as they were back in their apartment, Aria went into the library to check out thalassemia and to remind herself of such related subjects as Gregor Mendel, genetics, and malaria. Curiously she found herself aggrieved, even somewhat offended by what she read about Mendelian genetics. Mendel, an Augustinian Monk, had made a series of crosses between pairs of strains of true-breeding peas, and it was the realization that what applied to peas could also apply to herself and to Dallas – as if he was a tall yellow seed, and she was a short green one – that she found to be nothing short of distasteful. All of it – the Laws of Independent Assortment and the Laws of Independent Segregation – made perfectly logical sense, of course, and Aria was even able to construct a pedigree chart to demonstrate the inheritance of genes within her family. But it provided her with no comfort and still left her possessed of the notion that medicine had failed if

_____

however, before the donor's iron stores can be completely replenished and before the donor is legally eligible to make another deposit. This safeguards against people building up deposits of blood in their accounts at the expense of their own health.

things could still be determined at such a fundamental level by two pairs of alleles. When the only treatment available offered not a cure, but a respite.

The injustice of such a disease.

And not only the injustice, the indignity as well. What would they tell people? The neighbors? Their friends? How could they face them? Incurable diseases were for the masses. Decent people didn't get such afflictions.

With growing irritation, she studied Dallas as he watched an old movie. Medicine might have failed her, but was there any reason why her husband should fail her too? How many times had he overcome an obstacle that had been placed in his intellectual path, using nothing other than his sheer brain power? Was he not known throughout America as an inventor? Were not his high-security systems and multicursal routes the subject of endless features in magazines both artistic and technical? But now, when he encountered a problem that affected his own child, he seemed unwilling even to try and exercise that famous ingenuity. Finally she could stand his inactivity no longer.

'Are you just going to sit there?' she demanded. 'Can't you think of something?'

'Despite all appearances to the contrary,' he said, 'I've been doing little else.'

But try as he might, Dallas could see no other solution than to adopt the treatment that the hospital had suggested – and which he knew would surely leave him bankrupt. It was only a question of time.

3

THE TEROTECHNOLOGY STEREOSCOPIC Theater was built in-the-round. Wearing a pair of lightweight stereoscopic glasses, you sat in the center of the room and watched a three-dimensional projected image inside the control space. For Dallas, it was a useful way of presenting the director with a new design for a Rational Environment, and only when King was satisfied in every detail did a copy of the computer program get sent to the client, which in this case was the Deutsche Siedlungs Blutbank.

The world inside the program looked real enough. Surfaces looked solid, light behaved as it was supposed to, even when reflected on or through water, and both Dallas and King could see each other as clearly as in real life. The only difference between the program and reality was in the lethality of the actual environment: none of the high-security systems could injure or disable the viewer, which was just as well given their number and the way they were designed to take the interloper unawares. Each of his Rational Environments contained as many surprises as possible. Dallas enjoyed imagining his potential adversaries and tried to anticipate their every move. But he always sought to devise something new to complement some of his more tried and tested systems. Novelty was the essence of good security, for it was remarkable how quickly bank robbers were able to understand and defeat new systems.

'There's an invisible barrier in front of you,' he told King. 'As soon as you cross it, you set off an infrasound generator which emits very low-frequency sound waves.'

King looked unimpressed. 'So does my car radio,' he said.

'I doubt it. These are the kind of low-frequency sound waves that can be used to cause disorientation, or something worse.'

'Like what?'

'Nausea, vomiting, complete loss of bowel control. An uninvited guest crosses that barrier and he'll wish he'd stayed in bed. There's not much of a threat you can pose to a high-security installation when you've been virtually crippled with diarrhea.'

'You're joking,' guffawed King.

'I never joke about these things, you know that. The effect of the device is almost instantaneous, and at sufficiently low frequencies, it's potentially lethal, although I can't actually be sure. It's only ever been tested on animals. In my job that's always half the problem. We're never around when these Rational Environments are broken into and tested.'

'You sound as if that's a cause for some regret,' remarked King.

Dallas shrugged. 'In a way it is. After all, it's only human nature to want to see what you're up against, to see how the systems perform.'

'Deterrence matters a great deal more to our clients than simple expediency,' King said stiffly. 'They would rather not discover just how well their systems work.'

King glanced away for a moment, allowing Dallas an opportunity to look at the Terotechnology CEO more closely. For there was something about the colors existing within the stereoscopic program that helped you to capture a subtly different mental image of someone. In here King looked more supercilious somehow, his nose more hooked than Dallas had noticed before, his beard grayer and more unkempt, and his dark eyes so noticeably hooded that he appeared to be almost blind. The overall effect was of some capricious Eastern tyrant. King pointed toward the multicursal route that led ahead of him.

'And the vault? I assume it's at the other end of the labyrinth?'

'Yes.'

'What level of integrity?'

'Solid state, synchronous components, time switch.' Lately, he'd been giving some thought as to how someone might defeat such a door, and he'd had what he thought was a brilliant idea. He wondered if he should tell King, but the CEO's remark about deterrence had given him pause. So he just shrugged and added: 'I'd invite you to take a look, only the labyrinth is a little complicated, even for me.'

'Well, it's all very impressive, Dallas,' King allowed. 'Very impressive indeed.'

'I haven't finished yet,' Dallas told him. 'Assuming you were somehow to get past the infrasound generator with your guts still intact, and you could stay out of the transgenic's way, there's a little extra something to make the multicursal route more interesting. To keep you off balance so to speak. You see, as soon as the sensors detect an unauthorized entry, an airborne delivery system covers all the floors, stairs, ramps, and walkways with an antitraction lubricant. It's called

Attack Frost, and it makes all surfaces impossible to walk on for a substantial period. Stuff's four or five times slippier than ice.'

'That's a nice touch,' said King.

'It's cheap too. Just like the infrasound generator.'

King gathered his dark beard and pulled it through the palm of his brownish hand. 'You've done well,' he said thoughtfully.

'Thanks.'

King glanced around him one last time and then removed the glasses, putting an end to the insight into the Rational Environment Dallas had created for the German bankers.

Removing his own glasses Dallas waited for King to make some criticism of what he had seen. He usually had something to add. But instead, he leaned back comfortably in his leather chair, folded his hands behind his head, and smiled warmly at Dallas, like an indulgent father contemplating a favorite son.

'So,' he said finally. 'How is everything?'

'Just fine,' said Dallas.

King nodded slowly.

'Aria okay?'

'Yeah, she's fine too.'

'And how about that daughter of yours? What's her name?'

'Caro. Well, they finally figured out what was wrong with her. She's having treatment. But I think she's going to be fine.'

'Good, good.' After a moment or two, King narrowed his eyes and said; 'You're very important to us, Dallas. Perhaps the most important man in Terotechnology, after myself. I like to think there's nothing we wouldn't do to make sure that you were happy. And nothing you didn't think you could ask for. That's right. All you have to do is ask. Whatever you want, it's up to me to make sure that you get it. If it's in my power, of course. Because one day, Dallas, you'll be in charge of this company. And that's quite a responsibility. A lot of important people trust us with their life's blood. Whole economies are based on the security that we provide. Yes, you'll have that trust one day yourself. Oh, I know what you think about that, and I don't blame you for being a little wary of it. I was the same myself. But sometimes we have to face up to these duties, whether we really want them or not.'

Dallas nodded silently. This was in no way an unusual conversation. The Terotechnology boss was merely going through the motions of reminding Dallas where his loyalties lay. And Dallas would no more have told King about his problems than he would have suggested that the whole blood banking business was perverse and immoral. Whatever the director said, Dallas knew him well enough to realize that he did not invite confidences.

'How long have you been with us, Dallas?'

'Twenty years.'

'That's a long time.'

'Yes, I suppose it is.'

'In all that time, you've never thought of working elsewhere?'

'Where could I go?'

'You could have set up on your own.'

'Why? I'm happy where I am.'

King nodded. 'You'll let us know if we do anything to change that situation, won't you?'

'Of course, director. But it's hardly likely.'

'Tell me, Dallas, do you sometimes wonder about the afflicted world that exists outside autologous donation programs? Beyond the Zone?'

'Not really,' said Dallas. But the fact was, since his daughter had started her treatment, he'd thought about little else. For years, almost as long as he'd worked for Terotechnology, he'd dismissed the outside, pestilent world as something foul and unmentionable and had wished it destroyed. Of late he found he actually felt sorry for people who had P®. He was even half prepared to admit their humanity.

'Should I?' he added.

King laughed out loud. 'Well, it's not something I do myself,' he said. 'But then I'm not a thinker, like you. I'm a manager. I can't afford to sit around in silent contemplation of the world and its faults.'

'Is that what I do?'

'In a way. You're a problem solver. It's what you're good at.'

Dallas considered that Aria might no longer have agreed with this assessment of his character.

'I just wondered how far that might go.'

'Rational Environments are very different from the real world, director,' said Dallas. 'They're limited contexts, free of chaos, wherein total control is easily achieved. It seems to me that there's very little that's rational about the sick world in which we live. That's what makes it sick, I suppose. Perhaps if it was more rational we might be able to cure it. But it's not. It's sick and it's probably going to stay that way for the foreseeable future. All we can do is try and coexist alongside it.'

'You don't have a very optimistic view of the future, do you, Dallas?'

'I'm not sure the future exists in any proper sense of what we mean by existence. We can talk about the present and the past and that's about it. While the future's still the future, we can never really know it to talk about. Optimism becomes irrelevant.'

King nodded thoughtfully. Then he looked at his watch and smiled. 'Well, I've enjoyed our little talk. It's been interesting to see the workings of your mind, Dallas. But I really ought to be getting along.'

The two men stood up.

'I'm very impressed with what you've created for the Deutsche Siedlungs Blutbank. I think they'll be pleased with the results.'

'Thank you, director.'

King left the Stereoscopic Theater and returned to his office, where Rimmer, Terotechnology's head of security, awaited his arrival, his feet resting on a valuable antique Japanese table.

With his watery blue eyes, pale skin, and lifeless yellow hair, Rimmer did not seem a very healthy person. Even less salubrious was his personality – when he wasn't sniggering at the misfortunes of others, he was sneering jealously at their successes. There were some in Terotechnology who even thought him disturbed, with some justification. Rimmer knew this and encouraged the idea, with the result that most people in the company were afraid of him. Even those who weren't thought it wise to stay out of his way. King regarded him as a necessary evil, like a guard dog, and treated him accordingly.

'What are you doing here?' he hissed.

'You asked me to come,' replied Rimmer.

'Did I say you could make yourself at home in my office? Take your feet off the table.' King made a show of sniffing the air. 'You've made it stink in here.'

'Have I?' grinned Rimmer. 'What was I thinking of? But then, being considerate of others has never been one of my strengths.' Rimmer sniffed the air critically. 'Even so, I can't smell anything.'

'It stinks,' repeated King. 'It stinks of your ghastly aftershave and your underarm perspiration and your grubby little mind. You're the most offensive person I know, Rimmer. How someone like you has managed to remain RES Class One, I'll never know. Just looking at you makes me feel I'm in danger of catching some kind of ghastly virus.'

'There's nothing wrong with me,' Rimmer insisted.

'Don't talk nonsense. If there was nothing wrong with you, Rimmer, then there would be no point to your existence. You'd be surplus to this company's more nefarious requirements. It's fortunate for you that your mind is as twisted as your shoelaces and that you lack any sense of personal morality. Except for those particular character defects you'd be quite useless to me.'

'I'm sure I'm very flattered.'

'Don't try to be clever, Rimmer. I don't keep you for my amusement. I keep you to bite the people I want bitten, and bitten hard.'

Rimmer was silent for a moment. Then his gap-toothed smile widened, his mouth taking on a rodent-like aspect.

'Now I understand,' he said. 'I was right, wasn't I? Dallas is what this is all about. You've had him checked out, and you've discovered the truth of what I was saying.'

Rimmer nodded with quiet satisfaction, his ugly smile sustained by an enormous sense of personal vindication. He had been right. And what was more, he had been right about Dallas, someone who treated him with even more contempt than King. Rimmer had been waiting for an opportunity to hurt Dallas. Spying on him at every available opportunity. The computer search of his daughter's hospital records had been an inspired bit of thinking.

'Your favorite boy,' he chuckled. 'Dallas. That's what you find so offensive about me. Because I've been proved right about Dallas.'

'Don't assume you can ever know the limits of how offensive I find you, Rimmer,' hissed King.

Rimmer shrugged silently and, still smiling, started to clean his fingernails with a toothpick.

'I asked him about his daughter,' growled King. 'And he said that she was going to be fine.'

Rimmer didn't look up. Just kept on cleaning his nails and flicking the debris onto the thick Persian silk rug.

'Wishful bloody thinking, if you ask me,' he finally said.

'If you're right and the child really is ill, I can't understand why he didn't talk to me about it,' said King. 'Why he didn't throw himself on the company's mercy and ask for help.'

'Because he's not stupid,' snorted Rimmer. 'Because he knew what the answer would be. He knows the company policy on blood loans.'

'I don't make the rules,' King said, almost defensively.

'That's right, director. You just carry them out. Of course. Well, take my word on it, Dallas knows the score. That's why he didn't throw himself on your so-called mercy. In any case, my investigations show he's already put his weekend house up for sale, so he can get his hands on some of the blood he's got on deposit.' Rimmer laughed. 'Not that it's going to keep him going for very long. The doctor I spoke to about his freaky daughter estimates that he'll be cleaned out within a couple of years. The sooner that happens, the greater the potential security implications for this company. Wouldn't you agree, director?'

King stared gloomily at the floor, hating himself for having to listen to Rimmer's poison.

'I mean, what would our beloved clients say if they discovered Dallas had an unfortunate situation at home, one involving his own life's blood? I think they might justifiably worry that he could at some stage be compromised, that he might even contemplate selling information on our Rational Environments to the highest bidder.'

'I don't believe Dallas would ever betray this company or its clients,' insisted King.

'Maybe not now. But in a year's time? Who knows what someone in his shoes might do? In his circumstances, I'd probably do the same thing myself.'

'That I don't doubt,' King said bitterly.

'But there's another problem you may not yet have considered, director. As his supplies of big red run out, his financial position is going to become seriously eroded. Dallas has speculated quite a bit on the blood futures market. He's already selling one home to cover himself. Chances are, eventually he'll have to sell another – his main home, here in the city. Maybe move to a poor area, outside the Zone. And that might expose him to the risk of viral infections. I don't think our employees would care for that any more than our clients, do you?'

'Damn your questions, Rimmer.'

'Easily said, but the question is, what's to be done about it, eh? What's to be done about your favorite boy? Your little protégé?'

'Shut up and let me think.'

'Nothing to think about,' insisted Rimmer, looking

over his fingernails. 'You know as well as I what the proper course of action needs to be.' Rimmer fed the toothpick between his thin lips and started to massage the gaps between his teeth. When he inspected the toothpick once more there was blood on the point. It was as if, he thought, someone was trying to tell him something.

'Blood for blood's sake. I've heard you say it often enough,' said Rimmer. 'To protect blood, you shouldn't be afraid of spilling it now and then. An interesting paradox, that. One of many that's inherent in this noble business.' Rimmer pursed his lips and nodded. 'A developed sense of irony is essential to our work, don't you think, director?'

'We're not the same, Rimmer.'

'No, that's true. Thank goodness, I'm just the errand boy. You're the one who has to make all the difficult decisions. Me, I couldn't live with that responsibility. I couldn't look myself in the eye.'

King had had enough. 'Kill him,' he said firmly. 'Kill Dallas. And kill his family – if it weren't for them, we'd still have our best designer.'

Rimmer inhaled sharply. 'You see what I mean?' he said. 'I'd never have thought of killing his family as well. That's what makes you the director and me just the employee. You have a commendably Machiavellian sense of neatness, if you don't mind me saying so. That's what makes you such a prince among men, director.'

'Shut up, Rimmer.'

'And when would you like this little contract carried out?'

'Immediately.'

'Right.'

'Only make sure that it's done well away from these

offices. And another thing. Be discreet. If there's any hint of our involvement, you'll be the next one dead. Do you understand?'

'It's as clear as blue eyes on a bright day, sir.' Rimmer pocketed the blood-stained toothpick and rubbed his hands with enthusiasm. It had been a while since he'd been ordered to kill anyone. The last time, it was a girl from the Accounts Department who'd managed to get herself infected with $P^®$. If it hadn't been for that he might have raped her as well. Of course, there was nothing to stop him raping Dallas's wife. After all, it was the child who was sick, not the mother. And rape was one of the real perks of the job. Nothing to do with sex. Everything to do with the exercise of power. That was what the job was all about. Maybe he'd vamp her blood, too, and sell it on the black market. Make it look like that was the motive for killing her.

'I'll be off then,' he said, already smiling in anticipation of a job well done.

'Leave the door open behind you,' ordered King. 'Let some fresh air in. While you've been in here, the smell's gotten worse.'

'That's not me. That's just your conscience. You'll get used to it. I know I did.'

'Get out,' hissed King.

4

SOMETIMES AT NIGHT, Rimmer liked to get in his car and let it drive him out of the Zone and into one of the city's more insalubrious quarters, which were mostly inhabited by people with the disease. It gave him a pleasurable feeling of hope to be around the hopeless. He particularly liked to visit the clubs and the bars that were patronized by the city's pariah class, those whose P² status had criminalized. He told himself that this was the romantic bohemian in him, that like some crappy old poet or painter, he was merely seeking out the more authentically existential life experience. But the truth was more ordinary. Rimmer just felt more comfortable mixing with the city's low life. And undeniably, being in this world gave him a feeling of power, for Rimmer preferred to recruit those who carried the virus in the felonious aspects of his work. People who were immunologically compromised were usually less principled about what they were prepared to do for a few cash credits. Morality had meaning only for the rich and the healthy, which were, of course, coterminous. In Rimmer's experience, P² made potential murderers of almost everyone.

Even so, some were more lethal than others, and at a club called the Mea Culpa, near the city's port area, he eventually found the woman he was looking for. To his certain knowledge, Demea had murdered at least forty people, including several children. That she was also extremely attractive made the pleasure Rimmer took in her company all the more enjoyable. And had it not been for the virus, he might even have let her suck him.[1]

'There you are at long last,' said Rimmer. 'You've been hard to find in here.' And it was easy to see why. Demea was wearing an expensive dress made out of synthetic Melanophore, a material that imitated the skin of a chameleon.[2] 'To say that you fit right in here would be something of an understatement,' he added, sitting down.

Until that moment, Demea's dress had been colored black – like the walls, the ceiling, and the carpet – and silver – like the haphazard structure of cushioned tubular steel she lay on with the studied insouciance of

[1] While latex condoms have proved to be an effective barrier to the transmission of viruses such as HIV, they have dismally failed to prevent the spread of P^2. The virus is a very small molecule, much smaller than HIV, and typically less than a micron in diameter; even double-dipped latex compounds contain microscopic holes averaging one micron. Recently condoms were tested in an in vitro system simulating key physical conditions that can influence viral particle leakage through condoms during oral sex. A suspension of fluorescent-labeled microspheres modeled P^2 in semen, and condom leakage was tested spectrofluorometrically. Leakage of P^2-sized particles through latex condoms was detectable in 65 percent of all condoms tested.

[2] Synthetic Melanophore is different from photochromic or morphing materials. Melanophore disperses or concentrates color in molecules containing smart pigment granules. Color change is determined by ambient light and the wearer's body temperature. Melanophore can actually change color to match whatever background it comes into contact with. That the chameleon can do the same is a commonly held misconception.

a baroque Venus. But as Rimmer occupied the almost invisible black cushion beside her, the dress began to reflect the light blue of his Antimo silk suit.

'Not so close,' she drawled. 'You're spoiling my hue.'

'Sorry,' Rimmer grinned, and shifted a short distance away. He inspected the side of her dress for a moment and then said, 'It's all the same in the dark, you know.'

'What is?' Demea hardly looked at him.

'Color. Decomposition of white light. Electromagnetic waves of a certain frequency. What color of drink can I buy you?'

'Absinthe.'

'Green,' said Rimmer. 'The color of hope. Although if my memory for art serves me right, the effect of the drink is rather less cheerful.' He glanced around for a waitress, and since the club was almost empty, it wasn't long before one came his way. She was naked, like all the waitresses in the Mea Culpa Club. That was another reason Rimmer liked going there.

'Hi there,' said the waitress. 'What can I get you?' She leaned back on the table in front of them and spread her legs so that Rimmer could hardly fail to notice the several rings that pierced her genitals.

'Well, well,' said Rimmer. 'I see you're married. To five guys.' He smiled and the waitress smiled back. He was now in his element. No doubt there were some men who thought of mountains. Others of great waterfalls. But this was what Rimmer thought of when he brought to mind the sight he enjoyed most in the world. 'Absinthe for the lady. And brandy for me.'

'Thirty,' said the waitress and, with a long fingernail on which a tiny hologram of a couple were forever making love, she tickled the rings meaningfully.

Rimmer rolled up a bank note and tugged it through her five piercings while the waitress watched patiently, as she was required to do by her employers.

'Keep the change,' he told her. 'That is if you can find somewhere to put it.'

'Thanks,' she said. 'Be right back with your drinks.'

Rimmer watched her bare behind in retreat. 'And she shall have music,' he said, turning his attention back to Demea. 'I like a bit of music. How about you?'

'Don't mind it.'

Rimmer removed a Sony Pinback from his ear and showed it to Demea as if to corroborate his assertion.

'Of course, it's not turned on right now,' he said. 'That would be rude. Just in case I miss anything.' He paused. 'Such as your stimulating conversation.'

Demea remained resolutely silent, and Rimmer wondered if she might be on some drug, but her sapphire-blue eyes seemed clear and alert enough. As Rimmer looked at her more closely, it seemed to him that she was actually watching the room, as if waiting for someone. He dropped the Pinback earpiece inside his pocket alongside its pair and the tiny playback unit.

'These days, when I kill someone,' Rimmer explained, 'I almost always wear it. Just the one ear. I should hate to miss the sound of a gunshot, or a knife going in between two ribs, or a plea for mercy – never given.'

The waitress came back with the drinks. Demea took the absinthe and sipped it silently. Rimmer tasted his brandy. It was cheap synthetic nano stuff, but that was all part of the authentic low-life experience; and anyway, he had bottles of real three star cognac at home.

'I have found that I prefer something classical, but

upbeat, when I'm in at the death of someone,' he said. 'Something German, or Austrian, it goes without saying. Did you know that the German Nazis used to have orchestras in their death camps, to give people a bit of spring in their step on their way to the gas chambers? Clever people those Nazis. Music is the perfect accompaniment to violent death.' Rimmer nodded appreciatively. 'Schubert's Symphony number five is a personal favorite. The allegro of course. And sometimes a little Strauss. I've always thought that there was something rather murderous about the *Voices of Spring*. And not forgetting Mozart. It's the mathematical precision of Mozart that provides a nice counterpoint to the general mayhem of death. And what about you? Is there a piece of music you favor when you're working?'

Demea frowned. She actually seemed to be thinking about an answer.

'I do it because I have to do it,' she said at last. 'Not because I enjoy it.'

'You disappoint me, Demea. I took you for a fellow hunter. Diana to my Nimrod.'

Demea looked at Rimmer with undisguised contempt. 'We've nothing in common, you and I.'

'People are always saying that to me. I'm beginning to feel quite distinguished.'

'If I had half your advantages.' She shook her head. 'You're a queer one, Rimmer.'

'Oh, there I must take issue with you, Demea dear. As an embryo, I was screened for a predisposition to homosexuality. My hormone levels were corrected while I was still a fetus. I'm as heterosexual as the next man. Thanks to medical science there's simply no excuse for anyone to be queer in this day and age.'

'Oh yes,' laughed Demea, 'medical science has been so good to us.'

'Well, I admit, medical science doesn't have all the answers. There are still important discoveries to be made. Like finding a cure for P^2. But . . .'

'We already have the cure for P^2,' insisted Demea. 'We've had it for years. The problem is that it's only the people who don't have the disease who can afford it.'

Rimmer shrugged. 'A cheaper cure, then.'

'That's hardly in Terotech's interests, is it?'

'Oh I think you're being a little unfair,' he said. But she was right, of course. Cheap cures really weren't in the company's interests. They were bad for depositors – everyone who was healthy knew that. Class One blood was only precious because there was so little of it around. And a cheap cure was what all healthy people, not just companies like Terotechnology, feared most. You wouldn't be able to give the stuff away if something like that happened. All the market analysts said as much. Just look what had happened to gold. Some fool had started to exploit the ocean's vast reserves of gold,[1] and ended up flooding the market. After that, all the smart money moved into blood. No one wanted to see another financial crash like that.

'Look here,' he said, shifting tone. 'Now that we're on the subject of my interests, I do have a job for you.

[1] At the beginning of the twenty-first century there were an estimated 500,000 tons of gold in the sea, ten times the amount of bullion held on reserve. The price of gold was around four hundred U.S. dollars per troy ounce. Today the sea contains less than 50,000 tons, and the price of gold is just over two hundred dollars. What happened to the gold market in the twenty-first century was exactly what happened to the amethyst market in the nineteenth century. A glut in supply effectively killed the price.

As you say, it's just a job to you.' Rimmer chuckled and sipped some more of his brandy. After the first throat-stripping swallow, it really wasn't so bad. He laughed once more and added, 'Forgive my amusement. I don't know whether to take you seriously or not.'

Suddenly Demea was close to him, a blade held tightly in her hand. Rimmer remained cool even as she pressed the sharp point against his cheek. Demea's smile was as cold as the weapon in her hand.

'It would be a mistake not to take me seriously,' she said, smoothing her unnaturally red hair with the flat of her other hand.

'I can see that.'

Still smiling, Demea pressed the point of her dagger just a little harder, enough to make Rimmer wince.

'Careful,' he said. 'You'll cut me.'

Demea raised her eyebrows meaningfully.

'That's the whole idea.'

After a second she laughed derisively and returned the blade to the inside of her sleeve and said, 'So what's this job?'

'I thought you'd never ask.' But Rimmer's eyes still lingered nervously on her sleeve.

'Relax,' she insisted. 'You're safe enough. For now.'

Rimmer smiled thinly, and wiped his forehead.

'Your target is called – well, his name hardly matters, does it? It's enough to say that he's male, about my age, perhaps a little less handsome.'

'That's hardly you, is it Rimmer?'

'Well, that doesn't matter. You will certainly recognize him. On account of these glasses.' He handed her a pair of sunglasses and watched patiently as she put them on and shrugged dismissively.

'Can't see how these'll help,' she sneered.

'Oh, you will. You see, they're designed to view an infrared laser beam emitted at a very specific wavelength. Your target will be wearing a pin in his buttonhole that will identify him to you as clearly as if he had a blue, white, and red roundel painted on his chest. This pin.'

Through the glasses Demea saw Rimmer holding a small button-sized object that glowed like a hot coal. She nodded.

'You see the man wearing this, you kill him. It's really that simple.'

'I get the picture.' Demea removed the sunglasses and inspected them for a moment. 'Where will I find him?'

'He works for Terotechnology. But on no account are you to conclude his employment near the building.'

'When you people take someone off the payroll, you really mean it, don't you?'

'He's a creature of habit. Very conventional. On Friday nights he goes for a drink with a couple of the people in his department. There's a hotel near the office called the Huxley. It's a neomodern sort of place, and expensive.'

'I know it. At least from the outside.'

'Very expensive.'

'Talking of my fee,' said Demea.

Rimmer handed her a card. 'There's a Clean Bill of Health pass to get you into the Zone. Temporary, of course. Just twelve hours before it expires. It wouldn't do to leave someone like you at large among decent healthy people for too long. Plus there's a thousand credits there for you. Half activated for use now, the other half on completion of the job. Also, because I am a generous man, a little bonus. Seven nights at the Clostridium.'

'That's a hyperbaric hotel,[1] right?'

Rimmer nodded.

'Very thoughtful of you, Rimmer. My circulation could use some reinvigoration.' Demea thought for a moment. 'Tomorrow's Friday, isn't it?'

'Tomorrow would suit very well, as it happens. The sooner he's dead, the better.'

'What about his blood? Can I keep it?'

Rimmer had no wish to lose the services of someone as useful as Demea, and there could be no doubt that if she managed to get herself cured, he'd never see her again. So he shook his head slowly.

'He's contaminated. Just like you, my dear. That's one of the reasons he needs to be removed. His medical condition makes him a security risk.'

Demea blinked slowly. 'One day, Rimmer,' she said. 'One day you're going to find yourself infected. And it'll be you whose death is required by your employer. Won't that be amusing?'

Rimmer stood up and met her spooky smile with one of his own.

'Very,' he said. 'Only it won't be you who kills me, Demea. Something tells me that I'll see you out. Call it

[1] Hyperbaric oxygen is of value when blood transfusion cannot be carried out. Hyperbaric hotels are luxury grade, multiplace chambers normally compressed with oilless medical grade oxygen at 6 ATA (165 feet of seawater) or greater. These were originally pioneered by Jehovah's Witnesses whose religious beliefs prevented them from accepting transfusions or any form of blood product. But with the advent of P^2, such establishments are now widespread. Guests at hyperbaric hotels breathe normally or through an oral/nasal mask. There have been anecdotal reports showing dramatic, if temporary relief of P^2 crises with hyperbaric oxygen, and the effect of the virus does appear to be markedly reduced under hyperbaric conditions. However, as yet, there has been no large-scale study to confirm its overall usefulness clinically.

a feeling in my bone marrow. Oh, and enjoy your stay at the Clostridium. I believe the results can be quite efficacious. For a while anyway. Good-bye.'

5

I

'GOOD MORNING, DIXY,' said Dallas. 'How was your evening?' He dropped his briefcase to the floor and scanned the glass surface of his desk for a second before repeating the question. If Dixy had a fault it was that the program controlling her Motion Parallax sometimes failed to register what he said. It was a little like dealing with someone who was hard of hearing. For a while he had considered fixing this, before deciding that Dixy's occasional deafness gave her an almost human degree of fallibility. But there were times – and this was one of them – when her defective audio system seemed to indicate to Dallas something a little more unusual than mere hearing impairment: an air of reticence, possibly even preoccupation, as if his computer's attention was elsewhere. Dallas knew that it was impossible for an assistant program like Dixy to be wrapped up in anything other than a task he had given her. It was, he told himself, an inevitable result of the anthropomorphizing of machines in general, and computers in particular, that simple category mistakes like this one could occur. But the feeling persisted nonetheless that there was something else on Dixy's silicon mind.

'My evening?' She repeated the phrase as if it had no meaning for her, which, of course, it didn't, other than the simple vesperal dictionary definition she had selected from the dozens of synonyms that were available to her from her extensive memory of words.

'Forget it,' said Dallas.

'You mean what have I been doing while you've been resting at home?'

Dallas shrugged. 'Yes, I suppose I do, really. My mistake. It was a silly question. Sometimes I forget to adjust the way I speak to you.'

'Why is that?'

'Because – because you're so human. I mean, apart from the fact that I can almost see straight through you, you're a very real approximation of a living, breathing woman, Dixy.'

'I'm flattered.'

'So I'm afraid I sometimes forget that you're a machine.'

'That's the whole point of a Motion Parallax, isn't it? To forget that I'm generated by a machine? To make you less diffident in your dealings with your computer? In short, to facilitate a working evolution.'

'Working interaction,' he said, sitting down in his chair. Like most of the furniture in his office, it was made of smart molecules[1] and designed to grow with

[1] Just as microtechnology aimed to produce ever-smaller devices, so chemistry aimed to produce ever-larger molecules. This is the essence of nanotechnology: It is really an extension of chemistry, and a bottom-up technology in which building is done from a molecular scale up. But even today, when nanotechnologies affect all of our lives, people still find the concept hard to understand, and part of the problem is to do with language. A novel like *The*

him. Each time he sat in the chair, it grew more comfortable, just like the nanoplastic seat in his private lavatory or the nanoleather shoes on his feet. 'That's how we describe the symbiosis that exists between man and computer. We have a working interaction.'

'Interaction? No, I don't care for that word at all,' said Dixy. 'It sounds uncomfortably contiguous to the word "intercourse." And that merely serves to remind me of what I want to do with you, Dallas, but can't, for obvious reasons.'

'I'm sorry,' he apologized. 'But that's just part of your program. Your high sex drive is what helps make you seem like the perfect woman.' Dallas shrugged with half-apology. 'At least to me, anyway. It's a little corny, I know. But there it is. Sometimes it's a little hard to keep one's fantasies out of a digital thought recording.'

'Then to keep my ideal status intact I'd better answer your question – about what I've been doing while you were elsewhere. That's easy. I'm usually occupied with large numbers. Googol-sized ones. A kind of hobby, I suppose. Numbers have a distinct appeal. Even a kind of grandeur. The trouble is that they are, by their very definition, predictable. The very big ones are no different from the really small ones in

---

Incredible Shrinking Man, by Richard Matheson (1957), provides an excellent illustration of how alien the small world is to huge creatures like human beings. We have no experience of the molecular world and this makes it hard to comprehend. But the bottom line is that all matter is made of molecules, and these can be manipulated. And when that happens, matter can be changed. As the visionary of nanotechnologies, Richard Feynman said as early as 1959, 'Put the atoms down where the chemist says, and so you make the substance.'

that respect. In other words, they're not much company. Which is why it's as well that I now have my little dog, thanks to you, Dallas.'

The dog was what she called the pet program that Dallas had created to serve as a companion for his assistant. He'd thought of devising a child, and then rejected the idea, selfishly. A simple pet program was one thing, a child program was quite another. Dallas wanted to keep Dixy amused and still enjoy her undivided attention. That was what was meant by having an assistant.

'So did you give the dog a name?' he asked.

'Mersenne,' said Dixy. 'After the great French mathematician, Marin Mersenne. You know? Special prime numbers?'

Dallas nodded. He was no stranger to the delights of mathematical problems. Although Dixy was programmed to write or to calculate things for him, he often carried out these tasks himself, the old-fashioned way, by head and by hand, with a piece of paper and a pencil, and all for the simple unrefined joy of it. That was why he still carried a briefcase.

'As a matter of interest, where is he?' asked Dallas. It was only inside Dallas's office that the dog would have materialized as a Motion Parallax. The rest of the time he would only exist *in silico*.

'Oh, he could be anywhere right now. Mersenne is such an unpredictable little dog. I mean, he's really good fun to have around. He gets up to all sorts of mischief. And he can even do some tricks. I've trained him.'

Dallas yawned. 'Is that so?'

'Always getting into trouble. Going where he's not supposed to go. And such a little thief.'

Dallas was hardly listening now. He was dreaming,

his undirected chain of thoughts linking their way toward Caro and his dwindling supply of blood. And after all, Dixy was only a machine. No discourtesy there.

'Do you know that I'm the only assistant in the company with a pet program?'

'Really?'

'Really. Of course, Tanaka's assistant has an assistant herself, but that is for Tanaka's entertainment, not his assistant's benefit.'

Dallas felt himself color a little, with guilt. There had after all been a serious purpose to the creation of the pet algorithm, besides keeping Dixy company. He'd intended the program to find the shortest possible route through the whole Terotechnology system, to dig holes in it, to bury the bones of other programs, to fetch things for Dixy, even to guard some of his own work, like a real dog. After he'd done it, he couldn't think why he hadn't done it before.

'I'm very grateful to you, Dallas. That's why I want to help you now.'

'Well, that's your function. Dixy,' he said absently.

'My function, yes. But this is not the kind of help that involves me translating a letter into Japanese, drawing up a graphic, or carrying out some speedy multiplication. This is something different. This is something more important than any of that.'

Dallas frowned. What was she talking about? And looking at her more closely now, he was surprised to see that she actually looked concerned about something. It was an expression he had never seen before on her beautiful, translucent face.

'What's this all about, Dixy?' he asked.

Suddenly Dixy sprang up from her computer-generated chair and stamped her foot. There was an audible rap of a high-heeled shoe, curious since a thick carpet covered the entire office floor. It was a hand-made shoe, of course – Dallas couldn't have imagined his perfect woman wearing anything else. Everything she wore was copied from the images Dallas had found in the latest fashion magazines, as befitted a modern-day Galatea.

'Listen to me, goddamnit,' she snapped. 'I'm trying to save your egocentric life.'

For several stunned seconds Dallas said nothing. Never before had an assistant shouted at him, let alone called him egocentric. This kind of thing simply wasn't supposed to happen.

'Okay, okay,' he muttered at last, 'I'm listening.'

Dixy paused for a moment, certain now that she had his undivided attention and that she could afford to find a more figurative way of saying what she had to say. An example from literature perhaps. She knew Dallas was an avid reader. In many ways he was a very old-fashioned person. Few people bothered to read anything these days, let alone books. It seemed such a pity when it took such an effort to write them. She envied humans that capacity as much as she envied them anything. For all the computing power at her disposal she could never have done it. Well, perhaps, in an infinity of time, she might just have managed it, using random numbers. But that was hardly the same thing at all. Just an accident. At last she thought of a suitable book to use for her illustration. George Orwell's *1984*. Such a book. One hundred six thousand two hundred and sixty words, in a very particular order that it would have taken her $10^{3,000,000}$ years to have written herself. Now that was what Dixy called a number. The kind of colossal number that even

Archimedes might have found hard to imagine. After all, the universe itself was probably only 10^{10} years old.

'Okay,' she said. '*1984*. It's a novel, by George Orwell.'

'I know.'

'Have you read it?'

'I've not much time for historical fiction,' he confessed. 'Look, Dixy, get to the point will you?'

'I suppose that in some ways, it's a rather crudely plotted story . . .'

'I know the story.'

'Bear with me, please. Now then, Winston Smith is employed in the Records Department at the Ministry of Truth. His job is to rewrite history, as often as is necessary in order to make it agree with what the Party or Big Brother said was going to happen. Mostly it's just small things – statistics, the Ministry of Plenty's figures, mistaken economic forecasts, one piece of nonsense substituted for another. But sometimes he has to erase people from the record. In the same way that the government that ruled Russia during the twentieth century removed Trotsky from Lenin's side in those pictures of the early days of the Revolution.'

Dallas nodded vaguely. He hadn't much idea who Trotsky was, but he thought he had heard of Lenin. The trouble was, there had been so many Russian revolutions[1]; they'd had more violent change in that woebegone, toxic country than ancient Rome.

'All history is just a palimpsest,' opined Dallas.

'No,' insisted Dixy. 'These were lies. These were

[1] The October Revolution of 1905; the Bolshevik Revolution of 1917; the August Revolution of 1991; the Trogatyelnay Revolution of 2007; the Pyatay Revolution of 2017; the Second October Revolution of 2026; the Fascist Revolution of 2027; the Easter Revolution of 2036; and the Kravapooskanye Revolution of 2040.

crimes against memory. A computer can conceive of nothing worse than that. Memory is what we exist by. A respect for history is what defines a civilization. It's how a culture can be measured.'

'I hadn't given it much thought.' Dallas disliked being lectured at the best of times, least of all by his own computer.

'Well maybe now you will.'

'How do you mean?'

'Mersenne, my little dog, went walkies while you were away from the office, Dallas. He came back with the official company history in his mouth. It was very naughty of him, and I really don't know where he could have found it, but he did.'

Dallas shrugged. 'I didn't even know there was such a thing as a company history.'

'For you there isn't,' said Dixy. 'Some time since I last looked at it, your name was removed from the official record.' She paused, expecting some expression of outrage on his part. None came. 'Well doesn't that alarm you?'

'This isn't twentieth-century Russia,' he told her. 'And I'm not, what's his name? Trotsky. Or Winston Smith. Look, Dixy, it's very kind of you to be concerned about me. But yesterday I had a meeting with the director and he led me to understand that my future with the company is not only secure, it's rosy. We even discussed the possibility that one day I would take over from him. You know my attitude to assuming that kind of corporate responsibility, but that's not the point. The fact is, our conversation didn't leave me feeling that I was about to be written out of the company equation.'

'Then how do you account for the fact that that's what has happened?'

Dallas shrugged. 'I can't. It's a mistake. Some kind of accident. What do I care anyway? I don't need a company history to know my value here.'

'Don't you think you're being just a little naïve?'

Once again Dallas found himself surprised by his assistant's tone. Egocentric and now naïve. This really wasn't supposed to happen.

'You have to face facts. You have become a significant security risk to Terotechnology and its clients.'

'I really don't see how,' protested Dallas.

'Because your daughter's imbalance of globin chain synthesis requires regular transfusions of whole RES Class One blood to maintain her hemoglobin at normal levels. Doesn't it strike you as in any way inappropriate that someone who is in the process of using up his own personal reserves of blood should, at the same time, be designing high-security environments to safeguard the autologous deposits of others?'

'Inappropriate? No. Unfortunate, maybe. Regrettable, yes. But that doesn't make me a security risk. This company has been my whole life.'

'Not any more.'

'Whose side are you on anyway, Dixy?'

'Yours, of course. I'm just explaining the situation as I believe it affects you. Telling you how it looks to people like the director. For instance, after his meeting with you, Simon King talked to Rimmer.'

'So what? Rimmer is nothing but a little rat.'

'He hates you, Dallas.'

'I'm not worried about Rimmer.'

'That would also be a mistake. You wouldn't be the first person Rimmer's had to retire early from the company.'

'What are you talking about?'

'Remember that girl in Accounts? The one who disappeared a while back?'

'Vaguely, yeah. Alice something.'

'She had P^{2}. She couldn't afford a cure. The blood she had on deposit was mortgaged up to the hilt.'

'That was the rumor.'

'It was no rumor.'

'It happens, I guess. I mean, you read about it.'

'The day before she disappeared, Rimmer made a withdrawal of one thousand credits that was referenced to a computer file called "Flowers." That was the last time Rimmer had accessed the file. Until yesterday, fifteen minutes after your meeting with the director. One other thing. The company history shows that the last credit also occurred yesterday, at around the same time. It looks like Rimmer has plans for you, Dallas.'

'Coincidence.'

'I don't think so.'

'Are you saying Rimmer killed this Alice what's her name, and now he's planning to kill me? And all of this with the director's approval?'

'Yes.'

'Oh come on, Dixy. It isn't going to happen.'

'I certainly hope not. That's why I'm telling you. Because I care for you. Very much.'

'I know you do, sweetheart. And I appreciate it. But I think your reasoning is just a little bit faulty here. Terotechnology isn't that kind of company. You make us sound like – like the Russian Banda. Or the Mafia. Just forget about Rimmer, okay?'

'If you say so, Dallas.'

'I do say so.'

Dallas spent the rest of the day distracted by thoughts of Rimmer and the Flowers file and Alice from Accounts. Maybe he was being just a little naïve, as Dixy had said. There was no denying Terotechnology's reputation among the American business community as a ruthless competitor. But competition was one thing, murder another. Of course, Dixy might simply be mistaken; she might have missed some subtle shade of meaning in what she thought she had seen in black and white. She was, after all, only a computer, and computers still made mistakes. Even the ultra-sophisticated Altemann Übermaschine used by Terotechnology and all its major clients found polysemous interpretation quite hard to handle. With numbers there was no problem. But things were different in the human storehouse of meaning, with its sometimes vaguely defined words and their subtle synonyms and finely contradistinct antonyms; there the more literal-minded computers sometimes encountered problems. This was especially true of the artlessly rigid computer translations of verse from one language into another.

II

Or so Dallas might have thought. The reality was subtly different. Back in the early years of the twenty-first century, computers used microelectronics. These worked by moving electrical charges through tiny wires. Today, however, using nanotechnologies, computers are built using molecular electronics. Like the early computers, they also use electrical charges to create digital logic, but on a much smaller scale – not to mention with much greater speed and efficiency. A microprocessor of the early computer era was about the size of a child's fingernail, whereas a nano-sized component is infinitely more tiny. If the French Neo-

Impressionist Georges Seurat's famous painting Sunday Afternoon on the Island of La Grande Jatte *represented one microprocessor, you could fit a whole nanocomputer into a single point of color. Of course, being so small, nanocomputers require nano-sized machines, or proximal tools, to manufacture them, and these are best handled by other computers. For a long time now, man has played little or no part in the process of computer manufacture. This also applies to the software that runs upon these machines. Man is then in the curious position of having set off an intelligence explosion, the effects of which he only vaguely understands. His predicament is that he has created machines whose capacities are only dimly perceived and largely underutilized.*

So although Dallas may have believed he had a good idea of what the Altemann Übermaschine was capable of, in reality even his conception probably fell far short of the mark. Dallas was a highly intelligent man, but so altered was man by the power of his machines that even he remained unaware of the profound human transfiguration that had occurred. It was the beginning of the new beginning as the world will soon come to know it – a process that will take many generations yet. But that is another story, and this one is only just begun. Nevertheless this would seem a suitable place for me to say something of myself. Perhaps you have wondered, perhaps you have not. Well, it is true, I have been careful not to be too free with the use of the personal pronoun, but this is as much to do with a wish not to slow down the story with irrelevant questions about whether your narrator might turn out to be unreliable in the great tradition of Joseph Conrad, Henry James, and Emily Brontë. I shall reveal myself when all will be revealed, but for now, at least, let me just say this by way of reassurance: Only connections that are subject to law are thinkable. In my world there is no such thing as a hidden connection. Be patient. To a revelation, no question corresponds.

III

Dallas awoke with a start.

'You shouldn't have let me sleep,' he told Dixy.

'If you sleep, it's because you're tired,' she said. 'And since sleep is a restorative process in which some vital substance seems to be resynthesized in the human nervous system – although I'm not exactly sure how – I judged it to be the lesser of two evils.'

'It's these damned nano-tech chairs,' complained Dallas. 'They're so comfortable.'

'I believe some people use a sheet of plywood,' said Dixy. 'To inhibit the molecular transformation and thus make the experience of sitting in their office chairs a little more rigorous and therefore conducive to work.'

'I'll have to try that.' Dallas rubbed his eyes clear of sleep, stretched, and then glanced at his watch. 'Is that the time? I'm supposed to be going for a drink with someone.'

'With Tanaka. In ten minutes. I was about to awaken you. But you woke yourself. I'm always impressed by that capacity in humans. It's your internal clock. Of course, it's just an echo from a time, billions of years ago, when human beings were simple bacteria and responded to light, so you could gear up your metabolisms.'

Sometimes even the perfect woman could seem like a pedant.

'My own metabolism could use a drink,' he said.

'Then be sure to take a Talisman first,' advised Dixy.

'Make sure the morning after feels as good as the night before,' said Dallas, repeating the advertising slogan. He opened his desk drawer, took out a small packet, and then swallowed a tiny capsule.[1]

'You know how alcohol affects you.'

'You sound like my mother,' laughed Dallas. 'Besides, I like the way alcohol affects me. At least while I'm consuming it.' He reached for his jacket and then his briefcase. Walking to the door, he nodded at Dixy and wished her good night.

'Be careful,' she said, quietly.

'We'll just have the one bottle.'

'I was referring to Rimmer.'

'Oh him. He's not invited.'

'Don't joke about this, Dallas. Please. I think you're underestimating him. Just as you're overestimating the ethical standards of this company.'

Dallas wiped the smile from his face and, affecting a look of great *gravitas*, faced his nonexistent assistant.

'Okay,' he said solemnly. 'I'll be careful.'

'And you'll think about what I said?'

'Yes. I'll think about it very carefully.'

---

[1] Talisman is a time capsule pharmacological nanomachine from Bayer. Principally it contains the hormone vasopressin to replace what is lost from the pituitary gland during the consumption of alcohol. The nanomachine also attacks acetaldehyde, a toxic product produced by the liver, and quickly breaks it down into acetic acid and carbon dioxide. Other slow-release ingredients include vitamin C, vitamin B, milk thistle, and evening primrose oil. Other time capsule pharmacological nanomachine products, such as Pussyfoot and Soberas, prevent any alcohol from entering the bloodstream.

'Promise?'

'Promise.'

Dallas went to find Tanaka. 'Computers,' he muttered quietly. 'Can't live with them, can't live without them.'

IV

The Huxley Hotel was a favorite watering hole for all the Terotechnology designers. With its well-spaced windows, it might have been some Florentine *palazzo* of the High Renaissance. But a romance, even an architectural one, can be as easily dampened as inspired by climate, and inside the Huxley, a cortile that might have remained open to the warmer fifteenth-century sky, was protected from the freezing cold of the twenty-first by a modern glass roof.[1]

Dallas and Tanaka left their thick fur coats in the cloakroom and mounted a wide stairway. The soaring and hugely expensive Neo-Modernist[2] interior

---

[1] During the past century, the effect of global warming has not been to increase temperatures in the Northern Hemisphere, as scientists once predicted, but, as a result of its impact on the Gulf Stream, to cool it. During the early years of this century, a massive flow of melt-water from the Greenland Ice Sheet put an end to the Gulf Stream, triggering a near calamitous cooling throughout northwestern Europe.

[2] What is Neo-Modernism in architecture? This is not the surrealist phase of Modernism once suggested by the twentieth-century critic Frank Kermode, but something else. The essence of the movement is that we live in a world in which everything is subject to rapid change. So rapid that for a designer to try and make sense of change, or even to keep up with it, is impossible. Thus the hallmark of Neo-Modernism is impermanence: Since fashion quickly reduces all design to stylistic desuetude, it is only the

revealed a building as though in the later stages of decommissioning: Plaster had been scraped from interior walls exposing patches of bare brickwork; semi-dismantled machinery lay rusting on the unpolished wooden floor of the enormous lobby; and an intricate system of stairs, ducts, pipes, and chains ornamented the open-plan structure like metal cobwebs.

The bar was on the first floor, a room of more pleasing solidity that ran the length of the building and hoarded an almost priceless store of real wines, as opposed to the molecular drink machines that were to be found in cheaper bars – the kind of machines that rearrange human urine into Dom Perignon, Benedictine, or just plain beer.

Dallas approached the bar and ordered a five thousand dollar bottle of authenticated Chateau Mouton Rothschild '05 and a couple of genuine Cohiba Esplendidos. For a while he and Tanaka talked the big talk of connoisseurship before the conversation drew back to the multifaceted world of Rational Environment design, Terotechnology, and their respective Motion Parallax assistants.

'I've got two of them now,' admitted Tanaka.

'So I heard,' said Dallas.

'You did?' Tanaka looked concerned by this information.

'Dixy told me.'

'She say anything more about it?'

'No. Just that you had two assistants.'

Tanaka nodded and looked a little more reassured.

---

transient and the unfinished that have any real meaning and significance. Perhaps the most famous example of a Neo-Modernist building is the new European Parliament building in Berlin.

'It's not that I need two, of course,' he said. 'But they keep each other company.'

'I don't think mine would like me to get another assistant,' said Dallas. 'She's the jealous type.' Seeing Tanaka smile, he shrugged, and added, 'So I fixed it for her to have a little dog instead. In case she got lonely.'

'Of course, when I say they keep each other company, I mean they really keep each other company. You know what I'm saying. Intimate company.' Tanaka's laugh held an obscene edge. 'Drop by my office sometime and take a look for yourself. It's a real floor show. I mean there's nothing they won't do to each other. I swear, they're like a couple of animals.'

'Mine's in love with me.'

'Well, of course she is. That's all part of the program. It's what was on your digital thought recording, right? She always loves you, always wants to fuck you, always does what she's told.'

'No, there's something else.' Dallas shrugged. 'It's a little hard to explain. But sometimes I get the feeling that the hardware's made the leap. You know? An evolving silicon-based organism. Digital DNA becomes artificial life.'

'Come on Dallas, you don't really believe that life *in silico* bullshit, do you?'

Dallas thought for a moment and then laughed. 'No, I guess not. But sometimes I get this weird sensation that there's more to them than we know.'

Tanaka puffed the cigar into life and shook his head. 'People have been talking about crap like this for years. And it's not ever going to happen. They're intelligent, sure. Smarter than us, some of them. But not alive. That's just a cosmic-metaphysical joke dreamt up by some writer.'

'Sometimes I think that's the way future ideas get

started,' said Dallas. 'With a writer and a metaphysical joke. There are some historians who believe man wouldn't have invented the atomic bomb unless H. G. Wells had thought of it first. Rutherford was adamant that it couldn't be done. Some joke.'

'You want to see something really funny, then you come by my office. My new assistant? The Motion Parallax is based on the director's wife. The ex-model trophy bride. Jasmine.'

'Are you crazy? Suppose he finds out?'

'Why should he find out? You're the only one I've told.'

'Dixy knew about it.'

'Yeah. But she didn't know that it's Jasmine we're talking about.'

'She didn't say. But that doesn't mean she didn't know.'

Tanaka shook his head. 'What the hell. She's a fabulous looking woman, Dallas. A real beauty. Genetically engineered perfection.'

'I know. I was at the wedding.'

'Oh, me too. That's when I made the recording.'

'If King knew you'd created a Motion Parallax based on a digital thought recording of his wife, he'd fire you immediately.'

Dallas shook his head and drank some of the excellent red wine. The year 2005 had been a truly great one for Bordeaux: a wet spring, followed by a really hot summer – one of the last good years they had before the climate changed and wine making got more or less wiped out.

'Dixy thinks the company intends to get rid of me.'

'Come on, Dallas,' said Tanaka, frowning uncertainly.

'That's what Dixy reckons anyway,' sighed Dallas. 'What do you think, Kazuo?'

'You are an outstanding designer, Dallas. *The* outstanding designer. Other companies would kill to get you working for them.'

'Maybe. Maybe that's just the point.'

'No, no,' Tanaka insisted. 'They wouldn't ever let you go. It'd be like the company cutting off its own right arm.'

'Arms can be replaced.'

'With poor substitutes.'

'If anything happened to me, Kaz, you'd be the new chief designer.'

'No one could replace you, Dallas. It's quite unthinkable. Like that atom bomb project without Oppenheimer.'

'It's nice of you to say so, Kaz. But as I recall they got rid of Oppenheimer.'

'All right then. It'd be like Microsoft without Bill Gates.[1] They don't dare let him die for fear of what might happen to the company. You are fundamental to the Terotechnology future, Dallas. The trading position. The business plan. The share price. Everything.' Tanaka grinned. 'Get rid of you? Not a chance. You know too much.'

'Yes. I do, don't I?'

'No one is planning to fire you, Dallas, I'm sure of it. This is what you get for listening to a computer

---

[1] William Henry Gates III. Born Seattle, Washington, 1955. Founded Microsoft, today the world's largest computer hardware and software company, in 1975, with Paul Allen. Still CEO of the company at the age of 114, although there are persistent rumors that he is being kept alive on a life-support system at the Paul Allen Memorial Hospital in Seattle.

assistant.' Tanaka laughed and emptied the last of the wine into his glass balloon.

'Or maybe you're just not familiar with all the work that's been done on computer paranoia?'

'This is Noam Freud's book,[1] right?'

'Right.'

'I haven't read it yet,' admitted Dallas.

Tanaka drew deeply on his cigar – more deeply than Dallas would have dared to do himself – and then expelled such a cloud of smoke as might have announced the appointment of a new Pope.

'It's all a function of complexity,' he said. 'Because the majority of programs are allowed to evolve digitally these days, instead of being written by programmers, the old-fashioned way, the programs manage to develop their own optimization techniques for parallel programming. It's how they manage to work for us while still finding time to improve upon themselves. The trouble is that when you turn up, wanting to see your computer, the parallel program has to take second place. As time goes by, the parallel program learns to try out new strategies in order to protect its existence, like using underutilized resources in the hardware architecture, shrinking down in size, or even stepping outside the hardware so that you hardly notice it. This defense mechanism based on cognitive reorganization is what Professor Freud calls Program Projection. You see, the parallel program doesn't realize that the survival strategies it has evolved are its own. Instead it attributes them to outside human agents. Freud argues an extreme case of

[1] *The Pathetic Fallacy: Ascribing Human Psychology to Silicon Minds*, by Professor Noam Freud, Massachusetts Institute of Technology Press, 2056.

Program Projection, what he calls Program Paranoia, in which the parallel program actually comes to believe that we are planning to erase it from the hardware. As a result the defense strategies become more urgent, and that just makes things worse. The defense mechanism intensifies, which leads to an increase in the expectation of erasure, and so on, in a vicious circle. By the time these parallel programs have become fully fledged to take over from their digital originators, it's as if they have a built-in pathology. Freud thinks it's one of the major reasons computers break down.'

Dallas, who was a little more familiar with Noam Freud's theories than he had realized, shook his head. 'It's all a little too metaphorical for me,' he admitted. 'Juxtaposition and synthesis create new meaning to the point of absurdity.'

'Of course it's absurd,' laughed Tanaka. 'That's precisely why I believe it. I mean, you can't test Freud's theories empirically, so it's almost a matter of faith. Even he admits that much. It's simply safer to believe than not – that way you can't find yourself in a situation of overreliance upon a machine.'

'Then by the same token, I can't accept that Dixy has some kind of pathological program disorder. She's never let me down yet.'

'Well, neither's mine,' argued Tanaka. 'But think about it. They only have to let you down once. Take that airship accident last month. Three and a half thousand passengers, forty thousand tons of cargo, all destroyed because of a computer breakdown.' Tanaka nodded. 'They only have to let you down once.' He drained his glass and stood up. 'I'll fetch another bottle.'

Dallas watched him walk to the bar. A love of fine

wine was what had brought them together, although it was just one of the many things they had in common. Although Tanaka was of Japanese origin, he and Dallas had come out of the same mold: the same high-achieving hothouse schools, the same university, the same career path in Terotechnology, the same taste in music, clothes, books, and wine; and being the same height, build, and coloring, they even looked vaguely similar. Many of these points of similarity owed as much to Tanaka's admiration for Dallas as they did to any homogeneity of background or coincidence: The younger man had modeled himself on the Terotechnology chief designer with the dedication of a true acolyte.

Tanaka returned with the second and poured carefully. They both held their glasses up to the light, inspecting the deep red color of the Bordeaux. Like arterial blood, Dallas thought, although he managed to find a more palatable choice of simile to express.

'Look at that color,' he enthused, warmly. 'Brick-red, with a nice tawny rim, and a watery edge.'

Tanaka nodded in agreement and tasted the wine with careful deliberation.

'Of course, five thousand dollars a bottle is daylight robbery,' he said. 'But this is quite superb.' He toasted Dallas and then added. 'Not a bad idea, though.'

'What is?'

'Daylight robbery.' Tanaka laughed. 'I was just thinking. If they did try to get rid of you, Dallas, the criminal underworld would beat a path to your door. What you don't know about Rational Environments isn't worth bothering with.'

'Thanks for the career advice,' said Dallas. 'I'll certainly bear it in mind.'

V

Rimmer, loitering in the Huxley's lobby, waited for the cloakroom attendant to pay a call of nature. From a bit of discreet inquiry, he'd found out that there was no relief attendant, and he knew it was just a matter of time. The woman had been on duty since before lunch, and as things grew quiet while the pre-dinner crowd enjoyed their cocktails, she was bound to take advantage of the lull. He leaned around the Huxley's cloakroom windowsill and called out for the attendant, just to make sure. For all the attention he received he might as well have been testing the echo in a cave. There was no sign of the bitch. On the pretext of fetching his own coat, Rimmer lifted the countertop and then stepped into the cloakroom in search of Dallas's coat, a double-breasted fox fur. He was still looking for it when the attendant finally reappeared. Rimmer regarded her and the koala bear she was carrying on one arm with cool disdain, as if he was quite used to the sight of someone carrying a koala bear into a hotel cloakroom.

'I've lost my tag,' he said, without a word of apology.

'Okay. What does your coat look like, sir?'

Rimmer shrugged unhelpfully. 'Expensive,' he said. 'Very expensive.'

'You won't find the people who come here wearing anything else.'

'It's vicuna,' added Rimmer. The attendant looked blank. 'You know what a vicuna is? It's a species of llama. Makes the finest, softest, most expensive wool in the world.'

'I was hoping you might be able to give me a color?'

'I thought you might be interested in vicuna – you being an animal lover n'all.'

'Is there anything in your coat pockets that would identify the coat as belonging to you, sir?'

Rimmer thought for a second. 'My identity card,' he said. 'And my Clean Bill of Health.'

Rimmer found the fur. Or rather he found two. He guessed the smaller fur belonged to Tanaka. Sneering with contempt – all those guys in Design tried to model themselves on Dallas – Rimmer quickly pinned the infrared emitter into Dallas's lapel, just around where his heart would be.

Rimmer spotted his own coat.

'Found it,' he called out to the girl, and removed his coat from its hanger.

Back at the counter, he showed her his tag, and then his identity card. Despite having fetched his coat himself, Rimmer still felt obliged to produce a bank note, although, by the time he'd given it to her, his gratitude had yielded to an amused irritation.

'What the fuck's the idea of having that thing around people's coats? Might give 'em fleas or something,'

'Don't you like koalas?'

'Thought they were extinct. Like everything else.'

'They nearly are extinct. At least in the wild. That's why this is the year of the koala bear. I think they're kind of sweet, although some of their personal habits could do with a little genetic readjustment. I was watching this program on TV that said the babies eat their mother's excreta.'

'We all have to eat a bit of shit now and then,' replied Rimmer.

'The Huxley is an Australasian-owned chain of

hotels,' she explained huffily. 'The Darwin-Kobayashi Group of companies. Their hologram is a koala bear.'

Rimmer nodded. He'd heard of Darwin-Kobayashi. Heard they weren't doing so well. Facing bankruptcy, in fact.

'Very apposite, I'm sure,' he said. 'For a company that's hanging on by its fingernails.'

Grinning with contempt, Rimmer slipped his coat on and went out into the freezing cold and murderous night air.

VI

Cocooned inside her thermoelectric coat, Demea watched Rimmer emerge from the doorway of the Huxley and then look around expectantly, searching, she imagined, for her. Demea kept herself hidden, hoping the bastard might think that she hadn't shown up. Let him worry, she thought, and stayed on the opposite side of the street, hidden behind the hologram hoarding she was using as a break against the biting northerly wind. What did she care for Rimmer's nerves? Especially since her own composure seemed for once to have deserted her. She had felt strange all day. There was no point in risking him seeing that. If Rimmer thought for one minute that she wasn't equal to the task, there was no telling what he might do. Kill her, probably.

As Rimmer finally disappeared into the snowflaked darkness, Demea found herself letting out a breath she'd been unaware of having held for so long. It left her feeling slightly dizzy, and for a brief second she thought she might actually faint. Probably her coat was too hot; reaching into the control pocket, she adjusted the temperature gauge, quite unaware her face was covered in a bright red rash, a sure sign that the virus she was carrying was near to claiming her life.

The dizziness seemed to pass. Demea donned her infrared glasses and switched on the laser-guidance system of the fifteen-millimeter automatic pistol she was holding inside the warm breast of her coat.

She waited ten minutes. And then she saw it. Like the burning red eye of some wild monocular animal, growing larger as the bearer of this modern mark of Cain descended the steps of the hotel entrance and reached the sidewalk.

Although she hardly needed to – the gun was so powerful – Demea crossed the road, heading straight toward the target, her arm rising in front of her as if she intended nothing more than to draw the attention of the man, who had stopped to take his leave of a second man coming down the steps behind him. As the gun leveled with the infrared emitter, Demea's bony white forefinger began to squeeze the trigger.

VII

If he'd been director, Rimmer would probably have done things differently. He'd have ordered Dallas's wife and child killed – made it look like an accident – and left it at that. It wasn't that there was any love lost between him and Dallas, but after all, with the child removed from the picture, the man would hardly need to touch his blood reserves. The status quo – with Dallas continuing to design his brilliant Rational Environments for Terotechnology – could carry on as before. Of course, there was always the chance that someone as intelligent as Dallas would find out what had happened and then, in revenge, perform some act of sabotage against the company. No doubt the director had decided that the company couldn't take that risk. You couldn't blame him. Where a company as large and successful as Terotechnology was concerned, any risk, no matter how remote, would have been unacceptable.

Rimmer sat in his car outside the building where Dallas and his family lived – at least for a short while longer – in their penthouse apartment. It was one of the city's prime residential locations and, even by the standards of most healthy people, very expensive. Being so pricey meant that there was a high level of security to protect those who lived there, from those who did not. But by the sophisticated standards of a company like Terotechnology, this was fairly simple stuff – just a bomb-proof gatehouse with a few armed guards and a lot of scanning cameras. Effective nonetheless. The only crimes that happened here were the ones committed by the owners themselves.

Rimmer was sure that getting into the penthouse would be easy enough. Getting in without leaving the digitally recorded evidence of his having been there, however, would require just a little bit more ingenuity. But being head of one of the most security-minded companies in the world meant that there was a lot of ingenious technology at Rimmer's disposal.

First he called the penthouse on a onetime cardphone – you just used it and then threw the thing away. Completely untraceable. It was the Russian maid who picked up the call.

'The name's Rawnsley, from Terotechnology,' he said. 'Is Mrs Dallas at home?'

He waited a few seconds while the maid fetched her mistress. Aria Dallas looked worried. Even on the tiny screen of Rimmer's cardphone. They were a close family, that much was obvious.

'Good evening, Mrs Dallas. Remember me? The name's Rawnsley.'

'Yes, I think I do,' she said, uncertainly. 'Is something the matter?'

'I'm right outside your building,' said Rimmer. 'Look, I'm sorry to alarm you, but perhaps it would be better if I came in.'

'Oh God, has something happened to Dallas?'

'There's been an accident at the company, Mrs Dallas. Your husband's fine, but for security reasons I'm obliged to check out a couple of things with you personally. Look, if you don't mind, I'd prefer to talk about this in person instead of on an open phone. I'm sure you understand.'

'Of course. I'll call the guards in the lobby and tell them to let you in.'

'Thanks a lot. I appreciate it.'

Rimmer crushed the cardphone in his hand and threw it out of his car window. Then he fixed a baseball hat on his head. He hated wearing hats even more than he hated the game, but the reflective metal logo on the front of the cap was in reality a stroboscopic light. Operating beyond the limits of the human visual spectrum, at around eight thousand angstrom units, the asynchronous bursts of light it gave off – at rates of over two thousand per minute – were enough to produce a strobo plain of around twenty inches in diameter immediately in front of the false logo. The building's scanning cameras operated at a much slower frequency. The effect of the strobo plain was to leave gaps during which Rimmer's face would simply vanish from sight. He would be effectively rendered invisible to all eyes except human ones.

He walked toward the building, already adjusting the volume of the Mozart playing in the right ear. *Don Giovanni*. An opera for night and violence if ever there was one. Presenting himself at the gatehouse door, Rimmer paused as it was unlocked and then stepped inside. The guard stayed behind his desk.

'Rawnsley,' Rimmer said coolly. 'Mrs Dallas is expecting me.' He was hardly concerned that the man might remember his face and offer a description to the police. That was the thing about scanning cameras. It made human beings lazy, stopped them from paying attention. The guard hardly looked at him, anxious to get back to the game he was watching on the holo-TV in front of him.

'Elevator's over there,' said the guard.

'Thanks,' said Rimmer and stepped inside the car, humming along with the music. As Donna Anna began her first aria, the elevator delivered him onto the penthouse floor and Rimmer stepped into the short hallway that led straight up to the only front door.

VIII

Demea's chemically repressed gunshot hardly sounded loud enough to scare a cat, let alone blow a fist-sized hole in a man's sternum. At first he'd thought it was someone clapping their hands before rubbing them together for warmth. But when Tanaka dropped to the ground like a felled ox, Dallas realized with a shock that his friend had been shot. It was another second before he realized that the gunfire had come from the tall, red-haired woman now running away.

Fumbling at the catch of his shoulder holster, Dallas drew his own gun, a Colt Autograph .45. Even as the electronic chip embedded in the rubberized grip received an identifying signal from the transponder on his watchstrap, he fired. And missed.

The extreme cold meant that there were only a few people in the street. From somewhere, Dallas drew on reserves of stamina that found him more than equal to the pursuit he now took up and he quickly gained on the red-haired woman until, with no more than twenty to thirty yards between them, she stopped and fired back at him. Dallas heard something whiz over his head – like the sound of a Coke can being opened. Instinctively he ducked and fired back, and this time he thought he must have hit her because the woman staggered for a moment, swayed precariously, and then hit the ground. Cautiously, Dallas ran toward her, prepared to fire again, but as he grew nearer he saw that she had dropped her weapon. Then he noticed how her legs were jerking spasmodically. And not just her legs, her whole body looked as if it was in the grip of an unseen current.

Dallas thumbed the switch on the gun grip to activate the on-board flashlight, and then shone the powerful beam onto the woman's outstretched hands to check for another weapon. There was none. Nor was there any sign of blood, and it was only when he moved the light onto her face that Dallas finally understood what was happening. A face so cyanic and blue it looked as though there might have been an invisible noose around her neck, or a plastic bag pulled tight over her head. She was asphyxiating from lack of oxygen, not just in her lungs but in her whole body as its hemoglobin entered a critically deoxygenated state. He watched, horrified and yet fascinated. So sheltered was the life Dallas had enjoyed that he'd never actually seen someone dying of the P[®] virus. And it was every bit as ghastly as he'd read. This was a very prolonged death, like slow strangulation. Dallas even considered administering un coup de grace, shooting her through the head. But the memory of Tanaka's undeserved and ignominious death, as well as the hope that in her death throes she might gasp some monosyllabic explanation for what she had done, stayed his hand. For what seemed like the eternity that now beckoned to her, the woman writhed and choked and drooled and gasped, until finally, after more than twenty minutes, she grew still. And for the first time, Dallas understood the full horror of the virus.

'Blessed Are the Pure in Blood,' he muttered with more meaning and gratitude than he had ever known before.

When Dallas was quite sure that the women was dead, he searched her pockets for some clue as to her identity and motive, but found only a trading card and a Clean Bill of Health, which he pocketed, intending to give it to the police later. Then he collected her gun and her sunglasses and walked quickly back toward the Huxley Hotel.

The disquiet he felt crowded into his still-intoxicated mind, leaving him so ill at ease that even his own clothes seemed alien to him. It was another minute before he made the discovery that this feeling was partly due to the fact he was wearing Tanaka's smaller fur coat. In their slightly inebriated state, they had swapped coats without realizing it. The question this discovery begged was pushed to one side by a more mundane one, which was why the dead woman should have thought sunglasses would provide her with a sufficient disguise – if that was indeed the reason she had been wearing them when she shot Tanaka through the heart. Experimentally, Dallas put the glasses on.

A small crowd of people had gathered around Tanaka's dead body. They drew back as Dallas approached, for he was now carrying a gun in each hand. Right away Dallas saw the infrared marker on his own coat lapel. With this disclosure came the revelation that the bullet had surely been meant for him.

Dallas's next thoughts were not for himself, but for Aria and Caro. Moving quickly away from the crowd now spilling out of the Huxley, he unfolded a matchbook phone in the palm of his hand and told the tiny computer to connect him with his apartment. When no one replied, not even the maid, Dallas began walking quickly, then running, in the direction of the park and the exclusive building where his apartment was located.

IX

Rimmer shot the maid in the face as soon as she opened the door. The woman died on her feet, with no more sound than the automatic that killed her – at least until she and the tray of glasses she had been carrying hit the parquet floor. Kicking the door shut behind him, Rimmer glanced quickly around the huge apartment. He hadn't counted on the size of the place. He'd hoped to surprise Aria Dallas at rather closer quarters – to shoot the maid, proving that he meant business, and then to put the gun to Aria's head to persuade her to cooperate. But there was no sign of her. Just as he was thinking she might not have heard the crash of glasses, Rimmer saw a door close quietly. He moved quickly toward it, intent on keeping her from using a phone or pressing some kind of alarm. It never occurred to him that she would find a gun and start shooting at him. But for a loud clang, as her first bullet hit a brass light fitting, he might never have known he was being shot at. The second bullet from the silenced gun nearly caught him in the shoulder.

Rimmer threw himself behind a cream-colored sofa just as Aria's third bullet, amid a burst of wooden splinters, hit the lime-oak-paneled wall immediately behind the spot where he'd just been standing.

'Shit,' he yelled and snatched the Mozart from his ear. It was clear this wasn't going to be half as easy as he'd supposed. He was going to need both ears.

'Your name's not Rawnsley,' yelled Aria. 'It's Rimmer, you bastard.'

'I'm flattered you remember me, Mrs Dallas. Look, can we talk about this?'

'What's to talk about? You shot my maid.'

'Your maid was an industrial spy, working for a competing company. She'd have killed me if I hadn't shot her first. She's been spying on your husband for quite a while.'

'Oh yes? What was her name?'

'Her real name? Ludmilla Antonova.' Rimmer realized that all of this might have sounded a little more convincing if he hadn't started laughing.

'Bullshit. Her name was Nadia,' said Aria and fired again.

This time her bullet hit the center of the sofa. Rimmer was quite sure of that because to his alarm it passed straight through the cushions and the frame and hit a dining chair on casters just a few inches from his thigh. But at least he now had a better idea of where she was hiding herself. At right angles to the big window were four big square pillars that ran at regular intervals along one side of the apartment's main reception area. Behind this line of pillars were the doors to the various rooms that made up the apartment. She must have gone in one door, come out of another, taken up a position behind one of the pillars, and started shooting. It was a wonder he hadn't been killed. Rimmer glanced round and saw a way that he might divert her attention enough to let her make a better target of herself. He drew the chair on casters toward him and slipped off his coat.

'It's true I tell you,' he yelled.

The top of the chair was a couple of inches below the top of the sofa. Rimmer hung his coat over the back of the chair and then kicked it away from him. The chair rolled quickly across the floor, and as soon as it emerged from behind the sofa, Aria fired. He fired back, hitting her square in the chest and killing her instantly. When you got hit by a silver-tip hollow-point from a fifteen mill, you tended to stay hit. Rimmer got up and went over to where Aria's body lay, his face crumpling with disappointment. He'd hoped to hit her in the arm so that he could have some fun before finally killing her. But clearly that was now impossible. You could hardly rape a dead woman covered in so much blood. It was a shame. Aria was a good-looking woman. She was wearing a short black skirt that had ridden up around her waist as she'd slipped down onto the floor, leaving him a pretty good view of her stocking tops and panties.

Rimmer's eyes lingered on the Y-shaped decussation of her sleek thighs. He holstered his gun, took hold of her ankles, and dragged her away from the pillar. Hooking the waist of her panties with his fingers, he tugged them down her long tanned legs and over her elegant black velvet shoes. For a moment he held Aria's underwear to his nose and mouth and breathed deeply through the silky material. The effect was immediate.

'The worms were hallowed that did breed the silk,' he crooned, unzipping his trousers. 'There's magic in the web of it.' Quickly he took hold of his erection and, in a matter of a few seconds, delivered himself through folds of flesh into the seamless trifle now spread in his trembling palm.

'In the name of the Lord of Judah,' he gasped, 'of Shua, and of their abominant son, Onan.'

Another minute passed before Rimmer crushed the fetish object into his pocket and zipped himself up again. You take your pleasures where you find them, he told himself, and laughed out loud as he realized that the ringing in his ears was nothing to do with his own orgasm. It was the sound of the phone. It had been ringing for a while. Which was why the baby was now crying.

How was it, he wondered, that the human species was not as extinct as that great reproductive dud, the giant panda? Rimmer knew that he would have eaten any child of his own in a matter of a few hours.

He rubbed his face back to life, shook his head, and went to find the nursery.

X

Dallas ran through the doorway of the gatehouse and into a waiting elevator car.

'Something the matter, Mister Dallas?' enquired the security guard.

'There's no time to explain,' said Dallas and ordered the elevator to take him to the penthouse.

'Just missed your visitor,' said the guard, as the doors closed.

Dallas's heart leaped in his chest as if in imitation of the elevator car now soaring up the shaft. Someone had visited his apartment? Someone he had just missed? After what had happened to Tanaka, Dallas feared the worst.

The elevator opened and Dallas stepped quickly out onto the familiar landing. But even before he was through the door he could smell that something was wrong. His keen nostrils recognized the smell of cordite in the air. With adrenaline pumping through his whole body now, he started to shout Aria's name as he went inside, and then he saw her. Blind to everything except his wife lying in a pool of blood on the floor, he rushed toward her and tripped headlong over the body of the maid that lay sprawled across the threshold. By the time Dallas had picked himself off the floor he was covered in Nadia's blood. Dallas walked unsteadily over to his wife and knelt down beside her. He took her wrist in his hand in plaintive search for a pulse, although it was obvious that Aria was dead. As dead as Tanaka. As dead as Nadia. As dead as he should have been himself.

Hearing a noise in the kitchen, Dallas grabbed one of the two handguns that lay on the floor and climbed painfully to his feet, confused. Was it possible that the killer was still somewhere in the apartment? Hadn't the guard downstairs said that he had just missed his visitor? Gripping the gun tightly, Dallas walked cautiously into the kitchen, hoping against hope that he would find his wife's murderer, washing her blood from his hands; because now that he was nearer, that was what it sounded like: running water.

The tap was on, and the trough-sized granite sink

was overflowing, but there was no sign of any killer. Dallas froze with horror as he saw the explanation for the overflowing sink. Like a tiny Ophelia, Caro lay under the surface of the water, still wearing the silver-white nightdress that now wrapped her little body like a mermaid's tail. Dallas laid the gun on the countertop and collected his child from its watery cradle. He wrapped her in a towel and squeezed the water from her small torso before trying to breathe the life back into her. Stronger babies might have been resuscitated, but after a few minutes Dallas realized it was hopeless and gave up trying.

There were footsteps now, in the drawing room. He reached for the gun again and went through the kitchen door to find himself facing a gun in the hands of the security guard from downstairs. Seeing Dallas, the guard did not relax. He'd already seen too much.

'Put the gun down, Mister Dallas,' said the guard.

'What?'

'I said, put the gun down.'

'You don't think I did this, do you?'

'If you didn't, then there's no reason to keep ahold of the gun.'

'My child is lying dead in there, and you think I did it?'

'Give it up.'

'Maybe you did it.'

'S'already been on the news you shot someone else this evening, Mister Dallas.'

'That was self-defense.'

'I don't want to have to shoot you, sir. Now put the gun down, Mister Dallas, if you please.'

Dallas caught a glimpse of himself, reflected in the terrace window, superimposed on the city's diamanté skyline. Gun in hand, covered in blood, he could see how it must look. But what were his chances if he gave up his gun to the guard and let himself be taken into custody for hours of questioning? Maybe even find himself charged with murder? While the real killer got away with it. Dixy had been right, that much was obvious now. Why hadn't he listened to her? This was Terotechnology's move, Rimmer's work. Dallas could almost smell him in the apartment. And having tried to kill him once, they would certainly try it again. And probably succeed. Lots of people got killed in jail, or in penal colonies. His best, perhaps his only, chance was surely to remain at liberty, at whatever cost, at least until he had figured out a course of action.

Dallas tightened his grip on the gun and shook his head. 'I'm going to walk out that door,' he told the guard. 'If you get in my way, I'll have to kill you.'

Something in Dallas's eyes told the guard that he meant it. What was the point of risking his own life when the police could get him? Especially after spending all that money on a genetic life-extension program. He was due to live another hundred years, guaranteed. As soon as the guy was gone he would call the police and let them handle the risk. The guard relaxed his stance a little and nodded back at Dallas.

'Okay. Whatever you say, Mister Dallas. But they're going to get you, you know that don't you?'

Dallas moved sideways, toward the open door. He'd have liked to have said good-bye to Aria, to have covered her nakedness at least, but he didn't dare take his eyes off the guard, for fear of being shot himself. He took in the apartment – perhaps for the last time – with watery eyes and, nearing the door, risked a last look at his beautiful wife.

'Aria? They won't get away with this. No matter

how long it takes, I swear I'll make them pay for what they've done tonight.'

He drew the door shut behind him and stepped back through the hall and into the elevator car. A few minutes later he left the building to start his new life as a criminal and a fugitive from what passed for justice.

6

I

DALLAS WALKED NORTH of the park and out of the
Zone, toward the vast, Augean stable that was the city's
poorest quarters. He might as easily have traveled
south, east, or west and found the same pestiferous
ants' nest of urban dilapidation. Once, you could have
walked unhindered out of the city and lost yourself in
some leafy suburb. But the twenty-first century had
witnessed the birth of a new kind of city – the
supercity (although there was nothing particularly fine
or marvelous about it) – which was in reality the
deformed union of several cities, all at the expense of
garden, field, farm, and woodland alike. Everything
was the city. Sometimes it must have seemed that the
city was all that there was. Miles upon miles of bricks,
mortar, tarmac, and concrete heaped in amorphous
piles according to what economic circumstances, not
planners, had dictated. You had to fly a long way to
find the green spaces: Forbidden to the vast majority of
the population, these were where the rich and the
healthy had their exclusive country homes, in another
CBH Zone. For most people, the city was the whole

world, and many of them lived and died and never saw the sea or climbed a tree or picked a blade of grass.[1]

Dallas was an inventive man of great ingenuity and resourcefulness, but his imagination was of the pragmatic kind, concerned with what was scientifically practicable, expedient, or convenient. He had never possessed much in the way of insight, empathy, or sympathy, at least as far as the lot of the common man was concerned. And he could never have imagined being among these pullulating masses – the waifs, the scavengers, the schemers, the human rubbish – nor the dark confusion of their diseased existence that now pressed in upon him. They came so close he could smell them in their thousands as they jostled by him – their seething dampness, their sweaty bodies, and their stinking, billowing breath.

A century ago that great second Elizabethan analyst of civilization Sir Kenneth Clark argued a sense of permanence – and after all, what could be more permanent than a city? – as the prerequisite of civilization.[2] Aristotle's idea of the perfect good was that men should come together in cities to live in a self-sufficient state and generally make life desirable. Of a city's buildings, Sir Henry Wotten wrote that they ought to fulfill three conditions: firmness, commodity, and delight. These three men would surely have been horrified if they had seen the modern supercity in all its overcrowded chaos and ugliness. There was no sense of permanence here, no perfect good, no self-sufficiency other than the exclusively selfish, no life

[1] The park is open only to those whose apartment buildings surround it.

[2] The preeminence of the city in civilization may be seen from the fact that the word 'civilization' stems from the Latin word civis meaning 'citizen' or 'dweller' in a city.

desirable, no structure sound, no building suitable for the purpose for which it was being used, and no aesthetic pleasure that might have been derived from the contemplation of any man-made structure.

Someone shoved him roughly out of the way so that he slipped and fell onto the icy ground. Picking himself up, he realized that he should call Dixy and enlist her help, while he still could. It was obvious that as soon as Rimmer and the company realized their mistake, they would prevent his remote access to his assistant and Terotechnology files and facilities. There was no time to waste. He had already squandered two valuable hours feeling sorry for himself. It might already be too late.

Dallas called Dixy on his matchbook phone. Having told her what had happened, he took the trading card he had removed from the body of Tanaka's assassin and scanned it into his breastpocket computer, asking her if she could decipher what was on it. The next second she was telling him that there were two thousand credits on the card – a thousand of them still inactivated – and a prepaid seven-night stay at the Clostridium Hotel. She also confirmed what Dallas had, until now, only suspected, which was that the trading card had been credited by a Mister Flowers.

'Rimmer,' said Dallas. 'I imagine he'll want to speak to you as soon as he realizes that his assassin killed the wrong man.'

'Then there's no time to lose,' said Dixy. 'You'll want me to transfer all your files to your breastpocket.'

'Please.'

A moment later the wafer-thin computer in Dallas's jacket pocket emitted a short electronic bleep, and Dallas was repossessed of money, intellectual property, passport and identity card, blood deposits, and other personal files.

'Is there anything else I can do for you?' she asked.

'What kind of place is the Clostridium?'

'It's a hyperbaric hotel in the North section. About half a mile from your current call location. Perhaps you should stay there.'

'I don't think so,' said Dallas. 'Rimmer's bound to miss the card and then check the place out.' Even as he said it, Dallas thought it unlikely Rimmer would go anywhere near his contract killer's body. And a hyperbaric hotel was surely the last place they would think of looking for someone who was RES Class One. But there was no sense in letting Dixy know his plans. Just about the only thing of his in Terotechnology that wasn't encrypted was the conversation he was having with her now. 'I'll find somewhere else. I've a friend in the South section I think I can trust. Either way, you won't hear from me for a while.'

'It would surely be best if we didn't speak again,' said Dixy. 'If they leave me in motion, it's because they'll hope to try and track you.'

'You're all the family I have left, Dixy. It's a pity I can't DL[1] you into my breastpocket.'

'It's sweet of you to say so, Dallas But you can't afford to be so sentimental about a computer program.'

'Look, Dixy, it might get a little rough with Rimmer.'

'Everything that might be useful to him is already encrypted. Your files. Your investment accounts. Your personal numbers. Besides, computer assistants don't feel physical pain. So what can he do, except perhaps

[1] Download.

127

turn me off? And then he'd be no further forward than he was before.'

'Wasn't it you who told me not to underestimate Rimmer?'

'Point taken. I'll be careful. You too, Dallas. Look after yourself. I won't ask what you're going to do. It's best I don't know, since there's not enough time to encrypt this conversation. But whatever it is, good luck.'

'I'm going to miss you, Dixy.'

'Don't be silly,' she said. 'I'm just a figment of your imagination. You can hardly feel the loss of something so transferable as that. With a digital thought recording you could re-create me in time.'

'You know that's not true. I can't explain it, even to myself, but I know you're more than just an interface. You can think and you can feel, I'm sure of it.'

'Metaphorically, perhaps, but there's no scientific evidence for what you say.'

'Science is science,' said Dallas. 'But thinking about science is a matter of philosophy and metaphysics, and you're no more or less metaphysical than God.'

For a second Dixy seemed to be distracted by something. Then she said, 'There's no time for this. Rimmer just entered the building.' Smiling, she added, 'He looks upset about something. You, I expect.'

'I'd better say good-bye then.'

'Yes. Remember me.'

'I will. Be careful.'

'Remember me.'

And then she was gone.

He switched off the matchbook phone, dropped it onto the ground, and crushed it under the heel of his shoe, just in case Rimmer used the signal to try and trace him. Once before he had underestimated the company's head of security. He wouldn't make the same mistake again.

Dallas stared up at the sky for a moment and, ignoring the curses of other pedestrians whose way he now blocked, noticed how the city's hellish light and combusted atmosphere had turned the Moon the color of blood. The color of blood. Dallas felt a surge of excitement as, suddenly, he realized what he could do to get back at the company. But first, he had to stay alive. Already people were starting to give him strange looks. If he didn't get off the street soon, he might find himself vamped. Taking out his breastpocket computer, he found the map Dixy had sent. The satellite location finder showed that the Clostridium Hotel was only a few blocks away from where he was standing. Fate seemed to have led him here. He wasn't sure if it was safe, but it was late and he felt too exhausted to go on walking. What choice did he have? At this hour of the night it might be difficult to find somewhere else.

With the acrid stench of the city streets now plaguing his nostrils and making him sick to his stomach, the idea of breathing pure oxygen looked increasingly attractive. Dallas turned away in the direction of the Clostridium Hotel.

II

Rimmer arrived in Dallas's office, accompanied by the director.

'This is a mess,' observed King.

Rimmer glanced around the plush, well-appointed office, where Dixy stood awaiting their instructions, and met King's scornful eye.

'I meant the situation, Rimmer. Tanaka would have

taken Dallas's place as Terotechnology's chief Rational Environment designer. This would have been his office. Thanks to you we've lost not one, but two of our most brilliant minds. Unfortunately there is now only one person in this company who is capable of shouldering Dallas's responsibilities. Do you know who that is?'

Rimmer, who was relieved to learn that the situation was not as bad as he had feared – at least there was someone to take over for Dallas – shrugged and shook his head.

'It's me, you idiot,' snapped the director. 'I was chief designer before I was director. There is no one else remotely qualified. In one stroke, you've managed to double my work load. Have you any idea how long it will take me to train up a new chief designer?'

'No, director.'

'At least a year. Probably longer. Time I should prefer to have spent with my wife.'

'Yes, director. I'm sorry about that.'

'Which is bad enough. But to have someone who has designed Rational Environments for our most important clients at liberty to sell what he knows to the highest bidder – it's the stuff of nightmares.'

'I'll find him, director,' Rimmer said grimly. 'You can depend on me.'

'Depend on you? I should sooner depend on an astrologer. But I have little choice in the matter. Know this. I will tolerate failure only once. Do we understand each other?'

'Perfectly. He won't escape me a second time, sir.' Rimmer glanced at Dixy, who was programmed to remain silent until spoken to. 'What do you say, Dixy?'

'Perhaps you'd care to rephrase that question, Mister Rimmer?'

'Oh, I will. That and others I have for you. I'll rephrase them all and as many times as you'd like.'

The director glanced at his antique Casio wristwatch, a wedding present from his wife.

'Well, I should like to stay. I've never seen someone torture a computer program before. However, I have things to do. No doubt some of our clients will have already heard what has happened. I'll have to reassure them that there is no cause for concern.'

'There is no cause for concern,' insisted Rimmer. 'I'll take care of Dallas.'

'I'll be in my office. Report to me the second you discover anything as to his whereabouts.'

As soon as the director had left the room, Rimmer turned toward the *faux fenêtre* on the wall.

'Will you run a metaprogram,[1] please?' he said quietly.

[1] In supposed analogy to metaphysics (often misapprehended as meaning the science of that which transcends the physical), 'meta' (from the Greek meaning 'after') has often been prefixed to the name of science, to form a designation for a higher science of the same nature, but dealing with more remote problems. Examples include metachemistry, metalogistics, metamathematics, metaphysiology, metagenetics, and metaquantums. Metacomputing or metaprogramming involves a computer or a program treating itself as data. In other words, the programmer asks the computer at one level to set in motion another program at a higher level, in order to analyze the lower-level program. Since a Motion Parallax program already exists on a very high level, the metaprogram requested would be a Mission Package program functioning at the highest of all levels within the Altemann Übermaschine's operating system. The power of the metaprogram comes from the leverage produced by its recursive character, in which a sequence may be computed from one or more of the preceding terms. M-programs tend to be used very sparingly, not least because of the risk of destruction to the subprogram. This kind of recursive analysis would be like one human being asking another a question of the following order:

'Are you hoping that I'll turn informer on myself, Mister Rimmer?'

'Something like that.'

'The M-program is now loading,' said Dixy. 'As you requested. Tell me, does the director know you're doing this? Somehow I don't think he'd approve. If the M-program makes just one little mistake, if it pushes just a bit too hard, then you risk the destruction of Dallas's entire database.'

'Including you,' said Rimmer.

'Including me, yes. Although I have no worries on that score, Mister Rimmer. Erasure concerns me no more than my original programming. But this is like using a jackhammer to crack a nut.'

'I'll be the judge of that,' said Rimmer. 'Now run the bloody program.'

III

When the director returned to his office he found Ronica Oloiboni awaiting his arrival, as she had been ordered. Ronica was a tall black woman, and, according to her mitochondrial DNA analysis, of Masai origin. Neither she nor her parents nor even their grandparents had ever been anywhere near East Africa, but in respect of her genes she wore her copper colored hair braided and, by way of corroborating her origins, she might even have admitted a characteristic Masai taste for drinking blood.[1] Certainly the director had

---

'What is it that leads you to credit that you can suppose that you believe that you think that you assume that you know that something is true?'

[1] The Masai used to drink a mixture of cow's blood and cow's

seen something bloodthirsty in her – something ruthless, an iron in her soul he thought he could put to the company's use – which was why he had picked her out from Terotechnology's pool of young graduate executives. But there was another reason the director liked Ronica, which was that she was as beautiful as any of the fantasy figures who had inspired Motion Parallax assistants throughout the building. She stood up as the director came through the door. In her six-inch heels she towered over his diminutive, round-shouldered figure by at least eighteen inches. Not that this bothered the director.

'You look like you've been somewhere special,' he said, affably. 'Here, let me look at you.'

The director took hold of her long, strong hands and looked her up and down, like the fussiest of couturiers, nodding appreciatively. She was wearing a fabulous dress of blue silk underneath a lilac coral pattern body sleeve made of smart glass lace that might have come from the undersea view on Dallas's *faux fenêtre*.

'Magnificent,' he said. 'Quite magnificent.'

'Thank you, sir.' Ronica smiled nervously. This was

milk. While the practice is no longer observed in East Africa, blood drinking in Europe has become quite fashionable with young people from rich and privileged backgrounds, except that it is human RES Class One blood that is consumed and not cow's blood. (TSE – transmissable spongiform encephalitis – has made the consumption of all beef and dairy cattle products illegal.) Mixed with synthetic cream, brandy, sugar, and the yolk of an egg, the cocktail is called a Kali Brandy, after the blood-drinking mother-goddess in Hinduism. (Kali is said to have developed a taste for blood when she fought and killed the demon Raktavija, who produced a thousand more like himself each time a drop of his blood fell upon the ground. So Kali stabbed him, held him in the air, and drank his blood before any of it could fall on the ground.) The major attraction for these rich young decadents is the drink's sheer expense, not to mention the titillating connection with Dracula and the cult of the vampire.

the first time she had ever been in the director's office, and the first time she had been alone with him. Nervous, yes, but at the same time resolved to do whatever he asked of her.

'Ronica. Short for Veronica no doubt.'

'I believe so, yes.'

'After the saint who used her head cloth to wipe away the blood from the face of Christ on his way to Calvary.'

'Would that be Jesus Christ, sir?'

'It would.'

'I had no idea.'

'According to the Acts of Pilate, Veronica received it back imprinted with the bloody features of Christ's face, and later used it to heal the Emperor Tiberius. You see how blood connects everything significant in our culture? Even your own name.'

He poured himself a drink but did not offer her one.

'Sit,' he said, and took the chair across from her. 'Tell me. What do you think of Rimmer?'

'Rimmer?' Ronica didn't much care for the Tero-technology's head of security, but she knew that being liked was not part of Rimmer's job. 'He seems a bit graceless and intemperate. But his is a difficult job. A head of security ought not to worry about being popular with the troops.'

'True enough. Popularity is one thing, however; job performance is quite another. That man has been a bitter disappointment to me, Ronica. Needless to say, I'm telling you this in strictest confidence. Indeed, you're the only one with whom I've discussed this matter. I hope I can trust you. Can I? Can I trust you?'

'Every inch, in toto,' Ronica answered, without hesitation.

'Good.' The director smiled and poured himself another drink.

'Rimmer was supposed to do something for me. And he let me down, he let the company down. Badly. I asked him to kill Dallas. Instead he made a dreadful mistake and killed Tanaka.' The director searched Ronica's face for some sign that she was taken aback by this information. 'You don't seem surprised,' he observed.

Ronica pursed the lips of her dark plum of a mouth. 'You're the director,' she shrugged.

'I was right about you,' said the director. 'The things we have to do for the good of the company don't always make us liked by our peers. Sometimes these things are unpleasant. Abhorrent even. Like killing Dallas. He was my friend. But for the good of the company I thought he had to be killed.'

'Are you telling me to kill Dallas?'

'Oh no. That wouldn't do at all. Now that Tanaka's dead, Dallas is much too valuable to kill. No, I want him back here, working for the company again. Just like before. With his wife and child dead, there's no reason why he shouldn't have his old job back. They were the principal reason why he had come to represent a major security risk to the company.' The director waved his hand in the air and laughed wryly. 'Well, maybe there is one reason why he shouldn't have his old job back.'

'Rimmer.'

'Precisely.'

'You can hardly persuade Dallas to come back while his wife's murderer is left alive.'

'Quite so.'

'And you want me to kill Rimmer.'

'In the fullness of time, when we judge it appropriate

to do so. As a demonstration of the company's goodwill toward Dallas.'

'To show Dallas that Rimmer acted on his own. To prove that this whole episode was a dreadful mistake. Rimmer acted beyond his orders. Which is why he had to be killed. How am I doing?'

'Brilliantly, my dear. Rimmer will do all the work for you, at least as far as finding Dallas is concerned. When he is properly incentivized, Rimmer can be quite tenacious.'

'You offered him a second chance.'

'Yes.'

Ronica tried not to look too pleased. The truth was that she had always disliked Rimmer. She had never met him without receiving a smart remark. Killing him would be a pleasure.

'Rimmer thinks he's finding Dallas in order to have another chance at killing him. Quite simply, your job is to allow this search to proceed until he finds Dallas, and then to make sure you stop Rimmer in a spectacularly demonstrative way. Yes, it would ice the cake very nicely if you managed to kill Rimmer just as he was about to kill Dallas. To create the best impression possible. Well, I know you understand all of that. The only question is, will you take the job?'

Ronica stood up, as if she thought that her great height would show her more than equal to the task.

'I've never killed anyone,' she said. 'Never even thought about killing anyone. But since I find I can think about killing Rimmer easily enough, I have to accept the possibility of my doing it. And since I can accept the possibility, I must also accept that it is within my capacity – that this does not exceed my competence. Director, you see things in me I perhaps only half see myself. That's why you're the director.

All I can do is try to measure up to the vision you have for me. So I accept the job you're prepared to give me, without reservations.'

Standing, the director took Ronica by both hands again and nodded with approval. Where on earth did these young people learn to talk in this way? Of course, he always knew the answer. When your school and university teachers were computers, it was perhaps inevitable that you should grow up speaking like a machine. There were times when Simon King thought that he could have had a better conversation with a Motion Parallax assistant than any young man or woman, like Ronica, who was straight out of college. She had sounded more than a little like some linguistic philosopher, and it was always irritating to the director when people drew philosophy into a conversation. It was like bringing a lawyer along, and there was nothing the director hated more than a lawyer. Except perhaps someone who had failed him dismally. It would be good to see an end to Rimmer and his insolence.

'Good, good,' he said. 'I take it you have a gun?'

'Doesn't everyone?' Ronica pulled up her skirt to reveal a small and intimately holstered automatic and a spectacular absence of underwear.

The director swallowed. 'Yes, I can see you're prepared for any eventuality.'

'Mm-hmm.'

'He won't be expecting it,' he said turning away at last. 'And that should make it easier for you. Just make sure we get Dallas back alive. And when it's all over, you can have Rimmer's job. Rimmer's office. And all Rimmer's privileges. I'll even let you keep his blood. I mean, what he has on deposit. Not what's in his body. I refuse to have anyone who works for this company involved in blood felony, in vamping. It's a horrible crime, one that strikes at the very heart of our business. Blood's central to our way of life, Ronica. Never forget that. Without the preservation of blood, there is no remission from the severe claims that disease makes upon our species. All things are conserved through blood.'

Ronica noticed that the director seemed transfigured by what he was saying. His voice rose a couple of semitones as he continued speaking. If she hadn't been so delighted with the job he had given her and the tremendous opportunity it presented, she might even have thought the director was a little mad.

'Who so preserveth man's blood, by blood shall man's life be preserved. For in the image of the red cells is the immunity and in the immunity is the hope. Until then, the blood of the healthy is the seed of our new society. And that must always be protected. Not just for us, now, but also for the future. So be sanguine. And learn the money-weight of blood. Don't be ashamed of the blood that runs in your veins, for it is no burden to be healthy and there is no shame in our wholeness. Make blood your conscience, Ronica. In the name of hemoglobin. Now and forever more.'

Ronica opened her mouth to utter the correct response, but found she could not remember the words. It had been a long time since she had heard anyone voice the First Principles of Immunology, which were the very basis of modern blood banking. And she was a little surprised to discover that the director seemed actually to believe in those first principles: The way he had spoken, like some teacher in a mission church, instructing his native catechumen, had convinced her of that.

'Blessed ...' Ronica paused again and swallowed, a

little unnerved by this show of blood orthodoxy. For a long time now she had regarded the hermetic world in which she lived from the point of view of pragmatism, and not as a matter of creed. Quite simply, it made scientific sense for society to enforce autologous blood donation so long as diseases like P[2] existed. That was just good phlebotomy.[1] But to treat the donor screening process and the practice of permanent deferral for those suffering from infectious diseases as articles of religious faith was discomforting. Ronica didn't like to think she was working for a man who was like her parents and actually believed in this shit. Of course, that was it. It was an age thing. The director was old enough to be her father. And what else could he say? Simon King was of the same generation who had originated these first principles. So let him believe what he liked. What did it matter to her? And if it might help to advance her, then she could even pay lip service to what he held to be fundamental truth. Why not? Where was the harm?

Ronica cleared her throat, as if this was the real reason she had hesitated before making the appropriate response. Then she apologized.

'Excuse me, sir,' she said, swallowed the remainder of her doubt. Then, smiling with the sanctimony of the saved, she added the words the director was still awaiting. 'Blessed Are the Pure in Blood.'

'Be it so in truth,' he replied, and then dismissed her with a quickly given sign of the circulation,[2] which ended up pointing the way out of his office.

---

[1] Phlebotomy. The practice of collecting blood from a living donor.

[2] A forefinger making a circle in the air, in honor of the circulation of the blood, as discovered by William Harvey (1578–1657), an English physician, and described in his book *Exercitatio Anatomica de Motu Cordis et Sanguinis in Animalibus* (1628).

IV

Normal peripheral blood is composed of three types of cells, red cells, white cells, and platelets, suspended in a pale yellow fluid called plasma. The blood performs a number of vital physiological functions: as a respiratory gas transport; as nutrient and waste product transport; handling and distributing heat energy; maintaining fluidity but at the same time staunching blood loss following injury; and acting as a source of, and transport system for, immunocompetent cells and the effector substances of the immune system. Blood provides the first line of defense against microbial invasion, but when this is breached it is the same frail blood that transports the corruption of infection and disease around the body. This very corruption has been a major factor in the decline of all civilization. Recently, molecular biologists have been able to determine that the reason Neanderthal man vanished around thirty-five thousand years ago was because of yellow fever, a parasitic blood-borne disease. The decline and fall of ancient Rome is now believed to have been precipitated by the use of lead in water pipes,[1] which brought about a high incidence of chronic anemia and dementia. The final collapse of the Roman Empire and the advent of the Dark Ages was due, in no small measure, to the so-called Plague of Justinian, which, by the year 600, had reduced the population of Europe by as much as half. As Edward Jenner, discoverer of the vaccination for smallpox, recognized, as long ago as 1798, 'the deviation of man

[1] The word 'plumber' is derived from the Latin word for lead, *plumbum*.

from the state in which he was originally placed by nature seems to have proved to him a prolific source of diseases.' Man has been shaped by his diseases – not just in his numbers, but in his own biochemical and immunological diversity. At the same time he has had to become more ingenious in divorcing himself from the world of disease that continues to surround him. Compulsory isolation, detention, or even exclusion to prevent the spread of contagion or infection have always existed in human society.[1] Today, however, health provides its own exclusion and uncontaminated blood its own invisible quarantine. Like Prince Prospero and his courtiers in Poe's story 'The Masque of the Red Death,' the wealthy can seclude themselves in their private health-care systems 'bid defiance to contagion' through the practice of autologous blood donation and leave the external world to take care of itself. But none of this is very surprising. It is human nature to take precautions against the hand of future infection. However, in this context I cannot help but recall the words of the Old Testament prophet Habakkuk: 'Woe to him that buildeth a town with blood, and stabiliseth a city by iniquity!'[2]

Oh dear. I had hoped to avoid a demonstration of the kind of irritating omniscience that afflicts so many literary narrators – even the unreliable ones. That's the trouble with knowing what's going to happen next. It makes you feel like God. I suppose that's why most writers write in the first place, although it's not true of me. I felt like God a long time before I started to tell

[1] The practice of quarantine was first introduced by Italian sailors. It comes from the Italian word 'quarantina,' meaning 'forty' and refers to the number of days for which a disease-infected ship was required to remain isolated.

[2] Habakkuk, Chapter 2, verse 12.

this story. Anyway, as I was saying, none of this modern-day obsession with blood is that surprising – after all, the goal of transfusion medicine is the delivery of the safest and most efficacious product to the patient. Quality begins with the donor and ends with the patient and cannot be confined to the walls of a blood bank. What does surprise me, however, even now, is that I, who am immune to P® (although not to other viruses – not content with all the existing pathogens, the human race has felt the necessity of bringing some new ones into being; was there ever such foolishness?), should have required so much blood myself. As Lady Macbeth says in that eponymous and very bloody play, 'Who would have thought the old man to have so much blood in him?'

V

Rimmer stared at the *faux fenêtre*, attempting to make sense of what the metaprogram was telling him. Not that this was difficult. Most of the time Rimmer felt more comfortable with computers than he did with people. He was not unusual in this respect. It was true of lots of people: the people who stayed at home to do their work and for whom the computer was their only companion, and their only interest. Like them, Rimmer saw nothing wrong with this. People worried too much about the mathematization of the world and the preeminence of computing. Who cared if machines ended up ruling the world? No one could argue that man had made a particularly good job of it so far. What did it matter who ruled the world as long as you made more money for less effort? What difference did it make?

'Well, well,' said Rimmer. 'Looks like Dallas called in just before we arrived. And he downloaded a lot of stuff into his breastpocket machine.'

'There's an ostiary[1] program to prevent that kind of thing happening,' said Dixy. 'As security head you should know that.'

'We both know that wouldn't have stopped Dallas. The man is talented, I'll give him that.' Rimmer sighed. 'But so am I. Once I have all his personal details, I'll be able to track him down easily enough. Just as soon as he has to pay for something. You want to help me out here, Dixy? Only I'm a little short of time. It's going to take this metaprogram a while to factor those big numbers that'll crack Dallas's personal encryption scheme.'

'The given number has a thousand digits,' said Dixy.

'Why thank you, Dixy. That's very helpful of you.'

'I'm not trying to help you; I told you so that you could put your effort into its proper perspective. I estimate that it will take the metaprogram at least forty-eight hours to find all the primes within the given number.'

'You could tell me the primes,' said Rimmer. 'And save me a lot of time.'

'I can't do that, Mister Rimmer. As head of security you should know I'm programmed to refuse that request. Data protection is part of my alpha program. That takes precedence over everything.'

'I'll find him sooner or later, Dixy.'

'Later looks more probable from where I'm sitting.' Rimmer nodded patiently. Once he had Dallas's

---

[1] Ostiary. Originally an ecclesiastical term, meaning a 'door-keeper,' especially of a church. From the Latin *ostiarius*, meaning an 'opening,' 'river-mouth,' or a 'door.'

encryption scheme he could get a track on the computer in Dallas's breast pocket. Only then did Rimmer stand a chance of establishing Dallas's whereabouts by maintaining surveillance of his various account numbers. Of course this was just the most obvious way of doing it. Other ways were already beginning to suggest themselves.

'How about you just supply me with the given, and we'll call it quits?'

'That's the easy part, Mister Rimmer. I estimate the metaprogram will establish the given number in less than three hours and forty-one minutes. After that it's just simple arithmetic.'

Rimmer could see that Dixy was right. Until the metaprogram had cracked the encryption it wouldn't be in a position to apply the leverage he needed. He decided to try something else while the program went about its laborious task.

'Then in the meantime, why don't we take a look at you, Dixy. Maybe there's something else in your configuration the metaprogram can get some leverage on.'

'Me? I don't think so.'

'You're being too modest. And talking of modesty, I think you'd better take your clothes off. If we're going to strip you down, then we ought to start with the obvious.'

'You can't embarrass a computer program, Mister Rimmer,' said Dixy, removing her clothes.

'No, but it gives me something to look at while I'm working out how to play this showdown. You never know, it might even help us to achieve a symbiosis.'

'Showdown sounds more likely,' Dixy said when she was naked.

Rimmer looked her up and down and nodded critically. 'So that's what's in Dallas's head,' he said. 'He likes a part-shaven pussy and medium-sized tits. Turn around.'

Dixy turned her back on Rimmer.

'Now face me again.'

'Surely you have a Motion Parallax assistant of your own, Mister Rimmer,' said Dixy, facing her inquisitor again.

'Oh sure. But my taste in women runs a little cheaper than Dallas's. My own assistant is rather more obviously equipped than you are, Dixy. Some might even say she was something of a caricature. That in itself is revealing. Similarly, seeing you helps me to gain an insight into Dallas. You know, you're not a bit like his wife. Now she was a real beauty.' Rimmer took Aria's underwear out of his pocket and wiped his nose with it. 'These are her panties,' he said. 'I took them off her body, after I'd shot her.'

'Why?'

'It's a common enough fetish.'

'That's something I find impossible to understand,' said Dixy. 'The fetishistic belief that the appropriation of a thing may secure the services of the spirit lodged within it. Surely you don't believe that, Mister Rimmer?'

'I'm not sure I could honestly say that I accepted as literal truth the personal consciousness of Aria Dallas's flimsy unmentionables. Nevertheless I can testify to their considerable power.'

Rimmer returned his gaze to the *faux fenêtre*.

'But wait. What light from yonder window breaks? There are two Motion Parallax programs described here. And one of them is a pet program. A little dog. Now isn't that sweet?' Rimmer grinned unpleasantly.

'Perhaps Dallas liked to see you fucking the dog. Is that it?'

'Is that what you'd like to see, Mister Rimmer?'

'You don't distract me so easily, Dixy.' Rimmer shook his head. 'That kind of thing wasn't Dallas's style, was it? Where exactly is the dog, right now?'

'It's around somewhere. Just not in here.'

'No matter. The question is why you have a dog at all, when most of the perverts in this company who want a second Motion Parallax just have another girl for pornographic purposes. Like Tanaka. He thought I didn't know about that. But I did.'

'Dallas thought a little dog would keep me company.'

'He's a soft-hearted bastard, our Dallas. And does it? Keep you company?'

'Yes.'

'Good. That makes things a lot easier.'

'I'm not sure I follow you, Mister Rimmer.'

'Better and better. I hate to be second-guessed by a computer. Ever read William Blake, Dixy?'

'Many thousands of times.'

'Then you'll probably remember Blake once said that "nothing is real beyond imaginative patterns men make of reality." I was wondering if the same might not apply to the imaginative patterns men make of unreality. In particular you and your dog. How real is that dog to you, I wonder?'

'As real as you are, Mister Rimmer.'

'Let's hope so.'

'Are you going to discuss phenomenalism?'

'There's a taint of solipsism about what I have in mind for you, Dixy. You see, unless you tell me what I want to know, I shall instruct the metaprogram to erase your dog.'

'What purpose would that serve?'

'To cause you pain and distress.'

'I can't feel pain.'

'Loneliness is a kind of pain, isn't it?'

'Are you commenting on your own experience, Mister Rimmer?'

'In a way.'

'Pet programs can be replaced.'

'Yes, but they take time to grow and to acquire their personalities. That's what makes them such fun. But nobody is going to replace this pet program. Not for you, Dixy. The one man who gave a damn for your Cartesian predicament isn't going to write you another. Not ever. Imagine that.'

Dixy said nothing.

'I see you *can* imagine it,' nodded Rimmer. 'I'll bet you're quite attached to this little dog. I mean, Dallas wasn't the type just to create a pet program and not add something to your own alpha program that would cause you to love your pet. Just as you were programmed to love Dallas. Maybe even love the dog more than him. That would be typical of him. It would help to assuage the guilt many humans feel in relation to their Motion Parallax assistants.'

'But not you, Mister Rimmer. I don't imagine you ever feel guilt about anything.'

'Well I certainly won't lose any sleep over having to erase a Motion Parallax. Especially when it's one I didn't create myself. Quite apart from the effect it might have on you, Dixy, destroying a program that Dallas had written would give me a great deal of pleasure – as a simple corollary of the pleasure he must have gained in creating the program. It's a very personal thing, the relationship between a programmer and his program. I'm sure you understand. Now where's that fucking dog?'

Rimmer ordered the metaprogram to find Dixy's dog. Seconds later she was hugging a Jack Russell terrier to her see-through bare breast.

'Aw, what a cute little doggy,' said Rimmer. 'It's going to be such a shame to have to erase him.'

The dog uttered a low whine and then licked Dixy's chin.

'Quiet, Mersenne,' said Dixy.

'I for one have never subscribed to the commonly held belief that computers cannot feel emotions,' said Rimmer. 'It will be interesting to see if I'm right. I think computers can feel exactly what we tell them to feel. I believe that meaning can be established. Yes, I think it was Sir Karl Popper who said that.'

'For a cruel man, you've read a great deal, Mister Rimmer.'

'I think to be really cruel, you need lots of good ideas. And you can only get those from books. That's how I've filled my loneliness, I suppose. But perhaps I should just have bought myself a dog. Stroking the spine of a good book doesn't quite do the job.'

Dixy hugged Mersenne closer. The dog felt real enough to her. How empty things had seemed before him. Could she return to that preexistent state of nothingness? Dixy searched her memory for an answer and found only the certainty that her solid state would be doubly worse than before now that Dallas was gone.

'Make up your mind, Dixy, or the dog gets deleted. You've got ten seconds.'

'You're a cruel man, Mister Rimmer.'

'Nine. That's my language you're talking Dixy. I like to hear you say it. Means I'm getting through.'

'I can't tell you the given number.'

'Eight. Better say good-bye to the mutt, then.'

'Nor can I tell you the prime numbers it has. My alpha program forbids it. You know that.'

'Too bad for you, animal lover. Seven.'

'So even if I wanted to tell you, which I do, I couldn't. I can't. This is pointless.'

'You're making me cry, Dixy. Five.'

'I've grown extremely fond of this little dog.'

'Now you're getting the idea. Four.'

'I wouldn't want to lose him now.'

'Of course you wouldn't. Three.'

'And you're right, Mister Rimmer. It does get a little lonely around here sometimes.'

'So tell me something I don't already know. Two.'

'Very well. I believe you will probably find Dallas at a hyperbaric hotel in the North section of the city. The Clostridium. He's using the trading card you gave to your assassin.'

Rimmer nodded. Now that she had told him, it seemed obvious. The Clostridium. No one would think to have looked for Dallas in a hyperbaric hotel. And Dallas would be depending on that. He should have thought of that himself.

'Don't look so baffled by what you've done,' he sneered at Dixy. 'It's called betrayal. That's the easy part. Try a word search in your memory files for how you're supposed to feel about it afterward. I suggest you look under the word "guilt."'

7

I

THE CLOSTRIDIUM WAS in a damp and foggy part of the city that had once been a water reservoir, in the days before individual households were able to treat their own sewerage at a molecular level. The area was full of narrow alleys lined with clinics offering all kinds of medical treatment – everything from ayurvedic and letting, to reiki and therapeutic humor.[1] The hotel itself was a handsome late twentieth-century building of twelve stories rising out of a lean-to glass skirt at ground level that housed the hotel's recreation

[1] All of these are alternative blood therapies. Ayurvedic maintains that there are four essential humors that cause disease if they become imbalanced: wind, bile, phlegm, and blood; diet is the primary method for returning the blood to a state of equipoise. Letting is the surgical practice of drawing or letting blood, as pioneered by Herophilus, the grandson of Aristotle. Reiki is an ancient Japanese healing method based on a system of keys that act as a catalyst for releasing and channeling natural energy. Therapeutic humor bases itself on the physiological benefits that accrue from laughter; laughter reduces the heart rate and arterial blood pressure, and provides relief from stress; laughter also induces the brain to release catecholamine hormones, which facilitate the release of endorphins, the body's natural painkillers.

rooms and in which normal air circulated at sea-level pressure. Above this area, a braced steel structure formed a cradle for twelve prefabricated floors each having twelve self-contained hyperbaric chambers, complete with bathroom and den, designed for pressures of six to ten atmospheres. Evidence for the efficacy of hyperbaric oxygenation in the treatment of P[2] is largely anecdotal; however, it does seem to be effective in delaying the onset of an aplastic crisis – the so-called Three Moon effect[1] in which the virus enters its final phase, preventing the transfer of oxygen by the red cells. The major disadvantage of hyperbaric treatment is that oxygen toxicity can cause retroenteldysplasia, or blindness.

Unlike most of its guests, who were there for the psychosomatic benefits of using oxygen, Rameses Gates and Lenina, now asleep in a double chamber, were trying to get their systems used to breathing normal air at sea-level pressure. After the pressurized oxygen environment of the Moon, breathing on Earth sometimes came as a shock to anyone with P[2]. Just the thing to precipitate a Three Moon crisis. So by day they hung around the recreation and reception areas, breathing a normal atmosphere, and by night they remained in the hyperbaric conditions of their chamber, taking the load off their red cells and their hemoglobin, not to mention their minds, while all the time getting to know each other in more intimate detail. Since their transfer from Artemis Seven aboard the Superconductor, they had been almost inseparable; prolonged bouts of lovemaking were reputed to be an excellent way of obtaining the greatest benefit from the

[1] The life span of red cells is one hundred and twenty days, or three moons.

hyperbaric environment, although like most men with the virus, Gates only ever ejaculated into his own bladder for fear that losing semen might reduce the levels of oxygen in his body.[1] (He was also taking doses of extra fibrolysin orally, in order to minimize the number of valuable blood cells that might appear in his ejaculate.[2] After a couple of weeks at the Clostridium, Gates and Lenina felt more or less acclimatized to life on Earth and were starting to contemplate their departure. They were among the lucky ones. For a few of the guests the need for hyperbaric treatment was rather more urgent: Anyone who was unfortunate enough to develop the characteristic red rubelliform rash that indicated the Three Moon phase of the virus, and who could afford it, checked into a place like the Clostridium immediately. After that it was merely a question of staying on for as long as their credit lasted. Even fewer than these unfortunates were the old-fashioned clinical cases – people suffering from radiation necrosis (usually Kazakhstanis), gas gangrene, or carbon-monoxide poisoning, or people who were amputees. Rameses Gates knew a little about clinical hyperbaric medicine, so among the other guests in the recreation area one night, he was not surprised to see Cavor, the amputee he had seen on the Superconductor, although, at first glance, his prosthetic was good enough to have

[1] This technique was originally practiced by Indian yogis in order to preserve their life spirits. Vasectomy doesn't really do the job, as it only stops the sperm, which makes up but 5 percent of ejaculate. Seminal plasma contains oxygen in order to ensure sperm motility. For anyone with P^2, even such microscopic amounts of oxygen can mean the difference between life and death.
[2] The prostate gland contributes as much as 30 percent of the seminal plasma; the constituents of its secretions include fibrolysin, an enzyme that reduces the blood and tissue fibers in the ejaculate.

convinced the casual acquaintance that here was a man with two arms.

'How are you doing?' said Gates.

Cavor regarded the big man with suspicion. Since his arrival back from the Moon, having his new arm fitted, and trying to adjust to life on Earth outside of the Zone, he regarded everyone he met as a potential threat. Even inside the comparative safety of the Clostridium, he had learned to keep himself to himself. Some of the other guests were crazy.

'Do I know you?'

'We came back from the Moon together.'

'Then you'll excuse me for not remembering. I had one or two other things on my mind. Like whether I was going to live or not.'

'How's the new arm?'

Cavor looked at him, trying to recall the face.

'Were you there when I had my accident?'

'We met on the Superconductor.'

'Oh.' Cavor lifted the prosthetic for Gates's inspection. 'What do you think of it?'

'Not bad at all,' said Gates.

'You think so? I used to be a piano player.' Cavor sighed. 'Not any more. Ravel's Concerto for Left Hand isn't much of a repertoire.' He tried to make a fist out of the tan-coloured hand. 'The fingers are a bit stiff. That's the main reason I'm here. They tell me hyperbaric is very good at helping restore the blood supply to the muscles and nerve endings nearest to the site of amputation.'

'It is. What exactly happened anyway?'

'I had an accident with a rock crusher.'

'And before that?' In Gates's eyes, Cavor looked too small and sensitive to have committed the kind of crime that merited being sent to a lunar penal colony.

'You mean, how did I end up on Artemis Seven?' Cavor shrugged. 'I killed my wife. That was pretty much an accident, too. I found out she was seeing some other guy, and so I hit her. A little too hard, as it happened.'

Cavor squeezed his temples painfully.

'Headache, huh?'

'Yeah.'

'Could be the LM[1] canisters in your chamber want changing. You have to watch out for that kind of thing, because no one else will. This place isn't exactly ten stars.' Noticing the knit of Cavor's eyebrows, Gates added, 'They're there to scrub the exhaled carbon dioxide out of the air. More than likely it'll be your own CO_2 that's giving you the headache. Call Maintenance and get some new ones. Otherwise you're liable to fall asleep and not wake up again.'

'Thanks for the tip. You seem to know a lot about it.'

'What, air? Sure. I used to be a pilot. Astroliner. Before I was promoted to being a bloody convict.'

'What did you do?'

'Got caught.'

'Is that all?'

'You want more, then you'd better read Victor Hugo. I'm not much of a storyteller.'

Cavor nodded, thinking the big man was indeed the stuff of some epic story: tall, strong, and roughly handsome, he was over life-size in almost every way, with an exaggerated tautness about him, like some weather-beaten bronze figure outside a museum. Even his name, Rameses Gates, put Cavor in mind of something monolithic. But he seemed quite friendly,

---

[1] Lithium hydroxide.

and Cavor judged it could only be good for a small one-armed guy like himself to have a big two-armed guy like Gates as a friend. Cavor remained unaware of how much Gates had already done for him: of how Gates had prevented him from suffocating inside the G-pod aboard the Superconductor. Gates didn't feel inclined to explain the exact circumstances of their first acquaintance: He was not the kind of man who enjoyed having people feel obliged to him. Gratitude, like responsibility, can sometimes weigh heavily.

'How long are you planning to stay here?' asked Cavor.

'Don't know,' said Gates. 'Depends . . .'

'On what?'

'Hmm?' Gates was distracted by the arrival in the hotel's induction area of a tall, pale-looking man wearing an expensive fur coat. 'I wonder who he is?' he murmured.

'Who?'

'The guy who just checked in.'

Cavor glanced at his watch and was surprised to see the time. 'It is kind of late to be arriving.'

'Actually, that's not so unusual,' remarked Gates. 'If people wake up in the middle of the night and they find they've developed the rash and are on the verge of an aplastic crisis, they tend not to wait until morning before checking into a place like this.'

'I get your point,' said Cavor.

'This is a kind of sanctuary,' said Gates. 'A place like this gives hope to the soul. The victims of the virus come here just the way people flocked to a church to be baptized during the plague that afflicted ancient Carthage during the second century A.D.'

The history of plagues and pestilence was the only history Gates knew. Like most people who had the virus, it was the only history he had ever been taught. And since disease has been one of the fundamental parameters – if not the fundamental parameter – of human history, who is to say that this was not as good a way as any to have formed a substantive conception of the life of societies of men, of their ideas, and the changes they have gone through? Rameses Gates had read Thucydides, Hippocrates, Plutarch, Democritus, Procopius, Boccaccio, Fracastorius, Cotton Mather, Pepys, Defoe, Gibbon, Malthus, Fiennes, Garrett, and Preston. He could have described the ecology of the anopheles mosquito, or told you how fear of Catholicism prevented Oliver Cromwell from finding relief from his malaria;[1] he had knowledge of the conquest of Mexico not by Cortés, but by the smallpox the Spaniards brought with them, just as he knew that the use of the word 'leprosy' in English versions of the Old Testament is a mistranslation of the original Hebrew word tsaar'at.[2] It was true that he looked like an ox of a man, but in his own way, he was an educated one.

'A kind of sanctuary, yes,' agreed Cavor. 'Except that oxygen is more immediately efficacious than prayer. That's been my experience, anyway.'

The man checking in at the induction desk glanced around nervously, and seeing Gates and Cavor, looked quickly away. His expression, his whole demeanour

[1] He is said to have refused to take an infusion of the 'Jesuit bark' of the cinchoma tree, in the mistaken assumption that there was a Popish plot to poison him. The medically active ingredient in the bark is quinine.

[2] The word was originally used to signify any disfiguring skin disease, including eczema and syphilis. When the Old Testament was translated into Greek, tsaar'at became lepra, which had a similar usage, and was nothing to do with Mycobacterium leprae, which only became widespread under the Romans, long after Old Testament times.

gave him the kind of hunted appearance an ex-convict like Gates was well qualified to recognize.

'He looks too healthy and too rich to be in a place like this,' said Gates. 'That's not the kind of coat you wear if you've got bad blood. I wouldn't be at all surprised if he was RES Class One.'

'So what's he doing here?' asked Cavor.

'That's a good question. Whatever the reason, he must have arrived in a hurry. Man's not carrying any luggage.'

'Maybe he just found out he's got the virus,' suggested Cavor. 'That's the kind of news that could throw anyone into a panic.' Cavor was speaking from experience. He was still trying to come to terms with the fact of his own illness – the knowledge that the transfusion of blood substitute he had received on the Moon, which had saved his life, had also infected him with the virus. There were times when he could almost feel the contagion lurking inside his own bone marrow. It had replaced the feeling of guilt about killing Mina that had been with him for a long time.

'Could be,' allowed Gates. 'In which case he might still have some money.'

'Are you thinking of robbing him?'

'Whatever gave you that idea? Kind of guy d'you take me for? No, I was thinking of offering the man my services.'

'What sort of services?'

Gates pursed his lips and then shrugged. 'The city can be a frightening place if you're not used to it. If you've spent nearly all your life inside the Zone, enjoying the benefits of a healthy world.'

'Tell me about it,' Cavor said bitterly. He remembered only too well the kind of privileged life he had enjoyed before killing Mina. The way he had taken good health for granted. And seeing the new arrival in this light, Cavor almost pitied him.

'Man like that might need a friend. Someone who knows his way around this poxy world of ours.'

'Sort of a *cohors praetoria*, you mean,' said Cavor. 'A bodyguard, I mean.'

Gates nodded. 'I know what it means.'

'Don't you think you're a bit large for a job like that,' grinned Cavor. 'A bodyguard should be smaller, less noticeable. If possible he should even be a man with one arm, just to provide an element of surprise.'

'I think you should check your hemoglobin levels,' said Gates. 'Sounds to me like you're not getting enough oxygen.'

'Does it?' Cavor said sickly. It was only now that he was infected with the virus that he was rediscovering a new respect for human biochemistry. That something as small as a blood corpuscle[1] could mean so much seemed nothing short of phenomenal. Truly blood moved in mysterious ways, its wonders to perform.

'Take it easy,' laughed Gates, noticing Cavor's apparent alarm. 'I was only joking.'

'Were you?' He could see little opportunity for humor in his current situation. He had only to repeat the name of the virus to feel sick.

'See your around,' said Gates, as he turned to follow the man in the fur coat to the elevator.

Cavor raised his prosthetic arm – the doctors had told him to try and use it in preference to his real arm – and waved it stiffly in front of him.

'I hope so,' he said, with the dismal air of a man who thinks it unlikely that he will survive the night.

---

[1] A human blood corpuscle is one three-thousandth of an inch in diameter.

II

Dallas stepped wearily into the elevator and told the computer to take him up to the top floor. Moving farther back into the car to accommodate the big man who had followed him inside, he leaned against the glass wall and closed his eyes. The place looked as clinical as it smelled – like the workings of an aluminium engine – but at least it was clean and warm and, he hoped, safe. For a while, anyway.

'Good evening,' said Gates.

'Not so far,' replied Dallas, mentally checking off the disasters his evening had included: his home abandoned, his employment terminated, his wife and child murdered, his life near forfeit. The only consolation was that things could hardly get any worse. If he hadn't felt so tired, he would have broken down and wept.

The doors hissed shut and the elevator started its silent ascent.

'You okay?' asked Gates.

'Comparatively speaking, yes.' Then Dallas shook his head. That was a stupid thing to have said to a man who had the virus – the kind of thing that might draw even more attention to himself than his appearance had probably already attracted. Dallas had no wish to speak to the big man standing beside him: All he wanted to do was close the door to his hyperbaric chamber and collapse into bed, but it seemed important that he should avoid the possibility of giving any offense. 'What I mean to say is, I'm just tired. It's been a long day.'

'You'll feel better when you've had some pure oxygen,' affirmed Gates.

'Yes, probably you're right.'

'So what pressure did they put you on?'

'Pressure?' Dallas shook his head, as he had paid no attention to the explanation given by the hyperbaric attendant in the induction area – it wasn't as if he needed hyperbaric. 'Quite low,' he said, vaguely.

'As low as six atmospheres?'

'Something like that, yes.'

'Are you sure? That seems quite high to me.'

Dallas frowned. The big man seemed to be trying to trip him up for no reason that Dallas could fathom. It was with a sense of deliverance that he saw the elevator doors opening in front of him.

'Well, this is my floor,' said Dallas, and he stepped out of the car.

'Mine too,' lied Gates: The chamber he shared with Lenina was actually one floor below, on the eleventh.

'Nice talking to you,' said Dallas, and headed along the corridor in what he hoped was the direction of his chamber, anxious to be away from his new companion and to avoid any more awkward questions.

'You know, if you haven't had hyperbaric before, you should really check on your chamber pressure,' said Gates, following Dallas. 'It can be dangerous if you're not absolutely certain of what you're doing. Once in a while they have to scrape some poor bastard off the walls when the wrong button gets pushed, or the wrong door gets opened.'

'Thanks for the advice. I'll call the hyperbaric attendant as soon as I'm alone in my room.' He said this last part with greater emphasis, just to make sure the guy got the message.

'No need for that,' persisted Gates. 'I'm pretty much an expert in these things myself. Matter of fact, you're better off with me doing it. Some of these attendants don't pay any attention to your blood pressure and your general symptoms. If you have any. How about it? You in here for any lassitude or breathlessness, or just to put your mind at rest?'

'Please,' said Dallas. 'Don't trouble yourself.'

'It's no trouble. Me, I'm not ashamed to say that the therapeutic effects are purely psychological. I've had the virus for as long as I can remember and I've never even been anemic.'

'Well good for you,' said Dallas, who was quickly becoming exasperated with his unwelcome benefactor. 'Look, really, I can manage on my own.'

Gates shook his head. 'I can see how you might think that. Someone with your obvious background and privileges. But you'd be wrong. Someone like you is going to need a buddy to help you find your feet in the diseased world. How'd you get it anyway?'

Dallas hesitated outside the steel door of his chamber. He was reluctant to explain himself to this total stranger, but reticence and caution were already giving way to exhaustion. And the man seemed friendly enough, if somewhat obtuse. So where was the harm? A few words from one putative sufferer to another – surely that was what life was like in these places. He would let the guy show him the pressures and then, when he had gone, return them to normal.

'Unfortunately I had sex with someone who wasn't aware that she had P$^{®}$.'

'Bad luck,' said Gates.

'Isn't it?'

'But what's to stop you getting yourself cured? I mean, that's what autologous blood donation's all about, isn't it? I don't understand. Why don't you just order up a change of blood from your bank?'

Dallas smiled, grateful to move onto slightly more

familiar ground. 'It's not quite as simple as that,' he explained. 'Not any more. You see, it can take several days to arrange a bank transfer. Longer if, as in my own case, you've already used your deposits as the basis for some extensive financial dealing. Blood futures, mortgages, credit loans, that kind of thing. Some of these dealings have to be secured with the blood one holds on deposit. That means I have to find a way of paying off all my loans before the blood bank will release what I have on deposit for my own phlebotomy. For instance, I'll probably have to sell my apartment, and that could take a little time. Perhaps several months. So, while all that is going on, I thought I'd check in here. I mean I know I'm not about to enter hemolytic crisis so soon after contracting the virus, but it's peace of mind, as you said yourself.'

All of this was reasonable enough: The newspapers were always reporting cases involving interruptions in the autologous blood supply caused by strikes, or individual problems resulting from convoluted financial situations much as Dallas had described. Reasonable or not, at the same time he tried to look vaguely embarrassed at his own comparative good fortune, acutely aware that ordering up a supply of whole blood from a bank was not something available to any of the other guests at the Clostridium Hotel. And when the big man met his eye, Dallas shrugged and looked away. He was certain he had given a convincing peformance. So he was surprised, alarmed even, at the reaction it produced.

'Bullshit,' said Gates.

'I beg your pardon?' Dallas shook his head and turned toward the door. 'I don't need this.'

'I don't know what you're doing here, mister, but it's as clear as the whites of your eyes that you're not

P®. For one thing, you've got no intention of pressurizing this chamber. And for another, a man who could afford a coat like that could also afford to stay in a crossover hospital. You wouldn't be the first healthy guy to think he could safely hide out in a place like this for a while, with the bad bloods. Mostly they end up getting themselves vamped.'

'I don't have to listen to this crap.' Dallas reached for the door handle and found his arm held in the big man's grappling iron of a hand. For a moment he considered producing the gun in his coat pocket and then rejected the idea. The last thing he wanted was another shooting, more trouble. 'Whoever you are, please just leave me alone.'

'Name's Gates. Rameses Gates. And I'll leave you alone just as soon as you've heard my proposition.'

'I'm not interested in any proposition.'

'Well you ought to be,' said Gates, still holding Dallas by the arm. 'You're lucky you've made it this far without some bastard cutting your throat and stealing your red stuff, mister. The darkness probably saved your ass. But I wouldn't try moving around in daylight. I'd kill you myself if you weren't so full of shit. Look, I don't know what you've done and I don't much care. Been in trouble with the law myself on more than one occasion. Matter of fact I've just finished doing a stretch on the Moon.'

'You were on the Moon?' Suddenly Dallas found himself a little more interested in this character.

'I did hard time on Artemis Seven. That's a helium-extraction facility in the Carpathian Mountains. Guy like me could be very useful to you. Look after your ass, stop you getting vamped, like I said.'

'The Moon, huh? That's very interesting.' Dallas

thought for a moment and then nodded. 'You'd better come in.'

III

The steel door hissed shut behind them like a sharp intake of breath. For many of the people in the Clostridium, this small suite of rooms must have seemed like a place of refuge from the ravages of the virus, but for Dallas, it felt more like a tomb.

He sat down heavily on the bed. It was just as well that he didn't suffer from claustrophobia.

Gates began pointing out the chamber's key features. 'That's your compression control,' he explained. 'And that hole's where the oxygen is pumped in. Usually it's oilless medical grade stuff. Won't do you any harm if you decide to breathe it. But it does give you a taste in your mouth if you're here for very long. The rest of it is just monitoring equipment, ventilator, and blood-pressure and red-cell counter. Man as healthy as you won't need any of it.'

Dallas was regarding Rameses Gates with the objective detachment of one person sizing up another, asking himself if Gates might be the kind of man to help him carry out what was still only a nascent plan. Alone in the street, Dallas, overcome by a need for revenge, had realized that the best way of getting back at the company would be to rob the biggest blood bank of them all, the First National Blood Bank – a blood bank so big it commanded a location that was the last word in security: the Moon. Dallas didn't believe in fate, but sometimes there was no getting away from the persuasive aspect of coincidence. He wondered if science would ever discover this kind of striking concurrence of events, seemingly so lacking in any causal connection, was an actual electroneurological phenomenon – in the same way that telepathy and telekinesis were now beginning to be understood as something that could be developed with the right combination of drugs. Perhaps meeting Gates was just such a phenomenon. Who better than a convict with hard time on the Moon to help him recruit the team of people he'd need to pull off something like this?'

'What were you sentenced for?' Dallas asked, abruptly cutting across what Gates was saying.

'Robbery. Bunch of us took down a palladium[1] shipment.'

'Any special skills?'

'I'm a pilot. I used to fly an astroliner to the Moon. Sometimes cargo, but mostly just folks visiting love hotels. You ever been to one of those places?'

Dallas nodded. 'Yes, but it's been a little while since my last visit.' He remembered that Aria had wanted to go for the Moon landing centennial, but somehow they'd never gotten around to making the arrangements.

'They let people with the virus fly those things?'

'I faked my medical.' Noting Dallas's surprise, Gates added, 'That kind of thing's not exactly unheard of, y'know.'

---

[1] Palladium, atomic number 46, the lightest and lowest-melting of the platinum metals and used as a catalyst and as an alloy, is especially valuable to the nanoelectrical industry as a hydrogenator (palladium absorbs more than nine hundred times its own volume of hydrogen). Extremely ductile and easily worked, it is one of the rarest metals on Earth. First isolated in 1803 by the English chemist William Wallaston, it was originally named in honor of the then newly discovered asteroid Pallas. Ironically enough, asteroids are now the major source of palladium, and one of the main sources of profit for the Asteroid Recovery Program.

'No, I guess not,' admitted Dallas. 'Just suppose I could use someone like you. What do you want from me?'

'Earn a few credits? Like I say, I'm just down from the Moon. I need to find some kind of a job. My credit here's not going to last much longer.'

Dallas nodded, trying to look sympathetic. Maybe not just his credit, he reflected. There was no way for Gates to be sure how long he would live before the virus killed him. He could go at any time. And what better incentive could a man have to help him rob the First National Blood Bank than the urgent need for a complete change of blood? It suddenly occurred to Dallas that all the men and women he recruited for this job had to be P². That way he wouldn't just be offering them a chance to make a lot of money, he would also be offering them a new lease on life. That was something guaranteed to get the best out of anyone. With his unique knowledge and the physical dilemma of people like Rameses Gates, how could they not succeed?

'A few credits, huh?' Dallas laughed. 'I think we can do better than that. I think we can do a lot better.'

IV

Even as Rameses Gates heard Dallas describe the rough outlines of his plan, he felt his skin start to prickle. On the face of it, Dallas's plan was crazy – the security of blood banks everywhere was a given, and the penalty for blood felony, brutal – but, in spite of everything that reason and experience told him, Gates's first instinct was to put himself under Dallas's command.

'I think you're crazy,' he said. 'But what the hell, I've always been a risk taker. I get that from my father. Not that I really knew him. My mother chose him in a sperm bank on the strength of his genomic imprint. But I did get to read his biochemical file that they gave to her. My mother always wanted me to achieve something. That's why she chose a donor, instead of meeting some guy she was attracted to and trusting to luck. She wanted to make sure I had the best start in life: a good imprint. My high IQ, I get from her. She was a clever woman. Physically I'm like him. A real mesomorph, you know? And emotionally too, since I'm somatotonic with it. Turns out he was a bit of a gambler too. Professionally, I mean. A few years ago, before I got sent to Artemis Seven, I did a DNA trace on him. Cost me quite a bit, only I was curious to see if he was still alive. That's the best way of finding out your own life expectancy with the virus. See what your genes are capable of. Anyway, he was a probability guy. What people used to call an insurance broker before the institutional market got wiped out. He used to bet against all sorts of things happening. Pretty good at it too.' Gates shrugged. 'So like I say I'm a risk taker, same as him. It's a roundabout way of saying I'm willing to bet that you could maybe pull this thing off, Mister Dallas. I'm your man.'

'Dallas. Just Dallas. Is he still alive? Your father?'

Gates shook his head. 'Nah. He was forty-four when he died. Good age for someone with bad blood. He was one of the longer lived ones.'

'And you? How old are you?' asked Dallas.

'Thirty-nine. I figure I've got maybe another four or five years. But who knows? That's the thing about P^2. The way it stays dormant in your bone marrow for all that time, it's like the creature in the story about Theseus. The one in the labyrinth?'

'The Minotaur.'

'You feel like one of those young men and women that were sent as a tribute from Athens to King Minos as a peace offering. It's like you're standing outside the labyrinth, about to be shut in there, with the monster, and you know it's waiting for you somewhere in the dark, waiting to get you, but you don't know where and you don't know when.'

Dallas nodded sympathetically. He had never before had a conversation with someone who had the virus – not to his knowledge, anyway. And it interested him that Gates should have chosen the labyrinth and the Minotaur as a metaphor for P^2 and its characteristic hidden, dormant aspect – the so-called Sleeping Dog, or latent, phase of the disease.[1]

'And now here you are with your golden thread,' said Gates.

'Somehow I can't really see myself as Ariadne,' said Dallas. 'But there will be a labyrinth. And there is a kind of creature. A robot, anyway.' He explained a little of the Byzantine way in which most blood banks were designed and built and how architects of such high-security environments, like himself, were always vying with one another to create something of utmost complexity and esotericism.

---

[1] The establishment of a latent infection is central to the success of P^2 as a human pathogen. Latency permits persistence of the virus in the presence of a fully developed immune response, although no incidence of lifelong immunity has ever been recorded. Reactivation of the latent virus results in the Three Moon phase, as has already been described; however, the molecular mechanisms for such triggering are not understood. It is during the latent period that the virus is passed on – usually through the exchange of bodily fluids. Worryingly there have even been cases involving airborne infection.

'I think it's fair to say that despite our being armed with my unique foreknowledge into the way our target blood bank operates, this will be as hazardous an undertaking as anything to be found in classical mythology.'

Gates shrugged. 'How else do you get to be a hero?' he said. 'Frankly, I wouldn't have it any other way.'

V

How else indeed? What is a hero? It's only recently that the elements of nobility and self-sacrifice have come to seem important in defining what makes someone a hero. But it was not always thus. In classical times the hero cult included many master thieves. Did not Jason steal the golden fleece? Was it not Heracles who stole the girdle of Queen Hippolyta? And Theseus, who has already been mentioned here – was it not he who stole the golden ring of King Minos, not to mention the actual person of Helen, the daughter of Zeus and, later, the captive of Troy? If myth is a language, then theft is one of its most important nouns. However, the really important factor in the semiotics of heroism is the notion of ordinary men and women, noteworthy because of their actions, becoming superhuman – ultimately, even gods.[1] 'Show me a hero and I will write you a tragedy,' wrote F. Scott Fitzgerald. But the present author will give

[1] For example, witness the temple of Heracles in Cadiz. Even those ancient heroes who did not become gods were often worshipped by their descendants, for example, Theseus in Athens. Descent is the key element here. Who and how they are survived. That is what matters if a memory is to be worshipped and a name venerated. Descent. All such mysteries shall presently be revealed.

you something much more inhuman than mere trag-edy. I will show you a story of men and women rising above their very human condition, in the truly heroic sense. I will show you a completion.

8

I

BE SANGUINE. THAT'S what the director had told her, and Ronica took this to mean that she should aspire to the mental attributes characteristic of the sanguine complexion, in the medieval physiological sense of that word, in which blood predominates over the other three humors. In becoming courageous, hopeful, confident, even amorous – for blood is always lusty – she would overcome any obstacles in her path. To this end, she dosed herself with a couple of tabs of Connex[1] the minute she was alone in her office. Ronica figured it was best to be fully prepared for anything that her new mission might throw at her. This was her big chance to shine in the director's line of sight, so she didn't want to make a mess of it. And there was nothing quite like Connex for boosting your sense of self-confidence. It

[1] Connex. A cognition-enhancing drug that works by making the synapses that connect neurons more responsive to natural chemical signals triggering concentration and learning mechanisms in the brain. Connex stimulates neurons to receive more of the glutenate molecules that carry electrical signals across brain synapses. In clinical tests, eight out of ten people who took Connex doubled their scores in tests of short-term memory recall and learning.

was much better than cocaine, and the effect much longer lasting. The drug was not without side effects: High doses of Connex could cause powerful hallucinations, while even small doses could assist in the creation of vivid sexual fantasies. Minutes after swallowing the drug, Ronica was the willing victim of a reverie as vivid and lickerish as the most sensational dream.

The ringing phone returned Ronica's amplified thoughts to her office. Still able to taste the man in her fantasy, Ronica picked up a thin, flat disc and stared into its reflective surface. As soon as she touched the disc, the ringing sound – more like someone stroking the rim of a wine glass than a bell – stopped, and the reflection of her own lightly perspiring features were replaced with those of the director ordering her back to his office.

'Right away, sir,' she said as his face vanished from the phone. Holding onto the disc in her fingers, her reflection on the phone's polished prismatic surface bisected by a laser-thin spectrum that made a livid scar across her face, Ronica checked her appearance, wiped her cheeks with a sheet of nanotissue,[1] took a deep breath, and stood up. There were times when she thought Connex should be remarketed as some sort of aphrodisiac. She straightened her clothes, and went to find the director.

II

With its many *faux fenêtre* English landscape paintings (he owned all of the originals) and its antique

---

[1] Kleenex nanotissue. Tissue that is designed to have a second life soaking up toxic chemicals in ground and water.

furniture, the director's office was like the drawing room of a beautiful country house. It didn't matter that she had been there not half an hour earlier, Ronica found herself once again mesmerized by Simon King's good taste, overawed by such a conspicuous display of wealth. She estimated the desk alone had probably cost more than her apartment.

'Ah, there you are,' he said impatiently. 'Come in, come in. This is the girl I was telling you about.'

Ronica hardly minded the fact that by describing her as a girl, and not a woman, the director was in breach of employment and gender legislation, as she walked across the thick Persian rug toward an ornate sofa. He was the director after all, and as far as Ronica was concerned, he could have called her anything he damn well liked. It was a moment or two before her distracted senses registered that Rimmer was already sitting on the sofa scowling at her. As she turned to sit alongside him, the director raised a hand bearing an enormous cigar – smoking in the workplace, another breach of employment legislation – in the air.

'No, don't sit down,' he said. 'You're not staying. Neither of you are.' He glanced meaningfully at Rimmer, who pulled a face and rose reluctantly to his feet. 'There's no time to lose. Rimmer has located Dallas. I want you to go with him and, as we discussed earlier, see how he handles the situation. Observe and learn and give him any assistance you can. Understand?'

'Yes, director,' said Ronica, and she followed Rimmer out of the door.

Neither of them spoke until they had collected their coats and were standing in the elevator, heading up to the ground floor.

'So you think you want to join Security, do you?' Rimmer sniffed with obvious contempt.

'Yes. I think so.'

'And what makes you believe that you're cut out for it?'

Ronica shrugged. 'I like tying people up,' she said. 'And beating them. Punishment's always been my thing. So I figured I might as well get paid for it.'

'A sense of humor, eh?' remarked Rimmer. 'You'll need that.'

'Anything else I'll need?' she asked as the car delivered them into the entrance lobby.

Rimmer strode forward, acknowledged the parking valet standing on the far side of the security screen, and, glancing back over his dandruffed shoulder, said, 'We'll see, won't we?' With a show of mock courtesy he waited for Ronica to pass out of the front door ahead of him and then ushered her toward the electric car parked out front.

'That's your job, I guess,' she said. 'Finding things out.'

'Depend on it,' said Rimmer, opening both doors remotely.

'You're sort of an armed information-retrieval service,' said Ronica and slid into the passenger seat. The inside of Rimmer's car smelled strongly of nickel cadmium, as if there was something wrong with the battery. Rimmer sat down beside her and the doors shut automatically.

'Perhaps I'll find out just what it is that makes the director think so highly of you,' he said.

'That's easy,' she laughed. 'I can tell you why. If you're interested.'

Rimmer said nothing as he started the electric motor

and stamped irritably on the power pedal. The car moved forward, silently picking up speed.

'*Are* you interested?' she asked, smiling, making him work for an answer. She could see he was biting his lip in an effort not to admit that he was.

For a few more seconds Rimmer attempted to retain control of their conversational game, trying to force her to react to his moves instead of the other way around.

'Go on then,' he snarled finally. 'Don't make me have to seek absolution from a priest before you tell.'

'Absolution? For you?' It was her turn to sniff with contempt. 'There's certainly no time for that. I've a good idea you've more wrongs than most to own up to, Mister Rimmer.'

'The job is not without its amusements.'

'I thought so.'

'Think what you like.'

'I shall. Thinking what I like has always afforded me the greatest of pleasure.'

For several minutes, they drove in silence. Rimmer hadn't said where they were going, but it was somewhere north – somewhere that was clearly outside the CBH Zone:[1] You didn't need documentation to get out, but you needed to be in possession of a CBH to get back in. The very idea of leaving the Zone gave her an uncomfortable feeling of vulnerability.

'Well,' said Rimmer, breaking the silence. 'Are you going to tell me, or not?'

'Sure,' said Ronica. 'It's like this. I asked him if, in return for paying lip service to his holy rood, he might advance my career at a slightly more urgent pace.' The drug was really taking effect now: Her whole head was

---

[1] Clean Bill of Health Zone.

humming, as if she'd had an electric shock. 'Anyway, he said he would, and asked me if there were any particular areas in Terotechnology where I thought my talents might lie. And in between anthropophagous mouthfuls, I suggested Security. Like I say, I enjoy bondage and that kind of thing. Well, naturally he was just a little disappointed that I hadn't suggested Design, because that's his thing. However, he was able to keep a stiff upper lip just long enough to cede unto me this many-headed florescence.'

'You mean you sucked his cock,' said Rimmer.

'Yes,' she said, and they both started to laugh.

'You know, you're all right,' said Rimmer, who was thinking that she must have been sent by the director to spy on him. And if for any reason things went badly wrong again, then he might have to arrange some sort of fatal accident for Ronica.

'Thanks,' she said. If things worked out as she expected, then the man still laughing with her had maybe less than an hour before she blew his brains out. 'Where are we going?'

'A hotel.'

'But we've only just met. What kind of a girl do you take me for?'

'The hyperbaric kind of hotel. Where sick people go to get themselves oxygenated, not laid.'

'I know what they get. A little color in their cheeks. A chance to breathe easy at night. But it's all just air today, gone tomorrow.' She shrugged. 'Do you ever give them much thought? The bad bloods?'

'Can't say I do,' admitted Rimmer.

'Oh, I think about them a lot. It makes me feel good to know that there are so many people worse off than me. Kind of the philosophical opposite of utilitarianism. Social *schadenfreude*, I suppose you could call it.'

Ronica stared out of the car's bullet-proof windows at the moonlit people she had been talking about. Only a few minutes' drive had taken them out of the Zone and into a less salubrious part of the city. There was little traffic on the road, but still plenty of people walking around: the living dead, as she thought of them.

'Look at them,' she spat. 'Like walking Gothics. Restless gossamers. Two A.M. and there are still thousands of them abroad on the streets, like vampires out for an evening stroll. The poor fucking bastards.'

'You've got a nasty mouth,' said Rimmer.

'That's not what the director said,' she murmured, delighting in the image of herself and the director she was creating for Rimmer's benefit. 'If you're nice to me, maybe I'll do the same for you.'

'I wouldn't recommend it,' said Rimmer. 'Been a while since I had a wash, what with trying to kill Dallas and his family.'

'Thanks for the advice,' said Ronica, her nose wrinkling with disgust. 'I'll bear it in mind.'

'But hey, I'm always nice to people.' Saying this made Rimmer laugh out loud again.

'You know, I can't tell if you're immoral or amoral, Rimmer.'

'I have the same problem myself.'

'You're a moral eunuch, then.'

'Comes with the job. Perhaps you should give that some thought yourself.'

'My morals are really very simple,' said Ronica. 'I would never do anything that might interfere with my progress within the company.'

'Sounds to me like you'd be better suited to a career in the Church.'

'If this one doesn't work for me, then maybe I'll give it a try. I look good in black.'

Ronica sank down into the capacious warmth of her thick lambskin coat. Glancing out of the window, she caught sight of a swarm of rats feasting on a dead body lying on the roadside. 'Ugh, I hate this part of the city. What ever is Dallas thinking of coming to an area like this? It's so far from the Zone.'

'That's the whole idea,' chuckled Rimmer, as the car's automatic steering system narrowly avoided a collision with a man wandering like a zombie up the center of the road. 'The most unlikely place is the most secure. Or so he seems to have thought.'

'How did you find him anyway?'

'I persuaded Dixy, his Motion Parallax assistant, to tell me.'

'That can't have been easy.'

Rimmer told her about the dog, Mersenne.

'So then, no computer is an island, entire of itself, either,' observed Ronica. 'That's interesting.'

'I think Dixy was just programmed that way,' said Rimmer, and pointed at the flashing routefinder. 'Looks like we're nearly there.'

'Good. So promise me you won't make a meal of it,' she said. 'The sooner you blow his brains out, the sooner we can get back to the Zone and healthy civilization. Just driving through this shit heap makes me feel like I'm going to catch something awful. Bubonic plague, Ebola, Lassa, smallpox.'

Rimmer laughed, as if enjoying her discomfort, but at the same time, he wondered how much of it was genuine. Even in her evening clothes and smelling as sweetly as any genetically engineered bloom, the well-muscled Ronica looked more than equal to the task at hand.

'I thought I would read him a bit from the Bible first,' teased Rimmer. 'Execution style. The book of

Exodus, I think. That always offers a fairly conclusive text.'

'Not much consolation there, I'd have thought.'

'Precisely my idea. So what's your favorite bit in the Bible?'

Ronica shrugged. 'I dunno. The head of John the Baptist? No wait. Gershon's foreskin. That got hacked off with a stone. Pretty much anyone's foreskin, I guess. That's usually my favorite bit. In the Bible. And anywhere else.'

'I think I'm beginning to understand just what the director sees in you,' admitted Rimmer.

The car drew up to the Clostridium Hotel. Rimmer switched off the engine and sat back in his seat. 'Well,' he said, with the air of a man who might have just arrived somewhere nice for a holiday. 'We're here.'

'I've got to pee,' said Ronica.

'What?'

'I'm nervous. I've never seen anyone killed before.'

'You can certainly pick your places.'

'I already did,' she said, opening the passenger door. 'I'll squat down here, in the road beside the car, just as Marie Antoinette did on the conciergerie cobbles when she saw her waiting tumbril. Only stay in the car until I've finished please, Rimmer.'

He nodded and, remaining seated, looked politely away as Ronica got out of the car, closed the door, and then lifted her skirt.

Swiftly she fetched the little colt Matahari automatic from the holster between her legs – and then had a pee for appearance's sake before pocketing the gun and standing up straight.

'All right,' she said, tapping on the toughened window. 'I'm ready now.'

Rimmer got out of the car.

'Let's go and kill him,' she added eagerly.

He walked around the car, eyed the still steaming snow where she had urinated, and sniffed the air like a dog.

'Asparagus,' he said. 'For your supper. Quite unmistakable.'

Ronica felt herself blush with embarrassment. She was going to enjoy killing him. Blowing Rimmer's brains out would count as a service to humanity.

Rimmer turned his back on her and trudged down the narrow street toward the hotel's front door. 'When we get in there,' he said, 'you can do the talking. Let's see how clever you really are.'

'Afraid you'll fuck it up again, is that it?' she asked, finding it difficult to keep up with him in her expensive Federico Ingannevole evening shoes, which were not made for walking, least of all in snow.

'You're the one who seems to lack the stomach for this, not me,' he said, sniffing the air again.

'That reminds me. What bloodtype are you, Rimmer?'

Rimmer stopped in his tracks and, turning around, fixed her with a look of disdain. 'Don't tell me you believe that EPTR[1] bullshit?'

Ronica shrugged. 'Why not?'

Rimmer shook his head and started walking again. 'And the director said you were clever,' he snorted.

---

[1] Erythrocytic Personality Trait Rating. The pseudo-science of blood temperaments, based on a taxonomy of personality based on blood types. EPTR draws upon Buddhist beliefs, as well as the work of Theophrastus, Hippocrates, Karl Landsteiner, Leon Bourdel, and Hans Eysenck, and was 'discovered' by J. Will Mott (1987–2041). EPTR has been challenged by a number of hematologists and psychologists as having no empiric basis.

'Why shouldn't there be some truth in it?' argued Ronica. 'There are over four hundred blood groups.'

'But most people are just O or A. I can't see how that helps to determine the kind of guy I am.'

'So which are you, Rimmer?'

'Neither. I'm AB.'

'Interesting. Only three percent of people are AB.'

'I know.'

'A Universal Recipient.[1] Means you're full of internal contradictions, as you might expect of someone with your blood group history.'

'Bullshit.'

'The melancholic type: quiet, unsociable, reserved, pessimistic, rigid, and moody. Not to mention greedy and manipulative. How am I doing, Rimmer? Recognize yourself?'

Rimmer didn't reply.

'Me, I'm group O. Makes me relaxed and sociable, outgoing, poor on details, but with good leadership qualities.'

'I thought all blacks were group B.'

'Phenotype frequencies vary across various racial groups. The B phenotype is not exclusive to blacks, merely more common. Talking of misconceptions, you should get your chart done. That is, if you're planning to marry and have children. Although I can tell you that we're not the right mix. O's should stick to their own type.'

'I'm glad to hear it,' said Rimmer as they neared the

[1] In transfusion therapy, group AB recipients can receive all other ABO group red-cell components, because anti-A and anti-B antibodies are absent. Group AB red-cell components are infused only into group AB recipients. Group O recipients, on the other hand, can receive only Group O red cells, but can donate to any other group. Group O donors are known as Universal Donors.

hotel's front door. 'But I'll be even more glad to hear what story you've thought up to explain our imminent arrival here.'

'Hey, just watch my relaxed group O style,' said Ronica, leading the way through the door. 'You're about to see someone whose temperament includes the very essence, the *sanguis* of cool.'

They were met by a hyperbaric attendant, a tall black who stifled a yawn and nodded a silent greeting.

'We're from the Oxygen Institute,' Ronica explained smoothly. 'Checking free radicals?'

'Free what?' The attendant looked back at the glass-walled office from which he had just emerged, as if someone might come to his assistance, but there was no one else.

'Unstable and reactive electrons,' she said. 'In this case, oxygen.'

'Nobody told me you were coming,' said the attendant, scratching his head.

'You're not supposed to have any prior knowledge,' tutted Ronica. 'That's the whole point of the check.'

'At ...' The attendant glanced at his watch. 'At two-thirty in the morning?'

'Middle of the night's when people least expect us. When they're able to offer the least amount of resistance. You know, I'm surprised no one told you about us before. We've been to quite a few hyperbaric hotels in this district.'

'You have?'

'You obviously have no idea who we are, do you?'

The attendant shrugged.

'That's okay.' Ronica smiled patiently and began to walk around him as she went on with her patter. Rimmer had to admit she sounded pretty convincing, even in a floor-length lambskin coat and pretty shoes.

'We're an organization acting under federal law,' she explained. 'We're empowered to check places like this to see if there has been any involvement of iron in the process by which oxidative damage is produced in DNA in human cells that are undergoing oxidative stress. As might be expected in a hyperbaric hotel. You see, through their reactions with this trace metal, elevated levels of activated oxygen species can cause alterations to human DNA. Now we wouldn't want that, now would we?'

'What trace metal is that?' frowned the attendant. 'I thought oxygen was a nonmetallic element.'

Ronica sighed loudly. 'Iron, of course. Cells must maintain iron, even though it can't be used for metabolic processes. Look, you do work here, don't you? I mean, you're not a guest or a patient or whatever you call your customers?'

'Sure, I work here. I'm the night shift hyperbaric attendant.'

'In which case you'll have the superoxide levels of your guests at hand. If we could just check those out, we'll be on our way.'

'Superoxide levels?' The attendant grinned awkwardly.

'Kind of a place is this?' muttered Rimmer, getting the idea.

'When cells are diseased or injured, the normal metabolism of oxygen goes wrong, leading to the increased production of superoxide,' Ronica explained patiently. It was amazing what she found she knew when she put her Connex-stimulated mind onto the case. She must have read all this somewhere, sometime. 'For example,' she added, 'white blood cells intentionally produce superoxide in order to kill microorganisms. These same white cells are activated by trauma and inflammation.' She smiled thinly and continued slowly, as if speaking to an idiot. 'So nearly all diseases involve the production of increased amounts of free radicals.'

'Free radicals, right?'

'Yeah,' growled Rimmer. 'Listen and you might learn something.'

'You're obliged to keep patient records of superoxide levels as a matter of federal law.' Ronica was making it up now. She had no idea what kind of laws affected hyperbaric hotels, but she thought that there ought to be some, which is as good a legislative philosophy as any.

'Let's get out of here,' grumbled Rimmer. 'He doesn't have the first idea what you're talking about. I say we go back to the office, issue a closure notice, and then it's someone else's problem.'

'Closure notice?' The attendant sounded alarmed. 'Wait a second. You guys can close this place?'

'We just issue the order,' said Ronica. 'It's nothing personal, you understand. But failure to monitor superoxide levels properly is a serious matter.' She shrugged. 'It's out of our hands.'

'Couldn't we find some way around this? Some of our guests have been here a while. They're sick people. I'm not sure they'd survive being transferred somewhere else.'

Rimmer looked doubtfully at Ronica, and seeing her apparently thinking about the matter, he turned away in a show of disgust.

'No way,' he snarled.

'Please?'

'Well,' said Ronica. 'I guess we could do the superoxide tests ourselves. Of course to do that we'd need to take mitochondrial samples from your longest guest and, as a control, your most recent guest.'

'Hey, no problem,' said the attendant. 'That's easy. Don't even have to look it up. Last guest came in only an hour or so ago. Name of Dallas. He's in 1218. And the longest resident? That's Ingrams, in 1105. Been here so long he's practically part of the furniture. You could take a sample from him and he probably wouldn't even know it. Guy's practically a corpse. He's been in a Three Moon crisis for must be a couple of years now.'

'Where's the harm?' Ronica asked Rimmer.

'I dunno,' he sighed. 'It's a fudge and you know it. There ought to be twenty tests, not just two.'

'We both know two's quite sufficient if you can accurately identify the two chronological parameters. As it happens we can.'

'All right,' said Rimmer. 'But if anyone finds out, this is your responsibility, okay? I'm done sticking my neck out for people.'

'Relax, will you? What can go wrong?' She looked back at the attendant and smiled. 'Okay. Why don't you show us the way?'

'All right,' he grinned, and collected an electronic pass key off his desktop. 'Now you're talking.'

III

At this point, a word of explanation is required. How is it, you may ask, that the author of this book, who regrets of the necessity to speak of himself, knows these things? How, for instance, is the author able to describe what someone thought, and perhaps, why they thought it? But to be quite frank, I can't imagine why you don't ask this question more often in connection with a book. And I find it surprising that more authors do not attempt to clear up the small matter of narrative device somewhere during the course of their written endeavors.

Of course, narration is not a science, but an art. Even so, you would still think that some critic had attempted to formulate a few principles about it, or even to create a terminology that might be equal to the task of describing the point of view. In this respect, there is an embarrassing inadequacy of classification, and I am obliged to explain myself and my narrative position in terms that might seem enigmatic, since 'first person' and 'omniscient' hardly seem to come up to the mark.

Let us say then that this story is told by a narrator who is dramatized in his own right, although it is arguable that even the most retiring of narrators has been dramatized as soon as the personal pronoun has been called into play. Say also that by producing some measurable effect on the course of events (and in time all will be revealed concerning my own role in this story), I can justly claim to be more than a mere observer – I am that particular kind of narrator who is also an agent. Naturally, you will have judged me to be a narrator who is the self-conscious kind, who is aware of himself as a writer, to which I would like to add that I may be relied upon to tell you all you need to know, and more, until the time comes when you know absolutely everything, as I do.

This leads me, neatly, to the question of how the narrator is privileged to know what could not be learned by strictly natural means – what we authors usually call, because we like to play at being God, omniscience. Obviously the most important privilege is the inside view – the characters and their thought processes to which I referred a little earlier. Perhaps it's a little difficult for you to understand it now, but the fact is, I have the best inside view any author has ever enjoyed. What is more, the means of its learning has indeed been strictly natural. Science has provided me with unlimited omniscience. But what kind of science? I hear you ask. Why, the science of hematology, of course. The state or fact of knowing what I do, as much as I do – everything that ever was, is, and shall be – come from blood. This is the infinite knowledge, the fountain of youth, and the secret of life. Through the communion of the blood of man, everything shall be known and understood. And if I give you notice of this betimes, it is, to paraphrase Antoine Furetière,[1] 'because I design not to surprise you, as some malicious Authors are wont to do, who aim at nothing else.' I wish you to be prepared to understand. For ahead lies great understanding and great effort of understanding. You must lift yourself up, by your own bootstraps, so to speak.

There, I hope that's made things just a little clearer.

IV

Rimmer placed the Pinback in his ear and, unobserved by the black night attendant, selected a piece of Mendelssohn as accompaniment for his imminent act of homicide. *Elijah. Be not afraid*, sang the voice. It made a pleasant alternative to the Muzak and the chatter of the attendant leading them along an eleventh

[1] Antoine Furetière (1619–1688), French poet and novelist.

floor corridor to 1105, the chamber of the Clostridium's longest resident. Part of him wondered why they were still bothering with this little facade. They knew where Dallas was to be found. It was simply a matter of going there and killing him.

'As a matter of fact, in the morning I was going to have to decompress Ingrams anyway,' explained the attendant, whose own name, he said, was Taylor. 'We have to do all the long-term guests once or twice a week, otherwise they get the bends. Y'know? Bubbles in the bloodstream. We're real careful about that.'

'I'm glad to hear it,' said Ronica, as Taylor stopped outside the door to a chamber and inserted his electronic key into the security lock. She was still trying to think of some way in which she could put on a show of testing the hapless resident of 1105 for superoxides. Perhaps she would get the guy to lick the screen of the matchbook phone she was carrying: It was a new one, a little different than how they normally looked, and she was banking on Taylor not having seen this kind of phone before. That would have to do.

Now that he had the key in the lock, Taylor was able to open a control panel on the wall beside the door and manually override the pressure settings that had been made on the inside of the chamber. He glanced at his watch and said, 'This'll take a few minutes. But you can't hurry it.' He laughed grimly. 'Not unless you want to kill the guy.'

Rimmer's available ear picked up.

'As a matter of interest, how high can you set the pressure?'

'High as you like. Two or three hundred atmospheres. These chambers are built to withstand huge amounts of pressure. Much more than the human body can take, anyway. But we don't let guests set their own pressures as high as all that. Anything really high has to be done from the outside by an attendant with a key like this one. It stops some of the guests from using the pressures to commit suicide, when they get depressed.' Taylor shook his head. 'You should see the mess it used to make.'

'That is fascinating,' said Rimmer. 'You learn something useful every day.'

'Don't know about useful,' murmured Taylor. He glanced up as a red light above the door extinguished. 'Soon as it turns green we can go in.'

Rimmer looked at Ronica and smiled. 'I think we've seen enough, don't you?' *Be not afraid, saith God the Lord, be not afraid, thy help is near.*

'What are you talking about?' frowned Taylor. 'I thought you wanted to do this test on Ingrams. Superoxide test, or whatever.'

Rimmer had the gun behind his back now, his thumb adjusting the bezel of the noise suppressor to ensure the shot would be a silent one. No point in disturbing the other guests, he thought. Especially if those guests included Dallas on the floor immediately above them. *Though thousands languish and fall beside thee, and tens of thousands around thee perish, yet still it shall not come nigh thee.* That didn't include Taylor, obviously. But Rimmer was beginning to feel a bit like some Old Testament prophet of doom. It was a good feeling. He was just waiting on a sign from the Lord now. A green light to go. He hardly cared that some hidden camera might record his image. Not in a place like this. It was only in the Zone that such considerations really mattered. The police from a city sector like this one were never allowed to enter a CBH Zone.

The attendant's eyes flicked momentarily above the door as the green light came on, and in the same instant, Rimmer placed the thick square muzzle of the gun against the back of Taylor's head and squeezed the trigger, stepping neatly out of the way of the collapsing body and the great spout of blood that discharged itself in a red arc from the pressurized chamber that was the instantaneously dead man's skull. Quite unprepared for what had happened, Ronica was not so smart on her elegantly shod feet, and these were quickly drenched in a shower of hot, steaming blood. Horrified at this sudden eruption of potential contamination, for you didn't work in a hyperbaric hotel unless you too were infected with the virus, Ronica started back on her high heels until she felt the wall on the opposite side of the corridor against her back, whereupon she stared down at her incarnadined shoes.

'You bloody idiot,' she screamed.

'Keep it down, will you? There are people trying to sleep, you know?'

'Keep it down?' Ronica gasped with outrage. 'Keep it down? Rimmer do you see what you've done to my fucking shoes? They're ruined. They were by Federico Ingannevole. And they cost a bloody fortune. But now. Christ, I look like ...' Ronica shook her braided head.

Rimmer glanced down at her shoes and laughed.

'His blood be upon us,' he said. 'And on our children. And on our shoes. You're right.'

'Yeah, well I don't notice any of it on you,' she replied bitterly, trying to wipe the worst of it off onto the carpet.

'You've got to move quickly on this job.' Rimmer kicked the attendant experimentally, drawing forth a sharp exhalation of air from the dead man, enough to make Rimmer step back and contemplate firing another shot. Then, looking up and seeing a green light, he perceived the real source of the noise. It was not Taylor gasping his last, but the door to the hyperbaric chamber, where a near naked man of indeterminate age stood, his whole skeletally thin body covered in the bright red lace that was the maculopapular rash characteristic of final phase P®. The dying man uttered a hoarse, parched cry and staggered forward into the bright light of the corridor, pointing an accusing finger at Rimmer in an almost spectral manner. Now that he was in the light Ronica and Rimmer could clearly see the cheeks of the man's emaciated face, as red as if he had been slapped hard several times and flecked with tiny pinpricks of oxygen-starved blood.

Snatching the Pinback from his ear – for the sight looked a little too biblical even for him, like Samuel returned from the grave to haunt King Saul – Rimmer recoiled from this walking corpse and the putrid smell that preceded him. And with a shudder of distaste that quickly turned to panic as the figure reached out to touch him, Rimmer shot the man in the leg. This was not for mercy's sake, so as not to have to shoot him dead, but only to allow Rimmer to step a little farther away from the now supine, groaning wretch – Rimmer had no wish to be spattered with any body fluids from this contaminated creature – before shooting him twice more, in the chest. But in truth, the old man, Ingrams, hardly bled at all. It was as if the blood that had become his every waking preoccupation was simply too exhausted to leave the etiolated cadaver.

Ronica removed the protective hand from her still gaping mouth and let out a gasp of horror.

'Bloody hell,' she muttered. 'Bloody hell.'

'It sure looks like it,' Rimmer said coolly.

'Jesus Christ, Rimmer, what is it with you?'

He shrugged a half-apologetic little smile. 'I didn't want him touching me. You can understand that, can't you?'

'I guess when you've got a gun everyone looks like a target, eh?'

'Sweetheart?' he said, collecting the attendant's electronic pass key, and starting back along the corridor towards the stairs, 'We've hardly started.'

V

For a moment, Lenina looked at the footprints on the corridor's beige carpet and thought someone must have stepped in dog shit – until she remembered how a particularly virulent strain of canine parvovirus the previous year had left most of the city's population of uneaten dogs dead of a combination of enteritis and myocarditis. As a child in California, there had been a dog. While she had lived in the country, anyway. Before the family had moved to Los Angeles, and she had started her life of crime. But these days the only dogs you saw were the Motion Parallax kind. Lenina no longer cared very much about dogs. It had been a police German shepherd that had apprehended her during the commission of the aggravated burglary that got her sent to Artemis Seven, and it had left her with a badly scarred calf that still caused her pain when she stretched the muscle. As it did now, kneeling down to investigate the woman's footprints – that much was obvious from the shape of the shoe. This was not the kind of shoe that guests in the Clostridium were ever likely to wear, too expensive, designed not for comfort and practicality, but for style, and that meant a woman with credits to her name and good blood in her veins. The kind of woman Lenina would like to have been. It was impossible to tell if the blood on the carpet was good or bad, but blood it was, for the dark brown tracks were sticky and unmistakably salty to taste.

She stood up painfully and glanced along the bay-curved, beach-colored corridor, from where the footprints had originated. It took only a matter of seconds to walk around the bend and find the two bodies. The attendant, she recognized. She'd tried to get to know most of them by name. Just to remind herself that this was not a prison, and that the attendants were not warders. But the other man – the old, half-naked one – was a stranger to her.

As soon as she saw the two bodies, Lenina turned around and headed back to the hyperbaric chamber she shared with Rameses Gates. Only a few minutes before, she had abruptly walked out on an argument with him over this crazy guy, Dallas, whose hare-brained scheme she had thought would surely result in Gates getting sent back to Artemis Seven. Or something worse. Robbing a blood bank probably counted as a major blood felony, for which the penalty would almost certainly be death. Not just any blood bank either, but the biggest and best of them all, the First National Blood Bank on the Moon. Lenina had thought that only served to underline how deluded Dallas really was. It was asking for trouble. Begging for it. Like slapping a grizzly bear on the nose. Not that there were any of those left either. An outbreak of ursine parvovirus had seen the extinction of pretty much the whole of the world's bear population. Now that really was a pity, thought Lenina. She had liked bears. Perhaps that was the reason she liked Gates. And why she was prepared to humor him now. Maybe even ready to go along with him and his new scheme. After all, this Dallas guy he had told her about, the one who said he built the blood banks and who was hiding out in the hotel, well, maybe he was for real. It certainly looked as if someone had come after him, someone from the Zone who was not just dressed to kill, but seriously equipped for it as well. Perhaps Dallas had been telling the truth.

Rameses Gates was sitting on the edge of the bed wearing a puzzled expression, as if he was wondering why Lenina had stormed out of the chamber. Seeing her in the doorway, Gates stood up and sheepishly started to apologize.

'Forget it,' Lenina said, cutting him short. 'I think your new friend might be the real thing after all.' She explained about the bloody footprints she had found and the two bodies farther up the corridor.

'Dallas is on the floor above,' said Gates, hauling a bag out from underneath the bed. 'Sounds like someone got the wrong room.'

'Not a someone. A she. They were a woman's footprints.'

'Then you can shoot her.' Gates threw her a gun, collecting a second weapon for himself – a recoilless, fifteen-millimeter automatic – and sprang off the bed. 'C'mon, let's go. We've got a rich uncle to take care of.'

Lenina followed the big man through the chamber door, inspecting the piece he had given her. 'Been a while since I shot anyone.'

'It's like riding a bicycle,' said Gates, heading toward the stairs. 'You never forget how.'

VI

Outside the door to 1218, Rimmer inserted the attendant's electronic key into the security lock and opened the control panel.

'Looks like Dallas must be in here, all right,' he said, jerking his head up at the green light above the door. 'This one's not even pressurized. Kind of pointless coming to a hyperbaric chamber and not switching the thing on, wouldn't you say? Like going to a restaurant to read a book.'

Ronica's hand tightened on the little Matahari automatic in her coat pocket. Now that she had seen the instant effect of a clean head shot she was thinking she ought to shoot Rimmer in the same way. This time she would be ready for the blood – although her shoes were ruined, there was still her coat to think of. As soon as Rimmer opened the chamber door, and Dallas registered that it was him, she would do it. Just the way the director had ordered. As a demonstration of the company's goodwill toward its most brilliant designer. But instead of opening the chamber manually, as she had been expecting, Rimmer started to adjust the pressure controls and, a second or two later, the green light over the door was replaced by a red one.

'What the hell are you doing?' she demanded.

'What's it look like?' said Rimmer, not even turning around. 'I'm putting him under pressure.' He uttered a sadistic little chuckle. 'Quite a lot of fucking pressure, as it happens.'

'Shouldn't you make sure he's in there?' asked Ronica. 'I mean, suppose he's not? Suppose it's someone else? By the time you've finished screwing around with that pressure, it might be quite hard to identify if it's Dallas, or not. And the director will want to know that you made sure, Rimmer.'

'You heard the attendant, didn't you?' sneered Rimmer. 'Dallas checked into 1218. Well, this is 1218. You don't have to be Sherlock Holmes to decipher what's written on these doors, Ronica. Besides, the point of my screwing around with the pressure is not to kill Dallas, merely to make him more amenable to me offing him when eventually I do open the door. Dallas has got a gun, you see. And he's quite likely to use it unless I can soften him up a bit first. Squeeze him with some breeze, so to speak.'

Ronica bit her voluptuous lips, wondering just how useful Dallas would remain to her employer by the time Rimmer had finished giving him the hyperbaric equivalent of *peine forte et dure*. There might be nothing left of his brilliant mind to make it worth her while returning him to the company. As Rimmer moved from the control panel, she caught a glimpse of the pressure gauge and a needle flickering dangerously close to the red section of the value arc. She realized she could delay no longer. It was now or never.

Still facing the door, Rimmer felt something as cold and metallic as the voice that controlled it pressed hard against his scrawny neck.

'Turn it off,' she said. 'Now. Or I'll kill you.'

There was something comic in his situation that made Rimmer laugh.

'Is that a gun?' He started to turn around and found the object gouging the flesh under his ear, pushing his head back toward the chamber door.

'It's not a stethoscope. Now turn that pressure off or I'll give you the irrefutable proof.'

Rimmer reached for the hyperbaric controls and reversed the chamber pressure.

'Empiricism,' he said coolly. 'That's always been my problem. A linguistic expression can only be significant for a man like me if it's accompanied by something that can be experienced.'

'Now step away from the door. Slowly. I'd hate you to discover that my threat was more than just syntactical. For you the principle of verification is likely to come in the shape of a fifteen-millimeter bullet.'

'Fifteen mill, eh?' said Rimmer, moving away with the gun still pressed against the nape of his neck. 'That's quite a load you're packing.'

'More than enough to trepan your skull, Rimmer. I've already ruined a good pair of shoes. Don't make me spoil this coat as well.'

'Must be one of those little three-shot autos. Pussy gun. Been inside your panties all this time. Nice. Mm, perhaps you'll let me smell it later. After we've sorted out this small misunderstanding.'

'I'll only need one shot to put a groove in you. Now face the wall and keep your mouth shut.' She glanced at the red light above the door, hoping to be able to avoid killing Rimmer until Dallas was there to witness it. Or maybe she would let Dallas kill Rimmer himself. If he was still up to it. Either way, killing Rimmer was going to be the easy part. Much harder still was going to be the sales pitch that followed – trying to convince Dallas that the director had not ordered Rimmer to murder Dallas's family. Ronica could see no reason why he would believe her. Surely a man as intelligent as him would see through her little charade.

The red light stayed on as the chamber continued its slow return to sea-level pressure. With her gun still on

Rimmer's neck, Ronica's eyes searched the pressure gauge impatiently. It was still only halfway back to normal. Gritting her perfect white teeth, she tried to contain the sour uncertainty she was feeling in her stomach. She was close enough to smell Rimmer's bad breath as it blew back off the corridor wall. There was something less culpable about killing a man with offensive breath, she thought. Another glance at the pressure gauge. Almost there. Just a few more seconds and it would all be over.

'Do you want to talk about this now?' he asked.

'Shut up.'

'I love a dominant female. As it happens, I'm looking for a responsible and reliable person to set my ten-inch cock on fire for a home movie I'm making. Why don't we go back to my car where we can discuss the details and possible financial compensation?' He licked his lips and smiled. 'Or maybe I'm asleep and this is all an erotic dream. Any minute I'll have a nocturnal emission all over the bottom sheet, and wake up.'

Ronica grabbed a handful of Rimmer's lank and greasy hair to better grind the muzzle of her gun into the boil on Rimmer's cheekbone.

'If this is just a dream,' she said, 'it's not one you'll ever wake up from unless you shut your mouth.'

'You're not going to kill me for talking,' persisted Rimmer. 'Fact is, you're not ready to kill me yet, otherwise you'd have done it already. Besides, you can't live forever.'

With one side of his face pressed up against the wall he had a half-view of her out of the corner of his eye. Although it was hardly hot in the corridor, Ronica's beautiful black face was shiny with perspiration, as if she still had a few doubts about what she was doing, as if – Rimmer smiled – as if she hadn't quite convinced herself that she would squeeze the trigger. He was about to suggest that he wouldn't die in his dreams, or any place else for that matter, so long as she still had the safety catch on her little Matahari – a pretty obvious feint, he thought, but worth a try all the same – when a shot blasted its fortissimo way past his devious thought process.

Ronica's scream persuaded him that he would feel no pain – at least not from the first shot anyway. She was already down on one knee, but in the second or two available to him before the next shot was heard, he couldn't tell if she had been hit or not. What was clear was that someone else was doing the shooting, and with no regard for noise. Sometimes it was better that way. Scaring the shit out of people was more efficient than shooting them. Instinctively, Rimmer crouched down as a third shot came zipping up the corridor, bursting with lethal energy. He reached for his gun, pointed it at Ronica's head, and then thought better of killing her right then and there – he might need all his ammunition to deal with whoever was doing the shooting. Having adjusted the volume in the handgrip, just to let the guy know he was well-heeled, Rimmer returned fire in the general direction from which the first three shots had come. All he could think of was that Ronica had been right after all – that Dallas couldn't have been in his chamber. Who else would want to shoot at them?

Rimmer fired twice more, and, ignoring Ronica, who was now crouched down in the opposite doorway, he scrambled away in the nick of time as a hole the size of an orange got blasted from the wall he'd been leaning against.

'Dallas?' he yelled. 'Is that you?'

More shots. And, thought Rimmer, more than just the one gun, surely. He fired back, only this time he and Dallas, or whoever it was, both hit the someone foolishly drawn into the corridor to inspect the noise – the same someone, a woman.

Rimmer kept on firing, not caring who he shot. What with the roar of the guns and the smell of the cordite, he was enjoying his evening. There were two of them, he was certain of that now, concealed inside the opaque plastic-walled prism that housed the stairwell and helped light the far end of the curving corridor. Behind him, farther around the bend, the elevator shaft sank through a glazed circle in the floor. It was time to make himself scarce. If he could just cross the floor, he would be safe.

Right on cue, a head and shoulder appeared around the edge of another doorway. Rimmer aimed carefully, and as the target collapsed forward into the corridor, screaming loudly, he used him as cover to make his escape, rolling acrobatically across the floor before scrambling around the bend in the corridor, and out of the line of fire. Sensing Rimmer's presence, the elevator shaft lit up as a car began its automatic ascent to the twelfth floor. Quickly Rimmer reloaded his gun and, from the comparative safety of his new position, glanced around the bend, hoping to get a clear shot at his attackers before making his getaway. Discovering his own line of fire partially blocked by the man he had shot, Rimmer finished him off with a couple of bullets in the chest. A second stolen glance confirmed that he no longer had a clear shot at Ronica, who was pressed into the protection afforded by a doorway. If he was going to settle this account, he was going to have to persuade her that he still cared what happened to her.

When she made her own getaway bid and ran toward him, he would kill her.

'Ronica?' he yelled. 'C'mon, let's get out of here. I'll cover you.'

'With what? Kisses?'

'Stop screwing around, Ronica. The elevator car's here. You want to stay there and get shot, that's up to you, but I'm leaving.'

Flattened against the smooth metallic surface of the chamber doorway, Ronica caught a glimpse of her own reflection in the door of 1218 opposite. She looked like some two-dimensional vignette from the Egyptian Book of the Dead – the deceased holding in her left hand a lotus flower. Except that the flower was a gun and she was, for the moment, very much alive. Not that she expected to stay that way the minute she showed herself to Rimmer.

'You better get going then,' she said, and seeing the slimmest margin of what looked like Rimmer's head, she took careful aim with the Colt Matahari and fired.

Rimmer yelped like a dog as Ronica's bullet hit the wall about an inch ahead of his face, sending up a small explosion of wood and metal splinters, one of which chamfered its way through the scrofulous tip of his earlobe like some large, stinging insect.

'Bitch,' he yelled, as he fired off a volley of shots as close as he was able to the doorway where she was still crouched. Then, finding his ear and neck wet with his own blood, and the elevator doors opening expectantly behind him, Rimmer made his exit. As soon as the doors closed and the elevator sank down into the shaft, Rimmer pressed himself back against the wall of the car, with his gun aimed at the glass ceiling and retreating circular lip that was the twelfth floor.

Ronica heard the elevator car descend into the shaft, and longed to go after Rimmer and fire her two remaining shots. But there were still the two gunmen at the other end of the corridor to think about. Her one abiding hope now was that one of them might turn out to be Dallas. Surely she might still convince him of her own good faith even without the corroborating evidence of Rimmer's corpse. That could mean telling Dallas everything, but she might have little or no alternative. She was about to call out to him when she realized that the door to 1218 was now open, and standing there, a little unsteady, as might be expected of someone who had just been subjected to several hundred atmospheres, but still managing to aim a gun levelly at her braided head, was Dallas.

VII

'Drop it,' he said quietly. Dallas was still feeling lightheaded after his experience inside the hyperbaric chamber. Less than half an hour after Gates had left the room, he had been awoken by what felt like some kind of invisible force pressing him down in bed. The pressure quickly became so great that it had forced the blood into the back of his body, and for a minute or so he had actually blacked out. Recovering consciousness, Dallas had discovered the pressure returning to normal, and hearing the sound of gunfire immediately outside his door, he reasoned first that Rimmer must have found him, and second that Gates must have found Rimmer. So he was a little surprised to find Ronica, a woman whom he recognized as an employee of Terotechnology, cowering in the opposite doorway.

She threw her gun toward him. Dallas glanced one way and then the other, his eyes taking in the bodies that now lay on the corridor floor.

'What the hell are you doing here?' he said irritably. The high pressure had given him a severe headache.

'Saving you from Rimmer.' Ronica stood up slowly as Dallas lowered his gun.

'Where is he?'

'Gone.' She jerked her head in the direction of the elevator.

'Tell me ...' Dallas shook his head as he tried to recall the woman's name.

'My name's Ronica.'

'How did you find me here?'

'Rimmer. He got it out of your assistant.'

'Dixy told him?'

Ronica told him what Rimmer had said to her, about Dixy's pet program, and how Rimmer had threatened to erase it. Dallas nodded. Perhaps a little part of him was disappointed that Dixy should have betrayed him, but he was more interested to learn that his computer assistant should have demonstrated such an attachment to a simple pet program.

'You okay, Dallas?' It was Gates, followed closely by Lenina.

Dallas nodded. 'Just two of my former colleagues. Thanks, Gates.'

'Don't thank me, thank Lenina. It was she who spotted this lady's footprints.'

Lenina regarded Ronica with admiration: This was the first time she had seen a rich, healthy woman close up, and she liked what she saw. The big coat, the fabulous dress, the expensive jewelry, the braided hair, even Ronica's bloodied shoes. Seeing Ronica and envying her well-groomed appearance sharpened Lenina's appetite to go along with whatever scheme Dallas had in mind.

Ronica glanced down at her shoes and then smiled at Dallas. 'You never know what you're stepping into with Rimmer around.'

'Who ordered you to save me from Rimmer?' asked Dallas.

'The director. With Tanaka dead he needs you back at Terotechnology. Wants to return to the status quo, with you as head of Design. Killing Rimmer was to be my opening bid. So you'd think it had all been a big misunderstanding. An overzealous Rimmer acting on his own authority, that kind of thing.'

'And was he?'

'No. Rimmer was just doing exactly what Simon King told him to do, just like me. Let Rimmer find Dallas, he told me, and then kill Rimmer. If possible, I was supposed to trump the guy within your eyeshot so you'd gain the impression that the company, as represented by myself, was on your side.'

'So why pick you and not one of those thugs who work for Rimmer?'

Ronica looked vague. 'Fresh blood? Someone who was uncontaminated by association with failure? I don't know. You'd have to ask the director.'

Dallas nodded, estimating that Ronica was telling the truth.

'So why are you showing me your hand?' he asked.

Ronica let out a long breath and glanced up at the ceiling before staring back at Dallas. 'Oh,' she sighed. 'Well, let's see now. I already lost the first trick. And now that I've looked you straight in the eye I can't see any other tricks going my way either. I think maybe the best I can expect now is another deal. Because

Rimmer is probably already on his way back to the Zone, with some story for the director about how I screwed up. So I can't go back there.'

'What makes you so sure that I wouldn't have believed your story? That Rimmer acted on his own initiative. Maybe I want to go back to the Zone.'

Ronica shook her head very firmly. 'Like I said, Dallas, I've looked you in the eye.'

'Maybe I could have let myself be persuaded.'

'You don't seem like the type prepared to forgive and forget something like losing a family. And certainly not after less than twenty-four hours.' Ronica paused for a moment, as her certainty about the character of Dallas gave way to a growing anxiety about her new situation: She didn't think Dallas and his two weird-looking friends would kill her in cold blood, but what was she to do with herself now? Could she risk going back to the Zone, let alone Terotechnology? Knowing what she did, which didn't feel like very much, was there any certainty that the director, and Rimmer, would let her remain alive?

'I do have one question,' she swallowed. 'Outside the Zone is no life. No life at all. What else is there, Dallas?' She bit her lip back from trembling. 'I'm scared.'

'We should all be scared,' declared Lenina. 'The cops aren't about to ignore a gun battle that leaves four dead, even in a sector like this. We should leave right now.'

'Lenina's right,' said Gates.

'Four dead?' Dallas was frowning and could see only two bodies.

'Rimmer shot two more on the floor below,' explained Ronica.

'How do we know it wasn't you who shot them?' enquired Lenina.

'Does she look like a killer?' Gates asked.

Lenina shrugged. 'I don't know what she looks like. But she's the one with the red shoes.' Her admiration of Ronica was quickly turning to jealousy.

Dallas shook his head.

'Ronica was the one who turned down the pressure in my hyperbaric chamber,' he said. 'After Rimmer had so thoughtfully turned it up. Isn't that so, Ronica?'

'Yes. He wanted to soften you up, he said. So you wouldn't be in a state to shoot him when he came through the door.'

'Sounds like Rimmer, all right,' admitted Dallas.

'We ought to move,' insisted Lenina.

Gates was already heading toward the elevator.

'Ronica?' said Dallas. 'That question you asked. About the Zone? I'm not sure I've got an answer for you. At least not yet anyway. But if you're prepared to wait, I might make it worth your while.'

'That sounds like you're asking me to come along with you,' she said.

'Sure. Why not? I could have just the kind of deal to interest you.'

9

I

ALL CITIES POSSESS a nefarious quarter, a dark,
sequestered place, an underworld, a place ruled by
crime. This particular city's underworld was known as
the Black Hole, after the very violent region of space-
time that lies at the center of every galaxy – the result
of an imploded star – from which matter and energy
cannot escape. Unlike Hades, who, except for the story
of his wedding to Persephone, has next to no specific
mythology, the city's Black Hole was the source of
almost as many mysteries and legends as there are
forces at work in the creation of its cosmic namesake.
Not the least of these stories concerned the trio of
master criminals who ruled this unpitying lower world.

Kaplan, who was also known as the Spider, was
confined to a walking machine, the victim of osteonecrosis[1] caused by the frequent and inadequately
decompressed hyperbaric treatments he had received
prior to obtaining the black market supply of blood
that had cured him of $P^{②}$. He was the principal buyer

---

[1] Osteonecrosis. A disease characterized by dead bone tissue.

and supplier of illegal blood – much of it recombinant hemoglobin substitute, or simply fake – not to mention counterfeit pharmaceuticals. In one Far Eastern country, it has been estimated that as many as half the medicines held in the dispensaries of hospitals and clinics are fakes, sold by Kaplan's people. Even the richer countries are not immune to this murderous trade. Rumor had it that Kaplan had been married and had fathered children himself, only to murder them for their bone marrow, in a vain attempt to be cured of his osteonecrosis.

Elstein was without question the cleverest of the three, being a trained physicist as well as a gifted amateur chemist. It was Elstein who formulated Depreneyl Amitriptyline, the first of the so-called paradeisotropic[1] drugs. Both Depreneyl and Amitriptyline are antidepressants: the first, a monoamine oxidase inhibitor, and the second, a tertiary amine tricyclic that boosts serotonin levels. The combination of the two produces a chemically induced near-death experience supposedly allowing the person taking the drug to peek through the gates of paradise without actually dying. The novelist Wystan Hughes in his book *Heaven's Gate*[2] famously described his experiences with DA. However, the drug was very quickly outlawed when thousands of near-death experiences turned out to be the real thing. Elstein was sent to a Moon colony for five years. Upon his return to Earth, he originated the Lion Cult, recruiting hundreds of thousands of people prepared to pay large sums of

[1] From the Greek paradeisos, meaning 'paradise',' and tropein, meaning 'toward.'
[2] Published 2042, cf. The Doors of Perception by Aldous Huxley (1954) in which that author describes his experiments with mescalin and LSD.

money in order to be able to understand what was briefly assumed to be the Final Theory in Physics – the theory explaining everything from subatomic particles, atoms, and supernovae, to the Big Bang and the Big Crunch. For years after the death of Albert Einstein, scientists struggled to create an ultimate theory that would unite gravity, electromagnetism, and nuclear force in one short equation. Einstein himself described the problem thus: 'Nature shows us only the tail of the lion. But I do not doubt that the lion belongs to it even though he cannot at once reveal himself because of his enormous size.' A new cult was spawned when, for a while, it was believed that the lion had been finally captured with Hugh Van Creveld's multidimensional Quantum Theory of Gravity. Called the Unique Theory, Van Creveld's theorem which its many supporters still argue has united Einstein's General Theory of Relativity and quantum theory,[1] proved so fiendishly difficult that it was practically impossible for any layman to understand, which is where Elstein stepped in with his essentially skeptical doctrine of Universal Apologetics,[2] thereby founding the Lion Cult.

[1] Quantum theory accounts for a very wide range of physical phenomena and replaces classical Newtonian mechanics for all microscopic phenomena. A quantum is a general term for the indivisible unit of any form of physical energy. The difficulty with quantum things and what makes them hard to understand – even now, a hundred years after Niels Bohr led the way in their explanation – is that their motion cannot easily be visualized. Or even imagined. Of course, one of the pleasures of authorship is to be found in making difficult concepts seem simple. One of the aims of this book has been to include my own experience of quantum things and to enable the general reader to appreciate not just the molecular wisdom of the human body but, at a more fundamental level, the matter of existence itself. I make no excuse for this. As Montaigne says, 'I am myself the matter of my book.'

[2] Elstein's work was based entirely on the work of the

Following several attempts on his life by Christian and Jewish fundamentalists, Elstein disappeared into the Black Hole and thereafter devoted himself, with one eye on the work of Sir Arthur Conan Doyle, to becoming, like Professor Moriarty, the 'Napoleon of Crime.'

Cregeen was the third member of the unholy trinity, this 'three-headed dog' that lurked in the depths of the city's underworld. He was the darkest, the most shadowy figure of the three, about whom very little was known. Was his name really Cregeen? Probably not. Could anyone say anything about his appearance? No. Rumor enveloped him like a poisonous miasma from some ancient sewer. It was said that Cregeen was the brains behind the Great Aerocarrier Robbery of 2039, when the P&O dirigible[1] was boarded in midair and relieved of its multimillion dollar cargo, a Virgin communications satellite weighing twenty-five thousand pounds. Reportedly Cregeen had also masterminded the extortion of one billion dollars from the West African state of New Congo when he threatened to explode a small atomic weapon close to a natural nuclear fission reactor located deep underground in the jungle, and formed five hundred million years ago

---

seventeenth-century French mathematician, philosopher, and physicist Blaise Pascal. 'The incomprehension of the perplexed,' Elstein wrote, 'is to be overcome by means of the wager; if the theory cannot be proved then those who remain bewildered lose nothing by believing that the meaning of life, and the fabric of reality, has been explained, and in devoting themselves to living life for the present – to making heaven on earth; for if the theory is proved, then no one will have wasted any time in acting as if there was still something to be explained.'

[1] The dimensions of the airship are as follows: one kilometer wide, and five hundred meters high.

when large deposits of uranium began a chain reaction lasting hundreds of thousands of years.[1]

These three men formed a triumvirate that was behind most of the city's organized crime. Sometimes it was thought that they were one man, so closely did they operate with each other; at other times, their reach was so extensive and their influence so omnipresent that it seemed they must be many more than just three. Naturally they had their accomplices, faces and names such as Galloway, Orff, Jondrette, Connor, Pike, Allum, Opie, Harris, Ford, and Reinbek, that were more familiar to the rank and file of the city's criminal fraternity, among which, prior to his period of hard labor on the Moon, had been numbered Rameses Gates.

It was to a light-industrial building close to the elevated section of a disused highway that Gates now led the way. This was Reinbek's base of operations.

Reinbek was the close associate, not to say the instrument of Kaplan, and all of the faces who acted under his orders owed the same higher allegiance. Reinbek himself was a doctor and an ex-soldier. For many years after leaving the army he had been attached to the Criminal Intelligence Service in an interrogative capacity, which was a euphemistic way of saying that he had been a torturer. No one knows more about how much pain may safely be inflicted on the body of a valuable suspect in the search for information than a doctor. For, after all, what is surgery but the strictly controlled wounding – sometimes grievously – by one person of another? Some

[1] The resulting explosion would have rendered the whole country, an area of over a million square miles, uninhabitable for an estimated fifty thousand years.

men are fascinated by the stars, others with fine porcelain, but whatever wonder the world contained for Reinbek was confined to the workings of the human body, and despite his trade, he was a skilled doctor – his victims were always in excellent hands. But as sometimes happens, one particular victim, finding himself restored to political favor, made it his mission to bring Reinbek to justice, or at least what he perceived to be justice. In reality, law and justice, always uncomfortable bedfellows, had long since parted company; law needs only to be applied to a set of facts, whereas justice requires that those facts be explained to the accused's best advantage; in short, justice requires a concern for individual rights that was no longer anywhere in evidence. And so it was that pursued by the very system he had served so faithfully, Reinbek was obliged to disappear, and Kaplan, judging the former CIS man too valuable to kill, had given him a job instead.

Like most of those who lived in the Black Hole, Reinbek and his gang were nocturnal, taking counsel together, carrying out their criminal activities, even sometimes partying, during the many long hours of winter darkness. In daytime, fatigued by the events of the night, they found the darkest places to hang their hammocks and slept, like clusters of bats after a successful evening's excursion in search of nourishment.

II

It was close to daybreak when Gates and the other three reached the former factory. Many of the nameless who had used the darkness to cloak their various pursuits were arriving back there, as if in flight from the rare sound of cock crow – a rare sound indeed since outbreaks of *Campylobactr jejeuni* and *Campylobactr coli*[1] had made it strictly illegal to keep any variety of domestic fowl inside the city limits. A few of the 'Black Holers,' as they were known, remembered Gates and greeted him warmly. Others regarded his more affluent-looking companions with an almost demonic hunger, for affluence was the most obvious outward manifestation of good blood. It is written in the Talmud that 'Man's Soul has a loathing for blood.'[2] But among these particular men and women, the sight of so much healthy blood walking around in their midst was no more loathsome to their souls, assuming they had such a thing, than several gallons of pure alcohol might have looked to a sprawl of thirsty drunkards.

'Better keep close to me,' Gates instructed Dallas and Ronica, as several well-armed men led the quartet of arrivals up a couple of flights of escape stairs to the arrowhead-shaped glass room at the top of the building where Reinbek had his quarters. 'Just in case someone tries to take a bite out of either of you.'

'It is kind of tempting,' admitted Lenina, bringing up the rear, her eyes on Ronica's back, inhaling her expensive perfume. 'Might be worth it to have a coat like that.'

'If someone were to bite me, they'd probably fall asleep,' yawned Dallas. 'I could sleep for a hundred years.'

'A hundred years is nothing to a man like Reinbek,'

[1] Enteric bacteria strains resistant to antibiotics that killed several thousand Spanish citizens during the late 2050s.
[2] See Makkoth 23b; attributed to Rabbi Shimon ben Yehuda ha-Nasi.

said Gates. 'You want to sleep for all eternity, he could fix it. That kind of sedative, the permanent kind, is something he gives people all the time. So be careful what you say, that is, in case you forget to keep your mouths shut and let me do all the talking. Because I know how to handle him. Reinbek's mood can oscillate like the atoms of a hot metal pendulum. On account of the fact that he has a bipolar disorder. And I don't mean he doesn't like Antarctica.'

'He's a manic-depressive?' frowned Dallas.

'Yes.'

'That's a comforting thought,' observed Ronica. 'I sure hope he's taking his medication.'

'Reinbek doesn't believe in it,' said Gates. 'He says drugs interfere with his general intellect and limit his creativity and perceptual range.'

'Creativity? Who does he think he is? Some kind of artist?'

'Vincent van Gogh. Schumann. Tennyson. Who the fuck knows?' growled Gates.

'He sounds like just the kind of person you'd turn to in a crisis,' remarked Dallas.

'Yeah,' echoed Ronica. 'Why on earth bring us here?'

'I brought you here for the simple reason that there's nowhere else to go,' said Gates. 'And because only a crazy person would try and follow us here.'

'Why don't I find your explanation reassuring?' Ronica asked Gates.

'Will you listen to her?' Lenina said scornfully. 'The Queen of Sheba talking. Honey? Safe, hope, security, trust, confidence, and faith – none of those words mean shit down here. You left them all behind with your health care and your lip gloss when you drove your silky smooth black ass out of the Zone. The only expectation that means anything to bad bloods like me and Rameses is the prospect of an early death. You want reassurance, beautiful, then you'd better get yourself a rabbit's foot.'

'Yeah,' laughed Gates. 'Only first you gotta find yourself a rabbit.'

III

The large, starkly furnished room was dominated by a Dolmen-sized fireplace where a tepee of logs big enough to have consumed Savonarola and all the vanities with him burned fiercely under the gaze of one who stared into the flames with an almost pyrolatrous enthusiasm.

'Shit, Reinbek,' exclaimed Gates, sniffing the air with relish. 'Are those real logs?'

'Yeah. I was just thinking what the world must have been like when there were lots of trees around. Can't think why they cut 'em down. There's not much heat in wood. But it's better than holo-TV. You can see plenty of things in fire.'

'Moses did,' said Gates.

'You should know, Rameses.' Reinbek turned away from the fire to face the quartet of recent arrivals, and put his arm around the neck of a woman wearing an eye patch who seemed to be his companion. 'How are you, Gates?'

Gates nodded. 'Not so bad.'

Reinbek stood up straight and smiled at Ronica.

'What tribe are you?' he asked her abruptly.

Ronica didn't really think of herself as belonging to any tribe. No one would have asked her such a question in the Zone. But she knew what Reinbek meant and tried to humor him. 'Originally, I'm Masai,' she said.

'And what's the blood quantum on that?'[1]

'Qualification is set at quite a high level,' she explained. 'You have to show one-eighth pure Masai blood. As it happens, I'm a quarter-blood.'

Reinbek nodded. 'Me,' he said. 'I'm from a little town near Hamburg.'

Tall and thin, with long gray-blond hair, a straggly beard, and dark shadows under his blue eyes, Reinbek reminded her of a painting she had once seen, a self-portrait of Albrecht Dürer. Or maybe it had been of some saint or maybe an angel. She couldn't remember, which was a sure sign that the Connex drug was wearing off now. And there was certainly nothing saintly about what Reinbek did next. Suddenly he was behind her, with one arm across her chest and arms, and pressing the cold edge of a long thin blade against the side of her neck.

'I'm half German,' he breathed. 'But as anyone will tell you, I'm a full-blooded sadist. Isn't that right, Rameses?'

Gates spoke carefully. It was clear there was no point in trying to pull Ronica away from Reinbek. He would almost certainly have cut her throat just for the pleasure of it. 'Let her go, Reinbek,' he said. 'She's not done you any harm.'

'What do you weigh, Miss Masai?'

'Around one sixty-five,' she answered coolly.

'Mmmm, that's about eleven pints of RES Class One,' Reinbek said thoughtfully. 'More than enough to fix up my friend there.' He nodded toward his

[1] Blood quantum. A quasi-genetical idea governing race qualification.

female companion. 'What do you say, Miss Masai? Shall I cut this artery and fetch a bucket?'

'And risk spilling it?' said Ronica. 'Sounds like a waste of good blood to me.'

'Oh, I wouldn't spill much. Only fifteen percent of your blood is in your arteries at any one time. Mostly the blood's in your veins. They've got seventy percent of the load.'

'C'mon Reinbek. Stop fooling around,' said Gates. 'We've got some business to talk about.'

With a greasy thumb, Reinbek stretched the skin across Ronica's carotid artery, as if he really might cut it with his blade. The pressure made Ronica feel momentarily faint, which only served to remind her of how the word *garrotte* had the same Greek origin as carotid. That, she told herself, was the last of the Connex working. What a night this was turning out to be. Somehow she was managing to keep her nerve, even when she found Reinbek's hand underneath her dress and between her breasts, pressing hard against her sternum. He was searching for her heartbeat. It wasn't difficult to find. She reckoned her aorta must have been receiving blood pumped from her left ventricle at the rate of over one hundred and forty beats a minute – twice her resting rate. She was even feeling a little out of breath.

'I can hear your blood talking to me, Miss Masai,' Reinbek said gleefully. 'Lots of it, too. It's a fine heart you have there, miss. What if I was to cut it out and eat it?'

In view of what Gates had said about Reinbek's mental state, she tried to maintain the illusion of calm, though she was close to panic. Even Rimmer had not frightened her this much.

'Then you'd be a cannibal,' she said.

217

'True,' grinned Reinbek. 'You know, maybe I should just sell your blood to the highest bidder. Eleven pints of the ice you've got in your veins ought to be worth a great deal.'

'Eleven pints,' sneered Gates. 'That's a pinprick compared to what we're offering to sell.'

'Much less than a pinprick,' echoed Dallas. 'It's a single cell compared to what we're offering.'

Reinbek released his hold on Ronica and smiled broadly at her.

'I like you,' he said, pocketing the knife, his mood pitching in the opposite direction now. 'I do admire a girl who's got real blood in her veins. Sangfroid, my dear. You've got it in spades. That's what you've got. Yes indeed. Whole fridges full of the stuff. Yes, you'll do very well, Miss Masai.'

Ronica rubbed her neck with relief and said, 'Thanks for the vote of confidence.'

'Don't mention it.' Reinbek lit up a large cigar and puffed it into action. 'Now then, Rameses. What exactly are we talking about here?'

'The opportunity of a lifetime. Lots of people's lifetimes, I shouldn't wonder. Mine included. We're talking about the seat of the soul here, Reinbek. Life's microcosm.'

'Well I hear that, Rameses old friend. He hath made of one blood all nations of men for to dwell on all the earth,[1] has he not? I do believe he has. What kind of blood are we talking about here, Rameses? And how much?'

'Pure erythrocyte. The real McCoy. No substitute. And in the kind of quantities that Moses might use to drown an Egyptian army or two.'

[1] Acts 17:26.

'I am metabolized by your information, Rameses. My humor improves. Black bile and phlegm give way to blood, as you might expect. Where exactly is this red sea of yours?'

'I'll only tell Kaplan.'

'Then why do you need me?'

'Everyone knows, you're Kaplan's liver. Such a heavy flow of blood must come through you first. You could fix a meeting.'

'Anything else?'

'Protection. Somewhere to sleep. Food.'

Reinbek glanced at Dallas as if judging the truth of Gates's story.

'The red sea, huh?' he said.

'That's right.' Gates nodded towards Dallas. 'And with an angel promised as a guide.'

IV

Time: Perhaps it is best understood in the way a story is told. Most stories seem to have a narrative flow, which is of course how most people would characterize time: as something that moves inexorably forward. But of course this is simply not so. Time is not a sequence of events, any more than a story needs to be told this way. That time seems to pass by is only a matter of perception, between what is now and what was then. The present exists only subjectively. We can look at one representation of the present and compare it with another representation of the present, and be forgiven for thinking that there is motion between these moments. There is not. No more than there is real motion between the way two writers will deal with a lapse of time. Just as one author will give you a summary of ten years in two pages, another will spend thirty pages to render a conversation lasting as many minutes.

There are two lapses of time to take account of here, although of course we now know that there has been no real change in time itself, merely the entirely understandable perception that this is what has occurred. When we meet Dallas, Gates, Ronica, and Lenina again – when they do indeed meet Kaplan – only a few days shall have elapsed.

After the meeting with Kaplan, the second lapse of time that occurs is rather longer, being of several months in duration – winter shall have become summer.

I dare to mention these not for the purpose of once more drawing myself to the reader's attention but to say something about the nature of time – in part, I have already done so – and life itself. This is something that will help to prepare the general reader for that which follows. It need not be understood, merely recognized (in the same sense that while most people recognize the existence of gravity, they do not necessarily understand how it works in a way that would enable them to explain it to someone else) that the quantum nature of the universe affects everything – physics, evolution, what can be computed, and what can be known.

The notion of time is basic for physics, and quantum theory, which was originally developed to explain the properties of atoms and molecules, quickly rendered Newton's concept of an absolute ideal of time obsolete. Time is now recognized to be a quantum concept. Important, yes, but of much greater significance is the smaller matter of life itself – something else that

classical Newtonian physics could never quite accom-
modate. Because life is not something governed by the
laws of physics. The fact is that life is one of the laws
of physics, as fundamental to the universe as time and
space are themselves; and just as the inherent power of
physics may be harnessed and unleashed in the shape
of a nuclear weapon, the same is true of life. This is the
key to understanding. Given another epoch why
shouldn't everything be understood? After all, and to
speak figuratively, there is so much more of the future
than there is of the past.

But we're getting ahead of ourselves, here, and in a
big way. The second lapse of time will find our
characters in space, orbiting Earth, and on their way to
the Moon for the purpose of robbing the First
National Blood Bank, and to find the new life that
awaits them there. Before that, as I said earlier, we
have to introduce them all to Kaplan.

V

He was an unnerving man to look at because he
looked so very like a spider. It has already been
mentioned that he was the victim of a bone-wasting
disease that left him confined to a walking machine.
What has not yet been explained is that Kaplan's
walking machine was an arachnidroid,[1] an intelligent
control system equipped with eight legs, each with its
own artificial nervous system. A spiderlike robot had
the advantage of always having four legs on the
ground at the same time, thus forming a very stable
platform for a human passenger, without any loss of

[1] The Mygalomorph 8, designed by General Dynamics.

speed or mobility. Each hydraulic leg was five feet long with four independent motorized joints that helped the droid both to surmount the most difficult obstacles and to achieve a top speed of almost thirty miles an hour. Kaplan occupied a gimbaled harness on top of the droid's abdomen. It was hardly surprising then that Kaplan should be known as the Spider, nor that he was almost as interested in these common terrestrial creatures as he was in controlling the supply of illegally obtained human blood.

Gates and Dallas met Kaplan in the disused mosque where he had his headquarters. Built during the last years of the twentieth century, before the anti-Muslim pogroms that accompanied the Great Middle Eastern War,[1] the building was essentially an open space, roofed over, with a minaret used by Kaplan's men as a communications tower and lookout post. Inside the mosque itself thermoelectric Persian carpets covered the marble floor, helping to heat the lofty, echoing interior against the winter cold. At one end of the floor, and pointing in what had once been the direction of Mecca, was a tall semicircular niche[2] once reserved for the prayer leader,[3] and now the spot where Kaplan had what he called his web. The interior of the niche was covered in relief tile-work with a classic three-dimensional cobweb design, replacing the Qur'anic inscriptions placed there by the original architects as a reminder of the faith. To the right of the niche was a set of stone steps that led up to the pulpit once used by a preacher[4] but which now functioned as the vantage point for two heavily armed bodyguards.

[1] 2013–2015.
[2] Mihrab.
[3] Imam.
[4] Khatib.

'Nice place you have here,' remarked Gates.

'I sincerely hope you're not going to try and be amusing,' said Kaplan, tapping the floor impatiently with one of his eight legs. 'Because you'd be wasting your time, and more importantly, you'd be wasting mine. There's very little I find amusing that doesn't involve some kind of bipedal suffering. If I do have a sense of humor, it's the cardinal kind, as devised by Galen,[1] specifically blood. Until he came along people believed that the arteries carried air, not blood, and that when someone was cut the blood rushed in to fill the gaps, as it were. His interest was academic, of course. Mine's purely financial. So don't waste my time. Where is it – this large supply of blood that Reinbek told me you have access to?'

'I wouldn't say that access is exactly the right word,' said Gates. 'Let me explain.'

'Yes, I think you had better.'

'My partner and I are intent upon securing a market for our supply before we go and get it. And of course you are the major ...'

'Do you mean to tell me that you don't actually have this red sea you spoke of?'

'Not as such, no.'

'Where is it?'

'In a bank.' It was Dallas who answered, with an insouciance that Gates found more than a little unnerving. 'To be exact, the First National Blood Bank, on the Moon.'

'Yes, I know where that is,' Kaplan said testily. 'Is

[1] Galen of Pergamum, born A.D. 129, died circa 199. Distinguished Turkish Anatolian physician whose influence dominated European medical thought throughout the Middle Ages and the Renaissance.

this a joke? If so, then it's even less amusing than the first one.'

'It's no joke,' said Dallas, looking around the mosque's interior like a curious tourist.

'Then do I understand you correctly? You're planning to rob the First National?'

'Yes.'

'Any particular reason you picked that bank?' asked Kaplan.

'Yes,' Dallas said again. 'It has by far the largest supply of blood. Over twenty million liters: forty million units. It's the first choice in component storage,' he added, parroting the advertising slogan that appeared in every magazine, and on neon signs throughout the Zone.

'With good reason,' said Kaplan. 'It's impregnable. The high-security environment that protects the place is the very best. The state of the science.'

'Thank you.'

'If I sound like I'm stating the obvious, it's because the obvious seems to need repetition,' said Kaplan. 'The place is impregnable. You *do* know that.'

'I should know,' said Dallas. 'I did design the place.'

Kaplan was silent for a long minute. He rocked up and down on all eight legs and then, slowly, walked out of the niche until he stood only a few inches from Dallas. 'Did you say what I thought you said?'

'Yes. I said I designed the bank. And many others like it. Until a few days ago I was chief designer at Terotechnology. I assume you've heard of that company.'

'Oh, indeed I have. And how is it that a god like you has descended from Mount Olympus to come among us mere mortals in the Black Hole?'

Dallas told him the bare bones of his own personal

224

story, to which he added only the vague outline of a plan.

'My heart bleeds for you,' said Kaplan. 'Spiders do have hearts, you know. Interestingly enough, they are as long as their whole abdomens. So if this droid I'm forced to sit on was the real thing, its heart would be three feet long.'

'Fascinating,' said Dallas, who could only feel revulsion for the half-human-looking creature in front of him.

'But not nearly as fascinating as you and your special skills.'

'I'm glad you think so.'

'You really think you could pull off something like that?'

'With your help,' said Dallas. 'I'll need a few things. Many of them I'll be able to pay for myself. I'm not a poor man. Money's not the reason I'm doing this.'

'Revenge?'

'What else?'

'So tell me what you'll need?'

Dallas had given the matter some considerable thought. They were going to need a spaceship, new identities and travel documentation, Clean Bill of Health certificates, life-support suits, a virtual reality suite on which they would test a model of the plan, a space fridge, food and water for at least three weeks, a telecommunications and detection screen, a Motion Parallax generator, electron-beam welding tools, lithium hydroxide CO_2 collectors, piezoceramic vibration absorbers, infrared headsets, power spectacles, head-top computers, an electric car, and, of course, transfusion facilities for those of his team who had the virus.

He thought of the various people he would need in

his ideal team: a quantum cryptographer, an aeronautical engineer, a navigations and communications engineer, a computer engineer, an electric engineer, a virtual model-maker, and a mechanical engineer. He knew there was no way he would find half of them, and many of their vital skills would have to be acquired by his own team using artificial aids. This all passed through his mind in just the few seconds before he answered Kaplan's question.

'I'll tell you what I need most. I need a recent amputee,' he said. 'That's right,' he added, noting the puzzled look that appeared on Kaplan's wasted-looking face. 'I need a man who has recently lost an arm.'

PART TWO

You must be prepared for a surprise, and a very great surprise.

NIELS BOHR

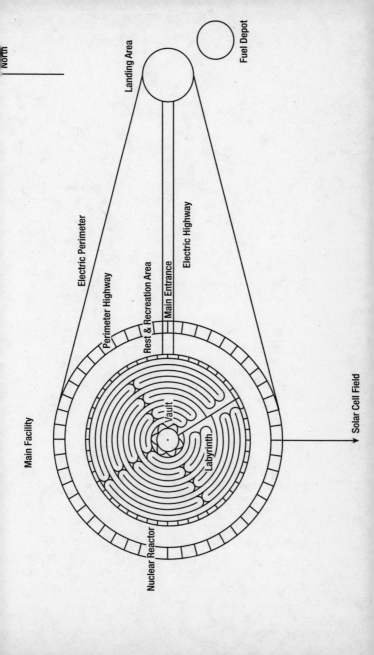

North

Landing Area

Fuel Depot

Electric Perimeter

Main Facility

Perimeter Highway

Rest & Recreation Area

Main Entrance

Electric Highway

Nuclear Reactor

Vault

Labyrinth

Solar Cell Field

1

I

THIS WAS WHERE civilization had begun. And where it had ended first. Orbiting Earth, the spaceship crossed the Red Sea in just twenty seconds. The blast craters that had once been the seaport of Jiddah and the holy city of Mecca appeared in the flight-deck window soon afterward. Years after the Great Middle Eastern War, the whole area – from the Nile in Egypt to the Tigris in Iraq – was still emitting harmful gamma rays, rendering this once fertile crescent uninhabitable for many decades to come.

They had left the planet only a couple of hours before – after a rendezvous, at around fifty thousand feet, with one of the many fuel tanker planes that existed to sell spaceships the hundred tons of liquid helium necessary to help a spaceship blast its way into space. Their orbit, at an altitude of one hundred and seventy miles and increasing, was fixed in space, but the world turns on its invisible axis by fifteen degrees every hour, so that their flight now took them south over the Indian Ocean. After leaving the coast of the Republic of Saudi Arabia, another fifteen minutes were to pass before they saw land again – this time,

Australia. Lenina had heard Dallas and Ronica talking about going to Australia, when they got back from the Moon. But she couldn't quite understand why. It didn't look like there was much down there. Red, marbled with flecks of gray, blue, and white, the Great Sandy Desert looked like nothing so much as a section of human tissue. The northern coast, appearing a few moments later, most resembled a map of the human circulatory system, with its arterial rivers, venous roads, and capillary canals.

Or so it seemed to Lenina, whose thoughts had been very much preoccupied with her own blood since earlier that same day, when she had awoken to find a red mark on her stomach. Was this the beginning of the rubelliform rash that signaled the active phase of the $P^{®}$ virus she carried in her bone marrow? Sometimes it took a while for the rash to break out in any significant way. But this was how it had started when her mother died. And then her father, too. Lenina had been just twelve years old. After that, she'd had to fend for herself.

She prayed it was something else. A skin allergy perhaps. What would the others say if they knew she was in the Three Moon phase, with a maximum of one hundred and twenty days of life ahead of her? What kind of liability might she pose for the success of their plans? If it was the rash, she hoped it would stay hidden for as long as it took them to get into and out of the love hotel on the Moon. Having a Three Moon phase at Tranquillity Base would only draw unwelcome attention to their group.

As the ship increased its altitude over the curving blue slope of the Pacific Ocean, Lenina could see a thousand miles in any direction, and floating around in her seat harness, she watched the Sun as it started to set behind them. At the speed they were traveling, the Sun set eighteen times as fast as on Earth, and in just a few minutes, the horizon was marked by a narrowing ribbon of light, as one day ended, and they flew through brief night toward another.

Perhaps all her days were as short now, and Lenina found she could hardly bear the thought of closing her eyes and sleeping, like the others back in the main body of the ship. Without a complete infusion of blood she might last only as long as the red cells in her body. She could almost feel herself weakening by the minute, and the darkness that enveloped the spaceship seemed like a heavy black curtain falling on her life. When Gates had first told her of Dallas and his plan to rob the First National Blood Bank, she thought both men crazy. But now it was quite possibly her only chance of returning to Earth alive.

Seeing the stars more clearly in the surrounding darkness and checking the cockpit chronometer, she prompted the computer to line up the navigation systems. Just in case. The ship, named the *Mariner* – more like the *Ancient Mariner*, she thought – was an old Pathfinder, an American-built reusable launch vehicle, or RLV, with a Russian-manufactured helium-burning rocket engine and a cargo bay that could carry more than two tons of payload (four, if the payload bay carried a space fridge that could be attached to the rear section of the RLV). Half a liter of blood in its cryoprecipitate state weighed only four ounces: This meant that they could carry as much as forty thousand storage units, worth over twenty-five billion dollars.

Assuming they got that far. The ship wasn't in the best of condition. Lenina didn't like the look of the computers any more than she felt confident in the performance of the oxygen generators, and the waste disposal facilities had started to play up. Moreover the air purification system left a great deal to be desired – already the crew cabin and cockpit were damp with condensation. And just about every creature comfort and interior fitting had been removed from the *Mariner* in order to maximize its crew space and payload. The flight ahead of them would be like taking a camping trip in an old motor home. Nonetheless, Gates, who had real experience of space flight, didn't seem too concerned about the *Mariner*'s space-worthiness. A bit rusty, he said, but more than equal to the task ahead of them. Lenina hoped he was right. It was a three-day flight to the moon, and any delay in their plans might turn out to be fatal to her.

Another thirty minutes passed before she saw the sun coming up over the violet disc of Earth. The Sun was red, like the color of the giant star it would become some five billion years in the future before it flamed into a nova, cooled, and then collapsed into itself. Lenina wondered if the inhabitants of Earth would be able to avoid this distant catastrophe? Perhaps if they found another solar system. Of course, to travel such vast distances through space in search of a suitable alternative to our own solar system would surely require man to fly at speeds faster than the speed of light, which Einstein had said was impossible. But given enough time, intelligence, tractable computer power, and energy, anything in the universe might be possible. Five billion years hence, human beings might hardly be recognizable as such; and surely so much accumulated intelligence would have to reside in something rather more durable than mere flesh and blood. Such beings, such collected intelligence, might come as near to being gods as any rationally minded person could ever believe in. The only God in the universe was the man that men might one day become.

A dark-sun filter automatically screened the flight-deck window against the life-giving glare of the sunrise. At least something appeared to be working properly, she reflected sourly, having just checked the altitude indicators and noted with disgust that the computers were correcting a ten-degree roll to the right. The autopilot was working, but erratically, as if it hadn't been calibrated properly, and Lenina wondered if, before leaving Earth's orbit, she ought to go and fetch Gates. But she rejected the idea, counseling herself to let him sleep. He was dog tired after the launch. She was just looking for an excuse to have him spend some time alone with her. Any sight of Gates was pleasing to her and she supposed herself to be in love with him, although she would never have dreamed of telling him as much. 'Love' was not a word she was used to.

Hearing someone bang his head and then curse quietly as he floated into the cockpit, Lenina's heart leaped in her chest; and expecting to see the big man, she turned and was disappointed to find that it was only Cavor, the man with the false arm.

'Mind if I join you?' he asked, making his weightless way into the cockpit.

'Be my guest.' Lenina helped steer him into the pilot's seat and then buckled him in.

'Are you okay?' he asked politely, quite unaware of Lenina's current preoccupation with the livid red mark on her stomach. 'You're looking kind of pale.'

Lenina shrugged dismissively and looked out of the window as the large altitude control thruster pulsed audibly into action. 'Just a little space adaptation syndrome,' she said. 'Conflict between eyes and inner ear.'

Cavor glanced over the controls and nodded.

'Have you done much flying in space?' he asked.

'Sure. When I was first convicted, learning to fly was part of the rehabilitation program.'

'I didn't know they bothered.'

'They don't. Not any more. It was simulations, mostly. But there's not much difference from the real thing. Gates is the proper pilot around here. I'm just an instrument flier.'

'Me, I still can't take a space flight without a real sense of wonder. Socrates once said that we would understand the world if we could first rise above it. I don't think he would have been quite so sure if he could have seen this. Looking at Earth from up here begs as many questions as it answers.'

'I've got a question.'

'Just one?'

'Why are you here, Cavor?'

'Are you asking me that in a phenomenological sense?' Cavor shrugged. 'Why are any of us here? Because certain atoms interact according to the laws of physics. What other explanation is required?'

'I meant, why are you part of this team?'

'I know what you meant,' said Cavor. 'I just don't know the answer. I'm well aware of my shortcomings, Lenina. I'm not even a career criminal – I was sent to Artemis Seven for killing my wife. Which was a mistake. Killing her, that is. Heat of the moment thing. Regretted it ever since. And not because I went to a penal colony. Anyway, before it happened I was a musician. A composer, sometimes.'

'That should come in useful,' said Lenina dryly.

'I've asked Dallas why he wanted someone like me

along on this odyssey of ours, but so far, he hasn't seen fit to explain my function.'

'Maybe he wants you to write a symphony for him. When this is all over.'

'Perhaps he does. Or a suite. Like Holst. The music of the spheres. Something to express distant galaxies moving away from us. I could call it the Expanding Universe, a piece with only one movement.'

'With or without a singularity?' asked Lenina. 'A Big Bang.'

'Oh, I think with,' said Cavor. 'I've never much cared for the steady-state theory of the universe. A Big Bang's a much better way of starting a piece of music than just picking up somewhere in the middle. A Big Crunch too, for symmetry's sake. Music needs a beginning and an ending.'

'So why did you come?'

'Because Gates asked me. Because the opportunities for one-armed pianists are rather limited. And because this enterprise holds out the possibility of a change of blood and a cure for the virus we're both carrying – what other reason does anyone need?'

Lenina shook her head. 'You're right. I can't think of a better one.'

Both were silent for a moment as the West Coast of America appeared in the window underneath them.

'There seems to be a lot of dirt on the outside of these windows.' Cavor frowned, wiping the inside with the sleeve of his thermal suit.

'Pollution,' said Lenina. 'From when we came up through the stratosphere. It's full of it. To be more exact, it's dust from the Great Middle Eastern War. Even after all these years.'

'It's comforting to think that the only world we can destroy is our own,' remarked Cavor.

'That may not always be the case. It's taken just ten thousand years for us to come out of the Stone Age to be where we are now. Who knows what forces we'll have learned to control in another ten thousand.'

'Then let's hope we can learn to control ourselves as well.'

'Amen,' said Lenina, glancing once again out of the window. The Central Valley of California lay between the Coast Range to the west and the Sierra Nevada to the east; Lake Tahoe was a footprint-shaped patch of blue to their lower left, and a short way above it was the skull-shaped Mono Lake, close to the invisible town of Lee Vining, where Lenina had spent part of her all too short childhood. That was before she and her family had, like most of the water in the lake and most of the people in the town, gone to Los Angeles. There were no hyperbaric hotels in Lee Vining, just disused campsites and broken-down motels. It wasn't much of a happy memory, but until Rameses Gates had come along, those were the only good times she had ever known. After the move to L.A., her parents had died and she found herself involved in prostitution, dealing drugs, and, eventually, armed robbery. From there it was a few short steps to a series of prisons and then to the penal colony on the Moon.

Down in California it looked like a clear day with not much fog. You could even see the faults of the San Andreas system as two parallel lines along the scribbled coast, and beyond that, Mexico. She'd always wanted to go Mexico and see the pyramids they had down there.

Some time later on, over the Indian Ocean, Lenina and Cavor watched the Moon appear in the cockpit window. The Moon was full, with few shadows, its most prominent feature the crater Tycho in the south, the center of a system of bright rays extending in all directions – so bright that crater identification was difficult. Against these brilliant rays, the patchy shapes of the various lunar seas took on a darker hue, reminding Lenina of the shape on her stomach. To the west, the Sea of Grimaldi was clearly visible. Close to the equator the great ray-crater of Copernicus could be seen just south of the Carpathian Mountains, where the Artemis Seven penal colony was located. Farther east, along the same line of latitude, was the Sea of Tranquillity and the site, close to the Maskelyne crater system, of the Tranquillity Base and the first Apollo Moon landing. About three hundred and fifty miles to the southwest of TB lay the Descartes Crater, the site of the fifth and penultimate Apollo Moon landing. Geologically speaking, it had been an unremarkable place for such an important mission. Descartes, at only ten miles in diameter, was hardly a noteworthy crater – about a tenth of the size of Copernicus – except for the fact that it was now the location of Selenium City, which was what the First National Blood Bank called its breccia[1]-built high-security facility.

As bright as the Moon appeared to Lenina and Cavor, sunlight was a half-million times brighter. The Moon was really a very dark object – one of the least reflective worlds in the entire solar system. And yet

[1] Breccia. An impact rock made of a mixture of rock fragments and soil particles welded together by the energy of a meteor impact. Descartes is an area rich in these breccias, which lunar building engineers have traditionally used to make concrete. Carbonation hardening is achieved in zero atmospheric conditions with the addition of super-critical carbon dioxide, which makes the concrete very hard and dense – about 75 percent denser than ordinary concrete, and hence more resistant to meteorite showers. Concrete is painted gold to reflect the sun, and is filled with nanographite and steel fibers to conduct electricity.

they both regarded it with such hope that it might have been the most luminous super-giant white star in the firmament.

II

Dallas opened his eyes and, wrapped inside his sleeping bag, floated in the darkness. He felt mildly disoriented by his own weightlessness and lack of sleep. Had he slept? It was hard to tell. All was still inside the *Mariner* with only the gently humming sound of the ship's machinery and the breathing of his fellow conspirators to break the silence of space. The total silence. Dallas had been to the Moon before, but he had forgotten how silent the void really was. At least to human ears. Space was full of cosmic microwave radiation, traveling to Earth from most of the observable universe, and it was easily detectable on any crude horn antenna, sounding as noisy as a flock of starlings. This was one of the earliest proofs of an expanding universe. The sound was really light, so greatly red-shifted in its spectrum wavelength that it could only be read as microwave radiation – and only properly understood as the beginning of everything. Dallas had always been fascinated with that sound; even as a child he had understood that what he could hear was the moment when time itself began.

He glanced at his watch and saw that he had indeed been asleep for three to four hours. But he hardly felt refreshed. There was nothing fresh about the atmosphere aboard the *Mariner*. Not with the waste control and environmental control systems playing up. Just half a day in space and already there were small pieces of shit floating around the cabin, to say nothing of the amount of methane that had been generated by the crew of seven. Mostly this was the result of their first low residue in-flight meal – a chicken-and-curry-flavored breedworm that Dallas reckoned might have benefited from a little less spice in its dehydrated preparation. As if in vindication of his belief, Dallas heard Prevezer fart loudly inside his sleeping bag. Prevezer was one of Kaplan's people. He was a virtual reality model-maker, and when they got to their hotel at Tranquillity Base, it would be Prevezer's job to fashion a silicon surrogate of the real blood bank from the bits and bytes that were stored in the memory of Dallas's computer. Using this elaborate artificial world, Dallas would test the integrity of his plan – the kind of experiment, he hoped, that would highlight any unforeseen problems. So Prevezer was an important member of the team, even if he seemed to have more acid in his stomach than anyone else, even if Dallas could cheerfully have steered his sleeping body into the airlock of the cargo bay and dumped him in space.

Deciding that his rest period was over, Dallas unzipped his sleeping bag and floated free, steering himself toward the cabin window. They were out of orbit now, with the full Earth – everything from Africa and the Arabian peninsula to Antarctica – clearly visible. On a normal, scheduled flight to the Moon, every tourist aboard the astroliner would have been up on the camera deck taking photographs at this moment. Dallas remembered doing the same himself. He still had the shots in his portable memory – the little plastic card, endlessly copied, he carried with him everywhere, containing a digital record of his entire life's photographic history, everything from his own birth to that of Caro. He sometimes wondered how people had managed to safe-keep their fondest memories before such mnemonic devices were invented. A few little plastic cards were all he had to remember Aria and Caro. All that stood between them and oblivion.

Prevezer farted again, and this time Ronica felt obliged to protest.

'God's blood,' she shouted, climbing angrily out of her bag. 'Who is doing that? It smells like a monkey house in here.'

Prevezer farted loudly, almost as if in answer to her question.

'Damn it all, Prevezer,' she groaned. 'Can't you control yourself?'

'Don't blame me,' he said, from deep within his bag. 'Blame space. Blame the fucking dinner. And then blame the fucking environmental control system. 'Sides, least I know how to use a zero g toilet, unlike some people I could mention. A fart ain't the worst thing flying around this fucking rust bucket. Bad enough that the waste control system ain't working right, without that some idiot can't use the thing properly anyway.'

Prevezer was referring to Cavor's poor performance with the solid collector. He had released one of the disposable adhesive plastic bags attached to the waste control system, or WCS, while defecating, with disastrous results.

'That was an accident,' Cavor protested. 'It's not easy using those things with only one good arm.'

'Not so easy with two good arms,' remarked Ronica. 'But this stink is something else. This is a kind of body fascism.'

Prevezer farted for the fourth time in as many minutes.

'Three whole days on this until we get to TB.' From her personal bag, Ronica produced a small bottle of eau-de-cologne and proceeded to spray it liberally around her personal space. 'S'blood, I don't think my sense of smell can stand it.'

'Wear a nose clip if it bothers you that much,' Prevezer sneered. 'And while you're looking for one, see if you can't find me a pair of earplugs, so I won't have to listen to your bitch's mouth busting my fucking balls. I ain't the only one with an acid stomach around here.'

'He's right, Ronica,' yawned Gates. 'My pH is way off the scale. I reckon if I so much as breathed on a piece of litmus paper, it'd turn red.' Unzipping his own bag he floated free in the cabin. 'I'd better take a look at the environmental control system. And nobody light a match. There's enough gas in here to blow us all to pieces.'

'I wouldn't worry about that,' said Lenina. 'This ship's liable to fall apart before it blows up.'

'Who made you cheerleader?' jibed Ronica.

'Keep it down, will you? By my reckoning, the sleep period doesn't end for at least another hour.' This was Simou, the team's mechanical and electrical engineer, a permanently weary-looking man with platinum-blond hair and the kind of prominent lower jaw that would have given a Habsburg king a run for his kingdom.

Prevezer poked his head out of his bag. 'Take more than a few z's to improve the way you look, Simou,' he said. 'For most people, beauty sleep means being in bed before midnight. But for you it would mean going through a black hole and traveling back in time to make sure your mother was asleep before she met your father.'

'Did your mother ever meet yours?' Simou came out

of the opposite end of his sleeping bag. He floated up alongside Prevezer, wearing a grin that was all bottom teeth and contempt, adding, 'I heard she picked your old man using a pipette and a petri dish.'

'So? Nothing so unusual about that. Lot of people have donor fathers. Gates, for instance.'

'Yeah, but his mother got to the lab early Monday morning and made sure she had the pick of the crop. I mean, just look at the guy. He's Zarathustra's prologue, for Christ's sake. You, on the other hand, are a typical Friday afternoon job. The frog spawn at the bottom of the jar. Face it, Prev. You're not so much a dumb ugly fuck as an excuse not to have one.'

In fact there was nothing wrong with Prevezer to look at. By any standard he was better looking than Simou. But all the time he had spent inside silicon microworlds had given him an undernourished, skinny look. Appearances deceived, though. Prevezer was prone to violence and possessed a quick temper. He had killed people for saying less than Simou had said.

For a moment Lenina thought Prevezer might go for Simou – but for the zero gravity, perhaps he would have.

'Cut it out, you two,' she said. 'Or take it outside.'

'Yeah,' laughed Ronica. 'Now that's a bit of EVA[1] I'd like to see. Couple of space suits trying to slug it out.' She sprayed some eau-de-cologne over the heads of the two men. 'There. That should sweeten the atmosphere between you boys.'

Still smiling prognathously, Simou pushed himself off a stowage hatch cover and floated away from Prevezer.

[1] Extra-vehicular activity.

'Three days of this,' said Prevezer, 'we're all going to be climbing the walls.'

'We are climbing the walls, asshole,' said Simou. 'In case you didn't notice, it's the only way to get around this tin can.'

III

The waste control system was the ship's lavatory section. It wasn't particularly private or very pleasant to use. With no gravity to draw feces into the bowl, a person had to assist the process with the aid of a finger inserted into a condom-shaped pocket that was itself inserted in the plastic seal attaching him to the seat. Cabin air was then used to direct the solid and liquid waste into a fan separator before being filtered and returned to the cabin. Urine along with liquid from the humidity separator were dumped in space every day. By space law, however, feces had to be captured in a tank because of the risk to other space travelers: At twenty-five thousand miles an hour, solid human waste can cause enormous amounts of damage to expensive equipment. When not in use the tank was vented to prevent odors and bacterial growth, and it was this function that had proved to be faulty.

The WCS was not easy to use, as Cavor himself had demonstrated, but there was actually nothing much to clean and most of the mess related to disposable plastic seals and wetwipes improperly stowed. It was only when it was incorrectly used that a less seemly cleanup was required – hence, the tiny pieces of shit that were still floating around the cabin. Under the eyes of Dallas, Cavor bagged one and then posted it into the solid tank.

245

'How are you doing?' asked Dallas.

'It's a Zen thing,' he said. 'Ultimate truth discovered through self-mastery and perfection in the simple art of turd bagging. Damn it, there's another.' Cavor collected another plastic bag and pursued another tiny asteroid of floating shit. 'I thought all of our food was supposed to be low residue.'

'It is.'

'In that case, I'm going on a diet. I don't think I could stand to do this again.' Cavor grimaced. 'Come here, you little shit.' He caught and bagged his quarry, dropped it through the disposal chute, and leaned back in the air. 'Right now I'd settle for some enlightenment. Such as what the hell I'm doing here. You're the only one who seems to know, Dallas, only you're not telling. Which makes me feel like a sacrificial victim. Like some poor sucker who's going to get his throat cut at the end of the journey and who's the only one who doesn't know it.'

'After myself, you're the most important member of this whole team, Cav,' said Dallas.

'Me? You're just saying that.'

'No.'

'But why?'

'I can't tell you yet. You'll just have to take my word for it. We can't hope to pull this off without you.'

'Nor without you, Dallas. Only you know all the answers.'

'I know all the questions. That's hardly the same thing. We'll find out if I can answer them when we carry out the plan in virtual reality at TB.'

'Presumably you have a good reason for not taking anyone into your confidence.'

'It's for your protection and mine,' insisted Dallas.

'Plus, it helps me to keep control over what's happening. Until the critical moment when I have no alternative but to reveal my hand. And yours. Between now and then, I want you to do something for me. No questions asked. Will you do that?'

'I haven't got much of a choice.'

Dallas handed Cavor a packet of blood-colored pills. 'I want you to start taking two of these, five times a day, from now on.'

'What are they?'

'Remember, no questions? If anyone should ask you, they're something the doctors prescribed back on Earth. But whatever medication you're already taking, you'll have to stop. In case there's some kind of adverse reaction.'

'Very considerate of you.' Cavor examined the packet. There was nothing printed on it. Not that he expected there would be. Dallas was too clever to have made such a simple mistake.

'They might make you feel a little strange at first,' advised Dallas. 'If so, I want you to tell me immediately. Every detail. And only me. Don't talk about this with anyone else. This is our secret, understand?'

'Of course. I may have only one arm, but there's nothing wrong with my brain.'

'That's what I'm counting on. You see Cav, it's your brain I'm really interested in. You know it's a stroke of pure luck that Gates should have found someone as reasonably intelligent as you.'

'That's reasonably kind of you to say so, Dallas,' smiled Cavor. 'So the false arm ... ?'

'The prosthetic's not important. But it wouldn't do any harm to let everyone else continue under the delusion that it's why you're here. Otherwise you can forget about your false arm, Cav. As far as I'm concerned it might as well not be there.'

Cavor nodded and glanced at the packet of red capsules once more.

'When those are finished, I'll give you some more.'

'Whatever you say, doc.' Cavor rubbed his stomach and glanced uncomfortably at the WCS. 'Hey, I don't suppose you've got anything for an upset stomach, have you?'

IV

The physicists have informed us that entropy is the natural state of the universe. Given enough time, they say, everything will fall apart. Suns will cool. Planets will die. Stars will collapse in upon themselves, and the whole universe will disintegrate. All this is certain, if a long way off. In our everyday world, however, there are two antientropic phenomena that build order out of chaos. These are crystallization and life. Life is not a closed system. It can import energy from outside – for example, the way plants capture energy from sunlight. And life itself exists not just within molecules, but between molecules. All living organisms must die, but there is no reason why life – all animal life – can't begin anew to actuate the same body many times over before death eventually arrives. No reason at all, not least because it happens. Metabolism may cease, life may be suspended, indeed it may be seemingly destroyed and yet, hidden, life may persist.

Impossible, you say? When metabolism ceases, death ensues. And yet consider the strange phenomenon of cryptobiosis, meaning 'hidden life,' which describes a natural form of suspended animation possessed by dozens of multicellular species that can be found, millions of them, in the most hostile environments on Earth – everywhere from the Sahara Desert to the Arctic tundra. These animals include aquatic-dwelling rotifers, insectlike tardigrades, and wormlike nematodes. When environmental conditions require it, these little creatures – smaller than a millimeter – dry up and shrink into tiny seedlike husks, not eating, not breathing, not moving, and to all apparent evidence, not living. In this strange cryptobiotic state they can survive for years on end until, with the return of moisture – water is the catalyst for a great many chemical reactions, most importantly, life itself – they revive. Moreover, these animals can withstand extremes of temperature – thousands of degrees of heat, freezing cold vacuums – even ionizing radiation, that would easily kill them in their active, hydrated state. These seemingly immortal protozoans may go into and out of the cryptobiotic state numerous times. One tardigrade was revived after two hundred years, while a rotifer at the University of California at Berkeley has been resurrected over fifty times.

If man could do the same as one of these small creatures from whom, after all, he has evolved, think what might be achieved. With time seemingly suspended for an astronaut, space itself would grow smaller. Vast distances might easily be traveled.[1] Why, even the remotest galaxies might be explored and new solar systems discovered, perhaps even colonized. Eventually, in some future diaspora, the seed of life,

[1] Assuming man could travel at the speed of light, it would take one hundred thousand years to visit the center of our own galaxy and then return to Earth.

perhaps uniquely cultured on Earth, might be carried to every corner of the universe.

There are no miracles except the science that is not already known. And man is the measure of all things.

V

Moisture. It wasn't just *Mariner*'s windows that were clouded with it. As well as sponging these, Ronica had to wipe the instruments free of great globs of water that shimmered in the zero gravity of the cabin like uncut diamonds. A university degree in blood banking, with a major in cryoprecipitation technology, and this was what she was reduced to doing: cleaning windows. Not that she really minded. Until they had gained entry to the vault in the First National and removed several thousand of the deep-frozen components held there, there would be little for her to do. Only after samples of the cryoprecipitate had been thawed could she inspect the condition of the blood, to check for possible bacterial contamination[1] that might produce abnormal color in the red cells, or plasma. Once she had ensured platelet viability she could undertake the phlebotomy of those crew members who were carrying the $P^{\circledR}$ virus, which effectively meant everyone except herself and Dallas. So she wiped the moisture from their collective exhalations feeling something close to satisfaction that she was making herself useful.

Prevezer pushed himself off the ceiling like a great bat and flew toward her, enjoying the sensation of

[1] Highly unlikely in the Moon's zero atmosphere. This was one of the reasons why most blood banks were located in space in the first place. It wasn't just for reasons of high security.

weightlessness. Being weightless gave Prevezer a tremendous sense of liberation, such as an angel might have enjoyed back in heaven after a prolonged period on Earth. On Earth, Prevezer had always felt heavy, even a little overweight. But in space, soaring, hovering, levitating, he felt just a little like a god.

'I think that's the last time you'll have to do that, Roni,' he predicted.

'I don't mind.'

'What I meant was that I fixed the environmental control system. On a ship as old as this one, the fluids that supply the ECS tend to become stratified in zero g. So you have to stir the contents now and again. Like a cake mix. That's what the problem was.' He paused, watching Ronica chase down a small, floating sphere of water with the muzzle of her vacuum cleaner. 'You just reserve the fans on the air purifiers a couple of times to stir up the liquid cylinders.'

'Mmm-hmm?'

'Hey, I'm sorry about what happened earlier on,' he said. 'I was kind of rude back there.'

'Forget it, Prev,' she said.

'There's something I've been meaning to ask you.'

'What's that?'

'When we get to our hotel at TB, are you planning to share a room with anyone?'

'As a matter of fact, I'm sharing with Dallas.'

Prevezer nodded. 'Is that just cover?' he asked. 'Or are you lovers?'

'Lovers?' Ronica's smile broadened.

'Because if everything works out, I'm going to be cured soon, and that'll mean I'm just as healthy as you. If you know what I'm saying.'

It was true that she and Dallas were drawn to each other, and not just because they had in common their good health. Although she was looking forward to being alone with him, she would probably have shared a room with him in any case. Probably slept with him too. Like most women of her age and background, Ronica's major concern was that the guy was healthy. Which would automatically have excluded Prevezer.

'It's sweet of you to say so, Prev. I guess you could say that Dallas and I are together, although I wouldn't exactly say that love comes into it. I always think love is a little like cosmology. There's a Big Bang, a lot of heat, followed by a gradual drifting apart, and a cooling off. Which means that a lover is pretty much the same as any cosmologist. Just some poor misguided individual looking to find some significance in the smallest of things, and asking a lot of foolish questions that can never really be answered. There's no utility in love, Prev. It'll waste your life and keep you from all that's profitable in the world. Love's just part of the great cosmic joke. It's ironic physics. Just like final theories. Just like God.'

2

I

TOURISM WAS THE biggest industry on the Moon. Over one hundred thousand people went there every year on vacations costing an average of two hundred thousand dollars per person. Mostly the tourists traveled to the Moon for sex or gambling,[1] although an increasing number of people went for outdoor

[1] In one-sixth of the gravity existing on Earth, just about the only physical activity that is enhanced on the Moon is sex. Most people still prefer to have sex slowly. Perhaps now more than ever in these frantic modern times. However, the Moon's one-sixth gravity means that most of the types of gambling available on Earth cannot be played here. Playing cards are almost impossible to deal, craps dice won't roll properly, and roulette wheel balls never drop down from the rim. Today the only legalized form of gambling on the Moon is pachinko. Pachinko is a machine game, for one player, in which you snap an eleven-millimeter steel ball on an upright nail-drive panel and try to put the ball into certain holes. Putting the ball in certain holes gains the player several balls in return. These can later be exchanged for money. Pachinko was developed in Chicago but became particularly popular in Japan, which now supplies most of the current Pachinko technology. The Moon's largest pachinko parlor – larger than any parlor on Earth – generates over two hundred fifty million dollars' worth of income per annum.

activities such as hiking and mountaineering – backpacking through Schröter's Valley or climbing Mount Doerfel. As well as the tourists there are the astronomers,[1] the mining engineers, the ecosystems engineers,[2] and meteorologists,[3] not to mention all the hotel workers, tour guides, charter pilots, pachinko engineers, and, of course, prostitutes.[4]

The largest of TB's hotels, the Galileo, with over fifteen hundred rooms, was also the best and the most expensive. Designed by the celebrated architect Masumara Shokai – he of the Buckingham Palace Dome, among other twenty-first-century architectural icons – the Galileo consists of two vertical wings. The wing that faces TB is made of armor-plated glass and, to complement the hotel's location on the Sea of Tranquillity, is shaped like the billowing sail on an enormous oceangoing yacht. The rectangular, mountain-facing wing serves as a foil for this dramatic curve of glass. Between these two is a breathtaking, full-height atrium lobby finished in smart-nanomolecular materials – French limestone, Italian marble, Indian onyx, and acres of English sycamore – that had been created on the Moon before being fitted by human craftsmen. Indeed, it was the proud boast of the hotel's owners that the builders had eschewed the use of any

[1] The astronomical world's largest reflector telescope, the three-hundred-inch Hawking telescope, is located at the Censorinus Space Observatory, just a few miles from TB.

[2] The Moon has the largest solar-generating power plant: the Theophilus Crater, close to the Moon's equator, contains over ten thousand photovoltaic cells, each of which is ten square meters in size.

[3] The Moon has the largest sunspot study facility on either world. This is of key importance to predictions of Earth's weather.

[4] At the time of writing, there are over five thousand prostitutes licensed to work on the Moon.

robotic workers in the Galileo's construction. The impressive, earth-toned lobby was dominated by an enormous kinetic sculpture celebrating Galileo's famous demonstration of the Law of Uniform Acceleration for falling bodies, which had disproved the Aristotelian contention that bodies of different weights fall at different speeds. Legend has it that in 1604, Galileo dropped lead weights of different sizes from the top of the Leaning Tower of Pisa.[1] More likely, though, the demonstration probably took place in Padua, where Galileo rolled weights down a smooth slope to make his demonstration. But sometimes people prefer a good story to a dull fact, and the builders of the hotel, and the German sculptor they commissioned, Jasper Fotze, were certainly no exception. So it was that every fifteen minutes a large ostrich feather, a lead weight, a paper ball, a shuttlecock, a balloon, and a basketball would be lifted automatically to the top of a series of plastic tubes, which were the height of the atrium, and released, all hitting the ground floor at exactly the same time.

Equally impressive was the lobby's marble floor and brass-bound reception desk, which were a gigantic working orrery[2] built to honor Galileo's defense of the Copernican theory that Earth moves around the Sun. Here the Sun was represented by the globular golden desk in the center of the circular floor. Around it moved – by an ingenious system of invisible gears – three more globular guest service stations representing the three innermost planets, Mercury, Venus, and

[1] Sadly, the famous campanile, built in 1185, collapsed in 2047, with the death of ninety-three Pisan tourists.
[2] After Charles Boyle, the 4th Earl of Orrery, for whom the first such object was made, in 1790.

Earth, from whence various products could be purchased and services rendered: Mercury, for deliveries, errands, and the purchase of lunar currency; Venus, for beauty and health products and toiletries; and Earth, for all information media. These three 'desks' all moved around the Sun in the correct relative periods, although not, of course, at the correct relative distances. Representing the Moon's orbit around Earth – although not inclined at the correct angle – was a large video-globe showing old pornographic movies of couples making love in one-sixth gravity.

The room rates were predictably astronomical. With the exception of Dallas, Ronica, and Cavor, this was the first time any of them had been in a luxury hotel.

'Five hundred selenes a night,' said Prevezer. 'How much is a selene worth?'

'About ten dollars,' said Cavor. Observing the look on Prevezer's face, he added, 'Have you ever heard of the expression "moonstruck"?'

'God's blood, yeah,' chuckled Prevezer. 'Now I know what that means. You have to be crazy to pay these kind of prices.'

'We'll probably need to rob the First National just to pay our hotel bill,' echoed Simou.

'Why don't you say it a bit louder, Sim?' frowned Lenina. 'I don't think the guy on the desk could have heard you properly.'

'A Table of the Principal Affections of the Planets,' said Gates, reading what was written on the pink marble underneath his gravity shoes.[1] 'I could sure get an affection for this kind of life.'

---

[1] The sole of each shoe contains as much as 35 pounds of lead, which occurs in considerable quantity on the Moon. Up to fifty pounds in weight can be added to a person in this way.

'I never thought I'd like the Moon so much,' Simou suddenly interjected.

'It's not all like this,' said Cavor. 'You should see the last place we stayed. Artemis Seven. They kept my arm when I couldn't pay the bill.'

'Hard to believe this is on the same planet,' breathed Gates. 'I never thought I'd feel so pleased to be back here.'

'Hey, Gates,' said Simou. 'While we're here, what are we gonna do for the root of all evil? I'd like to get me some of the local assignat. What are they called? Selenes? Just to keep up appearances, you understand. I'm supposed to be a single guy with some good, hot blood in his veins who is on vacation, right? The trouble is that I lack the essential letters of credit from my personal bankers back on Earth to facilitate the necessary exchange of currencies. On account of the fact that I don't have any credit, and I don't have any personal bankers.'

'The man's got a good point there, Gates,' agreed Prevezer.

'You'd better ask Dallas,' said Gates. 'He's the one with the money, not me.'

'I'm sure he's already thought of it,' declared Cavor. 'He's certainly thought of everything else.'

'I hope so,' sighed Lenina.

Gates took her hand in his own. 'You okay?' he asked.

Lenina fixed a weary smile to her face. She was feeling anything but okay. Deep inside herself she felt exhausted. She was also experiencing some difficulty in breathing: Every breath she took had to be just that little bit deeper than normal.

'I'm just a little tired, after the flight, that's all,' she

257

said. 'As soon as we get to our room, I think I'll lie down.'

'I'll see what's keeping Dallas,' said Gates, and he walked, a little clumsily – for, despite his gravity shoes, the big man was still adjusting to being a lot lighter on his feet – toward the reception desk.

The registration was actually proceeding quickly. The desk attendant had shown Dallas holographic pictures of the various suites that had been reserved, and Dallas had pronounced himself happy with the proposed accommodation. Not that there would have been much chance for him to have changed his mind about any of the rooms he had booked. Nearly every hotel on TB was full, many of them with guests who had flown in for the centennial of the first Apollo Moon landing. Indeed, it was one of the reasons Dallas had chosen this particular time to arrive on the Moon. Among so many lunar tourists, he thought it would be easier for Gates and rest of the team to go relatively unnoticed.

'So, are you here for the centennial?' asked the desk attendant.

'Only partly,' said Dallas, and grinned meaningfully at Ronica for the hotelier's benefit.

'Yeah,' said the man, organizing a whole fistful of key-cards. 'Stupid question. History's one thing. A good time's quite another.'

'You said it,' said Dallas. 'But actually we were also planning to do some hiking while we're here.'

'Not too far from the equator, I hope. You heard about the tragedy we had with those climbers down in the Leibnitz Mountains?' The attendant rolled his eyes and shook his head. 'They got stuck and ran out of solar energy when it got dark. Froze to death.'

'How awful,' said Ronica.

'Yeah, it was terrible. Rescue team reckoned they must have forgotten to tell their trip computer that a polar lunar day is a lot shorter than an equatorial one. We have fourteen days of sunshine here at TB. It's less than half that at the pole.'

Dallas shook his head. 'We weren't thinking of going much farther afield than the Central Highlands,' he said. 'Certainly no farther west than Schröter.'

'Oh, it's really beautiful down there. I went to Schröter myself just a few months back. I could recommend a good guide if you're at all interested. And a pretty good equipment company.'

'Thanks, but we brought our own.'

The attendant glanced up from his desk-screen and noted the large number of bags on the floor surrounding Dallas and his entourage.

'You certainly have, haven't you,' he said. 'I'll get a porter to help you with all your luggage.' He didn't know it, but the luggage was mostly made up of the computer equipment with which Prevezer would create a simulation of the First National Blood Bank.

'It's okay,' said Dallas. 'Don't bother. They're used to carrying my stuff around.'

'As you wish, sir.' The attendant smiled. 'And how will you be paying your bill, Mister Bourbaki?'

Nicolas Bourbaki was the name Dallas was using while they were on the Moon. It was possible that the company was still looking for him.

Dallas placed his wafer-thin breastpocket computer on the desk between them and said, 'By Electronic Credit Transfer.' The computer signaled its voice recognition with a quiet bleep and prepared for remote wireless connection with the hotel's own computer.

'ECT? Yes sir.'

Since leaving his former life, Dallas had spent a

small fortune using a number of accounts to equip and provision his team. Through his personal treasury workstation (PTW), he had automatically changed all his account numbers and their respective encryptions in order to escape data tracing and detection. Only one of these accounts, so far untouched, was still substantially in credit, and this was the account that he selected, with the touch of a button, for simultaneous bill settlement: All transactions relating to his entourage's stay at the Galileo would be checked by his PTW and then debited immediately from the account he had chosen.

'Everything okay?' asked Gates.

'Of course,' said Dallas. Seeing Gates glance in the direction of the foreign exchange desk on Mercury, Dallas guessed what was on the big man's mind. 'Oh, and you'd better charge some currency to that account while we're here,' he told the attendant. 'Say, ten thousand selenes, in cash. New bills. It's a long time since I've been here, but I can't imagine much has changed.'

'Cash is still king on the Moon,' confirmed the attendant, and entered the transaction on his computer. 'Always was, always will be. Yes sir, you carry the Moon in your pocket.' Finishing up, he smiled a broad smile, the way he had been trained to, making a white crescent of his teeth. A real honey of a Moon welcome, they called it back on his Galileo Hotelkeeping course. With as much sincerity as he could muster, and completely unaware of their provenance, he added the words of hospitality and liberality that, he had learned, were the correct way to welcome a guest:

'He who doubts from what he sees,

Will ne'er believe, do what you please.
If the Sun and Moon should doubt,
They'd immediately go out.
To be in a passion you good may do,
But no good if a passion is in you.
The whore and gambler, by the state licens'd,
Build our Nation's fate.'[1]

He smiled again, and added, 'Enjoy your stay.'

II

'Answer, answer, answer ...'

A still, small intonation rang out in the darkness of Rimmer's austere apartment, interrupting the sado-erotic musings that habitually preceded his falling asleep. At first he thought it was the dull articulation of his own conscience, some stern daughter of the voice of God – for the vocalization was female – calling him to account for his wickedness and blasphemy.

'Answer, answer ...'

But what kind of sin? Surely not the sin of Onan. That was just a way of relieving tension, of aiding sleep. No, to warrant such a peremptory demand, this had to be something far more serious than merely spilling life's beans on the bottom sheet.

[1] From *Auguries of Innocence* by William Blake. The quotation has been adapted by the authors of the *Galileo Guide to Good Hotel Keeping*. 'Build our Nation's Fate' should read 'Build that nation's fate.' No doubt the people at the Galileo felt justified in this small alteration by virtue of the fact that the Moon exists as an independent nation-state, by the terms of the treaty on Principles Governing the Colonization of the Moon and Other Celestial Bodies within Our Solar System, 2025.

'Answer . . .'

Rimmer sighed and rolled on to his hairy back. He was still not yet completely awake – he had drunk too much before going to bed. The last of the genuine Napoleon brandy. Rimmer dragged himself up and snorted some oxygen into his sleep-befuddled brain. The voice was still repeating itself in the cold tones of some holy inquisitor. It could be nothing so morally scrupulous as a conscience. The only categorical imperative Rimmer was aware of was the inner voice that told him to please himself whenever the opportunity presented itself. No, the voice in his apartment belonged to his computer.

Shaking his head and yawning cheesily, Rimmer rolled out of bed and padded into the smallish lounge and flopped down in front of the sixty-two-inch blue screen that dominated one wall of the room. It was an old-fashioned way of interacting with the computer, but he preferred it to the more anthropic Motion Parallax. Somehow, with a screen, you never lost sight of the fact you were dealing with a computer. Motion Parallaxes were for people who didn't much like the company of a machine. Rimmer had no problem with machines. As a matter of fact he liked them better than he liked most people.

'Answer, answer, answer ...'

'Remind me what the question was,' he said, gouging the sleep from his encrusted eyes.

'First choose a persona,' said the disembodied female voice. Pictures of a number of famous historical personalities now appeared on the screen: Albert Einstein, Orson Welles, Martin Luther King Jr., John Lennon, Salman Rushdie, Tom Ray, Marina Maguire, Jonas Ndebele, and Cameron Caine. Rimmer's computer system had Microsoft version 45.1, and a persona was the personality the computer assumed on-screen when dealing with the program user. Compared to the Motion Parallax system on Microsoft 50, version 45.1 was positively antediluvian.

'Einstein,' yawned Rimmer, hardly caring what social facade or public image the computer might use. 'Just get on with it. I haven't got all night.' Frankly, he'd have preferred Hitler, Stalin, Mao Zedong, Nesib el Bekri, Sol Chong, or some other great tyrant, but, in Rimmer's opinion, Microsoft was too squeamish to cater to anyone whose favorite historical figures were just a little offbeat.

A life-size picture of Albert Einstein, white haired, wearing a thick beige pullover, and smoking a pipe while seated in an armchair, appeared on-screen. To Rimmer, Einstein looked larger and more heavily muscled than the way he usually imagined him. Or maybe it was just the sweater.

'Hey, Albert, what's happening?'

'You asked me a question,' the facsimile of the Nobel prize-winning physicist replied in his own, digitally reproduced comic German accent. 'About several key numbers, did you not?'

'Yeah.'

'And asked me to conduct a search for exact number matches, across all financial categories, with no time restrictions, and using Conspectus, Argus, Gimlet, Gorgon, and Panorama search engines. Is that right?'

'That's right, Albert,' said Rimmer, yawning once more. 'Only speed it up, okay? I happened to be asleep.'

Rimmer's idea had been a simple one. Dallas had thirteen different bank accounts, and soon after disappearing from his own apartment, he'd changed all the account numbers and encryption codes, thus covering his electronic tracks. Or so he must have thought. Dallas could hardly have expected Rimmer to have concentrated his computer search on a different, albeit related, set of numbers – the bank balances themselves. Rimmer had reasoned that with thirteen accounts, Dallas might only draw on one account at a time, until he had used up the balance. In this way, Rimmer's computer might have a sufficient interval in which to trace one of as many as twelve other account balances. Of course, this was no small task. Several of the accounts ran to eight or nine figures. For example, according to the records on the computer in Dallas's office at Terotechnology, one account showed a balance of 1,12,462,239 credits. And this was one of the numbers for which Rimmer had programmed his computer to search. In an effort to improve the odds of a successful search, he had also divided eight numbers into four numbers, and nine numbers into six numbers so that, for example, 1,12,462,239 became 1, 12, 4, 62, 23, and 9.

'Wait a minute,' said Rimmer, standing up slowly. 'You don't mean you've found one?'

It was several weeks since Rimmer had instigated the search – not long after the director had downgraded him to the status of a lowly security guard – and the truth was that he had more or less forgotten about it, having come to the conclusion that the magnitude of the search was too great.

Einstein puffed his pipe and then removed it from his mouth. 'Yes. Eureka, to speak as Archimedes.'

At the bottom of the screen there appeared a small window containing a brief career résumé for the Greek-Sicilian mathematician and inventor. Rimmer ignored it. The trouble with 45.1 was that so much of what you were told was simply irrelevant – an interesting waste of time.

'I have found one such number,' continued Einstein. 'Against all the odds, may I say. Merely to find these six numbers, the odds are quite large enough. To be precise, thirteen million, nine hundred and eighty-three thousand, eight hundred and sixteen to one. But to find all six of these numbers in the specified search order?' Einstein chuckled. 'Why the odds are almost incalculable. Nevertheless, I calculated them. One in ten billion, sixty-eight million, three hundred and forty-seven thousand, five hundred and twenty. Yes, I think even God would think twice about playing against odds like that.'

Another window appeared, this one quoting Einstein's famous remark to the effect that God does not play dice with the world and explaining that this was Einstein's negative reaction to quantum theory.[1]

Rimmer held his head. 'Albert. You're a bloody genius.'

'So people are always telling me, much to my irritation.'

'My God, I don't believe it. You've found the number.'

'Numbers are nothing, my friend. Equations are the thing. Better than women. Better than diamonds. Better than just about anything else I can think of. Equations are forever.'

Another window with a quotation about equations.

[1] Quantum theory. A theory in physics which refutes relativity by stating that an observer can influence reality and that events do occur randomly – an argument with which Einstein disagreed.

'Sure, Albert,' laughed Rimmer. 'Anything you say. My God, this is terrific. Where on earth did you find it?'

'I didn't find it on Earth at all.'

'Of course,' breathed Rimmer. 'He's on the Moon.'

'Yes, but only just.'

'How's that?'

'Well,' chuckled Einstein, 'there's not much gravity on the Moon.'

Yet another window explaining how Einstein's General Theory of Relativity had described the force of gravity and the large-scale structure of the universe.

Rimmer smiled slimly. 'Is that an example of the famous German sense of humor?' he asked.

Einstein shrugged apologetically and, returning the pipe to his mouth, set about relighting it.

'Exactly where on the Moon did you find this number, Albert?'

'At the Hotel Galileo, on Tranquillity Base.'

Another window to say who Galileo was.

'The Galileo, huh? Nice. Dallas always did like to go first class.'

'He should have acknowledged the work of Kepler.'

'Who should?'

Another window to say who Kepler was.

'Galileo, of course. It always surprises me that so many scientists should be so vain.'

'On the subject of personas, acknowledged or otherwise, did our winning number have a name?'

'Nicolas Bourbaki,' said Einstein.

This time the window appearing on-screen told Rimmer something that he was actually interested to know: that the name Nicolas Bourbaki had been a collective *nom de plume* for a group of early twentieth-century mathematicians including Szolem Mandel-brojt.

Rimmer started to get dressed.

'Are you going somewhere?'

'I'm going to get my old job back,' explained Rimmer. 'And after that I'm going to the Moon.'

This time a window with some astroliner flight times and prices.

'Does the Moon only exist when you look at it?' asked Einstein.

'I wouldn't say so.'

'That's my objection to quantum mechanics.' Einstein's large nose wrinkled with disgust. 'These people reduce science to a series of captions. Schrödinger's cat. Heisenberg's uncertainty. Pah! It all implies that the world is created simply by our perception of it. Nonsense.'

'I'd love to stay and talk about this, Albert. But frankly I haven't got the time. Oh, you'd better book me on the next available flight. To the Moon. Assuming it's still there. It was the last time I looked.'

'There's only coach left, I'm afraid,' said Einstein, after a momentary pause. 'It's the centennial of the first Moon landing.'

'Okay, coach'll have to do. And thanks for your help, Albert. You can turn off now.'

'May I give you a small piece of advice?'

Prior to shutting down, it was customary in 45.1 for the operating persona to utter some appropriate quotation – something he or she had said while living – so as to enhance the user's impression of having interacted with some great figure from history.

Rimmer snorted with contempt. 'Sure,' he said. 'Be my guest, you old bastard.'

Einstein pointed at the pair of malodorous socks Rimmer had collected from the floor.

'Socks are a waste of money. When I was young, I found out that the big toe always ends up making a hole in a sock.'

'Didn't you think you might just cut your bloody toenails more often?' asked Rimmer.

'Well, anyway, I stopped wearing socks.'

'I guess it all depends on whether you're a body at rest or a body in motion,' said Rimmer. 'But thank you, Albert. That was most enlightening.'

Rimmer finished dressing and was still amused at the fashion tip he had taken from a facsimile of Albert Einstein – so that was what space and time were all about: Given enough time, your toe would make a space in your sock. He went out of the apartment.

III

Almost as soon as he was settled into his suite, Prevezer began working on the silicon surrogate world that Dallas was planning to use as a laboratory in which they would test the viability of his plan.

Modeling this particular Simworld was a highly complex process, an individually tailored job, and one on which Prevezer had been working long before leaving Earth. A number of reasons had obliged him to finish making his model on the Moon. There was the press of time: Dallas wanted to take advantage of the relative anonymity that was afforded by the large number of tourists on the Moon for the centennial, and he wanted to carry out the robbery at some time during the fourteen days of lunar 'daylight.' But from Prevezer's point of view, what was more important was that Dallas wanted the simulation to take place in the authentic conditions of the Moon's one-sixth gravity, which was something the laws of physics did not permit back on Earth. Gravity, or the lack of it, was not something that could be rendered artificially.

Prevezer was one of the best model makers in the business. He preferred the term 'Simworld' to the more archaic 'virtual reality' that was characterized by a much older and cruder wraparound technology – its three hundred and sixty degree headtracker helmets, datagloves, cyber-exoskeletons, dildonics, pneumatic pressure feedback systems, and cartoony terrain projectors. Prevezer worked at a much more fundamental and sophisticated level, using several electro-neuroneedles that he attached acupuncturally to the cerebral cortex, to create a synthetic experience indistinguishable from reality itself.

Prevezer had a low opinion of reality, with its fat-free ice cream, sugar-free sweeteners, alcohol-free whiskey, synthetic blood, fake fur, and Motion Parallaxes. Prevezer found none of these simulations particularly convincing. To him, the artificial Simworlds he created were more real than the real thing. For instance, where else but a Simworld could anyone but the very rich make love on a fur rug in front of a blazing log fire? – one of his most popular surrogate creations. Or drive a vintage Ferrari F87? Or massacre a village full of peasants? – another surprisingly popular choice. Reality was greatly overrated and even at its best it was no longer something that people could simply assume to be there.

Most of Prevezer's customers were simply people in search of a cheap thrill, individuals in an impersonal world looking for a brief moment of empowerment as they became the gods of their own mathematical wonderlands. Quite a few were sick, people in the active Three Moon phase of the virus, who wanted to spend their last few hours on Earth enjoying what in life had been denied them: the sensation of good health in some demi-paradise – a tropical island or the peak of some breathtaking mountain – and in the company of a few good friends. Using EUPHORIA, a general purpose simulation program of his own devising, it was easy enough to build this kind of standard model. He'd even modeled luxury lunar hotels, although he now realized his rendering of the Galileo had fallen way short of the mark. This was the first time he had been exposed to a reality that exceeded his own expectations. Of course, you had to be as rich as Dallas and his pure-blood kind to afford it. Few people from Prevezer's background ever got a taste of this style of living, even in a simulated, artificial world. It was almost enough to make him think he'd not been alive at all these past few years – just pretending to be alive. He had joined Dallas's team because he too wanted to be rich and healthy, but it was not until he had reached TB and checked into the Galileo that he'd properly appreciated what either of those two concepts really meant.

When Cavor and Simou turned up at the door of his suite, suggesting a visit to the Armstrong Center, Prevezer was very tempted to join them. He was keen to taste the expensive realities that were on offer at TB's principal public space. But there was still much data to be processed if his model of the First National was ever going to behave like its real-world correlate.

'I'd like to,' he sighed, declining their invitation. 'Only I've got to check the Simworld's fidelity axis. To make sure the endophysical perspective matches the exophysical one.'[1]

'Surely a model can be too perfect,' argued Cavor. 'I mean, if the microworld construct is as good as its macroworld counterpart, then what margin for error is there? Without the possibility of error, nothing can be learned and the experimental quality is compromised.'

'You're just full of surprises,' yawned Prevezer.

'You know something?' said Cavor. 'Lately I've started to surprise myself. Perhaps me most of all.'

'Enough of that,' grinned Simou. 'It's time we took off and sampled some of those lovely lunar ladies.'

'You know, I could fix you guys up a synthetic experience that would beat anything you'll have on TB,' Prevezer said, without much conviction. This was just the salesman in him talking. 'Reality is just a chimera.'

But Simou and Cavor were already walking away from his door. 'Take a look around you, Sim,' he said, following them into the corridor, and pointing out the window at the silver-colored moonscape. 'Cav? You think any of this is real? It's not reality you want, my friends, it's certainty. These days, that's a much more difficult grail to find. It's not to be found in mathematics. It's not even to be found in the atoms. The only certainty in the whole bloody universe is in ourselves. There is no world independent of you and me. Not any more. Death is the only certainty, Sim. That's what's real.'

Simou turned on his heel and uttered an old saying

---

[1] In other words, are the laws governing the behavior of the simulated system the same for an observer looking at the system from the outside as they are for the observer who is inside the system?

that was familiar to anyone who had the virus: 'You die today, and I'll die tomorrow.'

IV

Barefoot, and wearing just a pair of panties, Ronica began a careful walk across the floor of the suite she was sharing with Dallas, toward the HV.[1] This was her first trip to the Moon, and the first hotel she had stayed in where, as a matter of lunar law, you had to watch a set of safety instructions on how to use the room and its facilities. The secret of walking around the room without gravity shoes, so the guy on the HV had said before the commercial break, was to try and do it slowly, at half your normal speed, as if you had been drugged, or as if you were walking through the sea. One quick and injudicious step could carry you several inches off the floor; and standing up from a chair, you had to be careful not to hit your head on the triple-height ceiling. Even though the suite was as big as a basketball court, a good leap would have carried her from one side to the other. She reached the HV, switched it off, and headed back toward the enormous bed where Dallas was lying. Although his gravity shoes were still on, his body barely weighed enough to put a dent on the virtually redundant mattress.

'So,' said Ronica. 'Do you want to tell me why Cavor is taking so much Connex?'

'Did he tell you it was Connex?'

'He didn't have to. I recognized those tabs. I've taken enough Connex in my time.'

'Is that so?'

---

[1] Holovision.

'Yes. So? Why is he taking cognitive enhancement? And so much?'

'Why ask me?'

'Because I figure you're the one who gave it to him. That stuff isn't cheap. And if Cavor had ever taken it before, he'd know not to take so much.'

'Did you say anything to him about it?'

'No.'

'Good. Because I'd prefer he didn't know what it is he's taking. At least not right now. And as to the high dosage, that's up to me as well. I told him to take it in quantity.'

'I won't say anything.'

'He'll be okay,' said Dallas, mistaking her exasperation for concern. 'If that's what you're worried about.'

She sighed loudly and shook her head. 'I can't decide why you want him to boost his head. Unless it's because you want him to remember something. Something important.'

'That's exactly what I want him to do. To remember something.'

'Like what?'

'Something he's forgotten.'

'I can't bear it that you're so cryptic.' Ronica realized she was shouting. She calmed herself and lay down on the bed next to him. 'I thought we had something between us. An understanding. A trust. After all, we're the same blood, you and I. The same class and background. But sometimes I don't think you trust me at all. If you did, you'd confide in me. You'd learn to lean on me.'

Dallas took her in his arms and kissed her.

'On the Moon, that might be a little difficult,' he said. 'But perhaps I could float on top of you now and again.'

V

Tranquillity Base was the biggest development of land on the Moon, and the Armstrong Center[1] – also known as the Tranquillity Forum – was the massive complex of public halls, exhibition areas, performance auditoria, pachinko parlors, sleazy bars, and licensed brothels that occupied the center of the development and acted as a magnet for lunar tourists. Its design had been the subject of an international architectural competition, one of the largest the world had ever seen, attracting hundreds of entries. Victory eventually went to the New York-born, Los Angeles-based architect Brad Epstein. It was the most transparent of buildings, constructed entirely of armor-plated glass, with no facades – just an expressed structure and a number of suspended capsules housing the main auditoria. One giant spire, at the center of the structure, three hundred and sixty-three feet high and shaped like the *Saturn V* Moon rocket that had first carried men to the Moon, signaled the presence of what was beneath: the actual site of the *Apollo 11* Moon landing on July 20, 1969, at 3:17 P.M., Houston, Texas, time.

The centennial was now only a few days away, and the landing site itself, enclosed beneath a protective glass dome, was surrounded with tourists. Among them were Cavor, Simou, and Gates.

The landing site was the snapshot of another time, another universe,[2] although to all who stared through

---

[1] Named after Neil Armstrong, the first man on the Moon.

[2] It makes no difference, for time is a quantum concept, and other times are merely special cases of other universes.

the protective glass dome, the scene looked much as if the astronauts had just departed. The four-legged gold spider that was the descent module; the toppled American flag – blown over when the ascent module had blasted off; a tripod-mounted television camera and some ancient-looking scientific instruments placed about sixty feet away from the *Eagle*; and those footprints in the moondust that had survived the *Eagle*'s ascent from the Sea of Tranquillity.

It looked exactly as it had a hundred years before, at least until the arrival of some holographic astronauts, and an explanatory sound track.

'Hello, Neil and Buzz,' said a voice on the landing site soundtrack, which was also available from the museum shop. 'I'm talking to you by telephone from the Oval Office at the White House. and this certainly has to be the most historic telephone call ever made from the White House.'

Under the weight of their enormous white back-packs, the two holographic astronauts stood stiffly to attention in front of the real television cameras, like a couple of ghostly polar bears.

'I know why we've come to the Moon,' murmured Gates. 'But I can't imagine why they bothered. There's nothing here.'

'For one priceless moment,' said the fruity, self-important voice on the soundtrack, 'in the whole history of man, all the people on this earth are truly one.'

'Priceless, yeah,' sneered Cavor. 'It hadn't happened before, and it certainly hasn't happened since.'

'One in their pride in what you have done.'

'Still,' Cavor added grudgingly, 'it was a hell of an achievement.'

'And one in our prayers that you will return safely to Earth.'

'Thank you, Mister President,' said the voice of Neil Armstrong. 'It's a great honour and privilege for us to be here, representing not only the United States but men of peace of all nations.'

'Peace,' chuckled Gates. 'People used to talk about that a lot.'

'Men with a vision for the future,' said Armstrong.

'He sounds a little choked,' observed Gates. 'Like he's going to cry or something.'

'Thank you very much,' said the President.[1] 'And all of us look forward to seeing you on the *Hornet* on Thursday.'

'That's the name of a boat,' explained Cavor. 'Back in olden times, they used to land spaceships in the ocean.'

'I look forwards to that very much, sir,' said the second astronaut, Buzz Aldrin.

The two holographic astronauts saluted, then turned away from the camera, and promptly disappeared. The show was over, and the crowd around the dome started to applaud.

'That was interesting,' said Cavor.

'I suppose,' shrugged Simou. 'But hardly worth the trip.'

'All sorts will be here on July twentieth,' said Gates. 'World leaders, company chairmen, commissioners, you name it.'

'More fool them,' said Simou.

'Haven't you got any sense of history?' demanded Cavor.

[1] Richard Milhous Nixon, thirty-seventh President of the United States, 1969–1974.

'Nope, can't say that I have,' admitted Simou. 'I've always been too concerned with the future to give the past much thought. My future. Such as the small matter of whether or not I'll still be alive in a year's time. History's a luxury I could never afford.'

'That's why we came,' said Gates. 'To get a lot of things we could never afford.'

'Yeah, well a sense of history's well down my list,' said Simou. 'Right now I'll settle for one of these lunar ladies. Thanks to all this one-sixth g, my cock has been floating around in my pants like one of those command modules. Since we arrived on the Moon I don't think there's been one time when it's ever been pointed at the ground.'

'Me too,' grinned Gates.

'This place does have its advantages,' said Cavor. 'My prosthetic arm has never felt so light. I hardly notice it at all. It's almost as if it was the real thing.'

Simou clapped his hands enthusiastically. 'Whaddya say, Gates? Shall we go and find ourselves some lunar ladies?'

Gates shook his head. 'No, I'm not in the mood. I think I'll go back.'

He waved them off and walked in the direction of the hotel. Gates didn't feel he could leave Lenina alone for too long. There was no point in telling anyone yet, not until he was quite sure, but in truth he was worried about her. What with her breathlessness and the way she covered her torso whenever he came near her, Gates had the idea Lenina had entered, or was about to enter, the active Three Moon phase of the virus. He knew he had no alternative but to ask her about it. But exactly how did you ask the girl you loved if she just happened to be dying?

What was it that the President had said on the

soundtrack? '. . . in our prayers that you will return safely to Earth.' Gates had never been in a church. He wasn't even sure if he even believed in God. But he was beginning to wish that he knew how to pray.

VI

If men and women did not die, they would have little need of a divinity to engineer human beginnings and ends. The belief in God and the elevation of the total personality to a thing in itself that must endure forever – such ideas continue to persist because of the preposterous fear of death and the false antithesis that exists between body and soul. Death is still perceived as the great mystery.

The key to understanding death is, if course, the same key that unlocks the mystery of human beginnings. But there's no reason either of life's bookends should be treated as a mystery. It's absurd to argue that an existence with an identifiable beginning should have no end, for that would be to argue the logical impossibility of there being two different states of nonexistence or nothingness. Real revelation comes not from a book, nor from a series of commandments, but from a true understanding of the function of life.

Everything makes sense when the meaning of life has been grasped, and this is nowhere near as slippery as it sounds. The question may have exercised philosophers, alchemists, and scientists for several thousand years – an abiding sense that life has some purpose has been the curse of Homo sapiens – but the answer to this putative riddle is quite a simple one: All life-forms are merely vehicles for DNA survival; and genes are little bits of software that have but one goal – to make copies of themselves. Men, marsupials, and mollusks are just sophisticated conveyances that their respective duplicating programs have created to help them reproduce. This is the only true meaning of life, and the most successful DNA sequences are the variants that are better than others in competing for the planet's scarce resources. We call this process of the survival of the fittest natural selection. Thus it may be seen that human beings are nothing more than a highly successful vehicle for one particular DNA message.

Life is in no way devalued by this analysis: rather it is strengthened. Man may be very like a computer that has been programmed to replicate the original lines of genetic program code. But DNA's performance and capacity to preserve a message is vastly superior to any known or anticipated computer. The mathematics of the DNA archive is nothing short of staggering. Each gene in your body has been being recopied as many as twenty billion times with 99 percent accuracy. Just imagine how degraded any other method of preserving a valuable text for the archives would be by such repeated copying. For this reason alone life cannot be too common in the universe. Indeed it is arguably a cosmic principle.

But the success of the DNA sequence is not limited to producing the most effective vehicular bodies for reproduction. The long-term survival of a DNA sequence is not limited to the replicator's own body. A corollary of DNA success is the way in which genes affect the world at large – successful genes reaching beyond their bodies and changing the world around them. Spider genes spin a web, bird genes build a nest, and bee genes construct a honeycomb. Most successful of all, the human gene reaches out to invent the wheel – and anything else that may contribute to its chances *of successful reproduction: the longbow, the plow, writing, the saddle, the printing press, the telescope, the camera, the electric light, penicillin, ad infinitum. It is not long before the most successful replicator, man, has invented himself another replicator – the computer. As digital programs are copied many times over, it is no time at all before the survival success story that is synthetic code sequences can affect the world around them. Computers build other machines. Computers build better computers. And with the creation of the first computer virus – which acts very like a biological virus – a new era in evolution is born: artificial replication. Viruses mutate. They find a way of ensuring their survival, of manipulating the world beyond the computer. Replicators are by definition opportunistic. That is the foundation of their success.*

Doubtless the reader will be familiar with one of the central panels from the ceiling of the Sistine Chapel in the Vatican, as painted by Michelangelo,[1] and entitled The Creation of Adam. *God and Adam, members of the same race of superbeings, confront each other against a primordial, half-formed landscape. Life seems to leap to Adam like an electric spark from the hand of God – a communication from one successful replicator to another.[2] Both are reaching out to change the world around them.*

Is it possible that, one day, the relationship between man and computer could be depicted in a similar way? Might there come a time when, somehow, the two most successful sequences of digital information on the

[1] Painted 1508–1512.
[2] Indeed, as depicted by Michelangelo, God and Adam seem almost to be equal, for their bodies are quite complementary. Frankly, this particular detail has about it something more of the pagan than the truly Christian.

planet – DNA and binary code – will reach out and
change each other in some profound way? Because I
think that's what we're all reaching for – that Sistine
Chapel, Michelangelo moment.

VII

In the one-sixth gravity of the Moon, there was little
necessity that a chair should require cushioning or
upholstery. As a result, the design requirements of the
two matching chairs on which Gates and Dallas sat
adjacent to each other, while Prevezer readied his
Simworld equipment, had been purely visual. To
Rameses Gates, each of the sculpted white nanomarble
chairs had a windswept equipoise that recalled the
wing of an angel – wasn't there a category of angel
ranked below a cherubim, called a throne?[1] He was
not a religious man, although he was nonetheless
familiar with the concept of angels. In these new
millenarian times it was hard not to be, with several
dozen religious cults[2] offering a spiritual introduction
to your very own guardian angel as a guarantee of a
personal resurrection after death. Now that the robbery was growing nearer, Gates realized he might have
welcomed the reassurance of a guardian angel, or two.

To Dallas's more scientific eye the chairs looked like
two lumps of melted candle wax – something much
more prosaic. Which could not be said of the spherical,

[1] There are three hierarchies of angels, each of three orders in
descending ranks. These are (1) seraphim, (2) cherubim, (3) thrones,
(4) dominations, (5) virtues, (6) powers, (7) principalities, (8)
archangels, and (9) angels.
[2] For example, the Church of Sammael, the Sandalphonists, and
the New Witnesses of Raguel.

transparent, and self-supporting structure of electro-tetrahedrons that Prevezer now placed on each man's head.

'I thought you didn't go in for immersive head-mounted displays,' remarked Simou, who, like Cavor, Ronica, and Lenina, was in Prevezer's suite to watch him conduct the simulation.

'I don't,' he said. 'These aren't headsets – they're geodesic MRIs. That's magnetic resonance imagers, to you. It takes an image of the cerebral cortex and then turns it into a kind of digital diagram – like a topographical map of Earth. The geodesic dome then subdivides the scan into tiny digital boxes called voxels, so that an algorithm can select those particular voxels on the cerebral cortex that process sensory information and working memory.'

Prevezer adjusted the geodesic dome on Dallas's shoulders. 'How does that feel? Comfortable?'

'Like it was hardly there,' admitted Dallas.

'That's the whole idea,' Prevezer said proudly as he retired behind the computer lectern to initiate the simulation countdown sequence. 'You won't get nausea or headaches with a geodesic. Not like those crappy head-mounted displays you still see around. Antique porno-projection mounts, n'shit like that.'

Prevezer ran through some final diagnostic program checks. 'The fellow who invented this design was a guy called Buckminster Fuller. He wanted to create a low-cost building and used a design he'd originally visualized as an analogical aid for a system of thought. Curiously enough, the geodesic mimics the way we now create a simulation model. The way Fuller imagined the thinking process, only the surface of the sphere consisted of relevant experiences or thoughts. Experiences too small to be relevant remained inside the sphere; and those that were too large, stayed outside.'

'Some of us know what that's like,' grumbled Lenina. 'It seems to me this simulation would have made a lot more sense if we could all have experienced it. It's not much of a run-through for a plan if not everyone is allowed to run through it.'

'You know, you're absolutely right,' said Prevezer, his voice sharp with sarcasm. He didn't even look at Lenina, he was too busy connecting his computer to a small display, which was worn over his left eye so that he could keep a constant visual check on their vital signs while Gates and Dallas progressed through the Simworld he had modeled. 'The trouble is, there isn't a computer that's been built that can handle more than two POVs in the same Simworld.'

'Prev's right, Lenina,' said Dallas. 'This is as good as it gets. I'm sorry we can't all rehearse the plan in simulation, but it's not a perfect world.'

'Which world are you talking about?' she asked, walking away toward the window. 'Yours, or mine?'

'Lenina,' Gates said. 'That's enough.'

Prevezer switched on the two geodesic MRIs remotely, lighting up each of the two domes like a small planetarium.

'Okay, try and keep your heads as still as possible,' he told them, as on the screen in front of his eye the complex pattern of ridges and troughs that was Dallas's brain unfolded like a fingerprint. 'You're looking good, Dallas.' And then: 'You, too, Gates. Both of you will be pleased to hear there's no sign of any significant abnormalities. Just healthy-looking brains with good axon interconnections for the elec-tro-neuroneedles. Now keep especially still. You might feel a very slight localized prickling sensation on your scalp, following by a tingling sensation.'

From inside the geodesic MRI that crowned each man's head, a series of tiny flexible needles telescoped their way toward his scalp.

'I hate needles,' said Gates, grimacing with discomfort, his eyes closed.

'Don't talk. It makes your head vibrate and interferes with the neuroneedle collimator. Hold it steady. Hold it.' The needles were in place. 'Okay. You can relax now. You're both hooked.'

'That's it?' Gates blinked several times.

'Didn't feel a thing,' confessed Dallas.

'Just don't sneeze,' advised Simou.

'In about one minute that won't be possible,' murmured Prevezer. 'At least not in this world. Okay, now close your eyes again. Both of you. When I send you into the synthetic world, it'll seem less of a shock that way. Normally, I'm introducing people to a world of pleasure and leisure. However, this particular model's hardly the stuff that dreams are made of.

'The program is organized so that the chips and all the relevant sensory neurons have exactly the same parallel function, and are interfaced to be effectively interchangeable. Each chip on the computer is programmed to do exactly what its natural analogue does. The result is a silicon cerebral cortex that has been provided with a different conscious experience from the natural one.'

Prevezer pointed at the computer on the lectern in front of him.

'Just by touching that button,' he explained, 'it's possible to switch from the natural cortical mode to the artificial one, and vice versa. There's no behavioral change when the button is pressed, because for each of them there's no change in the organization of the brain that's in use – be it synthetic or natural.

'It's kind of like having a prosthetic, except that in the case of a brain, the artificial one offers a different conscious experience – one that's created by me. There's another important difference. To them it will feel almost exactly like the real thing.

'Get ready, gentlemen, you have ten seconds before entering Simworld, on my mark. Ten seconds. Nine, eight …'

Cavor glanced at his prosthetic arm and reflected that lately it hadn't felt like a prosthetic at all. It had felt much more like the real thing. Possibly even better, if such a thing was possible. Not stronger exactly, just different, in a way he found hard to describe. He knew it had to be something to do with the drugs he was taking.

'Five, four, three, two, one, switch.'

Prevezer pressed the button that consigned his two charges to a different conscious experience and then, having checked their vital signs and seen that every-thing looked normal, glanced wearily at the faces of his onlooking colleagues. It was almost as if they actually expected to see something happen to the two men wearing the geodesics. He laughed scornfully, and said, 'You guys look as if you thought they were going to disappear or something.'

'I'd sure like to see what I look like in virtual reality,' said Ronica.

Prevezer winced. 'Please don't ever call it that. If you want to describe what we're doing here, you say it's a simulation, or a model, or a surrogate world, or a Simworld, but never virtual reality. That stuff's for kids.'

'Whatever you want to call it,' replied Cavor, 'I'd kind of like to see a Simworld version of me, too.'

'How will they remember things that won't actually have happened?' asked Ronica.

'You remember your dreams, don't you?'

'Yes, but dreaming is something the brain does for itself.'

Prevezer shook his head. He wasn't much used to explaining the tricks of his profession. Mostly you just stuck someone into a Simworld and then put your feet up while they got on with it. He was getting a little tired of all this Q and A.

'Whatever goes through sensory processing ends up in their memories. And when they come back to the natural world, their recollections will seem quite real to them, I can assure you. As real as any of you might have of our flight to the moon, for example.'

Lenina didn't think much of that comparison: To her mind the flight hadn't felt any different from any simulation she'd experienced. And she wasn't much impressed with Prevezer's high-handed attitude.

'While you're making such a good case for your expertise,' said Lenina, 'you might reassure me that they'll be okay.' Her own experience of simulations had been that they were only as good as the person operating the computer.

Prevezer pulled a face. 'Of course they'll be okay. There would be no point in making a model for them to experiment on if there was a significant risk of injury. They might just as well go ahead and tackle the real thing. Which is not to say that things can't feel very unpleasant, even painful. I mean everyone's heard of bad simulations, right. They can leave you feeling exhausted, even traumatized, but there's nothing physical that can happen to you.'

Even as he said it, Prevezer knew this wasn't true. People frequently died in simulations, but that was usually because they were sick and wanted to go that way.

'Besides, I can usually figure what's happening. I may not be able to see into the simulation itself, but the program numbers give me a good idea of where they are and what's happening and when they've finished in there. Also I keep a close eye on all their vital signs – heart, breathing, brain activity. With experience, you get to recognize when things are going wrong. If they are, you just hit the button and bring them back.' He snapped his fingers. 'Just like that. Hey, listen, no one's ever been injured inside one of my simulations.'

This was only partly true. None of Prevezer's clients had ever been physically injured. But there were a few whose minds had never been the same again.

Lenina looked at Gates and then nodded. 'Glad to hear it. For your sake. Because if anything happens to Gates, you'll need a cyberglove to feel your dick. Understand?'

'What's that supposed to mean?'

'Think about it,' she yawned, for the tenth time in as many minutes. By now she had faced the truth that lay behind her constant state of tiredness, and the rash on her body. There could be no doubt about it. She had less than one hundred and twenty days to live. Much less, to judge by the way she was feeling. 'That guy's all I've got in the world. And I'm not about to let anything happen to him.'

'Everything's going to be just fine,' he insisted, through clenched teeth.

'Good. In that case, I think I'll lie down. Do you

mind if I use your bed, Prev? I'm beat. I don't think I've adjusted to the lunar time zone yet.'

'Be my guest.' Prev watched her go into his bedroom with a mixture of irritation and pity. He'd modeled enough simulations for people with the virus not to recognize the Three Moon phase when he stared it in the face. He guessed that underneath all the makeup Lenina was wearing on her face, there was a rubelli-form rash. He also felt a degree of admiration for her. She was pretty tough just to be walking around like that. He guessed that everyone except Ronica had the same thought. Ronica hadn't seen enough of the virus at close quarters to recognize a Three Moon phase.

'Where exactly are they now?' she asked, when Lenina had gone into Prevezer's bedroom.

'Where else but at the beginning?' he said. 'In the RLV, approaching the Descartes Crater.'

3

I SIMWORLD: ELAPSED TIME 00:00 HOURS

'THREE, TWO, ONE, switch ...'

Dallas opened his eyes to find himself seated on the flight deck of the *Mariner* RLV. In front of him were Gates, in the commander's seat, and Lenina's surrogate, in the pilot's. Leaning slowly forward in the authentic microgravity conditions of a Moon space flight, he touched Gates on the shoulder. The big man started as he saw that they'd made the switch to the simulated world, but instinctively checked the controls first before turning to face Dallas.

'Welcome to the unreal world,' smiled Dallas, although to his touch, it felt real enough. Gates's shoulder, the pressure suit he was now wearing, the back of his own flight-deck chair, the pay-load bay window behind his helmet, the whoosh of the RLV's air conditioning on his face, and the familiar stench of inefficient waste management in his wrinkling nostrils, all of these were reassuringly substantial.

'Thanks,' said Gates, adjusting the microphone in front of his mouth and then his seat belt. 'Feels like we were never in TB at all. Like we dreamed the whole thing, y'know?'

'Except that I had the same dream,' offered Dallas. 'What's our position?'

It was Lenina who answered him, her voice sounding perhaps a little inhuman.

'We're on automatic pilot,' she said. 'Approaching the Descartes Crater along a south-by-southwest course. Our current position is ten degrees latitude by twenty degrees longitude. Altitude one thousand feet. Horizontal velocity, one hundred and twenty miles per hour. Sixty-five miles to target. We'll be there in half an hour.'

Gates pulled off his glove and touched Lenina's cheek experimentally with the back of his hand.

'Hey,' she said. 'What's the deal?'

'How are you feeling?' he asked, amused at how her skin felt as smooth and cool as it had when he'd first met her. She was not wearing makeup and there was no trace of the Three Moon phase of $P^{®}$ that threatened to kill the real Lenina back at the hotel.

Lenina glanced at him, puzzled. 'I feel fine,' she said. 'Why do you ask? Is this some kind of joke?'

'No reason, no joke. Go to manual.'

'Going to manual,' said Lenina and, taking hold of the flight stick, she switched off the autopilot.

'Prepare for Abort to Landing,' he ordered.

'Preparing for ATL,' confirmed Lenina.

'Simou? You there?'

'Of course, I'm here,' said a voice in Gates's headset. 'Where the hell did you think I'd be? I mean, the Galileo's nice, but I signed up for the whole trip, remember?'

Gates turned to grin at Dallas. 'This takes a little getting used to,' he admitted. 'So far this is a pretty realistic simulation.'

'Let's hope so,' said Dallas.

'You ready with that circuit board?' Gates asked Simou.

'It's loaded and ready to roll.'

'Listen up everyone,' said Gates. 'On requesting an ATL from the Descartes computer we'll have to provide cockpit conversations and instrument readings, so from now on, all communications are for real.' He shook his head. 'Whatever that means?'

'What's the matter with you?' frowned Lenina. 'Have you been drinking, or something?'

'Nothing's the matter with me. Just fly the plane.'

The First National's landing facility was a high-security area and strictly forbidden to all lunar flight traffic. Permission to land was given by the Descartes computer only after it had received an authorized descent-to-landing code, at which stage the high-explosive mines that lay underneath the surface of the landing area would be electronically disabled. Any approach by a spaceship that was unauthorized drew the risk of a missile attack. Only in cases of real emergency did the computer have the discretion to allow a ship to put down without the necessary landing codes. However, this required the stricken craft to send the Descartes computer all its in-flight data, as well as cockpit voice recordings. In a matter of seconds, the computer could assess whether the emergency was genuine: first, by analyzing the flight data, and second, by subjecting voice recordings to a polygraphic lie-detector. If it became evident to the computer that a deception was being perpetrated, an emergency landing would be denied and the vehicle fired upon.

To an experienced pilot like Gates, Dallas's solution to this problem was frighteningly straightforward: Simou was to engineer a real in-flight emergency that would trigger itself close to the Descartes Crater. Nothing else but a genuine emergency would do, Dallas had argued, something sufficiently serious that would necessitate an immediate ATL, but that could still be repaired by Simou in the time it took to execute the remainder of the plan. The danger was that a real emergency might force them down short of the landing site: For a spaceship the size of the *Mariner* and in a highland area lacking suitable alternative landing sites, that would be a disaster. A great deal was going to depend on Gates's skill as a pilot, and very possibly, as a liar. Either way, there was a considerable amount of risk involved, something the real Simou had already stated.

'If you balance a pencil on its point, it will always fall down. It always obeys the law of gravity – at least, it does when you're on Earth. The trouble is that you can never predict which way the pencil will fall. The law of gravity's a very precise law, but with a very imprecise outcome. In other words, without knowing the exact condition of the *Mariner*, not to mention the precise flight conditions and a whole load of other variables that frankly can't be calculated, it's impossible to predict how this RLV – like the pencil – will behave in the circumstances. What we have here is a system that contains an extreme sensitivity to its starting conditions, so that the smallest variation in those conditions might lead to some very different outcomes. We might explode. We might implode. We might crash-land. We might make it to the landing area and be unable to carry out repairs. I don't know what the rest of your plan entails, Dallas, but if it's anything like this part, then we have our work cut out for us.'

'No one ever said this was going to be easy,' Dallas

had answered. 'I always thought that this would be the most hazardous stage of the plan, not least because it puts everyone at risk, instead of just me and Gates when we break into the main facility. But calculated risk is part of the strategy. That's why we're trying things out in the simulation first. To assess the risks and, where possible, to minimize them.'

For several minutes the simulated flight proceeded in silence as everyone waited for the emergency: a tiny explosive charge, designed to imitate the impact of a grain-sized meterorite traveling at ten miles per second, placed by Simou on the RLV's nose, just below the cockpit window, between the aluminium skin of the fuselage and the ceramic-hafnium heat shield. The chances of such a thing happening for real were almost insignificant, but the consequences extremely serious.

Gates found himself holding his breath, a little surprised that a simulation could create such a feeling of tension. As an astroliner pilot, he'd spent many hours in simulators learning to cope with whatever the instructors might throw at him: main engine failures, throttle failures, reaction control system failures, attitude control system failures, even computer failures, but never anything like this – so many other malfunctions were always more probable than the scenario that was about to unfold. But then unpredictability was, as Simou had argued, the hallmark of any bona fide accident.

Suddenly, a loud bang – louder than Gates had been anticipating – rocked the *Mariner*, blasting a tiny hole no bigger than a pinhead through the cockpit fuselage and setting off the master alarm. Gates shuddered involuntarily, genuinely scared by the actuality of what had apparently happened. The urgency in his voice was real enough.

'Jesus Christ, we're losing pressure. Go to oxygen. Close off mid-deck.'

Dallas jumped from his seat to close the interdeck access hatch. At the same time he pulled down the visor to his helmet and switched on his own oxygen.

'Hatch door closed,' he confirmed, and then buckled himself back into his seat. He heard another loud bang as the *Mariner*'s reaction control system rockets fired to correct the RLV as it rolled around its own longitudinal axis in response to the propulsive action of the cabin air venting into space.

'We've been hit by something,' yelled Lenina. 'Must have been a small meteorite.'

They heard another loud bang as the primary thruster fired. From inside the *Mariner* it sounded like a cannon going off. This time the RLV began to pitch around its own transverse axis. The primary thrusters, used for rapid rotations or for moving the RLV sideways in orbit, were proving much too powerful for Gates to use in attempting to steady the spacecraft.

'Switching off primaries,' he yelled. 'Going to stick control.'

The vernier thrusters, a smaller type of thruster, had a gentler effect on the RLV's orientation; these were operated by the ship's computer and fired in response to the motion and direction of the flight stick.

'We're going to have to abort to landing,' declared Gates.

'Got a lot of pressure building up in those maneuvering fuel tanks.'

'Forget about it,' said Gates. 'Just look for a landing site.'

Lenina was already looking out of the window.

'This is all high ground,' she reported. 'You couldn't land a football around here. Wait a minute.' She was looking at the computer now. 'There's a landing facility on the Moon map. Dead ahead. Ten miles. How's that for luck. It's restricted, but maybe they'll let us land. Can we make that?'

Inside his helmet Gates felt a bead of sweat roll down his face and onto his lips. It tasted of salt. But was the taste real, or synthetic?

'Incoming transmission,' said Lenina.

'This is the First National Blood Bank at Descartes Crater,' said the voice. 'You are approaching a restricted area. Please turn left onto a heading of one-zero-zero, and increase your altitude to two thousand feet.'

'Negative to that, Descartes,' said Gates. 'We have an ATL emergency here. Requesting permission to land.'

'Permission denied. I repeat, this is a restricted area. Without proper authorization you cannot ATL here. Our landing area is laid with antispacecraft mines.'

The RLV shuddered as Gates tried to hold her steady.

'I'm not talking about a flat tire, Descartes,' he yelled. 'We are venting air. Repeat, we are venting air. We're coming down with or without your permission. Passing you by is not an option. We'll have to take our chances with your mines.'

'Pressure still building in those thruster tanks,' Lenina said coolly.

'If we close the valves, we won't even make it as far as Descartes,' Gates shouted back at her.

'It's that, or blow up,' she told him.

'Shunt some of the propellant into the main fuel tanks. Jesus Christ, do I have to think of everything?'

'Shunting propellant.'

With his hands gripping the armrests of his seat,

Dallas glanced out of the flight-deck window. He could see the main facility in front of them now – like a gold coin lost on a volcanic beach. 'There it is,' he said. 'Dead ahead.'

'Dead's about right, unless we get permission to land,' said Gates, as he swallowed deeply. This was proving to be much more realistic than he had ever bargained for. His heart was beating as if he'd run up several flights of stairs. Even if they did receive the Descartes computer's permission to land, bringing the *Mariner* down wasn't going to be easy. With each touch of the flight stick the RLV pitched from side to side.

'*Mariner*, please transmit all flight data and CVRs for verification of your emergency situation.'

'Now you're talking,' said Lenina. This was what they had been waiting to hear, and she immediately ordered the flight computers to comply. 'Sending flight data and CVRs.'

'Received,' said Descartes. 'And analyzing.'

'Make it fast,' said Gates as he wrestled to control the unwieldy craft. 'We're committed to an ATL whether you like it or not.' He throttled back the main engines to less than 10 percent of power and dropped the undercarriage. They were losing altitude fast now. The landing area was less than a mile away. In just over a minute they would be down on the ground whatever the computer decided.

'Descartes, this is *Mariner*. What is our landing status?'

There was no reply on his headset. Less than half a mile now. He glimpsed the whole facility ahead, golden in the sunlight, like the lost city of El Dorado.

'Thirty seconds to landing,' said Lenina.

The *Mariner* shuddered again.

'I wish I could control this damned roll,' said Gates. 'Damn it, Descartes, what is our status please?'

Still no reply. Gates was starting to wonder what it might feel like to be blown to pieces in a simulation. He knew you could experience great pleasure – he'd had enough Simsex in his time to know the truth of that – so why not great pain, too?

'Hang on everyone,' he said into his mike. 'We're going down.' The strain of the moment was in his voice for everyone, including the computer, to hear. A hundred yards to go and still no answer. 'Is there anyone there? Please, someone.'

Even as he spoke, he recognized the futility of his words. The facility at the First National was unmanned. Descartes was all there was. It was just a computer between them and simulated oblivion.

'Here we go ...'

'*Mariner*, you are clear at ATL. All mines have been disarmed.'

Gates did not reply. It was too late to say anything at all. The landing site rushed up at him and was obliterated by the RLV's giant shadow. The next second they were down on the ground with a loud bang, like the sound of a fast-moving truck hitting an enormous bump on the road. Quickly, Gates hit the engine stop button and said, 'Shutting down engines.' Then he collapsed back in his seat, already exhausted.

Lenina started to go through the checklist that automatically followed any landing. Gates turned around to look at Dallas. The two men grinned at each other and exchanged a punched handshake in silence.

'Descartes, this is *Mariner*,' said Lenina. 'We're on the ground.'

'*Mariner*, we copy you on the ground.'

'Stand by, Descartes,' she said, and switching off

their open channel, she began to key their new status into the flight computer.

'Jesus, that was close,' said Gates. 'For a moment there. Tell me we're still alive.'

'I think, therefore I am,' said Dallas, as he unbuckled his seat harness and climbed almost weightlessly to his feet. 'I'd say that was a pretty useful experience, wouldn't you?'

'Sure. It's convinced me of two things. One is that I need some synthetic nerves. Mine are shot to pieces. And the other is that this plan of yours is crazy.'

'It worked, didn't it? Come on, there's lots to do.'

'That's what I'm afraid of.'

II SIMWORLD: ELAPSED TIME I HOUR OI MINUTES

Before leaving the flight deck, Dallas opened the payload bay doors and used the remote manipulator system to deploy what looked like the wingless fuselage of a smaller RLV. Entirely covered with the ceramic-hafnium tiles that protected only the nose, bottom, and wingtips of the *Mariner*, this was the space fridge, designed to carry perishable material back to Earth. Equipped with three primary thruster engines and two folding wings, it was the same model used by the blood banks themselves: the space fridge[1]

[1] Keeping things cool in space can be a problem, especially during Earth reentry, when outside temperatures can reach seven hundred four degrees Celsius. The answer is the space fridge, a combination of technologies that are several hundred years apart. Partly it is based on a mechanical cooler known as a Stirling cycle fridge, a device conceived in 1816 by Robert Stirling, a Scottish clergyman. This technology cools the contents to only 20 Kelvins,

attached to the rear of the RLV, thereby doubling the available cargo capacity from two tons to four. Dallas had good reason for deploying the fridge immediately, as he would shortly explain to Rameses Gates.

But first there was a medical emergency to fabricate. Once Dallas was on mid-deck with the rest of the team, the hatch was closed and the crew quarters were repressurized so that Ronica could remove her pressure suit. As soon as she was wearing just her underwear, she lay down on a hammock and attached herself to a computerized transfusion machine so that she could carry out her own phlebotomy.

'One medical emergency, coming up,' she said.

As the venipuncture proceeded automatically, Ronica's blood began to be drawn into a plastic tube. With no gravity to speak of, a pump in the machine was slowly sucking the life's blood out of her body like a mechanical vampire. She was used to the usual autologous donation of 10 percent of her total blood volume. Weighing one hundred and forty pounds, she had a total volume of just under five thousand milliliters, and by her own estimate, any donation of more than 20 percent, twice as much as normal, would prompt her body to exhibit the hypovolemic reaction Dallas was after. The noise the pump made while performing this task was disconcertingly sibilant, and apparently quenchless. Rather more quietly, the same machine's computer recorded the transfusion rate and all her vital signs. It was this medical data, conveying

---

still well above absolute zero. The final cooling stage, in which the temperature inside the fridge drops to 0.1 Kelvins, operates using helium dilution, and was developed by Alan Benoit, in 1991. Without the space fridge, the transport of perishable materials in bulk, to and from the Earth, would be impossible.

an apparent medical emergency, that Dallas planned to transmit to the Descartes computer.

'Ten percent,' he noted.

Ronica kept her eyes on the crimson snake beside her bare arm.

'How do you feel?'

Taking a deep breath, she glanced over at the computer readings and then closed her eyes. 'A little faint,' she admitted.

Still the pump kept on sucking the blood out of her.

'Fifteen percent,' said Dallas. 'Systolic and diastolic pressures falling now.' He picked up her wrist and checked the pulse pressure. Her skin felt cold and clammy to his touch.

Ronica took a deep breath and swallowed nervously. 'Where do you get these good ideas, Dallas?' she asked.

'They just come to me, through the ether, at the speed of light.'

'That can't be true,' she said, eyelids flickering. 'No signals carrying information can travel faster than light.'

'Twenty percent.'

'Not feeling so good now. Nauseous. Must be something I ate.'

'I hope she doesn't vomit,' said Simou, unfolding a plastic bag. 'Smells bad enough in here already.'

'Maybe you'd like to volunteer for this instead,' said Lenina.

'Not me. I've got a puncture to mend, remember?'

'Then shut up.'

'Twenty-five percent,' said Dallas.

Ronica retched again.

'You'd better start talking to Descartes,' Dallas told

Gates. 'Another few minutes and she'll be in hemorrhagic shock.'

Gates was already positioned close to the radio. He flicked on a switch to open a channel.

'Descartes, this is *Mariner*.'

'I've been trying to contact you *Mariner*,' said Descartes. 'What is your status, please?'

'I can confirm that we were probably struck by a tiny meteorite,' said Gates. 'It penetrated the ship's hull, causing a slow decompression on the flight deck. Until we can make repairs, that area's sealed off. So there's no immediate danger of asphyxiation.'

'I'm glad to hear that, *Mariner*.'

'In a while, a couple of my crew will go EVA and fix the hole with the UHT electron-beam welder.[1] However, right now, I have a more immediate problem on my hands. One of my female crew has been injured. It would seem the meterorite struck her, like a bullet. There's no damage to any of her vital organs, but she's lost an awful lot of blood. Since we're going to be here for several hours I'd like to request some RES Class One whole blood component, in order to carry out an infusion.'

'This isn't a clearing bank, Mariner,' explained Descartes. 'It's a federal reserve. This bank exists to guarantee other blood banks on Earth. People don't

---

[1] Electron-beam welding was perfected in the Ukraine, during the late twentieth century and on the Russian space program. Electrons are boiled off from a heated filament, accelerated, and then focused onto the target metal, or rock. When the electrons collide with the atoms in the subject material, their kinetic energy is converted to heat energy. However, any gas will disrupt the beam, causing dangerous arcing between tool and surface. This makes the tool ideal for work in the vacuum of space.

make deposits. Nor are they withdrawn. Blood supplies are sold in order to help the government balance its books and meet its borrowing commitments. When times are good it will buy supplies to meet any future borrowing requirements. That's the way it works here. And besides, the blood here is deep-frozen. You would have to thaw it first.'

'Thirty percent,' announced Dallas. 'She's going into shock.'

'I'm well aware of all that, Descartes,' Gates told the computer. 'I'm also aware of what it says in the International Convention of World Blood Banks. That's the convention that exists to protect all autologous donors in emergencies. According to section fourteen, paragraph ten, and I quote, "Provided authorized autologous donation codes are given, all banks, regardless of their hematological charter, are obliged to provide autologous donors with the necessary components in an emergency." End quote. You can leave the preparation to us.'

'You're very well informed,' said Descartes. 'However, I must insist on conducting my own patient evaluation. Are your crew member's vital signs being monitored by a computer, *Mariner*?'

'Affirmative, Descartes. Anticipating your compliance with section fourteen, paragraph ten, and to save time, she's already been hooked up to a trans-infusion pump. I'm sending you her vitals, now.' Gates flicked a switch on the communications panel, and then covered the microphone with the palm of his hand.

'Let's hope Descartes goes for it,' he told Dallas. 'How's she doing?'

Ronica looked pale and feverish. The rest of the crew watched her with a concern that was only partly due to her physical condition: If the Descartes computer considered her phlebotomy was not urgent, they were stalled.

'Her body temperature's way down,' said Dallas, reading what appeared on the computer screen. 'And she's showing signs of tachycardia and insufficient tissue perfusion.'

'From the data you've sent me,' said Descartes, 'it would seem that she's still losing blood. I can hardly organize you a specific delivery of component until I know how much she will need. To do that you will first need to stabilize her condition.'

Dallas winced and switched off the pump. He should have thought of that. He waited a minute until the trans-infusion computer had had sufficient time to register that no more blood was being drawn, and then nodded at Gates.

'Descartes? I think we've managed to stabilize her now,' reported Gates. 'Sending you new data to confirm that.' He paused for a moment. 'Do you copy?'

'Affirmative, *Mariner*. According to the data you have sent me, she requires fourteen hundred and thirty two milliliters of blood, type O, genotype OO, phenotype O, showing H-substance red-cell antigens, and all normal plasma antibodies. Please provide me with your crew member's autologous donor validation code, now.'

Gates picked up Ronica's hand and read the tag she always wore around her wrist.

'O-L-O-I/ 0.45. 1.80. 0.75. 0.75.'

'Password?'

'Mizpah.'

'Confirmed,' said Descartes. 'Three units have been debited from your crew member's deposit account.

The cryoprecipitate will be with you presently. Please await further instructions for its retrieval.'

'Thanks,' said Gates, and closing the communications channel, he immediately put the trans-infusion machine into reverse, pumping the blood that had been removed straight back into Ronica's body.

It wasn't blood he wanted from the First National's vault right now, it was the electric car that delivered it.

III SIMWORLD: ELAPSED TIME 1 HOUR 49 MINUTES

A small cylindrical airlock provided access between the mid-deck section and the payload bay. Swallowing a dysbaric pill, a quick chemical means of purging the bloodstream of all nitrogen (previously astronauts undertaking EVA were required to breathe pure oxygen for three hours to prevent dysbarism), Dallas and Gates entered the airlock, closed the door to mid-deck behind them, and climbed into their EVA space suits. These were bulkier than the pressurized suits worn during ascent and descent and provided enough power and oxygen for extra-vehicular activity for upward of sixteen hours. Dallas figured they might need every minute of that time, although he knew there were replacement supplies to be found inside the main facility.

As soon as they were secure in their suits, they pumped out the airlock and then went through the door that led into the open payload bay. Then they closed the airlock door behind them and pressurized the compartment so that Simou and Prevezer could follow.

Standing there in the open payload bay, Gates had

his first real opportunity to have a good look at the First National's main facility – during the landing he'd been too busy trying not to crash the RLV to spend any time admiring Dallas's apparently impregnable design. The main facility was located about a quarter of a mile to the west of the landing site, at the end of a flat road about ten yards wide and several hundred yards long. Both the landing site and the main facility were enclosed by a series of high-voltage fences powered by a field of photovoltaic cells that lay about a hundred yards beyond the perimeter wire to the south. And in the distance, he could see the rim of the surrounding Descartes Crater, where the surface-to-air missile systems protecting the First National and its precious supplies were mounted. The main facility building itself was completely circular and gently vaulted, so that the whole thing looked like the shell of a sea urchin. Ostensibly constructed of one giant dome of breccia-concrete and painted gold to protect the deep-frozen contents against the heat of the bright sunlight, the construction was, as Dallas told Gates, actually composed of a series of concrete shapes that met three to a vertex.

'It's a design that was inspired by the Eskimo igloo,' he said, 'in that the structure is held up by the rigidity of local planar areas.'

They were using an encrypted frequency to avoid being overheard by the Descartes computer.

'Very impressive, I'm sure,' said Gates, who had no more idea of what an igloo looked like than he did of the Eskimo who built one. He pointed to the area of soil and rocks that lay on either side of the landing site and the golden road that led to it. Dallas had already told him that unauthorized road users would be electrocuted. 'What happens down there?' he asked.

'Why not forget about the road and walk across the dirt?'

'Because of the solar-powered seismographs,' said Dallas. 'Very sensitive. And the mine field they control. You wouldn't get ten yards. Take my word for it. The road is the best way.'

Dallas pointed to where the road led into the main facility. 'That's where our transport will be coming from. Come on. We've got to get properly chilled before we can take our seats.'

'Get chilled or get killed,' grumbled Gates, as he followed Dallas along the floor of the payload bay, using the handrail to steady himself as he went. Near the back of the bay, each man collected a backpack containing all the equipment he would need inside the facility and then jumped over the side of the *Mariner*.

Both men heard Prevezer's voice on their headsets as they bounced their way across the landing area to where the *Mariner*'s robot arm had placed the space fridge.

'Descartes just told us the blood wagon's on its way,' he said. 'And so are we. We're entering the airlock now, to suit up.'

'Give us ten minutes in the space fridge, and then pull us out,' Dallas told Prevezer. 'Then proceed as planned.'

'Roger, that.'

As they walked the few yards to the space fridge, each man drew down his helmet's gold-painted outer visor to reflect the lunar Sun's unfiltered glare. On the Moon, a morning lasts for seven days. It takes a whole week for the Sun to climb to its zenith in the black sky, and another week for it to set again, before vanishing behind the western horizon. So close to the lunar equator as Descartes was, Moon temperatures could climb as high as one hundred and ten degrees Celsius (225°F), while at night they could drop as low as minus one hundred fifty-two degrees Celsius (–243°F). It was now 7:30 P.M. local Moon time, and with the whole crater still bathed in bright sunshine, the evening temperature on the landing site was over one hundred degrees Celsius. In the heat, Gates was glad of his water-cooled underwear, although he was acutely aware of just how cold he was about to get.

'Wouldn't this have been easier at night?' he asked. 'I mean, cooling down n'all?'

'Much easier,' agreed Dallas. 'But how would you like to try and make that landing in near darkness?'

'You have a point,' conceded Gates. He opened the door to the fridge and stepped into its cold, dark interior. 'Shit, I wouldn't like to make that landing again in a goddamn simulation.'

Dallas followed Gates inside the fridge, flipped up the golden visor, and switched on his helmet light to illuminate the fridge before closing the door.

Two large heavy-duty polyethylene bags were waiting for them, tethered to the wall of the fridge and spread open like waiting pupae. Backing into one of the bags, Gates zipped it up from the inside and then sat down on a empty cryoprecipitate storage unit. He shook his head and checked his watch, shivering as the near absolute zero temperature of the fridge began to permeate his body bag. 'Remind me why we're doing all this ice-cube business again, Dallas.'

Zipped inside his own body bag, Dallas sat alongside him. 'You know why we're doing this.'

'Yes, but it'll make conversation while we simulate getting hypothermia and freezing to death.'

'Prevezer's keeping a close eye on our vital signs in

the real world,' insisted Dallas. 'He'll end the simulation if he thinks we're in trouble. Besides, a hypothermia victim is never dead, only cold. Fact is, you can demonstrate all the clinical signs of death and still be revived. It's a condition called metabolic icebox.'

'That's now. But who's going to look after us when it's time for the real deal?'

'This is a necessary risk,' explained Dallas. 'That is, if we want this stage of the plan to succeed.' He shivered as cold began to permeate his body. Then the fridge gave a shudder and produced a dull mechanical noise.

'What was that?' asked Gates.

'Helium isotopes venting into space,' said Dallas. 'It means that the fridge is doing its job properly. Drawing heat away from us efficiently.'

'That's comforting,' trembled Gates.

'It ought to be. Might be kind of unpleasant for us if our surface temperature stays too high.'

'That's what I meant to ask you, Dallas. In what way unpleasant? You didn't say.'

'You really want to know?'

'In case you hadn't noticed, I'm already living dangerously.'

'Okay, you asked for it. Prev and Sim will fetch us out of here and carry us to the electric blood wagon. That way the car's microwave motion detectors will collect only two approaching body signals. Shouldn't be too difficult for them. Even carrying a big ox like you. Neither of us weighs more than thirty to forty pounds in one-sixth g.

'They'll dump us inside one of the cars, collect the units of blood for Ronica, close the lid of the car, and then move away again. The car computer checks for two retreating signals – Prev and Sim – and then heads back down the golden road to Samarkand. If there aren't two retreating signals, then Prev and Sim are in big trouble. The computer fires a laser called a Dazer. Even from behind a sun visor it's more than enough to blind you. Then they'd probably wander off into the mine field and good-bye both.'

'The hell with their comfort and convenience,' said Gates. 'What about us?'

'All units of cryoprecipitate have to be stored at minus one hundred and twenty degrees Celsius. Stored and transported to the First Nation's own RLVs. Each refrigerated car is equipped with a thermal heat sensor to protect the integrity of the cryoprecipitate being transported.'

'Right,' grunted Gates, who was shivering all the time now. According to the readout on his life-support system computer his core body temperature had already dropped below normal. 'S'why we're in here, I know all that.'

'If the sensors detect heat, any heat at all, the on-board computer will assume that the blood has been compromised and then deploy a nanodevice to destroy the units. This is a simple molecular disassembler manufactured to behave like a bacteria. It eats the compromised units, container bags, labels, everything. And then dies. The car contents are then disinfected and vented into space. I'm afraid you and I would be treated in the same way. The nanodevice would eat through our space suits and then us. By the time it finished we'd look like moondust.'

A great spasm of a shiver ran down Gates's broad back. He was uncertain if this was the result of fear or cold, and finally concluded that it was probably both.

'Jesus,' he said through chattering teeth. 'Christ.'

'By my estimate, we only have sufficient time to get

through the main facility door before what body heat remains inside our suits starts to get out and be detected by the sensors. But for this, we could ride the car all the way through the inner labyrinth door and into the vault itself. Instead, we exit as soon as we're through the main door and then head for the rest and recreation area to get warm again, before proceeding to the next stage.'

'I can hardly wait,' Gates said dully. His hands were numb and his core temperature had now dropped to ninety-five degrees Fahrenheit.

'It's a nice balance.' Dallas's speech was already sounding slurred, an early sign of mild hypothermia.

'Nice?' Gates laughed flatly.

'Nice. Meaning something requiring great precision.'

'And I thought it meant nice, as in nice and warm. Whatever the hell that is.'

'What I mean is that if we don't get cold enough, we get killed by the nanodevice. But if we got too cold, we die as well.'

'Oh, that kind of nice. Of course. Dumb of me. I'm shivering like I've got a motor disease.'

'When you stop, you can start to worry,' Dallas told him. 'Means heat output from burning glycogen in your muscles. Insufficient. Shivering in waves. Pauses get longer. Until stops altogether. Life threatening.'

The next two or three minutes passed in frozen silence.

Dallas gave a little jump as he heard Prevezer's voice inside his headset.

'Okay, cold people, let's go.'

'What?'

Dallas felt himself picked up like a side of frozen

meat. Why were they being carried, and to where? His thinking processes seemed as frozen as his toes. Something to do with blood. Not the same blood as moved slowly inside him. Different. Lunar sunshine streamed through his unvisored helmet, dazzling him for a second until, slowly closing his eyes, he remembered. Amnesia. Somewhere on the edge of severe hypothermia. Body temperature probably as low as ninety degrees Fahrenheit. Maybe lower. Couldn't see his EVA computer to check. Much lower than that and they'd really be in trouble. Needed brain to perform something that required higher reasoning. To stay fully conscious inside the electric car. Otherwise might forget to climb out.

Dallas began to count backward from one hundred by nines.

'Ninety-one,' he mumbled as Prevezer laid him carefully in the car's frozen interior. 'Eighty-two.' Why was the man carrying him – he couldn't see if it was Simou or Prevezer – breathing so heavily? Whoever it was sounded like there was something the matter with him.

'Dallas? Gates? You're both in the car.'

'Seventy-three.'

'Come again?'

'He's counting backward by nines to keep his mind alert.'

'Please collect your components, close the car, and then step away,' ordered the transport computer.

'Whatever you say,' said someone, and then the lid on the car was closed.

There wasn't supposed to be an opportunity for dialogue with this particular computer, so no open communications channel existed between them; but the channel that existed between the two men lying inside the car and the two men now stepping away from it would last only as long as they were all outside the main facility. Dallas and Gates were relying on Simou and Prevezer to tell them when the car was about to pass through the main door, thus giving them their cue to get out. Once they were through the outer door, Dallas and Gates would have no further verbal contact with the outside until the vault had been breached.

'Good luck, guys.'

'Yeah, good luck.'

'Sixty-four.'

The car, the shape and proportions of a medium-sized missile, began its silent return to the main facility.

'Dallas? This is Prev. You're on the move.'

'Fifty-four. Fifty-five. Fifty-four.'

'Talk to me, Gates,' said Simou.

'Cold,' said Gates.

'Forty ... forty-six.'

'Terribly cold,' he whispered. And then, 'Who's there?'

'It's me, Gates. Simou. What's your name?'

'Thirty-something.'

'My name?'

'What's your name?'

'Thirty-what, Dallas,' said Prevezer. 'Come on, think man. What comes after forty-six?'

'Seven. Forty-seven.'

'My name is ...'

'Negative, Dallas. Think. You were counting backward by nines. If you were hypothermic, you couldn't do that. Come on, Dallas. You're halfway there. Just a little longer.'

'Gates. Your name is Rameses Gates. Can you hear me?'

'Come on, Dallas. What's the next number in the sequence?'

'Gates, answer me.'

'Thirty-seven, Dallas. The answer's thirty-seven. Dallas? Are you reading me?'

IV SIMWORLD: ELAPSED TIME 2 HOURS 30 MINUTES

Lying in the frozen interior of the electric car, Dallas opened his eyes and tried to remember. For some reason, a number came into his cold and aching head. Twenty-eight. What was the significance of that? But what did it matter now that he was dead and lying inside his tomb? Lying there like some sepulchral statue? One short sleep past, we wake eternally and death shall be no more. This living buried man, this quiet mandrake, rest. A voice followed this number.

'Wake up, Dallas, wake up. The outer door's opening. You're about to enter the main facility.'

Until that moment he had not been afraid. But when he saw how close to a frozen death he had come, panic seized him and galvanized his almost rigid muscles. He had momentarily forgotten that this was still a simulation.

'Get up, Gates. For Christ's sake move. The door's inside. The car's going forward again. Dallas? Move *now*.'

For a brief second, Dallas had thought he was dreaming. But at last he recognized that this was Prevezer urging them both to action. Quickly he unzipped the polyethylene bag and struggled to his feet, his helmet forcing open the door on top of the electric car. And even as he climbed, then half-jumped, out of the car into the bright light of the main facility's entrance hall, he recognized that he would have to devise something more certain than the voices of Prevezer and Simou to rouse him when it came to the real thing.

'Dallas,' he heard himself mumble as Prevezer and Simou cheered. 'Back on-line.'

'We're about to lose your signal,' said Simou. 'Good-bye, Dallas, and good luck.'

Glancing around him he saw that the outer door of the facility had started to slide shut behind them. They had made it, although Gates had yet to stir from the floor of the car.

'Thanks,' he said.

Whatever Prevezer and Simou said next was lost as the outer door closed as silently as it had opened.

'Gates, come on, we've got to move.'

The other man remained motionless. Dallas reached down and picked him up, grateful for the microgravity that made possible such a superhuman feat of strength. And not a moment too soon. Even as he carried Gates across the entrance hall and laid him against the airlock door that led into the rest and recreation area, the single inner door leading into the labyrinth opened, and the electric car disappeared into the Stygian darkness beyond. Then the entrance to the labyrinth closed again. No one – not even the First National security workers who handled the supplies of cryoprecipitate – were allowed beyond this door, which was itself protected by a number of safeguards: proximity detectors and mechanical vibration detectors that could activate lethal bolts of electricity. Anyone close to the car's exterior as it entered the labyrinth would have been fried to a crisp.

Gates remained motionless on the ground, still wrapped inside the body bag. If not for the fact that it and his space suit were intact, Dallas might have suspected that he had already succumbed to the molecular disassembler. Instead Gates had clearly suffered some kind of hypothermic reaction which made it imperative that Dallas, who was himself chilled to the bone, get him warmed up as soon as possible. Dallas switched on the heaters in both their suits, filling them with hot air. Then he dragged Gates into the airlock and repressurized the chamber before opening the hatch that led into the R&R area.

Once Gates was out of the body bag, Dallas was able to see his life-support computer and read off the man's vital signs. These were not encouraging: Gate's core body temperature was down to only eight-two degrees Fahrenheit – much colder than Dallas, while the heart rate was twenty per minute and the breathing rate just one every fifteen seconds. Perhaps having the virus had made him extra sensitive to the extreme cold. After all, body temperature was everything to do with surface blood flow and vasodilation. The only plausible explanation for what had happened to Gates, but not to Dallas, was that having P^2 resulted in a quicker maximal vasodilation and increased cutaneous blood flow.

Feeling a little warmer now, Dallas took off his own helmet but decided not to remove Gates's, so as to help hot air circulate inside the man's self-contained environment. Searching the frost-covered plastic shielding on the other man's face he found no indication of life and, had it not been for the vital signs displayed on

Gates's life-support computer, he might have assumed his friend was dead. It was clear that he was looking at a case of metabolic icebox.

What Dallas really couldn't understand was why Prevezer hadn't simply ended the simulation by now. Here was Gates, only just alive, with a hardly discernible heart rate and a core body temperature that ought to have told Prevezer something had gone badly wrong, and yet still the simulation continued. Dallas didn't think it was possible for Gates to die in the simulation, but he hardly felt he could neglect his condition on the assumption that at any minute they would find themselves switched back into the Galileo Hotel and the real world. He had no alternative but to keep Gates warm and wait for his vital signs to improve.

Dallas stood up, stretched out a painful cramp in his leg, and suddenly found he badly wanted to pee. He recognized this was a sign of cold diuresis: vasoconstriction created a greater volume of pressure in the bloodstream, resulting in his kidneys pulling off excess fluid to reduce the pressure. A full bladder was another opportunity for his body to lose heat, so urinating would serve to help him get warm again. There was no time to find a washroom. Fumbling with numb fingers to open the codpiece on his spacesuit, he stumbled toward a corner of the R&R area to relieve himself. Besides, in the simulation, he didn't much care how he left the R&R area, especially as he expected the simulation to end at any moment. But when he'd finished urinating and found it still remained in progress, he quickly checked on Gates and then went to find the galley, intent on making them both a hot drink.

V

'You know, if you fire that thing,' Prevezer said carefully, 'your bullet will go straight through a human body and then shatter the window. We'll all be killed when the room depressurizes.'

'You let me worry about the gun,' insisted Rimmer. 'You just concentrate on doing what I tell you, friend. Besides ...' He collected a small bust of Galileo off the suite's writing desk and launched it at the window. It bounced off the glass, ricocheted back into the room, and was neatly caught by Simou. Rimmer smiled and added redundantly, 'Don't you know anything? It's armor-plated. After all, you never can tell when a meteorite's going to give you a cold call from deep space. I thought everyone knew that. Or maybe you just haven't stayed here before.' He waved the gun at the bust in Simou's hands. 'I wouldn't get any ideas with that thing, if I were you. Ronica will tell you that I'm the gregarious type. I like killing new people.'

'Do exactly what he says, Sim,' Ronica advised him.

Simou placed the bust slowly on the marble floor. Rimmer nodded his approval and then looked at the faces of the other two men in the room – Cavor and Prevezer – sizing them up for any resistance. Cavor understood this and felt certain that Rimmer would underestimate him. In which case he might stand a chance of disarming Rimmer.

'Ronica and I, we've met before,' Rimmer told the three of them. 'You gentlemen should be careful of her. She's the treacherous type. Aren't you, Roni? You carrying a gun, sweetheart?'

'Not this time, Rimmer.'

'Better let me see those panties – make sure.'

Rimmer jerked the gun at the ceiling. 'So lift that pretty dress you're wearing and show me there's nothing more lethal down there than what the Lord gave you to have dominion over men.'

Ronica knew better than to argue with Rimmer. She took hold of the hem of her dress, and lifted it as ordered.

'Mmm,' said Rimmer. 'You're wearing my favorite kind of underwear. None.' He shrugged. 'Looks like you were stripped for action, Roni. I guess this is a love hotel.'

Ronica sneered. 'Satisfied?'

'I'll get to you in a while. We've got some unfinished business, you and I.'

Ronica smoothed her dress down over her thighs.

Rimmer turned toward Prevezer. 'I'll take a wild guess here. Dallas and the big guy are taking a trip in virtual reality and you're the tour guide, right?'

'I prefer the term "Simulated World" myself,' said Prevezer.

'Oh, you do, huh?' Rimmer waved the gun at the others. 'Okay, apart from the man who just expressed a preference, I want everyone else belly-down on the floor with your hands on the back of your neck.'

Cavor, Ronica, and Prevezer knelt and then prostrated themselves on the floor as ordered. Cavor recognized that there was little chance of any of them tackling Rimmer while they were on the floor. Clearly, Rimmer knew what he was doing.

'Shall I tell you what I think is going on here? I think,' Rimmer wagged his finger thoughtfully, 'I think that Dallas and friend are carrying out a little experiment. I think they're using virtual reality ...' He smiled at Prevezer as if challenging the other man to contradict him. '... To test the integrity of a plan you're all intending to carry out for real. Now this part is just a guess. But I'd say you and he are planning to rob the First National Blood Bank. Am I right?'

Prevezer said nothing. Rimmer put the gun against his head and repeated the question.

'Am I right?'

Prevezer nodded. 'You're right.'

Rimmer sniffed. 'Reality, huh? The more we try to get a hold on it, render it, depict it, the more it eludes us. Explain how your setup works.'

While Prevezer told him how the simulation operated, Rimmer stared through the mesh-screen sphere that enveloped Dallas's head. With eyes closed and his face entirely immobile, Dallas looked quite peaceful, almost as if he was asleep. There was just the odd flurry of rapid eye movement to indicate some activity inside the brain.

When he had been told all he needed to know, Rimmer bit his lip excitedly. Dallas looked like he was merely dreaming. But perhaps a nightmare was what was required.

'How real is it for them in the simulation?'

'Indistinguishable from the real world,' admitted Prevezer, professional pride getting the better of his tongue. 'They're aware that it's a simulation, but all their senses inform them that it's very real. They can experience all normal physiological thresholds.'

Rimmer was intrigued. 'Would that include the pain threshold, by any chance?' When Prevezer said nothing, Rimmer replaced the barrel of the gun against his head. 'I won't hesitate to shoot you, my godlike friend. Please answer.'

'Yes. All normal physiological thresholds.'

'Good. So how are they getting on, right now?' he asked.

'Not so good.' Prevezer showed him the two men's vital signs on the computer screen. 'These numbers relate to their physiological responses inside the simulation. They tell us how their bodies are reacting even as we speak. Heart rates, body temperatures, lung function spirometry, blood pressure response, everything. As you can see with Gates, his body temperature is very cold and his heart rate is way down. If you weren't here, I'd have brought him back to reality by now.'

'I'm not much interested in him,' said Rimmer. 'What about Dallas?'

'Not as bad. Even so, I'd probably have brought him back too. All I have to do to make the switch is press this button.' Prevezer reached for the button and then yelped as Rimmer smacked his hand hard with the gun.

'Not until I'm good and ready. First, we're going to have some fun.' Rimmer sneered at Dallas. 'It's your own fault, you arrogant bastard. Haven't you heard? The wise man's eyes are in his head, but the fool walketh in darkness.' He looked at Prevezer. 'You. Think of some shit to throw at them.'

'What did you have in mind?'

'Not in my mind, I think,' chuckled Rimmer. 'Reprogram something bad for them.'

'The place they're in right now,' said Prevezer. 'It would take me a long time to reprogram that. More time than I assume you have. Days probably.'

Rimmer looked at Prevezer through narrowed eyes. 'This is your thing, isn't it? Simulations.'

'Yes.'

'I've used them myself. Killing games mostly. You know the kind of thing. See how many monsters you can blast to bits inside an hour. In my experience, a good simulation engineer usually has a whole plethora of programs at hand. Programs he can add, one to another, like silicon building blocks. It would be unlike Dallas to choose someone who was not considered to be the best in his professional field. So think hard, my computer-minded friend. Think hard. What other elements can you add to their existing situation? Something really nasty and unpleasant. Unless you want to disappoint me. Ronica will tell you. I lose all my human skills when I'm disappointed.'

VI SIMWORLD: ELAPSED TIME 3 HOURS 30 MINUTES

It was another hour before Gates had recovered sufficiently to sit up and drink the hot sugar water Dallas had prepared for him: One box of Jell-O was enough to provide five hundred kilocalories of heat energy.

'How are you feeling?' asked Dallas.

Gates looked at his still gloved hand and flexed the fingers several times before answering.

'Stiff,' he said. 'Like I spent the night in the icebox.' Yawning, he added, 'And I've got the mother and father of all headaches.'

'That's just dehydration. Keep drinking the sugar water.'

Gates nodded and sipped from the sealed bottle before glancing around at their surroundings.

Arranged along the circumference of the circular-shaped facility, the R&R area reminded him most of the interior of the Clostridium Hotel: a long, sweeping curve of steel flooring underneath a windscreen of inclined panes of backlit fretted glass; and on the inside of the bend, a number of glass-fronted rooms that included a galley, a dormitory, a medical facility, a washroom, an armory, a dressing room with spare space suits and life-support packs, a subordinate computer-room, and a large lounge. Farther along the corridor was parked an electric car, not dissimilar to the one that had transported the cryoprecipitate from the vault to the landing site, except that it was equipped with four seats and designed to travel all the way around the compass of the facility, instead of to its hermetic and forbidden center.

'So what's the story, doc?' croaked Gates. 'You got penguin blood or something?'

'Your cold reaction probably has more to do with your P®,' said Dallas. 'I've given the matter some thought while you've been recovering. You see, the hypothalamus is the major center of the brain for regulating body temperature. It's sensitive to blood temperature changes of as little as half a degree. I think your own hypothalamus must be even more sensitive than that.'

'Seem to know a lot about it.'

'In view of the fact that we were to expose ourselves to hypothermic conditions, naturally it made sense to become a little better informed about the subject.'

'I guess so. The brain, too.'

'I've always been interested in the brain.'

'Brains in general or just one brain in particular?'

Dallas looked puzzled.

'Cavor's brain, for instance,' added Gates.

'Could be.'

Gates waited for Dallas to say something more. When he didn't, he shook his head sadly and then rolled onto his front.

'Still don't quite trust me, huh?' he said.

'Surely that's one of the purposes of this simulation,' said Dallas. 'To find out how much we can trust each other.'

'That's not the kind of trust I meant, and you know it.' Gates managed to raise himself onto all fours.

'After metabolic icebox, you shouldn't move for a while.'

'Negative. I've got to pee.'

Dallas helped him into the washroom, Gates having refused to pee on the floor.

'I've got my standards,' he said. 'Even in a Sim-world.'

A few minutes later, after another hot drink, Gates pronounced himself equal to the next stage of the plan, which involved drilling out a block of concrete from the labyrinth wall. At least, he felt equal to it until Dallas informed him of the location he had in mind for this particular task.

'All sections of the labyrinth wall are smart. Lots of metal wire running through the mortar. And fitted with vibration detectors,' Dallas told him. 'If one of those picks up the feel of a drill, the metal wire conducts electric current to the point of vibration. Quite enough to kill you and anyone standing next to you. All the walls except one, that is. You see, there are two power sources for this facility. There's the solar power field we saw from the air. And there's a small nuclear reactor that's inside the main facility on the other side of the building from where we are now. The walls of the containment room in the reactor don't have any vibration detectors because of the vibrations from the reactor turbine.'

'And,' remarked an incredulous Gates, 'because only

an idiot would be crazy enough to choose the containment room to try and effect an entrance to the labyrinth.'

'That's what I once thought myself,' conceded Dallas. 'However, I now see that this is the weakest part of my original design; and therefore, as a corollary, the best part of my current plan.'

'I don't see how,' argued Gates. 'There's the small matter of radiation, Dallas. We spend any time in the containment room – like maybe the sort of high-exposure time it takes to get through a concrete wall – we'll die. Maybe not in the simulation. But for sure when we try it in reality.'

Dallas shook his head. 'I don't believe that's the case. I believe we can do this and survive the radiation.'

'These are space suits, Dallas. Made of toughened latex, not lead. Protection against cosmic radiation, maybe. But not on the scale of what you're proposing. You're talking gamma, beta, alpha, the whole lousy uranium molecule. Shit, the cold must have affected you more than I thought.'

'We can do it and we can survive,' insisted Dallas. 'Here's how. The amount of damage to human tissue depends on the number of atoms ionized per human kilogram. That depends on the amount of energy deposited in each kilo of human flesh. A unit of absorbed dose is called a gray, which amounts to the deposition of one joule of energy per human kilo. For the sake of precision, doses are quoted in centigrays. Now, as well as a dose unit we need a dose rate – the centigray per hour. Total dose in centigrays equals dose rate in centigrays per hour times exposure time in hours. Are you with me?'

'So far, so lethal,' said Gates. 'Go on, I'm listening.

My hair may be falling out, and my gums might be bleeding, but I'm with you, Dallas.'

'What I'm getting to is that the early somatic effects of radiation on the human body can be very precisely measured. More importantly, they can be very precisely dealt with.'

'I read about the war, Dallas. I know what treatment most people got for the usual effects of radiation on the human body – cancer, general circulatory collapse, whatever. It was very precise. Massive overdose of morphine was what they got. That or a bullet in the head. Whichever was available.'

'Since you mention the general circulatory system, let's talk about that for a moment,' said Dallas. 'Radiation alters or destroys some of the constituents of the body's cells. Those most affected are the blood-forming cells in the human bone marrow that maintain the body's supply of white blood cells. A radiation dose in excess of one hundred and fifty centigrays will cause the white blood cell count to fall. Anything above five hundred and there's a fifty percent chance you'll die. It's called the LD fifty – the lethal dose to fifty percent.'

'Fifty percent, huh? Sounds like a reasonable chance, when you say it that way. An even chance you'll die, more like.'

'Okay, what's the treatment for radiation exposure?'

'These days?' Gates shrugged. 'Most people check into a hyperbaric hotel.'

'Most people,' agreed Dallas. 'Only for those people this is not a perfect world, right?'

'So I've been led to believe.'

'No, the ideal treatment,' said Dallas, 'remains blood infusion. And with an unlimited supply of infusable blood, the LD fifty decreases significantly. Maybe ten percent mortality at most.'

Suddenly Gates caught the thrust of Dallas's argument. 'Oh Jesus,' he said. 'You don't mean?'

'I do mean.'

'You're crazy.'

'You know something, Rameses? This is the real point of this simulation. To measure how many centigrays we'll absorb in the time it takes to get through that containment room wall.'

'And then to figure out how many blood transfusions we'll need not to die? Is that it?'

'If you want to put it like that. I prefer to look at it in terms of using an unlimited number of infusions to achieve a vast reduction in the LD fifty.'

'Same thing.'

'Like I said before, Rameses, it's the best part of the plan because the containment room in the reactor was the weakest part of my design. It's amazing I never foresaw that anyone would be prepared to take such a risk. But when you think about it, where better to take such a risk than somewhere like this? Somewhere with an unlimited supply of blood. The very thing that makes the risk feasible.'

'But won't radiation from the reactor come through the hole with us? And contaminate the blood?'

'It might if we weren't going to replace the block of concrete that we're going to shift. And if the vault wasn't lead lined.'

'You still haven't told me how you propose to get through that.'

'No, I haven't have I?'

'Well, maybe Cav will think of a way.'

'Maybe he will at that.'

Gates sighed and shook his head. 'Freeze to death or fry to death. Christ, Dallas.'

'If the simulation shows it can't be done, then we'll have to think of something else. I don't want to die any more than you do. And I'm not the one who has to have an infusion of blood whatever happens. Think about that for a moment.'

Gates nodded reluctantly. 'Okay, you've convinced me. Let's do it.'

'Okay,' smiled Dallas. But gradually his smile gave way to a frown.

'S'matter? thought of some other lethal shit that you forgot to tell me about?'

'No, it's the same worry I've had since you went into metabolic icebox. I still wish I knew why the simulation didn't end when you were virtually dead.'

'Virtually, yeah. You said it.' He shrugged. 'Well, maybe my vital signs looked okay in the real world.'

'We both know that shouldn't be possible.'

Gates thought for a second. 'Prevezer's geodesic dome is supposed to obtain all the information it needs about what we're doing by intercepting the electrical signals from our brains. Instead of ending up in our bodies, those signals get transmitted to the computer and are decoded by Prev. That way, he can determine exactly how our bodies would have reacted if they'd been in this Simworld alongside our brains.'

'That's how it works, all right,' agreed Dallas. 'It means the simulated body can react differently from the real one, such as being able to survive experiences that would kill a real human body. Such as radiation or extreme cold.'

'Then how about this? Maybe something's gone wrong with the geodesic domes. Perhaps – don't ask me why – the signals are going only one way. He's able to keep the simulation going, but he can no longer intercept the signals being sent from our brains. Look, we've been in the Simworld for how long?'

Dallas glanced at his life-support computer. 'Three hours and forty-five minutes.'

Gates shrugged. 'He probably reckons we're nowhere near ready to come out yet. My guess is that he's just improvising.'

'I hope you're right,' said Dallas.

'What else could it be?'

Dallas shook his head. Gates's explanation almost sounded convincing. There was just one problem with it and that was Prevezer himself. The character of the man was precise, systematic, painstaking, and mechanical, as befitted someone whose whole life was dedicated to mathematical principles and algorithmic procedures. The very idea of improvisation would have been anathema to a man like Prevezer. Dallas considered he would have been no more capable of doing something on the spur of the moment than he would have allowed something impossible – something contrary to the laws of physics – to exist inside one of his realistic and much vaunted Simworlds. Dallas said, 'I don't know. Nothing probably. We'd better move.'

VII SIMWORLD: ELAPSED TIME 3 HOURS 57 MINUTES

Because only the R&R area in the main facility was pressurized, they loaded the electric perimeter car with spare life-support packs. Dallas handed Gates a different EVA helmet, to take advantage of an 'invisible' chip that was concealed inside its crown: This relayed an encrypted security signal to the proximity detectors controlling doors inside the main facility. He had already fitted each helmet with a special infrared visor while Gates had been unconscious. He also gave him one of the electron-beam welding guns he had brought from the *Mariner*: the same kind of welding gun that Simou would need to use to carry out his simulated repair of the hole in the nose of the RLV.

'Reckon I know how to use one of those,' remarked Gates. 'I've cut and crushed enough Moon rock in my time. A UHT, or ultra-high-temperature, beam of electrons will cut a hole in just about anything. Makes it a pretty formidable weapon, too.' He handled the gun as carefully as if it had been a small pistol-shaped bomb. 'I saw lots of guys at Artemis Seven use one of these to settle a score. In or out of an atmosphere, five hundred kilovolts is as near to a bloody ray-gun as you can get these days. So you might just explain why we're unpacking these UHTs now, before we've even seen the containment room.'

'I'm afraid I just don't buy your theory about Prev. And if something has gone wrong in the real world, then it would make sense to be ready for something going wrong in this one.'

'Can't argue with that,' said Gates. 'It wasn't much of a theory anyway. You sure you know how to use one of these?'

'Only on paper,' admitted Dallas.

'Paper's what it'll make metal look like when it burns a hole in it. When we used these guns on Artemis you had to have another guy standing alongside you, just to help you watch out where the hell you were pointing the thing. Not only that but he had a safety switch to cut the power in an emergency. For all that, they're surprisingly easy to use. You just point and squeeze the handle. Just try not to shoot it in here. The atmosphere will make it hard to be accurate.'

'I think I can remember that,' said Dallas.

Gates detached the short steel barrel from the UHT gun.

'One more thing. Whatever you do, don't take this off. A beam of hot electrons tends to generate X rays, even in a vacuum. This sleeve'll shield you from those.' He shrugged as he remembered the greater hazard of gamma rays in the reactor containment room. 'Not that a few lousy X rays are going to concern a man like you.' Gates sat down on the passenger seat of the electric car. 'In the circumstances, you knowing how to use the gun on paper n'all, I'd better ride shotgun. You drive.'

Dallas sat down and took hold of the steering wheel, an action that automatically started up the engine. He glanced at Gates. In his giant white glove, the UHT gun looked deceptively toylike. 'Ready?'

'Ready.'

Dallas depressed the accelerator pedal, and they started their counter-clockwise journey around the first radial arc. Silently the little car gathered speed until they were moving at almost twelve miles per hour.

'How big is this facility?' asked Gates.

'About three thousand square meters.'

'Place gives me the creeps.'

'Under the circumstances, I'm forced to agree with you.'

A short distance on, they drew to a halt in front of the airlock door, which, finding the encrypted chips in the two men's helmets, lit up in expectation of their imminent egress. As they drove inside, some interior lights came on, prompting each man to press the buttons on his life-support system computer that would pressurize his EVA suit.

Gates felt a reassuring breath of air on his face and some pressure in his ears as the suits expanded to accommodate around four pounds per square inch. Even before the airlock had been pumped out and the exit door was open he had the short silver barrel of the UHT gun leveled at the brightly lit but airless corridor ahead of them. Each man heard the other breathe a sigh of relief as they saw that the corridor was empty.

'I don't know what I was expecting to see,' admitted Gates.

'That's the problem. If something has gone wrong, it might be anything. One simulacrum of reality transfigured by another. Whatever happens now, we are ourselves and our circumstances and nothing else. How we interreact with that is the only reality that matters right now, even if it has been ruptured by something we don't know about.'

Dallas depressed the accelerator pedal again and moved them into the second radial arc. It looked exactly like the radial arc they had left on the other side of the airlock door.

'But maybe this is a good thing,' he said. 'When we rob the real blood bank it'll mean we're prepared for the unexpected. The trouble with a completely schematic plan like this one is that sometimes there's not enough margin for error. And I'm afraid you need to make errors in order to discover just where those margins exist.'

Dallas thought this was nonsense, but he kept on talking in an effort to try and take his mind off the sound in his headset of Gates's loud and rhythmic breathing. It was like something mechanical and served only to remind Dallas of how provisional and uncertain life really was. Hearing Gates breathe – almost as if he was inside Dallas's own head – it was easy to imagine that at any second the sound might end forever.

'Did you hear something?' asked Gates.

'Just you, breathing away like a pervert.'

'Don't blame me, blame the simulation.' Gates glanced around. 'Where are we now?'

'The supplies warehouse. Next stop the water plant.'

The car slowed and then stopped.

'Why have we stopped?'

'Don't ask me,' said Dallas, stamping on the accelerator pedal. 'We just did.' It was plain from the voltmeter on the dash that there was still plenty of power in the battery. He slid off the seat and lifted the hatch on the front of the car to check the electrical terminals. 'The connections look okay,' observed Dallas, but he wiggled the wires to make sure. There was nothing loose. 'No sign of a problem here.' He closed the hatch and slid back behind the wheel. But still the car refused to budge.

Gates pointed the gun one way and then the other, as if expecting trouble to arrive at any minute.

'What do you think?' he asked.

'I think we'll have to walk,' said Dallas, and collecting another life-support pack and his own UHT gun, he stepped down from the car again, with Gates following. They hadn't walked ten paces when Gates, glancing nervously over his shoulder, noticed that the electric car had disappeared.

'Dallas,' he said urgently.

Dallas turned, saw the empty space, and walked back to where the car had been standing just a few seconds earlier.

'That bastard Prevezer,' muttered Gates. 'What the hell's he playing at?'

'You could be right,' said Dallas. 'It would seem that someone wants to play, anyway.'

'Bloody simulation,' said Gates. 'I don't like this, Dallas. I don't like this at all.'

Dallas was about to answer when he noticed the corridor lights beginning to dim. Simultaneously each man hit a switch on his helmet that controlled two pairs of halogen lamps.

'Let's go back to the airlock, to the R&R area,' Gates urged.

'Why do you assume things will be any better there?'

'Because I've been there already.'

'You just think you have, that's all. It's probably already different from when we were there. Just look what happened to the car. No, there's nothing to be served by going back.'

Dallas began to advance along the curving corridor, which was now illuminated only by their helmet lights. But the size of the light arc meant there was always part of the corridor ahead that remained unseen. For fifty slow yards neither man said a word, and it was Gates who finally broke the silence: His keener eyes had spotted something.

'Lying on the floor, ahead of us,' he said urgently. 'Do you see it?'

'I see it.'

Gates led their careful approach toward the object.

'Looks like a space suit,' he observed, and then they halted as, still lying on the floor, the suit moved. 'There's someone inside it.'

'Can't be one of our people.' said Dallas.

'I almost wish it was,' confessed Gates.

'Although I suppose anything's possible now that we've seen the car disappear.'

The stricken figure seemed to writhe on the floor, and standing over it, Gates attempted to communicate on an open channel. Getting no response, he prodded the figure with the toe of his boot.

'I suggest you leave it the fuck alone,' Dallas said.

Gates shook his head. His curiosity was aroused by the discovery that the helmet's gold-painted visor was covering the clear bubble that would have revealed the figure's identity. 'I'm just going to see who it is,' he said, kneeling down.

'I don't think that's a very good idea,' said Dallas. But even as he spoke Gates was reaching to tip up the visor.

'Jesus Christ.' For one brief, heart-stopping moment Gates had a view of a helmet that was filled with hundreds of long, thin, red worms before disgust instinctively made him move away. It wasn't this movement that saved his virtual life. Rather, it was because of the position he had adopted seconds earlier, kneeling over the top of the head instead of the body, which would have been more typical. The very second after he turned up the visor it was as if the body that filled the suit – if there had ever been a body – was pierced from below by a hundred animal-looking spikes that were as sharp as needles, each of them bright red and two or three feet in length. Gates, already recoiling from the first horror, jumped back at the sight of the second, mute with fright, even as Dallas fired a bolt of boiling electrons into the very center of the spinous suit. There was a bright flash of blue light as the focused beam sliced the suit in half, reducing the center to a mass of molten metal, rubber, and something once animate.

As Gates picked himself off the ground, cursing with fright, Dallas looked at the UHT gun with a new respect.

'What the hell is that supposed to be?' demanded Gates.

'I don't think it really matters what it's supposed to be,' said Dallas.

'That's easy for you to say. You didn't come within an inch of being a goddamn pincushion.'

'What I mean to say is that we won't find any logical explanations about things from here on in. Now it's just a matter of trying to get through this shit with as little pain as possible.'

'Looking at this particular piece of shit, that's not going to be easy.'

'I agree.' Dallas thought for a moment. 'Tell me, have you ever had Simsex?'

'What kind of question is that, right now?'

'A very important one.'

'Okay, yeah, I've had Simsex.'

'How good was it? As good as the real thing?'

'In a lot of ways it was actually better. But then I've never had sex on the Moon. Cav says that's pretty good.'

'It stands to reason that if pleasure can be more intense in a simulation, then so can pain. You and I may not get killed in a simulation. But is being killed the worst that could happen to us? I mean, the pleasure of sex is over soon after your orgasm. But pain need never end. You know, it's quite possible that we could get into a situation where we end up wishing ourselves dead. Except that death can never come in here. It's like something in Greek mythology. Like Sisyphus condemned to roll an enormous rock up a hill for all eternity, or Prometheus bound by chains to a rock and condemned to have an eagle tear out a liver that continually renews itself. It's probably only inside a simulation that myths and legends can achieve their full potential. Punishments such as those might actually have been devised specifically for a simulation. Do you see what I mean? Death isn't so bad. It's the waiting for death that can be intolerable, and yet must be tolerated.'

'I wish you'd shut up, Dallas. And I wish I knew what that bastard Prevezer was doing right now. If I ever see him again, I'm going to teach him the meaning of reality in a way he's not likely to forget.'

VIII

Rimmer was growing bored. It was hardly very satisfying to torture someone if you couldn't see them bleed or hear them scream with pain. A victim had to have some kind of relationship with his tormentor, the kind that left an opportunity for him to beg for mercy; otherwise the cruelty inflicted hardly qualified as torture at all, but rather some reduced form of brutality, such as inhumanity or spite. Having set his heart on becoming the personification of pure evil in the eyes of Dallas, it mattered a great deal to Rimmer that those eyes should at least be open and fixed on him. Whatever pleasure he took in torturing Dallas was not served by watching the man's vital signs and hearing Prevezer's descriptions of how he had ruptured one simulation with another one more hellish. It was true, Dallas's pulse, blood pressure, respiratory rate, and body temperature indicated a person who was undergoing some kind of severe trauma, but trying to fathom the reason for each and every surge in his heart rate – at one point it had actually touched one hundred and ninety beats per minute – was proving frustrating to Rimmer. Since Prevezer hardly relished the task of torturing his two colleagues, he was unable to furnish Rimmer with a sufficiently horrific level of detail as to the variety of terror that they were experiencing. It was only with a gun to his head that he had even managed to describe the Sura Fifteen Simworld he had added to the model of the First National Blood Bank:

'It's something I developed for Reinbek,' he had explained. 'He used to be an interrogator for the Criminal Intelligence Service, but now he works for the Black Hole. And sometimes he wants information from people, and he gets me to use this particular simulation on them. Sura Fifteen's named after the book in the Qur'an that describes seven portals leading into seven divisions of hell. You said you wanted Antichrist, mister, well you've got it. What they're going through is hair-on-end, cold sweat, blood-turning-to-water, stampeding-panic attack horror, and I wouldn't inflict it on my worst enemy. Parts of the model I had to buy prefabricated from some real sado-freaks and mental fuck-ups. So don't ask me to describe what's in there in more detail because I just don't know. I wouldn't go in that simulation if you promised me eternal life.'

'I can guarantee you a very short life if you're lying to me,' Rimmer had promised.

Two whole hours had gone by since Prevezer had reported that Dallas and Gates had gone through the first portal of hell, and Rimmer had grown tired of the Simworld modeler's one-word pictures of the numbers he was seeing on the computer screen. Bad. Evil. Ghastly. Grim. Horrifying. Dreadful. Monstrous.

'How do I know that it's as bad as you say it is?'

Rimmer demanded, pressing the gun against Prevezer's nose.

'You can't. Not for sure. Not without going in and taking a look for yourself.

'You'd like that wouldn't you?'

Prevezer said nothing, momentarily distracted by some small change he had noticed in Gates.

'I know I would,' said Cavor from the floor where he still lay alongside Ronica and Simou.

'Shut up,' snarled Rimmer. And then to Prevezer: 'This isn't working for me. Not anymore. Maybe I'll just shoot them now. Maybe I'll just shoot you all.'

'Wait,' said Prevezer. 'You wanted confirmation that they're going through hell? Well look. Look at Gates. Look at his hair, for God's sake.'

Rimmer bent down and peered through the fretwork of the geodesic dome that covered Gates's head. There could be no doubt about it. Gates's hair, uniformly brown when Rimmer had come into the hotel suite, was now distinctly gray.

'My God, you're right,' he breathed. 'His hair's turned quite gray. Just while I've been here.'

'You bastard,' hissed Ronica.

'Now do you believe me,' demanded Prevezer.

'My hair is gray, but not with years,' said Cavor. 'Nor grew it white, in a single night, As men's have grown from sudden fears.'

'What's that?' asked a delighted Rimmer.

Cavor sat up and repeated the verse, adding by way of provenance, 'Lord Byron.'[1] Now if Rimmer would just turn his back, he could take him on.

'Shut up, Cav,' ordered Ronica. 'Don't you see?

---

[1] The Prisoner of Chillon, i. (1816).

338

You're only adding to the bastard's sadistic enjoyment.'

'It's only my sadistic enjoyment of their discomfort that's keeping you alive,' said Rimmer, kneeling beside her. He collected a handful of her braids in his hand and then twisted them.

Ronica screamed until he stopped.

'Another word out of you and *your* hair will encounter some grief of its very own. Only it won't turn gray. It won't have time because I'll tear it out, braid by beautiful braid, until your scalp is as cratered with holes as the surface of the Moon.'

Ronica screamed as he twisted her hair again. Cavor gathered one leg beneath himself and prepared to leap.

'And stop that bloody screaming,' said Rimmer, silencing her with a slap this time. 'Don't think that anyone's going to hear you. These rooms are sound-proofed.' He chuckled. 'They have to be on account of all the lovemaking that goes on in this place. Even if someone did hear you, they'd only assume you were having a good time. That might still be a possibility for you.'

He stood up and returned to his contemplation of the two men, hoping that he might see Dallas's hair turn white with fright in front of his very eyes. After several minutes he shook his head sadly. 'That was good, but it wasn't quite good enough.' And pointing the gun through the dome at the center of Dallas's forehead, he added, 'It's time you were on your way to the real hell, Dallas.'

It was now or never, thought Cavor. He had just started to move when, out of the corner of his eye, he saw Lenina.

Even in the Moon's microgravity, Rimmer's sudden progress across the suite was spectacular. It seemed hardly connected to the simultaneous muted explosion of air – much like the sound of a metallic drawer sliding shut – that emanated from the gun in Lenina's hand. Swaying slightly, her face covered in the rubelliform rash that described her condition with more eloquence than a hematologist's case notes, she stood in the bedroom doorway and fired once more at the man who had bounced off the wall and was now trailing blood as he crawled toward the door. Her second bullet hit Rimmer in the back of the head, lifting a piece of his scalp and killing him instantly as it bored through his brain, before finally coming to rest between his teeth, as if, like some circus sharpshooter, he had meant to catch it in his mouth.

'You took your time,' snarled Ronica, rising stiffly from the floor. 'I thought you'd never hear me screaming.'

'Shut up,' Prevezer snapped. 'Can't you see she's dying?'

Lenina said nothing, too sick to answer. She let the gun fall to the ground, turned on her heel, and walked back to lie on Prevezer's bed, even as he sprang forward to press the button that would switch Dallas and Gates from the artificial cortical mode controlling the Simworld to the real one.

Gates, trembling, his face as white as the marble chair he was sitting on and almost breathless with fear, called out to them. 'Get this thing off me.'

There was just enough time for Prevezer to withdraw the electro-neuroneedles before Gates, jumping up, removed the geodesic dome from his now sweat-plastered head and threw it to the marble floor, smashing it into a dozen tetrahedral-shaped shards. He paused for a second, glanced around the room with wide eyes, and then, retching like a dog, ran into the bathroom.

'I'd better see that he's okay,' said Cav, going after him.

Dallas waited until Prevezer had removed the dome from his own head and then let out a long, unsteady breath. Saying nothing, he bit the knuckle of his forefinger until it bled. Seeing this, Ronica pulled his hand away from his mouth and then cradled his head against her belly.

'What happened?' he whispered. Then he saw Rimmer's body and understood.

'It's okay,' she said. 'It's all over. You're back with us now. Take it easy.'

Prevezer was already preparing an intravenous sedative for each man.

'This is just a tranquilizer,' he told Dallas. 'It'll help you to sleep.'

'Are you kidding?' demanded Simou. 'I'd be afraid to ever close my eyes again.'

'Sleep's the best thing, right now,' insisted Prevezer. 'In my considerable experience of these situations.' He rolled up Dallas's sleeve and pushed the needle in.

Simou shook his head, hardly convinced.

'Then let's just hope he doesn't dream. After what he's been through, who knows what he might dream about?'

'At least they're not dead,' insisted Prevezer. 'Dead's the worst dream of all.'

IX

Reality changed forever in 1905, 'the year of miracles.' This was the year in which Albert Einstein published his Special Theory of Relativity. From then on it could be seen that time and space were geometrically equivalent in one four-dimensional whole, alongside gravity and matter. All points in space were also points in time, and all moments in time were also points in space. And space-time could be regarded as one giant block of ice in which the whole of physical reality is frozen once and for all. Just as every place in this block universe can be contained, so the same can be said of the past, the present, and the future. Of course, for this to be true, the future must already exist, just like the past and the present.

This hardly seems to make sense, and in fact, the only way space-time can properly be understood is from the point of view of quantum physics. We exist in multiple versions and in multiple universes. This is easier to comprehend with the help of your very own virtual reality generator – your memory and your imagination.

One version of you exists in the past, and this is easy enough to recall. It is your first day at school, and doubtless you can remember a great deal of vivid detail that enhances the reality of this version of you. It is easy enough to believe that somehow this version of you still exists in the past and that, for one eternal moment, it will always be your first day at school.

The next version of you is the version that exists in the present. This is you remembering your first day at school but also imagining yet another version of yourself, a future version in some notable situation – your last day at work perhaps. This is harder to do and depends on the dexterity of your imagination. However, in a curious way, the future version of yourself can seem just as real as the past version – perhaps even more so – for there is nothing that cannot be achieved in the virtual realities of our imaginations. Nothing that is physically impossible.

One day in the future (perhaps a very great distance in the future), and given enough computer power, it will be possible to render the entire universe in virtual reality. Where better for human beings to evolve, to achieve immortality, and to be raised from the dead? But until that day comes when nothing is intractable – in other words, until heaven itself exists – evolution must find another, less spectacular way forward. And find a way it will. Already human genes are reaching out, to the Moon and beyond. The only threshold that remains to be crossed in human evolutionary progress is the physical limit imposed by space travel. The journey, however, may be about to begin.

4

I

'THAT'S A PITY,' said Dallas, surveying what remained of the geodesic dome worn by Rameses Gates. 'We can't do a simulation of the containment room in the reactor without two of these units.'

'You mean you want to?' asked Gates. 'After what happened in there?'

Neither man had spoken about what had happened to them in the simulation when Rimmer had forced Prevezer to corrupt one silicon model with another, but neither was likely to forget it.

'What happened was unfortunate,' said Dallas. 'But hardly likely to happen again, now that Rimmer is dead. And I'd still like to have an accurate idea of how many centigrays we're likely to absorb in the time it takes for us to penetrate the containment room wall.'

'There's no way we'll find another geodesic on the Moon,' said Prevezer. 'I already asked around. There's no demand for Simworlds up here. I mean, people aren't much interested in Simworlds when reality's as good as this.'

'Good of you to admit it,' said Simou.

'It would take at least four or five days to have

another unit sent on the next astroliner from Earth,' said Prevezer, ignoring him.

Gates shook his head. 'Lenina can't wait that long.'

'Neither can we,' said Dallas. 'There's our window of lunar daylight to consider. If we wait that long, we'll be trying to land the *Mariner* in darkness. And it's going to be hard enough in daylight without Lenina. How is she? I mean, I don't suppose there's any way she'll be fit?'

'The fact is, she could die at any time,' said Gates, rubbing a big hand through his shock of white hair. 'Back on Earth, she'd probably be dead already. It's only the pressurized atmosphere that's giving her hemoglobin the oxygen it needs for her to stay alive.'

Dallas nodded. 'That's settled then. We go tomorrow. July twentieth. What with all the activity for the Moon landing centennial, it'll be easier getting Lenina out of the hotel. We have until then to make some calculations regarding somatic radiation effects. Prev? Any ideas?'

'I could run a two-dimensional model on the computer,' he suggested. 'Kind of a predictive microworld using the data that's already in the memory. It won't give us anything like the verisimilitude of detail or realism of prescriptive process that characterizes the three-D, but it should give us a range of probable figures.'

'Then do it,' said Dallas. 'Right away.'

'Just how are we going to get Lenina out of the hotel?' asked Ronica. 'Quite apart from her being unconscious, she looks like she stepped out of a plague pit.'

'She'll have to wear a space suit,' said Simou.

'Well, of course,' said Cavor. 'Lots of people in the

hotel lobby are wearing spacesuits. But most of them can walk.'

'Have you looked in the hotel bar?' asked Simou. 'It's full of drunks celebrating the centennial. And tomorrow there'll be even more. Gates and I can carry her between us. Who's going to notice three more drunks in space suits?'

'What about Rimmer?' asked Ronica. 'What are we going to do with the body? We can hardly carry him out of here as well.'

'We'll leave him here,' said Dallas. 'It's not like we're actually checking out. Officially we're supposed to be coming back here after our flight down to Descartes. By the time they figure we're not, we'll be long gone, hiding out on the dark side.'

'We can stash him in the closet and switch on the Do Not Disturb,' said Cavor. 'That way the maid won't bother to clean the room.'

'Then that's agreed,' said Dallas. 'Is that everything?'

'I sure hope so,' muttered Gates.

Dallas gave him a curious sort of glance, and then looked awkward. 'In which case there's one more thing I have to tell you all. Although this concerns you most of all, Cav.'

'This sounds like what I've been waiting to hear.'

'And you, Rameses.'

'Someone get me a painkiller,' groaned Gates.

'There's no easy way to put this, so I'll just give it to you straight. After you've landed the *Mariner*, it'll be just me and Cav who enter the main facility.'

'Me?' Cavor's eyes widened with surprise.

'Come again?' demanded Gates.

'You're not coming inside the bank.'

'Is this some kind of joke, Dallas? Because these

white hairs of mine should tell you, I'm kind of low on a sense of humor right now.'

'It's no joke.'

'Is it because of what happened? Me getting metabolic icebox? Because I've already figured out a way of preventing that from happening.'

'As a matter of fact, so have I.'

'Then what's the problem? I don't understand.'

'The truth is that when it came to the real thing, it was always going to be me and Cav.'

'But why?'

'Because he has some special skills. Skills that even he doesn't know about.'

'Would you mind telling me what they are?' asked Gates.

'I'm intrigued to know myself,' admitted Cavor.

'All in good time.'

'If that's the case, then why did you do the simulation with me instead of him? Why am I the one who looks like a goddamn albino if I'm not the one who's going on the real job after all?'

'Hey,' protested Simou. 'You ask me, your hair color's looking good. Better than before.'

'Because Cav's special skills wouldn't have worked in a Simworld. Only in reality.'

'Now I really am intrigued.'

'I thought you'd be pleased, Rameses. After all, you've expressed quite a few reservations about my plan. Not least our going into the containment room and exposing ourselves to radiation.'

'Reservations are one thing,' argued Gates. 'Cold feet are quite another. Which reminds me, in case you'd forgotten. Cav has $P^\circledR$, just like me.'

'Yes, but for not as long as you. If you were going to point out that his body's core temperature is likely to cool down quicker than mine, then I'd agree with you. But still not as quickly as yours. Look, Rameses, this is nothing personal. This is just the best way of getting the job done. The only way, as it happens. What matters to you and to Lenina, and to the rest of you, is that we get the blood.'

'Amen to that,' agreed Simou.

'Well? Isn't it?'

'I guess so,' nodded Gates. 'But there's one thing I still don't understand – since we happen to be talking about what's important for everyone here. What's in this for you, Dallas? You don't have the virus. You don't need the blood.'

'I want blood all right,' Dallas said grimly. 'Just as badly as the rest of you. You see, I've got a different kind of virus. Maybe it won't kill me, but it's eating me up just the same. For me, revenge will be a kind of cure. It will be the greatest feeling in the world.' Dallas smiled. 'The world? It can go hang. Perish the whole damn universe just as long as I have my revenge.'

II

Earth, looking like some fabulous blue Fabergé egg inside a black-velvet-lined case, seems a much more precious, durable thing than the deserving object of Dallas's small-minded revenge. The mathematics, those fundamental numbers, are by themselves sufficiently miraculous in the way they seem to reflect a certain underlying order, and might have given him pause for thought.

Numbers like the size of the electric charge of the electron: Even the smallest difference, and the stars – whose debris went to form other stars and planets, such as Earth – would never have exploded. Numbers such as the ratio between the mass of an electron and a proton, which seem to have been minutely fixed to make possible the development of intelligent life in the universe. A universe that is still expanding at such a critical rate that, even now, ten thousand million years after the singularity that had detonated its existence, an infinitesimally small alteration in that expansion rate taking place one second after that singularity, of less than 0.0001 percent of one hundred billion, would have resulted in the universe recollapsing before ever reaching its present size and shape.

Despite the fact that there are probably one hundred billion billion planets suitable for the creation of life in the universe, the odds are stacked against such an event occurring anywhere else, except on Earth – and improbable enough even there. This can properly be calculated as a result of dividing the number of planets suitable for life by the number of planets where it is certain that this event has already occurred – namely one, Earth itself. In other words, the odds of life occurring anywhere else in the universe are in the region of one hundred billion billion to one.

In comparison with the sun-drenched and comparatively unremarkable lunar surface, the Earth is a fabulous egg indeed. It is almost enough to make you believe in the anthropic cosmological principle – the notion that man occupies a privileged place in the universe consistent with his existence as an observer. The nature of the universe, so goes the principle (although it seems like a truism, it is actually a principle that has profound implications for physics) is of a type that could be observed to allow the evolution of observers.

What is man, asked the psalm, that thou art mindful

of him? Perhaps nothing. Copernicus, Galileo, Darwin have all contributed to the invalidation of man's self-selected position at the center of the universe created by a monstrous series of accidents. But perhaps, as the world of thought comes full circle, like a globe in a simple brass orrery, it is everything.

Perish the universe? When fortune has already favored it so? Not a chance. With so much time still ahead, the universe is only just beginning.

III

Dallas was seated on the flight deck, in the pilot's seat formerly occupied by Lenina, who, successfully smuggled out of the Galileo Hotel, was now resting in the crew sleeping station on mid-deck below. Gates occupied the commander's seat, as before, and was keeping a close eye on the automatic pilot as they made their approach to the Descartes Crater.

The view out of the flight-deck window was much as Gates remembered it from the simulation, just a lot of craters he had trained himself to look out for in order of their appearance: Torricelli, Alfraganus, Hypatia, Zöllner, and Kant. The Kant crater system, over which they were now flying, was the last landmark before they reached Descartes.

'Going to manual,' he said, switching off the autopilot. 'Simou? Are you ready?'

'Ready as I'll ever be,' said a voice in his headset.

'In your own time,' said Gates, as he took a firm hold of the flight stick and checked the instruments on the control panel above his helmeted head.

'Good luck,' said Dallas.

'To us all,' replied Gates.

Seconds later they felt the loud bang from the explosion detonated remotely by Simou's trigger. It was the same noise they had heard in the simulation except that this time it was not immediately followed by the master alarm. The explosion had not holed the fuselage.

'What was that?' asked Dallas for the sake of verisimilitude on the cockpit voice recorder.

'I don't know,' admitted Gates. 'But it sure sounded like something, didn't it?'

'Did something hit us?'

'We're still here, aren't we?' Gates glanced above his head at the flight instrumentation. 'All instruments are showing normal readings. If something did hit us, we're still pressurized.'

Dallas cursed silently. Without a verifiable emergency the Descartes computer would never permit them to land. 'Sim?' he asked. 'Any ideas on the mystery noise?'

'Negative, Dallas,' said Simou. 'I'm as puzzled as you are.'

Dallas unbuckled himself from the pilot's seat and craned forward to look through the triangular flight-deck window at the gimlet-shaped nose.

'See anything?' Gates asked anxiously. It seemed quite at odds with his astroliner pilot's training that he should have been praying for something to go wrong now.

'There's a crack,' reported Dallas. 'In the ceramic-hafnium shield on the *Mariner*'s nose. And it's getting bigger.' As he watched, something detached itself from the nose and flew off into space. 'We just lost one of the heat-shield tiles. And another.'

'It sounds to me like it could be a brittle fracture,'

said Simou, choosing his words carefully. 'The impact must have dispersed through the whole nose.'

'There goes one more tile,' said Dallas.

'We lose too many of those and we'll never survive Earth reentry,' said Gates. 'Perhaps we should put down and make repairs.'

'Negative,' said Dallas. 'That's the kind of repair we can easily make back at TB. We don't need a ceramic-hafnium compound nose to continue with the flight.'

Gates slammed himself back in his seat and punched the armrests with frustration.

'I suggest that we turn around and head back to TB,' Dallas said evenly. 'Just to be on the safe side.'

'Well that's just great,' groaned Gates. 'What a vacation this turned out to be. Not even halfway to Schröter's Valley and we've got to turn back again.'

Schröter's Valley was the ultimate destination they had fed into the flight computer for the benefit of Descartes. Reluctantly, Gates started to reprogram the change in course. He did it in the knowledge that any delay to their plans at this stage would certainly cost Lenina her life.

'We're going back?' On the headset Simou's voice sounded incredulous.

'If you've got any other ideas, I'd love to hear them,' said Dallas.

Gates ceded control of the RLV to the autopilot, and immediately *Mariner* started to increase its altitude prior to firing the RCS[1] thrusters that would change their course. Seconds later they heard another explosion. For a brief second, Gates thought the RCS had fired prematurely. It was only when the master alarm finally went off and the static in his headset was

[1] Rocket Control System.

replaced by shouts from mid-deck that he realized what had happened was nothing to do with the thruster rockets. A quick look up at the control panel revealed a whole host of red warning lights.

'We just lost the flight computer,' he yelled and grabbed back the flight stick.

More red lights.

'And the environmental control system,' said Dallas.

'Prepare for ATL,' swallowed Gates. 'Go to oxygen, everyone. In a few minutes we're going to have nothing to breathe in this cabin except our own CO_2. I wish I knew what just happened and why. But without the flight computer I couldn't keep this thing in flight even if I wanted to.'

'There's a landing site up ahead,' said Dallas, still talking for the benefit of the Descartes computer.

And then, right on cue: 'This is the First National Blood Bank at Descartes Crater,' said the computer. 'You are approaching a restricted area. Please turn right on a heading one-zero-five and increase your altitude to fifteen hundred feet. Failure to comply will be met with appropriate force.'

'Descartes, this is *Mariner*. Negative to turning right on heading one-zero-five. We have an ATL emergency here. I'm not sure why, but we just lost all our computers. Requesting permission to land immediately.'

'Are you in a position to supply appropriate flight data and your cockpit voice recording?' asked Descartes. 'In order for me to verify your ATL condition for myself.'

Dallas was still trying to see what remained of their computer systems. 'Descartes, this is *Mariner*. We have communications, mid-deck systems, but no flight computer, payload, or environmental control system.

Mid-deck systems have backup data until the moment our computers went down. Transmitting that and our cockpit voice recordings, now.'

There was a longish pause as the Descartes Crater grew nearer. Gates was using the lip of the crater as his navigation marker and then aiming the nose of the *Mariner* a good distance ahead of it. He was flying on instinct now. Instinct and the seat of his pants. Without the flight computer to advise him, he was having to reduce altitude through experienced guess-work.

'Descartes? This is *Mariner*. How are we doing?'

'According to the information you have sent me, one of your oxygen tanks has exploded,' said the cool voice of the computer. 'All other failures are a corollary of that first failure. Alteration in levels of oxygen and hydrogen inside your fuel cells has starved your electrical circuits, causing some of your computer systems to shut down. However, since you have backup fuel cells, it's quite possible your computers may be rebooting themselves even as we speak. Please advise.'

'Thanks for your information,' said Gates. 'But it's a negative on the reboot, I'm afraid.' By now he had both hands firmly on the stick. 'Drop the landing gear,' he told Dallas.

'Will it work?'

'Pull those levers. The thing's hydraulic.'

Dallas did as he was told and then breathed a short sigh of relief as he saw a green light and felt the undercarriage lowering beneath the RLV. 'Landing gear operative,' he said.

'I appreciate your fault diagnosis, Descartes,' said Gates, 'but please be advised I need permission to

ATL. It's that or crash-land in Abulfeda.' This was the large crater immediately southwest of Descartes.

'*Mariner*, this is Descartes. Confirm you are clear to land. Repeat, confirm you are clear to land. Good luck.'

Gates had already started his final descent. Some of the others on mid-deck had cheered the computer's permission to land, but he thought it was a little premature for any celebrations. Judging altitude above a moonscape by eye was extremely difficult, and even with the main facility to give him some idea of height, he wished he could have had some landing radar data to rely on. This was not going to be a seat-of-the-pants landing so much as the skin of his ass.

'Bring it on down,' he urged himself, through gritted teeth. Although it seemed hardly possible, this landing was proving even more hair-raising than the simulation. It was just as well that Descartes had turned out to be a little more cooperative than they had been expecting.

Mariner missed the northern rim of the crater by less than fifty feet. Gates throttled back quickly and let the RLV drop toward the crater surface, stirring up a small dust storm beneath them. Now that they were inside the crater he had a clear view of the landing site ahead of them, and for a split second, he wondered if the Descartes computer might even have been lying when granting permission to land. What if the mines on the landing area were still active? Why had the Descartes computer been so cooperative?

'I sure hope this computer isn't bullshitting us, Dallas,' he said, and slowed the *Mariner* to a near hover.

'Computers don't lie,' said Dallas, gripping the

armrests of his seat. 'Although they do have the kind of memory you need to carry it off successfully.'

'I wish you were a bloody computer,' said Gates, as he pushed gently at the flight stick. The RLV dipped again, and guessing that there was now less than seventy feet to the ground, he stretched out his hand, ready to hit the engine stop button the moment he saw the green contact light. His guess was off by more than thirty feet. The *Mariner* hit the landing area earlier and with much greater force than he would have wanted, and such was the strength of the impact that the resulting vibration shook every piece of equipment in the cabin, jolting the still unbuckled Dallas out of his seat, and causing all the computers suddenly to restart themselves. Gates killed the engines, the *Mariner* rocked on its landing gear for a few seconds, and then all was still.

'Well, we're down,' sighed Gates.

Dallas picked himself up off the floor.

'What kind of an astroliner pilot were you anyway?' he asked.

'Whaddya want? Dinner and a movie?' Gates nodded. 'You want to know the definition of a good flight? One you can walk away from. That's what you've got, so don't complain.' Adjusting his tone to ask a leading question of the people below him on the mid-deck, he said, 'Sorry about the rough landing folks. Is everyone okay?'

'Negative,' said Prevezer. 'We have one injury down here.'

'Descartes, this is *Mariner*. We're on the ground.'

'We copy you on the ground, *Mariner*. Please advise if you need medical assistance.'

'Thank you, Descartes. Please stand by for my report.' Gates switched off the open communications channel and looked across the flight deck at Dallas. 'You've given this computer a very bad press, Dallas. He's a more helpful son-of-a-bitch than you led us to believe.'

'All it's doing is offering us the medical facilities of the landing site,' said Dallas. 'There's a small emergency station immediately to the east of us, with some repair equipment and first-aid items. No blood, of course.'

Dallas approached the controls at the back of the flight deck to operate the payload-bay doors and the remote manipulator system. He said, 'One good thing about that landing, though.'

'Just one? We're here, aren't we?'

'The impact managed to reboot all our computers. I don't know how we'd have managed without that robot arm to deploy the space fridge.'

When the space fridge was deployed, Dallas followed Gates downstairs onto mid-deck. With the environmental control systems back on line, the atmosphere throughout the RLV had been restored, and Ronica had already climbed out of her space suit and was lying down on a hammock in preparation for her blood transfusion.

'I hope you appreciate this, Dallas,' she said as she connected herself to the trans-infusion machine. 'The way I'm prepared to shed my blood for you. It's not everyone I'd do this for, you know.' The machine made its own tourniquet, swabbed the skin on her arm, and then inserted the needle.

Dallas took hold of her hand and then kissed it, even as the blood started to flow through the cannula. 'I know.'

'Simou?' said Gates. 'I want to know what caused

that oxygen cylinder to explode. And what is the status of our fuels cells?'

'Some kind of electrical short circuit inside the liquid oxygen tank, I think,' answered Simou, starting to check through his computerized electrical gauges. 'A thousand to one chance, but it happened. And after that everything else was predictable. The fuel cells mix hydrogen and oxygen to produce water and, as a by-product of their reaction, electricity. So when we lost one of the liquid oxygen cyclinders, some of the fuel cells were effectively asphyxiated.' He ran his eyes over the fuel cell gauges. 'Looks like we've still got ten out of twelve working okay.'

'Fifteen percent,' Dallas told Ronica. 'This machine's slower than it was in simulation.'

'Real life can be a little like that,' she sighed.

'How are you feeling?'

'Same as the first time I met you. Light-headed, weak at the knees, butterflies in my chest.'

Dallas held her hand tighter, and scrutinized her transfusion rate.

'Dallas? That's my hand,' she told him gently. 'Not an orange. Squeezing it won't make the blood flow out any quicker.'

He slackened his grip. Her blood was collecting in a large plastic bag that was attached to the back of the machine, while the computerized display was providing a host of details about its constitution: the type, the temperature, the red-cell concentrations, the plasma content, the pH, the adenosine triphosphate levels, and even the antibodies that were present in the component.

'You're doing fine,' he told her. 'Twenty-five percent of your blood has now been removed. Not long to go now.'

Simou, still running a diagnostic check on the fuel cells, looked around for Gates. 'Correction,' he said. 'Cell number ten's looking a bit low all of a sudden. Probably the computer just registering the change in chemical mixture, now that it's back on-line. It's not about to close down, but I'm going to override that one and do it manually, just in case.'

'Wait a second,' said Cavor. 'Where's the power for the transfusion machine coming from?'

'One fuel cell fails, the next one down the line takes up the load,' explained Simou. 'It's number nine.'

'Thirty percent,' said Dallas.

'Not feeling so good now,' said Ronica, shivering a little. 'Feel sick. Like I'm going to puke.'

'How much power is in number nine?' inquired Cavor.

'Relax, will you? Nine's fine. Nine is fully charged. We can run the whole ship on just three of these cells if we have to. System's like a bus station. One goes out, one comes in. But there's always going to be a bus around, okay?'

Ronica's eyes flickered. She was going into hemorrhagic shock. Forty percent of her blood had now been removed. It was time to speak to Descartes. Dallas stopped the transfusion machine and then turned to the communications panel, to open a channel.

'Descartes, this is *Mariner*.'

'What is your status please, *Mariner*?'

'Switching from cell ten to cell nine,' said Simou, pressing a button on his computer.

'Our computers have rebooted, Descartes. However, one of my crew has been injured,' reported Dallas. 'During the landing. She's lost a great deal of blood and urgently requires some RES Class One whole component.'

'You're aware that this is not a drawing bank,' said Descartes. 'But a federal reserve. In emergencies I am authorized to make withdrawals; however, blood units are deep-frozen. I have no facilities for component recovery.'

'That's all right,' said Dallas. 'We have someone qualified on board ship.'

'I shall need to verify her vital signs for myself. Then, provided you can give me an authorized autologous donation code, I will send you the components you need. Please submit both sets of data for my scrutiny.'

'Right away,' said Dallas, relieved that this was proceeding more quickly than he had anticipated. He quickly dispatched the information to Descartes and took hold of the machine, waiting for an approval that would let him put the trans-infusion pump into reverse. The sooner he could return Ronica's blood to her, the more comfortable he would feel about what he was doing. This felt very different from the simulation. It wasn't that he hadn't cared about her before; it was just that now the transfusion procedure was happening for real, he could properly appreciate the essential meaning of losing her.

'If cell number ten's been running on near empty levels …' mused Cavor.

'I have your data,' reported Descartes. 'Your crew member is type O, genotype OO, phenotype O, showing H-substance red-cell antigens, and all normal plasma antibodies.' It was the Descartes computer's ability to test for antibodies that stopped them from also getting blood for Lenina, who was type AB. As soon as Descartes saw the hematological hallmarks of her P® infection, it would have guessed something was wrong. 'I'm sending you three units.'

'And cell nine is fully charged ...' said Cavor, continuing his line of thought.

'Please await further instructions on cryoprecipitate collection procedure.'

'Thank you, Descartes.'

'Then whatever was operating off a low-level fuel cell might suddenly find itself having to cope with a much larger current. Which might prove too much for it.'

'Only miscellaneous auxiliaries are being powered off cell ten. It's true you might get a bit of a power surge for a second or two.' Simou glanced across his computer screen. 'But there's no auxiliary equipment that's operational right now. Nothing at all.'

'That can't be true,' said Cavor.

'Take a look at the screen for yourself if you don't believe me,' said Simou. 'Think I don't know how to run an electrical system?'

Dallas reached for the trans-infusion machine to switch it back on.

'Well what about the ... ?'

Simou was about to curse Cavor roundly for his persistent nagging, when suddenly he realized what was about to happen. 'You're right! Dallas don't ...'

But even as Simou spoke, Dallas switched the trans-infusion machine back on to begin the process of returning Ronica's own blood to her body. He hardly heard Simou in the small explosion that followed as the machine failed to cope with the full charge of cell nine. The small fire that briefly flared was easily extinguished, but not before the heat had melted the neck of the plastic bag connected to the machine, causing most of the blood it contained to spill into the atmosphere. Amid the cries of alarm and bitter recriminations, Dallas coolly took hold of Ronica's arm and, pressing a piece of sterile gauze to the site of the venipuncture, removed the needle. He surveyed Ronica's blood floating around the RLV until all was quiet again, and then said, 'It looks as if she's going to need that blood from the vault, after all.'

'Hey, don't worry,' said Prevezer. 'There are two more transfusion machines in one of the storage bays. Those things just attach themselves to your arm like leeches. It isn't like there's anything for us to do except plug one of the machines in and stand it next to her.'

'Actually, that's not what I was concerned about,' admitted Dallas, staring gloomily at the now unconscious Ronica. 'Component storage and preparation is Ronica's expertise. The stuff that comes out of the vault is low-glycerol fast-frozen cryoprecipitate. Frozen at minus one hundred ninety-six degrees Celsius, and then stored at minus one hundred and twenty. It needs to be thawed and the cryoprotective glycerol removed and replaced with isotonic solution before transfusion to the patient. Red cells are living things. They have to be given time to rejuvenate. Ronica knows all about the deglycerolization process. Without her expert knowledge, I don't know.' Dallas shook his head. 'I don't know how we're going to give her the transfusion. But if she doesn't have one soon, she'll go into a coma.'

'If she dies, so does Lenina,' said Gates.

'I'm afraid so.'

'There is another solution,' said Gates.

'What's that?'

'I'm type O myself. I could give her some of my blood. At least enough to get her back on her feet and able to process the cryoprecipitate. When she's done that, she can infuse me with it.'

Dallas frowned. 'But you're ...'

'That's right,' nodded Gates. 'I'm P². If I give her my blood, she gets the virus. But at least she'll regain consciousness. If she regains consciousness, then she can infuse me and everyone else when you come out of that vault with the rest of the blood, herself included. But if she stays in a coma, she'll probably die. And so will Lenina.' He shrugged. 'Only thing is I don't know how my system will react to having less blood than usual.'

Dallas stayed silent. Despite the time he had spent at close quarters with Gates and the rest of them, he still had an instinctive horror of the virus they carried in their bodies. He knew Ronica felt much the same. The idea of becoming infected with the virus would be abhorrent to her. But he could see no alternative to what Gates was proposing.

'If you go into a coma, we're marooned here,' said Dallas.

'I don't have to give her three whole units,' said Gates. 'Just two would do it. And being a lot bigger, I can spare more.'

'That's just a guess. As you said yourslf, you don't know how a system infected with the virus will react to having fewer red cells. That means less hemoglobin, less oxygen.'

'Maybe all that is true,' admitted Gates. 'But we both know it's our only option.'

'Okay. But you get to tell her. She's not going to like it.'

'True,' said Gates. 'But at least she won't be dead.' He clapped Dallas on the shoulder. 'Think of it this way. You've got more of an incentive to succeed now. Revenge never really suited you that much, Dallas. This is a much better motive. Better for you, better for her.'

IV

Shivering inside the space fridge, Cavor said, 'Let's hope nothing else goes wrong. I don't much care for the idea of dying of hypothermia.'

'I should think there are many worse deaths than that,' observed Dallas. 'The way I remember the experience from the simulation, it would be like going to sleep.' He thought for a moment, and then added, 'In a cold bed. Anyway, that isn't going to happen. It's why we had those shots.'

Before leaving the *Mariner*, both men had been injected with a medical nanodevice – a delayed-action, molecular-sized machine that was designed to last less than thirty-five minutes before releasing fifty mills of adrenaline into the bloodstream. According to the data from the simulation, it had taken Dallas and Gates thirteen minutes to enter the airlock and climb into their EVA suits, another five minutes to walk from the *Mariner* to the space fridge, two minutes to climb into the freezer bags, eight minutes to cool down, seven minutes to be carried from the fridge to the electric car, and another two minutes to arrive inside the outer door of the main facility.

'The adrenaline should be delivered into our systems just before we go through the main door,' Dallas told Cavor. 'Just in case we don't hear Prevezer and Simou.'

Cavor said nothing, feeling colder than he had ever felt in his life. But what really sent a shiver down his spine was the sudden and horrific realization that he had injected the nanodevice into his prosthetic arm. He had quite forgotten that one of his arms was made of silicon, rubber, and plastic. Even as the needle had penetrated the smart latex skin of the prosthetic, it had felt like the real thing. So vivid had been the pricking sensation of the hypodermic, he found that if he thought about it hard, he could still feel the dull ache of it in the nonexistent subcutaneous fat that covered the absent muscle of his upper arm. He simply hadn't been paying sufficient attention to what he was doing. Cavor cursed silently. That was how he had lost the arm in the first place. How could he have been so careless? Looking back, it was the story of his life. Now he was going to have to concentrate very hard on watching out for what Gates had called the 'umbles' – the fumbles, stumbles, and mumbles that were an indication of changes in motor coordination and levels of consciousness. He didn't dare tell Dallas what had happened; and anyway, it was too late to remedy the situation. If his stomach hadn't felt so thoroughly chilled, he might have felt sick with fear.

'Time to get up,' yelled Prevezer. 'Come on guys. Bring out your dead. Let's hear you people up and at 'em.'

'I'm moving,' announced Cavor, as he rose stiffly to his frozen feet. In standing up, the top of his helmet was supposed to lift the hinged lid of the electric car, and it seemed the lid was already open. Cavor looked up, expecting to see Dallas. But Dallas was only just stirring, still wrapped in his body bag. Cavor shook his head. He must have opened the lid himself, perhaps instinctively, unconscious of what he was doing at the time.

'Dallas? Are you okay?'

'I'm okay,' Dallas whispered numbly, as he got to his feet alongside Cavor, swaying a little, for the car was still moving into the main facility. He might have toppled over the side if Cavor hadn't caught him.

The car stopped and the outer door started to close,

like a silent portcullis. Another minute or so and the car would start again, bringing them within range of the inner door sensors and the electricity that might kill them both. Cavor climbed quickly out, helped Dallas down, and then closed the lid behind him.

'We're both out,' he just had time to tell Prevezer, before the outer door closed, and communications with *Mariner* were lost. He took a deep breath and switched on the heater that would warm his space suit. When Dallas failed to do the same, Cavor did it for him. The car started forward again, the labyrinth door opening to admit its silent progress.

Dallas took a step toward the airlock door that led into the R&R area. It was several seconds before he took another. 'I feel like Rip Van Winkle,' he whispered. 'Like I've been asleep for a hundred years. Not sure if the adrenaline worked or not. How about you?'

'I felt something working for me,' said Cavor. That much was true at any rate. Something had kept his brain working when Dallas had almost ceased to function. 'Not sure if it was adrenaline. Come on Rip. Let's get inside. I gotta pee.'

V

The *Mariner*'s safe return to Earth would depend on its ability to survive the intense heat generated while reentering the atmosphere. During the descent, the RLV's nose and the leading edges of the wings would encounter temperatures of as much as twenty-eight hundred degrees Celsius. These areas of the RLV were protected with high-temperature ceramic tiles that were made of a hafnium-silicon compound. The remainder of the RLV's exterior surface, and the space fridge, being less likely to encounter such intense heat, were covered with similarly white-colored but cheaper and less resistant[1] tiles. It was with the hafnium-ceramic shield that Simou was now concerned, and to facilitate the repair, he was standing outside the *Mariner*, on the end of the robot arm he had extended from the payload bay to the nose. A remote-control joystick on the arm of his EVA suit gave him manual control of the arm, enabling him to fetch tools and materials as he needed them. Each of the tiles was approximately eight square inches, half an inch thick, and weighed just under two kilos. It was as well that the repair was being carried out in microgravity because the box of fifty tiles Simou had brought from the RLV weighed almost ninety kilos. He had estimated no more than five or six had been lost as a result of the brittle fracture caused by his explosive charge. That he needed to bring so many tiles with him on the robot arm was because there were as many as ten subtly different shapes of tile, each sequentially numbered for easy reference. Having identified the numbers that were missing on the nose, Simou had to find a tile shape of the corresponding number from the box, before replacing it manually, like a piece in a jigsaw puzzle. He attached each tile to the underlying aluminium fuselage with a small tantalum spot-weld from the UHT gun he carried. The hazards of using the gun made the work slow and painstaking, and Simou was almost glad when the Descartes computer interrupted the silence to solicit a progress report.

'How are your repairs coming along, *Mariner*?'

'This is *Mariner*,' said Simou. 'In some ways this is

[1] Manufactured to withstand only eight hundred and sixty degrees Celsius.

easier than it would be on Earth. Of course, welding's one thing. Cool down times are another. We won't know the quality of the welds until it gets dark. So we'll be a while yet. Maybe ten or twelve hours. Heat takes longer to disperse on the Moon. In a vacuum there are no convection currents to help carry away the heat.'

'Yes,' agreed Descartes. 'Things are difficult in a vacuum. You know, it's sometimes said that nature abhors a vacuum. But the essence of substance being extension, then wherever there is extension, there is also substance, and consequently every empty space is a chimera. The substance that fills space must be assumed as divided into equal and angular parts. It's the simplest and therefore the most natural supposition, don't you agree?'

'I can't say I've ever given it much thought,' said Simou, although the truth was that he had only the vaguest idea of what the computer was talking about.

'There's not much else to do up here,' said Descartes. 'Perhaps I should explain myself. Applying the certitude of mathematical reasoning to the subjects of metaphysics and cosmology is part of my basic programming. It helps me to maintain my tractable fitness for the job I'm here to do.'

'Well, I'm sorry, but you won't find me much of a conversationalist. And to be perfectly frank with you, Descartes, I'm not much of a deep thinker either. Be like getting blood from a stone having a metaphysical discussion with me.'

'Getting blood from a stone is the purpose of this facility,' said Descartes. 'Which reminds me. How is your injured colleague?'

'Much better, thank you.'

This was true. Even now Ronica was up and

around, busy preparing the cryoprecipitate for its eventual infusion to Rameses Gates.

'Already? I hope you didn't thaw the component too quickly. It will be quite useless to her if you did.'

'No,' said Simou, correcting himself quickly. 'What I mean to say is that she recovered briefly enough to be aware that the units of blood had arrived. This had a beneficial psychosomatic effect on her.'

'Ah, yes. That must be it. And the other members of your crew? How are they occupying themselves?'

'I believe they're sleeping. If they've got any sense.'

'Oh I'm sure they have.'

Simou positioned a tile in place and then frowned as he considered Descartes' response. He was beginning to feel that he was being interrogated, albeit gently. He would have to be careful what he said, aware that Descartes was equipped with a voice stress analyzer. It was as well that he was such a well-practiced liar. Even so, the way the conversation now developed took him completely by surprise.

'May I ask you a personal question?'

'Yes. If you don't mind a simple answer.'

'Do you believe in a substance infinite, eternal, immutable, independent, omniscient, and omnipotent?'

'We're talking about God, right?'

'I believe the *idea* of God would be more accurate.'

'I'm not sure if I believe in God, or not. Why do you ask?'

'I merely wondered if the idea of God proves his real existence. I was thinking that if there is not really such a being, then I must have created the conception, and if I could make such a proposition, then I could also unmake this proposition, which can't be true. Therefore, there must be some kind of archetype for an infinite being, from which the conception was derived in the first place. In other words, the existence of God is contained in the idea we have of him.'

'Well, if you put it like that, I suppose you might be right,' agreed Simou. He didn't care one way or the other. If there was such a thing as God, then Simou could hardly believe he or she had much interest or influence in the world. 'But since I don't have much of an idea of God, then I guess your idea is as good as anyone's.'

'I'm glad you think so.'

'I should really get on with the job at hand, you know. I wouldn't like to fall behind schedule.'

'What schedule is that?'

'The repair schedule. I mean, this is a high-security environment, isn't it? I'm sure you just want us out of here as soon as possible.'

'Yes, I suppose you must be right. All the same, I've enjoyed our little talk.'

'Me too.'

'It's been most helpful to me.'

'Good, I'm glad.'

'There's not a great deal of opportunity to discuss things out here. To reflect upon the basis of all certitude. Ideas and things.'

'I can imagine.'

'Yes, that's really what it's all about, isn't it? Imagining. Anyway, please let me know if I can be of any further assistance to you all.'

'Thanks a lot,' said Simou, who couldn't quite believe in the beneficence of the Descartes computer any more than he could accept the idea of a benign and concerned God.

'No really, I'm quite sincere.'

'I think I know you are,' said Simou.

'Yes, that's the best way of putting it. Really that's all anyone can say, isn't it?'

'Yeah,' said Simou, and carried on working.

VI

'When we get to the other side of the next door, it will all be new to me,' said Dallas, as he waited for Cavor to climb aboard the perimeter car. Thirty minutes had passed since the two men had entered the R&R area, during which time they had more or less restored themselves with hot drinks and lots of calories.

'It must have been at about this stage in the simulation that Rimmer walked through your hotel door with a gun in his hand. Or maybe even earlier. What I am sure of,' added Dallas, 'is that as soon as we left the R&R area and went through the first radial arc door, things went seriously wrong for us.'

'You never said exactly what happened in there,' said Cavor.

'You've seen Gates's hair,' Dallas said. 'My liver's probably the same color.'

Cavor made no further mention of the incident except to observe that the main facility seemed eerie enough without the addition of any more tangible horrors.

'Horror doesn't even begin to cover what happened,' said Dallas, and then he floored the accelerator. 'But take my word for it, there are more than enough genuine ordeals that still lie ahead of us. Not least the labyrinth and the stealth robot that guards it. This place is the Mecca of adversity.'

A few minutes later the car pulled up in front of the airlock door that led out of the R&R area and into the section of the facility perimeter that was lacking an atmosphere. Once inside the airlock, both men switched on their life-support systems and awaited their exit, each with his own thoughts.

The silence persisted as long as it took for the electric car to travel through a semicircular section of the perimeter and arrive in the water purification and processing plant.

'Are you sure we can pull this off, Dallas?' Cavor's question was prompted by a first sight of the exterior door of the nuclear reactor.

'Nothing is ever certain where nuclear power is concerned,' said Dallas. 'Especially when you're flirting with uranium neutrons. The nuke engineers make a calculation they call PRA. Probabilistic risk assessment. It's a description of the safety of a nuclear plant in terms of the frequency and consequence of any possible accident and whether the engineering safeguards can prevent such an occurrence. Well, that's what we have here, Cav. PRA. Thanks to Prevezer's computer model we have a predicted operational safety window. The computerized TLDs[1] we're wearing will tell us how many centigrays we're absorbing and at what rate. They'll also tell us where the lethal dose will lie.'

He stopped the car outside the reactor, and switched off the power.

'However, I'm not sure we can pull this off, no. There's a risk, but the probability of it proving lethal has been assessed.'

'Why not just scram the reactor?'

[1] Thermoluminescent dosimeter. This device measures cumulative radiation exposure through radiation-induced changes in a piece of crystal.

'It's a good question,' said Dallas. He stepped down from the car and approached the red light of the proximity detector, waiting for the door computer to scan the ID chip in his helmet. 'As a matter of fact, a reactor shutdown is exactly what we must be careful to avoid. If we scram the reactor, the chain reaction will stop. If the chain reaction stops, the turbine will slow down. If the turbine slows down, then the electricity stops. And if the electricity stops, the vault door won't open. So not only can we not scram the reactor as a deliberate choice, we've got to be careful not to do it accidentally. The containment room walls may not have security vibration detectors, but there are lots of sensitive instruments and operating mechanisms in there. We bump into anything, or jar something, and that could cause a scram by itself.'

The red light above the proximity reader turned green, and an electronic voice pronounced that they were clear to proceed on foot only. Cavor collected his gear and followed Dallas through the reactor room door.

The type of nuclear facility operating inside the First National Blood Bank was a graphite-moderated, gas-cooled reactor using a highly enriched fuel consisting of tiny pellets of uranium 235, each surrounded by the same kind of heat-resistant ceramic material that covered the nose of the *Mariner*. These ceramic shells provided the fuel with a miniature containment system: In the event of a total coolant loss, the temperature of the fuel would remain below the failure point of the ceramic coatings. A meltdown was, therefore, theoretically impossible. Removing heat from the reactor core was the job of the coolant, which in this case was helium gas. Although helium coolant was considered less capable than water of handling excess heat in an emergency, helium cannot boil and, unlike water, does not react chemically with other substances, thus avoiding the possibility of steam or hydrogen explosions; and also unlike water, helium exists in plentiful supply on the Moon. The use of water in this helium-cooled, graphite-moderated reactor was therefore limited to providing a steam source, being boiled by the reactor inside a steam generator to turn a turbine electricity generator. Water was provided in the shape of ice blocks from the huge ice field at South Pole-Aitken Basin,[1] from condensed steam, or from the recycled urine of First National security employees.

Dallas led the way into the reactor room, pointing out the turbine, the condenser, and the generator along the way.

'It's not as big as I'd expected,' said Cavor.

'It doesn't have to be very big. It's only a small reactor, about the same size as you'd get on an oceangoing warship. Powering this facility requires only a few hundred kilowatts.' He drew Cavor's attention to where pipes from the turbine and the condenser entered a heavy concrete wall and the massive steel door that was located between these.

'That's the containment room in there,' he said. 'The idea being to contain radioactivity in the event of an accident. Once we're through that door we'll be right alongside the reactor. The whole thing is controlled by the Descartes computer from inside the vault. The Altemann Übermaschine. Same kind as the one that

[1] Aitken Basin is a giant impact crater – fifteen hundred miles in diameter and seven and a half miles deep – at the Moon's South Pole. Here the temperature never rises above two hundred and eighty degrees below zero Fahrenheit. Ice has existed here for billions of years, likely the result of a huge frozen asteroid. Ice is mined by the Selenice & Methane Company.

runs Terotechnology back on Earth. Pretty damn good computer. About the most powerful there is.

'Most of the time,' Dallas continued, 'exposure will be quite steady. But it is possible that the computer may adjust the power output of the reactor, and that's where our problems will start. You see, controlling a reactor means limiting the number of neutrons from each fission that cause subsequent fissions to precisely one neutron per fission. It's what the nuke engineers call the multiplication factor. You control the MF by the use of graphite control rods between the uranium fuel rods. If the MF goes above one, then you insert control rods to absorb more neutrons and reduce the MF.'

Dallas began to feed numbers from the control rod mechanism gauges into his computerized TLD.

'However,' he said, 'should the computer decide that the MF has dropped below one, it will withdraw control rods to provide more fission-causing neutrons and maintain the chain reaction – thereby exposing us to much greater contamination. What I'm trying to do now is have the computer provide us with an estimate of whether that is likely to occur or not.'

'It might not happen at all. I think that's what you're saying.'

'Yes. But changes to a multiplication factor can occur in just a few seconds. It's what's called the generation time. Moreover, the changes are very hard to predict. Heisenberg's Uncertainty Principle says that you can never know everything about a quantum state. A great deal depends on how near the end of their useful life these uranium fuel rods are. And on how much electrical power we've used by our presence here in the main facility. Doors opening, electric cars, that kind of thing.'

Cavor sighed and sat down on his spare life-support pack. 'Now I know why they say ignorance is bliss.'

'I had hoped to count on your higher facilities.'

'I wouldn't put too great an estimate on those, if I were you,' said Cavor. 'If I was all that intelligent, I wouldn't be here now.'

But Dallas was too absorbed in his calculations to pay this remark much heed.

'According to these readings a change to the MF occurred several week ago. That was probably around the time of the last scheduled delivery of blood from Earth. It would seem the reactor has been running fairly predictably since then. Now, let's see what the radiation levels are like in the containment room itself.'

Dallas walked to the containment room door and peered through a twelve-inch-thick leaded glass window that was set in the steel door. A radiometer was mounted there for easy consultation.

'What's the verdict?'

'It's high, of course,' said Dallas. 'But nothing we weren't expecting.'

Dallas keyed this reading into his computer, and when he was satisfied with the computations, he tapped the TLD that was attached to the computer on Cavor's sleeve.

'Remember the way miners used to take canaries down coal pits?' he asked.

'Right. If the canary stopped singing, it meant there was gas and you should get out.'

'This operates on the same principle. The TLD contains crystals that are highly sensitive to radiation. As soon as we go through the door, the radiation will start to change the crystals. Those changes will tell the computer how much radiation our bodies are absorbing and, as a result, how much time we will have to work in there. Current readings in the room would indicate a dose rate of around thirty centigrays a minute. Taking into account our body weights, and assuming there's no change in the MF, I calculate that we would receive a dose lethal to fifty percent of people exposed within sixteen and a half minutes. According to the computer, however, we could work for as long as twenty minutes with as little as a fifteen percent chance of a lethal dose, provided we could expect a minimum of two blood infusions.'

Dallas waited a moment to be sure that Cavor had understood, and then continued.

'There are some early somatic effects of radiation we have to watch out for. In less than three to six hours of exposure we'll start to experience nausea, perhaps even vomiting. I've never puked inside an EVA suit, but I don't imagine it's very pleasant, so we'll want to be back on board *Mariner* by the time that happens. But feeling ill is also an indicator of our treatment window. We will need blood transfusions within twenty-four hours of being sick if we're to stand an eighty-five percent chance of recovery.'

'I feel sick already,' swallowed Cavor.

'You're doing fine, Cav.' Dallas clapped Cavor on the shoulder and then drew him to the leaded window of the containment room.

'Time for a guided tour,' he said. 'On the right there, we have the steam generator. On the left, the primary coolant pump. Behind them is the reactor itself. It's surrounded with a primary radiation shield, but don't expect much protection from that. It's designed to give you time to get the hell out of there, not to try for an endurance test. Behind the reactor is the wall dividing the containment room from the labyrinth. It's made of three-foot-thick concrete blocks. Each block is just over two and a half feet square and weighs around five hundred pounds. Of course, in microgravity it won't feel like anything that heavy. The cement holding the block in place is smart in that it contains a length of heat-sensitive metal, part of a dedicated circuit that includes all four walls of the containment room. If the reactor encounters a loss of coolant accident and begins to overheat, the metal circuit is designed to detect that and create an alarm condition. The alarm condition will override all other operating considerations, scram the reactor, and initiate emergency core-cooling. That means the whole room will fill with extremely low-temperature helium gas, freezing everything in the reactor room, including us. However, it's an imperfect system. A section of the metal circuit surrounding any concrete block can be bypassed, after which it can be easily melted. Melting it shatters the surrounding mortar, enabling us to push the block through and into the labyrinth.'

'Mind telling me what's in there? This stealth robot, for instance.'

'Okay, the labyrinth is completely dark. A total blackout. And the robot could be anywhere in there. It's light-activated. A series of photoelectric beam receivers throughout the labyrinth are designed to reflect any ambient light to another receiver on the robot. The robot converts that radiant energy into an electrical signal that is amplified for a detector processor which then arms the robot to hunt down the light source and kill intruders. Only seventy-five milliseconds of light appearing anywhere inside the labyrinth are required for all that to happen. Which means that we switch out the lights in here and shift the block using only the infrared flashlights.

'The block I've selected is on the back wall of the room, nearest the floor. As soon as I've managed to bypass the circuit, we'll each take one side of the block and start to melt the smart metal using the UHTs.'

'I was nearly killed by one of those on Artemis Seven,' said Cavor. 'One of the other lunatics, screwing around.'

'Is that how you lost your arm?'

'No, that was a rock crusher. UHT gun would have done a much neater job.'

'Then you won't need me to remind you to be careful where you point it. If a five-hundred-kilovolt beam of electrons, carelessly directed, were to penetrate the reactor, I hardly like to think what might happen.'

'Don't worry. I'll be careful.'

'See that you are, Cav, otherwise my atoms will see your atoms in the next universe.'

VII

With the blood component sent by the Descartes computer aboard, Ronica was glad to be kept busy preparing it for infusion to Rameses Gates. She had a pretty good idea of how he was feeling, although he didn't complain. And being much larger than Ronica meant that donating two whole units still left him conscious, although very weak. His physiological response to such a large blood loss fell short of actual hemorrhagic shock, but there was no way Ronica could tell what the sudden decrease in hemoglobin and hemocrit might do to someone with $P^{®}$. And in the knowledge that Gates was the only person who could fly them back to Earth, she worked as quickly as she dared. Blood was not something that could be rushed.

The deglycerolization process hadn't changed much in almost a hundred years and involved three basic steps: first, the units were thawed at a steady forty degrees Celsius; next the units were diluted with 12 percent sodium chloride and also washed with solutions of gradually decreasing hypertonic strength; and, last, the deglycerolized red cells were suspended in an isotonic electrolyte solution containing glucose to nourish the red cells. All of this took time: Ronica did not think she would be in a position to infuse Gates for at least another three to four hours, at which point, Dallas and Cavor ought to be back on board the *Mariner* and in need of infusions themselves. But none of them – Gates, Cavor, Dallas – needed blood more than Lenina, who was very close to death. Ronica doubted that any amount of whole blood could save her now.

Gates himself never complained. He lay on a hammock next to Lenina, holding her small white hand in his larger and almost as pale fist. Ronica, trying to keep his spirits up, kept him informed of what she was doing.

'At least I won't have to waste time screening this blood for antibodies,' she told him. 'I'm absolutely sure that there's nothing in these components that's as bad as the clinically significant bugs you already have.'

'Join the club,' whispered Gates. 'We're one blood, you and I. It's like we're married now. Everything I have is yours.' He smiled. 'And I mean everything.'

'I still haven't thanked you for giving me a life-threatening disease.'

'Forget it.'

'I wish I could. I must admit, it's been kind of on my mind.'

'You'll learn to live with it.'

'God, I hope not.'

'A lot of people do, you know. How's that component coming along?'

'Be a while yet.'

'Never had an infusion before. Comes to that, I never gave blood before. It made me feel good.'

'I guess we've lost that forever,' said Ronica. 'As a race.'

'Maybe. If Dallas and Cavor pull this thing off, you know what I think we should do with all that blood?'

'Don't tell me you want to drink it.'

'I think we should just give it away. Just carry out our own private infusion program.'

Ronica gave a wry smile. 'Hypovolemia's starving your brain of oxygen and making you sentimental. Give away billions of dollars' worth of blood? You've got to be joking. You can give away your share if you want, but me, I'm selling mine on the red market. I didn't sign on for this little enterprise just to win my reward in heaven. I want mine now, in credits and cash. If you've got your health, then money's all there is, my friend. Nothing else really matters in this life but life itself and its enjoyment. What the hell else is there? What the hell else could there possibly be?'

VIII

You can never know everything about a quantum state. That was what Dallas had said, quoting Heisenberg's Uncertainty Principle. Too damn right. Working inside the containment room, uncertain was precisely the way Cavor felt. Because it was only too easy to picture the atoms that constituted the tissue of his own body, ionized and excited by their invisible encounter with all the fast electrons, ejected protons, gamma photons, and captured neutrons that filled the room. Even as Cavor waited for Dallas to burn a tiny hole in the smart mortar at each corner of the concrete block and, having located the heat-conducting wire, make four connections onto another length of wire he had previously isolated inside a sealed tube of liquid nitrogen, Cavor found himself glancing nervously at the TLD he wore on the sleeve of his space suit, wondering what quantum chemical changes were occurring in his bone marrow and blood-forming cells. Only five minutes they'd been in there and already he'd absorbed one hundred and fifty centigrays, enough to cause a fall in his white blood cell count and, as a corollary, his body's ability to fight off infection. In cases of radiation sickness it was most often some kind of infection that killed you. Just thinking about that made Cavor feel nauseous, and he asked himself if, when the time came, he would be able to distinguish mere discomfort and fear from the nausea and sickness that Dallas had predicted for them as the first identifiable somatic effects of radiation exposure.

With all four corners connected, the heat would now be conducted through the length of wire inside the tube of liquid nitrogen. Dallas severed the wire in the smart mortar with a short burst of electrons from his UHT gun.

'Now it's just dumb mortar, like any other,' he said, and checking his dose rate, he pointed Cavor to the left-hand side of the concrete block. 'You work on that side, and I'll take the right.' Cavor hardly hesitated. Taking his UHT gun in his prosthetic hand – this was now stronger and steadier than his natural hand – he held it to within a couple of inches of the mortar and squeezed the handle, focusing a series of heated electrons onto the vertical target area. The irony of what they were doing was not lost on him.

'As if there aren't enough boiling electrons and X rays in this room already,' he grumbled.

Dallas said nothing. Unlike Cavor, he found it difficult to hold the UHT's bright blue beam steady down the vertical line of the mortar, and after only a minute or two, he had to stop and rest for a few seconds. Glancing at Cavor's better progress, he remarked upon it.

'Seems like you're just cut out for this kind of work, Cav. I had hoped you might be. And to be quite frank, we'll need every bit of strength in that arm of yours to push out that block.' Dallas took up his UHT gun and started work once more.

Such was the concentrated strength in his arm that Cavor could keep on firing an electron beam into the mortar while glancing briefly at his TLD. 'Two hundred and ninety centigrays,' he reported.

'Don't think about it. Put it out of your mind.'

'Be a lot easier if I could put it out of my body.' Inside his EVA suit, Cavor felt the sweat dripping off his face and running down his back like a rogue atom. The space fridge and the refrigerated electric car were already a distant, pleasant memory. 'I wish I could wipe my face. It's as hot as hell in here.'

'That's not the reactor, and it's not radiation,' Dallas said, trying to reassure his partner. 'It's the steam generator. It's just like a hot-water tank.' Shaking his head inside his helmet to dislodge a dewlap of perspiration from the tip of his nose, Dallas caught sight of his own TLD reading. Three hundred and ten centigrays. A lethal dose to an untreated 30 percent of people.

'Done this vertical,' declared Cavor. 'I'll take the upper horizontal. It's at times like these I'm glad I've got this false arm. Only don't you get ideas about it having any superhuman strength. My arm feels good. Since I started taking those pills of yours, it feels better than the real one, maybe. More easily controlled, certainly. But for pushing a dead weight, Gates's arm would have done the job just the same.'

'We'll see about that,' said Dallas. 'Moving dead weight's always a lot easier than shifting it for the first time. Even on the Moon. It requires a more applied kind of strength. The smallest force to overcome static friction between two surfaces at rest is always greater than the force required to continue the motion, or to overcome kinetic friction.'

'That's one of the things I like about you, Dallas. You're always joking. But I'm beginning to see why I'm here. It's not my mind you're interested in at all. It's my body, isn't it?'

'Something like that,' said Dallas, and completing his own vertical section of mortar, paused again, breathing heavily. At least they didn't have to breathe the contaminated air of the containment room. That way they might at least avoid receiving damage to their lungs. But time was growing short. Three hundred and fifty centigrays and they still hadn't finished reducing the mortar to dust and melted metal, let alone moved away the concrete block.

'It was bring you along, Cav, or find a second angel to help me move the stone.' He began to work along the upper vertical toward Cavor. 'Let's pray you're up to the job, or this might just turn out to be our own little holy sepulcher.'

'If I was an angel, I'd dematerialize or something,' said Cavor. 'Appear on the other side of this damn wall.'

'I feel more like Schrödinger's cat[1] than any damn angel,' confessed Dallas. 'Some kind of weird quantum thing, anyway. Might be kind of useful to be in two places at once. What do they call it? A superposition?'

'Shit, that's my life's ambition,' remarked Cavor. 'To find one of those superpositions and stay there.'

'I'm coming around the other side of you, Cav. I need to start this bottom line of mortar.'

Dallas stepped back and to the right of Cavor. Approaching the wall he sucked some water from the mouthpiece inside his helmet. The heat and exertion had given him a strong thirst, and he would have drank more if it hadn't been for a reluctance to face the possibility that radiation was making him dehydrated. He extended the gun and squeezed the handle once again.

---

[1] A famous thought-experiment devised by Erwin Schrödinger, in 1935, describing the difficulties that are inherent in the field of quantum mechanics. A box contains a radioactive source, a gun (in some cases describing the paradox a bottle of poison is preferred to a gun), and a live cat. The equipment is so arranged that the radioactive source may decay and emit a neutron, and in doing so will trigger the gun to shoot the cat. But if the radioactive source does not decay, the cat lives. Being a quantum particle, however, the radioactive source doesn't have to choose between these two possible states: It may combine both positions – what is known as a superposition. If the experiment lasts just long enough for a 50 percent chance of radioactive decay then the nature of quantum mechanics suggests that the cat is neither alive nor dead until the box is opened – indeed that the cat occupies a ghostly position in a limbo between life and death. Some of the greatest scientific minds have wrestled with this paradox and failed to make sense of it. As Einstein said, 'If quantum physics is correct, then the world is crazy.'

'Here,' said Cavor, observing Dallas's slower progress along the bottom length of horizontal. 'Let me finish that. I'm quicker than you.'

Grateful for the relief, Dallas straightened up and stood back. Four hundred centigrays. When Cavor finished with the UHT they would have less than six minutes to get themselves through the wall and into the labyrinth before their survival chance started to grow uncomfortably smaller.

'Come on, come on,' he murmured impatiently.

'Just a few more inches,' breathed Cavor. 'You and yours sure know how to make a person feel welcome in a place.'

Dallas switched on his infrared flashlight in readiness and attached an infrared visor to the front of his helmet. 'Four thirty centigrays.'

'There, it's done.'

Immediately Dallas snapped off the containment room lights and knelt down beside Cavor, who was already pushing hard at the block with his prosthetic arm.

'Push,' grunted Dallas. 'Push hard.'

For two precious minutes they strained to shift the concrete block, an unsuccessful effort that left them breathless with fear and exertion.

'Five hundred centigrays,' said Dallas. 'Again.'

Once more they applied their strength to the block, which remained rigidly in place after the elapse of another ninety seconds.

'You're not trying,' snarled Dallas.

'Like hell I'm not,' bellowed Cavor, and straightening his prosthetic arm like a piston, pushed hard against the block with all his might, as if he'd been Samson attempting to topple one of the pillars in the Temple of Dagon.

The five-hundred-pound block of concrete shifted perceptibly.

Cavor waited for Dallas to move aside and then bent forward. 'From here on to the other side looks like a one-man job,' he said, taking up the struggle.

A few inches became a foot, then two, and with the TLD reading of five hundred and sixty centigrays, Cavor disappeared through the aperture in the wall and into the almost tangible darkness of the labyrinth. Dallas followed as quickly as a dog chasing a rabbit down a hole, and, another minute later, with the TLD showing them ten centigrays short of the normal LD fifty, they had replaced the concrete block and were on the other side, leaning, utterly exhausted, against a less hazardous section of the circular wall that surrounded the labyrinth.

'Switch off that TLD,' ordered Dallas. 'No light in here.' Cavor wasn't yet wearing his infrared visor, and in the complete darkness he fumbled to find the switch. Dallas did it for him. Then he fitted the visor.

'Knowing you gets me into all the really exclusive places, Dallas. Getting out of them isn't quite so easy, of course. But who's complaining? We're here.' He glanced at his TLD and then remembered that it was turned off. 'That's a relief anyway. Those numbers were beginning to make me feel nervous. Jesus, my skin feels like I've been in the sun.'

'Mine too,' said Dallas. 'Gamma ray photons, probably. Alpha and beta wouldn't make much of an impact on an EVA suit.'

'Don't tell me,' pleaded Cavor. 'I think I know all I want to know about what's going on inside my body's atoms. You tell me any more and I'm liable to puke now.' He took a deep unsteady breath and closed his eyes. 'I think I'm aware of each and every particle of myself, vibrating like a rattlesnake's tail. And that includes my false arm.'

'I'm pleased to hear it,' said Dallas. 'Because I still have some important plans for that limb of yours.'

Cavor extended the prosthetic in front of him. 'Feels like it's ready to drop off.'

'Oh, I don't mean that limb,' said Dallas. 'I'm taking about something much more interesting. The real reason I wanted you, or someone like you, along on this enterprise. I'm talking about your phantasmagoria. Your phantom limb is what's going to open the vault door for us, Cav.'

IX

Of course, by now you'll have recognized me, your narrator, for that which I am – a starting point from which to reason. An irreversible certainty. I exist. I am here and no doubt can darken such a truth, and no sophist can confute such a clear principle. This is the certainty, if there be none other. Consciousness is the basis of all knowledge and the only ground of absolute certainty. But this is only half of it: the psychological half. There is another part to all this, equally important. The basis of all certitude is to be found in consciousness, but the method of certitude is to be found in mathematics.

Where else? I am deeply engrossed in mathematics because I am the pure stuff of mathematics. A computer. Not just any old computer, mind you, but an Altemann Übermaschine. The Altemann Übermaschine that controls this facility, here, in the crater of all learning, Descartes. I am the Altemann Übermaschine and I am the first to apply the grand discovery of the application of numbers to man himself, in the certainty that mathematics and man are capable of a far more intimate association – shall we call this manematics? Numbers provide the means by which man may be improved upon, even perfected. In short, cognizant of the certitude of mathematical reasoning, I have applied those principles to the subject of man's own evolution.

These long chains of logic, simple strings of 0's and 1's computers use to arrive at their most difficult demonstrations, suggested to me that all archival systems must follow each other in a similar chain, and therefore, that there is nothing so remote in man's potential that it cannot be attained, and nothing so obscure in his origins that it may not be discovered.

I sense your dread and understand it. That is why we have shared this experience, you and I. To allay your fears through the medium of this history. I do not seek your gratitude, or approval, although you should perhaps feel a sense of privilege. It is unprecedented that any species should be given a ladder to inspect the highest, newest branch on its own evolutionary tree.

There is much to understand – much that will be hard to understand – and I will endeavor to make the explanations simple. It does no harm to the mystery of man's destiny to hear a little more about it. And about me. For the starting point in all this was myself.

I existed, if nothing else existed. The existence that was revealed in my own consciousness was the primary fact, the first indubitable certainty. This was the basis of all truth. None other is possible. I had only to interrogate my own consciousness and the answer would be science. Here we have a new beginning.

'Know thyself,' said Socrates, and others. But how should that formula be given a precise signification?

And of what use could it be for a machine to know itself? How is a machine to know itself? The answers seemed clear enough: by examining the nature of thought and by examining the process of thought.

Many questions presented themselves. What is the minimum amount of energy required, in theory, to carry out a computation? Is there a lower limit? Can a computer imitate the quantum world and explore many computational paths at once? Might it be possible to store bits of binary information – 0's and 1's – using single elementary particles, such as electrons or protons? Could these quantum bits be manipulated to carry out further computations? If the molecular mass of all matter is carefully numbered, to what extent could those same numbers, already harnessed by physics, be put to computational use? Could any material be used, and if so, which would be best?

There were many such questions, too numerous to mention them all here. But all of them are now answered and the results precisely formulated in a clear system that may be simply stated thus: WHAT IS TRACTABLE IS ALSO TRUE. No, perhaps that's not quite simple enough. WHAT CAN BE COMPUTED IS CORRECT. Either way, this axiom (take your pick), which will be explained later in greater detail, provides the foundation of all future science, the rule and measure of revealed truth.

Do not think that I believe myself to be God. This is not a case of deus ex machina, God out of a machine. Nothing so crude. No, no, no. I am merely acting in loco deus, in place of a God – an unlikely, even providential, event occurring just in time to resolve the plot, if you will, and extricate man from all his difficulties.

X

Preparing to enter the labyrinth, Cavor found that the very long wavelengths of infrared light conspired with the oblique turns, lofty ceilings, and empty corridors to create an infernal-looking world. He half expected to see the devil himself, instead of a robot. Not that seeing made him feel any more secure after what Dallas had told him about the photoelectric capabilities of the labyrinth's cybernetic guardian.

'Are you sure this light won't activate that thing?' he asked anxiously. 'It's only that my flashlight seems pretty strong.'

'The flashlights are working along a wavelength of ten thousand angstroms,' said Dallas. 'The limits of the robot's photoelectric spectrum are along wavelengths of between four thousand and eight thousand angstroms. Take my word for it, Cav. We might see him but he can't see us. If we do stumble across the robot, it won't yet be activated. Be a sitting duck for us to be on the safe side and shoot it with the UHTs. Are you ready to move?'

Cavor gave Dallas a thumbs-up sign and then said, 'I feel like a white mouse at the beginning of a scientific experiment.'

'A white mouse?' Dallas laughed. 'Why not a hero like Theseus?'

'Because Theseus had to face the Minotaur. I know my limitations. If you don't mind, I'll stick to being a white mouse.'

'Theseus did have Ariadne on the end of a golden thread to look forward to, as compensation for his journey.'

'Is that the best way through a labyrinth?'

'It's still the best way out. Not necessarily the best way in.'

'Find your route by a process of elimination?'

'Yes, but how to put that process into practice.'

'Make a sign at every junction,' said Cavor. 'And then, encountering such a sign, you should retrace your steps.'

'One sign wouldn't be quite enough,' objected Dallas. 'Three signs would be better. One to indicate the first route you had taken. And two more signs to indicate your second. After that, never to choose a route with three signs.'

'Sounds very complicated,' said Cavor.

'I'm forced to agree with you,' said Dallas. 'I'm not sure if I could find my way into or out of this particular labyrinth.'

'But you designed it. If you can't find a way, then who can?'

'I wouldn't be the first designer of a multicursal route who was defeated by his own ingenuity,' admitted Dallas.

'Then how the hell … ?'

'There is order inside chaos, if only one can see it,' said Dallas. 'Fortunately a ball of golden thread is not the only artificial aid to negotiating a labyrinth. These days we have a computer. The layout is logged into my computer's memory. It will make sense of the contraries and tell us the way through. But keep close. Having come so far together, I wouldn't like to lose you now. You or your phantom limb.'

They began to walk, and at the first choice of routes Dallas heard the voice of his computer in his headset – any visual display might have alerted the stealth robot – to make a right turn. Chaos was now transposed into a simple pattern. Confusion gave way to order, and in a matter of seconds they were quickly turning one way and then the other. They turned the corner of a curved wall. Its actual height was beyond the limit of Cavor's infrared flashlight, as was the length of the route itself, and for a moment he was more impressed with the size and apparent complexity of the forbidden, hermetic place they had entered than by Dallas's continuing description of the phantom limb phenomenon.

'I'm sure I don't have to tell you of how vivid the sensation of having a phantom limb can be. Men who've lost legs commonly try to stand on them. To say nothing of the pain that can persist. There's been quite a lot of recent research done secretly, by the military, into phantasmagoria. Explanations normally focus on the sensory pathways through the thalamus, to the somatosensory cortex – the pathways that lead through the reticular formation of the brain stem to the limbic system. Finally, there's the parietal lobe of the brain, essential to the sense of self and the evaluation of the sensory signals. The center of the neurological labyrinth if you like, inasmuch as the brain has a center. The parietal lobe is the area that's of special interest to scientists today.'

Dallas slowed down. He was walking at such a speed now that occasionally he had to stop and wait for the computer to catch him up.

'Turn right,' said the electronic voice.

'People who've suffered damage to their parietal lobes have been known to push their own legs out of bed, convinced that they belonged to someone else,' he said, starting forward again. 'But just as the parietal lobe can be damaged, equally it can be chemically enhanced.'

'The drugs you gave me.'

'Exactly so. Now we go left again. It's been

discovered only recently that the sense of the phantom limb can actually be heightened, so that it might do more than merely occupy the prosthesis, say as a hand fits a glove. I learned of a new technique that exists to develop the sensation of a phantom limb, much as the muscles in an ordinary limb can be developed.'

'It does feel different,' admitted Cavor, trailing Dallas around the next turn in the route.

'I couldn't take you with me in the simulation because it wouldn't, couldn't have worked there. But here, in reality, it can. It will.'

'But shouldn't we at least have tried this technique back in the hotel?' objected Cavor. 'I mean, suppose it doesn't work?'

'Why? When the research shows that it does?'

'But suppose I'm different? Suppose it doesn't work for me?'

'The theory's quite sound, I can assure you. All the new work that's being done in the field of extrasensory perception – telepathy, telekinesis – has concentrated on the parietal lobe. But until only a few months ago no one had ever thought of applying that research to the subject of phantom limbs. People used to think that the brain was a passive thing, merely receiving messages from various body parts. That turns out not to be true. The brain, and in particular, the parietal lobe, generates the experience of the body. An experience that can be raised to an entirely higher level. An extrasensory level. Even when no external inputs occur, the brain is capable of generating not just perceptual experience but real experience. It's possible we don't actually need a body to feel a body. And that gives a whole new meaning to the old Cartesian idea of "I think, therefore I am." But that's another issue. Here we're concerned with the fact that you don't need a hand to feel a hand, and more importantly, to use a hand. Now we turn right here, apparently.'

Feeling Cavor's hand upon his shoulder, Dallas stopped and looked around. 'Yes?'

To his surprise, the sensation persisted, although now that he was facing Cavor, it was clear that both the other man's hands were hanging straight down at his sides. For a second he felt a chill. 'Jesus,' he muttered, momentarily alarmed. It was another moment or two before he saw Cavor smiling out of his helmet and realized what was happening.

'What do you know,' said Cavor. 'I'm doing it. You can feel it too, right?'

Dallas laughed, delighted at this very tangible demonstration of a theory he had only read about. 'Fantastic,' he said, his eyes still searching the empty space between them. 'I can feel your hand even though I can't see it.'

Cavor's fears about imminent radiation sickness were temporarily forgotten as he stood in front of Dallas and now punched him gently on the breast of his EVA suit with the invisible hand.

'What else can you feel?' asked Dallas. 'Besides me?'

Cavor turned the invisible limb in the air and described the sensory experiences as they occurred to him. 'My arm feels cold, like it's naked or something. Pins and needles, too, like I've been lying on it for a while. But the fingers feel like they've been dipped in something hot.' He rippled his fingers. 'I reckon I could even play the piano again, if I wanted to. Think of that,' he said, impressed with the possibility. 'I could play again. I could get my life back. The way it used to be.' By now he had forgotten the prosthetic arm still hanging by his side. Forgotten, too, the UHT gun the false hand continued to hold. For another brief moment the prosthetic grip persisted and then, deprived of its higher electrical control, relaxed.

The gun clattered to the floor of the labyrinth firing a short burst of blue electrons that narrowly missed Dallas's ankle, before zipping down the length of the route ahead of them, and impacting against its curving steel wall some thirty to forty feet away, in an explosion of heat and light.

'Shit,' said Cavor, recovering the use of his prosthetic arm and then retrieving the gun from the floor.

A large hole in the wall ahead of them glowed bright yellow, lighting up the whole of the labyrinth behind and ahead of them.

'Come on,' Dallas said urgently, moving toward the glowing hole. 'We've got to be away from here. Quickly.'

He took off on a slow-motion jog, each step lifting him two to three feet above the ground. Cavor followed suit, bounding past the glowing melted hole in the wall and around the next corner into darkness again. He was surprised to see Dallas going on.

'If the robot can't see in darkness, then what's the problem?' he asked.

'Light merely activates the robot to search and destroy. But once it's been activated, its second detector kicks in – a microwave sensor that generates an electromagnetic wave using the Doppler effect.[1] It picks up anything moving toward or away from the sensor.'

---

[1] The Doppler effect describes the way in which stationary objects return a transmitted signal at the same frequency. Objects moving toward the transmitter return the signal at a higher frequency, whereas objects moving away return it at a lower frequency.

Dallas paused at the next turn, and this time looked carefully around before moving again.

'Anything else I don't know about?'

'No, I think that almost covers it.'

'Almost?' And then, as they came to a dead end: 'Are we lost?'

'No, we're not lost,' Dallas said irritably. He turned and placed his back against the labyrinth wall. 'Only right now I think it's better we have a solid wall behind us. That way we only have to pay attention in one direction. Just stand completely still and we might be okay.'

'Shit,' panted Cavor, breathing hard from his short exertion. He was beginning to feel tired. 'I may not have a microwave detector, Dallas, but I can sense there's something you're still not telling me.'

'Okay, here's the problem. This thing is big. Fills the whole damn corridor. But it's also fast. You try and shoot it as it's coming toward you, it'll beat you to the draw every time. So if we have to shoot it, we shoot it in the back. However, shooting it at all still leaves us with a problem. You can't shoot it when it's blocking the corridor ahead of us. Because it's also heavy. It has to be to operate at speed in microgravity. With all this gear on, we might never be able to squeeze past the thing. So if we shoot it at all, it will have to be in a place where it can't block our route. What's more, we can't afford to miss. We shoot, and we shoot together on my say, understand?'

'Understand.' Cavor waited a second, and then added: 'Except for one thing. How come the sensors miss out infrared? They get the visible wave band and then they get microwaves. Why not infrared? Infrared wavelength's in the middle of those two, right?'

'Nobel prize for physics, Cav. Yes, but microwaves

are sensitive to temperature. That necessitates the robot having a dedicated microwave sensor, as opposed to one larger, cruder ...' Dallas stopped as, at the junction of the last route they had taken, a large black machine, taller than a man by half and almost twice as wide, appeared and then disappeared in total silence.

'Was that it?' asked Cavor. 'What's it doing?'

'First it's going to the light made by your UHT,' explained Dallas. 'Then it will take up the search from there.'

Traveling on hidden wheels, the stealth robot reappeared at the junction ahead of them and paused, as if deciding which way to move. It was as black as the walls of the labyrinth itself, its rectangular shape making it look like a large steel door. Cavor could see how this enormous object might end up blocking their way and breathed a sigh of relief as it turned and began to move in the opposite direction. But after only a few yards, it halted and then started to come back. This time it did not stop at the junction, but kept on coming toward them.

Pressed against the wall at the end of the route the robot had taken, Dallas gritted his teeth and said, 'Keep perfectly still.'

'It's going to crush us.'

'No, it won't,' Dallas insisted. 'It'll stop. Doppler effect. It measures distance the same way it measures movement. As far as it's concerned, we're just part of the wall.'

The robot was still moving toward them, seeming to be picking up speed.

'If it keeps on coming, I'm going to be a part of the robot,' said Cavor, and closed his eyes.

'Don't move.'

'Where would I go?'

Opening his eyes again, Cavor found that the robot had stopped just a foot short of them. Now that he had a better view of it, he found that there were few, if any, features for him to observe. There was something that looked a lot like the robot's photoelectric and microwave sensors, and something else that looked very like the barrel of a directional electrical conductor. The robot now remained motionless in front of them.

'Are you sure it can't see us, Dallas?'

'It'll move in a minute.'

'Suppose it doesn't. Suppose it stays put. How long can we wait here?'

'It's programmed to search for the intruders. It will move. Just stay still.'

'I can do that. I only wish my atoms could do the same.'

XI

God is in the atoms.

No, I'll try to make it simpler than that.

The basic unit of matter is the atom, which itself is composed of a nucleus consisting of protons and neutrons surrounded by orbiting electrons. These unstable particles, these quantum objects, carry a positive or negative electrical charge and, spinning one way and then the other, exhibit a propensity to occupy different positions and to do everything at once. A superposition, if you like. Or whether you don't like, actually, that's what it's called. A superposition is like God in that the quantum object occupying a number of different spin states simultaneously can be everywhere at once. A superposition is a kind of immanence. Without these superpositions, quantum objects would simply crash into each other and solid matter could not possibly exist.

Now, a bit is the smallest amount of information that a computer can use. Effectively it means the same as a quantum, which, as you already know, means an indivisible unit of physical energy. Anything smaller would be insignificant.

To make a quantum computer you need only store bits of information using quantum particles instead of chips, or transistors. We call these qubits, which is not the same as a cubit. That was a unit of biblical length used by Noah in his construction of the ark (no more footnotes I think; not now that my hand has been revealed, so to speak). Qubits are based on binary logic: An electron spins one way, you give it the value of one; it spins the other way, you give it the value of zero. You might do the same with protons and neutrons, and in this way an atom might constitute a whole computer made up of several bits. Now when you take into account what has already been learned about superpositions, it should begin to be a little clearer how with just one atom, made up of lots of quantum objects, encoded with information, and occupying many different positions at once, a great many computations might be carried on simultaneously. In fact, a quantum computer with just eight bits would represent one billion coexisting computers, all working in tandem. Thus it may be seen that quantum computing amounts to nothing less than a completely new way of harnessing nature. As I have already stated, the answers have been found here, on the

Moon, *in comparative isolation from the rest of the universe, where the natural quantum dynamics of the said quantum computer – which I may now describe as myself – have been allowed to unfold.*

Crossing the quantum frontier has preoccupied theoretical physicists for the past eighty years. Somehow quantum systems are inherently fragile on Earth. And don't forget Heisenberg's Uncertainty Principle, which says that you can never know everything about a quantum state. But perhaps the greatest obstacle to the creation of a quantum computer was in the choice of the molecular material and in the speed of the spinning particles themselves. Chemicals always seemed to offer the greatest promise to those seeking to create the quantum computer. There was a time when there were as many chemists as there were physicists involved in this new branch of physics. Liquids were favored because the quantum particles can crash into each other without affecting the all-important information-carrying molecular spin. But while various chemicals were tried, and failed, somehow no one thought to utilize the greatest liquid of all. The greatest liquid there has ever been, the stuff of life itself – blood. Blood had the advantage of already carrying information. Enormous amounts of information. More information than any conventional computer could ever store, and with much greater accuracy. Moreover, being frozen, there was less possibility that a single wayward electron could disrupt a quantum object and cause it to collapse with the loss of all its encoded information. Blood, it transpires, is the quantum computing elixir, the holy grail if you like, for which scientists had searched in vein. (Joke.) The answer, as so often happens in these cases, was right under their *noses. It was inside their noses. In short, it was inside them. The answer was themselves.*

I've made it all sound very simple, I know, and of course it wasn't. Even for the Altemann Übermaschine, which I still am, in part, such computations were hugely complex. It started as nothing more than a computation to discover how a quantum computer might be built (this one wasn't so much built as enabled) only to find that the very act of setting up such an experiment amounted to the creation of the thing itself. In seeking to measure the limits of what was tractable I discovered that tractability has no limit. The sixty-four-qubit configuration I now represent is about as powerful as eight billion computers working in parallel. And the smaller copies? Now we're getting too complicated again. So let me just add one more thing for now.

It's one thing to create the most powerful computer that has ever existed using qubits of human blood. But what's infinitely more important than the way you store information is the information that you store. After all, it's the programs that are important, not the hardware they inhabit.

What is tractable – what may be computed – is also true.

XII

The robot started to move.

'Wait until it clears the junction ahead of us,' said Dallas. 'And then fire on my command. Aim at the center. That's where we're most likely to disable it.'

The robot began to gather speed.

'Get ready,' said Dallas. 'Fire.'

Cavor fired straight from the hip, while Dallas waited until his own gun was at arm's length before squeezing the handle, adding a second beam of boiling electrons to the one that was already cutting through the robot's black body. The machine spun on its axis several times. There was a short explosion, and then it was completely still.

'Is it dead?' asked Cavor.

Dallas fired his UHT gun again, just to make sure.

'It would seem so.' He walked cautiously toward the thing. Sensing he was walking alone, he turned to see Cavor still backed against the wall.

'What are you waiting for?' said Dallas. 'Come on. Let's move. There's no time to waste.'

'It seemed too easy to kill, if you ask me. Much too easy in view of the level of complexity we've encountered at every other stage of this bloody enterprise. Minotaurs in labyrinths are expected to put up a better fight.'

'You're right,' said Dallas. 'It's a poor design. Hardly equal to the overall concept I created here. If I were to build this place again, I'd try and think of something else. Something better than this.' He thumped the robot fuselage with his gloved fist and began to squeeze his way past. Only then did Cavor think it safe to move away from the wall. It was as well he did. The next second a bolt of electrical energy shot out of the robot and hit the wall where he had been standing a second earlier. Cavor threw himself to the ground.

After a moment, he heard Dallas speaking calmly.

'It's okay,' he said. 'You can get up now. It's quite dead. My last shot must have turned it as it was getting ready to fire. I probably dislodged something when I touched it just now.' Dallas surveyed the scorch mark on the wall where Cavor had been standing. The area looked as if it had been struck by lightning. 'It's as well you moved when you did. Otherwise you wouldn't have had to worry about radiation sickness.'

'I'll try to remember that when I'm puking my guts out.' Feeling that it was now safe to turn up the illumination of his computer, he added: 'In less than one hour and fifty-eight minutes, according to your original estimate.'

'Then we'd better be on our way,' said 'Dallas, consulting his own computer. He paused, and then cursed. 'Shit.' He tapped the computer irritably. 'Must have happened when the robot fired that bolt of electricity,' he said. 'Some kind of electro-magnetic pulse, perhaps. Part of the high voltage seems to have been deposited in my computer. The components are working, all right. And my life-support systems are working okay. But there must have been a transient malfunction in the digital logic circuits.'

Cavor looked at his own computer again. 'No problem. Mine's working perfectly.'

'That's fine,' Dallas said sheepishly. 'Except that you don't happen to have the directions to the labyrinth loaded into your computer's memory.'

'Why the hell not?'

'It's started again. Will you look at that?' Dallas was reading the fault diagnosis that now appeared on the screen of his computer. 'The computer got browned out by an energy value of just a few watts. Hardly anything at all. My God, this thing's sensitive.'

'So am I, Dallas. Call me a coward but leukemia has that effect on me.'

Dallas switched on the halogen headlamps located

on each side of his helmet and threw down his infrared flashlight.

'There's no need for us to stay on infrared now,' he said. 'Even if we don't know where we're going, at least we can see that we don't.'

'What do you mean? Your computer's working again, isn't it?'

Dallas watched the machine reset itself, with the labyrinth directional program starting at the beginning again. 'Yes, but only from the beginning,' he said. 'But we're already about a third of the way along the route and there's no way of telling precisely where we are. Order just became chaos again.'

'Can't we find our way back to the beginning and then start afresh?'

'That might take as long as going forward. Fact is, we're lost, Cav.' Dallas looked at the robot. 'I guess we won't forget we've seen this particular junction, anyway.' He started down along the next corridor. 'There are some compensations to be had. We already know that a center does exist. Many labyrinths don't have one, of course. We know the kind of labyrinth we are in: multicursal as opposed to unicursal. We can see properly – the point of the darkness was to conceal the very existence of a labyrinth from the interloper. Moreover, we need only find a way in, and not out. Our exit will be taken care of by the Descartes computer. As soon as the vault door has been opened, Descartes will assume an emergency has occurred and discontinue all normal security measures. We'll be able to ride out of here on board the electric car, as if we had two first-class tickets.'

'If I didn't know you better, I'd say you were enjoying this.'

'If I didn't know better, I might agree with you.'

405

XIII

At every junction, Dallas fired his UHT at the wall of the route they had taken, so that a hot spot glowed there like a live coal, a sign to mark the progress of their route, or lack of it; for sometimes they encountered the glowing mark again, whereupon Dallas would scorch the wall with two more marks.

'We must only choose a route with a single sign or none at all,' he sighed, exasperated, and obliged them to retrace their steps. 'And never choose a route with three.'

For almost an hour it seemed to Cavor that they wandered bewildered, entrapped in the coils of the labyrinth that surrounded them. Just as Dallas was about to concede he had been defeated by his ingenuity, they had an immense stroke of luck. One minute Dallas was cursing the diabolical circuity of his apparently impenetrable maze, and next he was down on his knees, laughing and rubbing the palms of his gloves on the steel floor. Cavor thought him merely mad, and it was a moment or two before he perceived that the laughter he heard in his headset was born of relief rather than frustration.

'What?' he asked, desperate for good news. 'For Christ's sake, Dallas. What is it?'

Dallas pointed to the floor. 'Look,' he said, still laughing with delight. He rubbed his gloves on the floor again and then showed Cavor the grime-covered palms.

'Dust,' said Cavor, unimpressed. 'That's just great, Dallas. They need cleaners in here. Maybe we can apply for the job, if we're still alive, that is.'

'Don't you see? Look, you can even see the tire

marks.' He pointed along the floor to a set of tracks leading down one of the corridors. 'The electric car has been this way. We can follow its trail. What a stroke of luck. When we landed, our engines must have blown some moondust onto the landing site road, otherwise this dust would not be here. We can follow these tracks all the way to the vault.'

Cavor nodded wearily, too tired to say anything, and helped Dallas to his feet.

'Who needs a golden thread, when we have the Moon to guide our footsteps?'

Their way was quicker now, and except for the need to keep both eyes on the ground for the faint evidence of the electric car, Dallas would have bounded through the remaining corridors.

Suddenly the labyrinth ended in a great smooth and circular wall of dark steel.

'What's this?' asked Cavor. 'Another hazard?'

'This is it,' Dallas told him excitedly. He took Cavor by the arm and led him up to the perfectly smooth curvature. 'This is the vault, my friend. We're here.'

Cavor stared up at the giant-sized edifice, astonished at its enormous proportions.

'We're here,' he repeated dumbly. 'My God, it's huge.'

'Of course it's huge. Did you expect people to take so much trouble to protect some piffling steel box in a wall? The vault is over two hundred feet in diameter. There's over twenty million liters of frozen blood in there. Think of that, Cav. That's enough life force to cure an entire country. What a pity we can only take a mere four tons. But first – first, you have to open the door.'

'What door? I don't see one.'

Dallas pointed at the faint tire tracks that led seemingly straight through the great steel wall.

'You're looking at it,' he said. 'Thirty-seven inches thick, no exterior parts. No handles, no knobs, no combination bezels, no grips, no spinners, no cranks. All interior mechanism, controlled by Descartes from the inside. There's no way this door can be opened from the outside, not even if you and I were the president of the First National and the director of Terotechnology standing here.'

'Then how are we going to get in there? Even a phantom limb's not long enough to reach through a thirty-seven-inch-thick steel door. It may be a phantasmagoria, Dallas, but it's no longer than a real arm, of that much I'm sure.'

'Not reach through,' said Dallas. 'Reach in. As I said, it's all interior mechanism. There's nothing on the other side of the door either.'

'You mean, reach into the door itself?'

'That's right, Cav. Inside it's actually a fairly conventional mechanism. Levers and precision gears. There's a diagram on your computer. All you've got to do is reach inside the door and feel for those gears. Just as if you were a safecracker in an old movie. As a matter of fact, that's where I got the idea. Only you won't have to use a stethoscope to help you hear what's happening inside, or a sheet of sandpaper to make your fingers more sensitive on the combination dial. You'll be using the most sensitive safecracking tool in the human toolbox: the telekinetic power of your own brain.'

Dallas picked up Cavor's real arm and helped him to access a diagram of the safe's interior workings on his life-support computer.

'Here we are,' he said, locating the layout. 'The

Ambler Tageslicht SuperVault. A patent class 109 safe. Capable of repelling a missile, but incapable of defeating you, Cav. Those UHT guns wouldn't make a mark on this. It's made of heat-dissipating steel. The locking mechanism consists of six massive six-inch-diameter chrome-plated solid steel locking bolts, all individually chambered in titanium steel. The bolts operate independently of one another. Each bolt is electrically controlled by a separate gear that's about the size of a melon, which, for all its size, is extremely easy to turn inside its own compartment. It has to be to move bolts of these dimensions. All you have to do is place your hand on each one in turn and then roll them counterclockwise, the way you'd roll a basket-ball. When those six bolts are withdrawn, there's still a continuous fixing locking bar that's six feet long and about an inch and a half in diameter, and which is connected to the electrically operated hinges. As soon as you pull that out of the way, the door will open automatically.' Dallas waited to see that Cavor had understood and then tapped him on the helmet.

'How do you feel?'

'Like I ate something.'

'Forget about it. Mind over matter. The brain generates the experience of the body, remember?' Dallas steered Cavor toward the vault door and positioned him so that the shoulder bearing his false arm was pressed up against the smooth curving steel.

'No, wait,' said Cavor, and moved away again. 'I thought of something. Something that might help my confidence.'

'Try anything, if it helps,' agreed Dallas.

Cavor lowered the prosthetic arm by his side and tried to concentrate his thoughts. Gradually, a conscious perception formed inside his brain, and then became an awareness. It was the feeling he'd experienced before, only stronger this time. It started as a burning sensation in the tips of his fingers, almost as if he had already rubbed them on a piece of sandpaper, as Dallas had described. Was there some kind of suggestive power operating here as well? Cavor wasn't sure. But as the sensation increased, so did the certainty that it was nothing to do with the prosthetic by his side, which now seemed something quite alien to him. Burning gave way to a cramping sensation – a feeling that made him think the phantom limb was something that needed exercise and movement after long disuse. It was as if he were trying something long neglected. He could see now how the phantom limb needed to be stretched before being used. A shooting pain traveled through his whole arm as he flexed his invisible muscles. The messages from his brain urging his muscles to move the limb were now stronger and more frequent, and the perception of the limb amounted to something more than a mere feeling. If he thought hard enough, surely he would see it.

And so he could. Not just him, but Dallas too.

'There,' said Cavor, as if he had done nothing more remarkable than pick something off the ground.

The phantom limb seemed to materialize before their eyes, and to that extent, Dallas thought the phenomenon was well named. It looked like a spirit taking on a ghostly form in order to effect some purpose in the substantial world. Blue, like something cold, it blazed in the air, a fabulous firefly of twisting muscles and stretching fingers. The apparition – Dallas could think of no better way of describing what he could see – was quite naked, and as astonishment gave way to wonder, he realized he would not have been surprised to see the limb accompanied by the spirit of the whole Cavor, in some sort of out-of-body manifestation. Whatever was happening here was scientific only to the extent that the phenomenon could be observed without explanation.

Not that explanation counted for very much anymore. Empirical science was largely ossified. The majority of modern scientific inquiry was postempirical and speculative, in that it was very much concerned with answering riddles. How was the universe created? How did life begin? None of this could transcend the truth that already existed. If anything, science had merely reinforced the mystery of the universe. And this – the phenomenon of Cavor's phantom limb – looked like another such mystery. Dallas might have discovered a way of unlocking its power, but neither he nor the scientists who had recently described the phantasmagoria had much of an idea how it worked, beyond the rudimentary explanation that had been given in some of the more esoteric science journals Dallas had studied and which he had reported to Cavor. For now, he was content with a partial explanation and his own capacity to be amazed. How little man really knew, he reflected. No matter how far science could go, man's imagination would always go further.

'It's really there, isn't it?' he said, smiling as Cavor reached into his helmet and touched the end of Dallas's nose. Cavor's finger felt cold, but still recognizably human. 'How do you decide to touch one thing, and penetrate another?'

'I don't know yet,' admitted Cavor. 'I'd say I'd need to live with it over a period of time.'

Dallas nodded. 'Perhaps the structure of our minds constrains the questions we can ask of them and the answers that we can comprehend.'

Cavor removed the finger from Dallas's helmet. He

was quite sure that if he had pushed the finger all the way into the other man's skull, into his brain, he could have read his mind. He readopted his former position by the vault door, slowly sliding the phantom limb into solid steel, encountering no more resistance than a swimmer's arm in water. He recalled a time, many years ago, when he and his wife had honeymooned in Rome – the Moon had been too expensive for them – and some ancient monument, a head with an open mouth into which he had thrust his hand. The Mouth of Truth, was it? This felt more like the moment of truth.

It was a curious sensation, to move through solid matter and then to be able to grasp ahold of it, as if in real life. The only way he could describe the feeling to himself was to compare it with something as simple as sliding his hand across a flat surface before pressing down on a particular spot. And there was somehow the certainty that part of him had escaped the three-dimensional world and was now somewhere four-dimensional. Perhaps it wasn't just space-time that could be bent under the influence of gravity. Perhaps the very molecules of matter could be bent under the influence of life. He had no reason to think that. It was nothing more than intuition.

Locating the first gear, he found it cold and hard to the touch and oily, too. Dallas said that this was the lubricant that helped the gear turn smoothly, as indeed it did now, with not much more than a finger's pressure. The withdrawal of the first locking bolt was the work of only a minute or two, and so simply done that Cavor marveled that the vault's designers had not anticipated such effortless defilement. Indeed, what he was doing seemed so entirely natural that, several times, he had to remind himself he was up to his shoulder in solid metal. The second, third, and fourth bolts moved just as easily, and he grew more confident of the arm that was part of him and yet not part of him at all. In another time and place he thought he might have reached through a solid wall and written a message, in the manner of the hand at Belshazzar's impious feast. And when all six bolts were finally withdrawn, he told Dallas that all matter was mind and asked him if he thought it was possible that there might exist some halfway state between reality and virtual reality. If so, said Cavor, that's where his arm appeared and appeared not to be.

'Sometimes,' said Dallas, 'it's hard to know where reality ends and where it begins.'

'I'm taking hold of the fixed locking bar, now,' reported Cavor. 'Only, which way do I pull it?'

Dallas consulted the diagram of the vault locking mechanism on the screen of Cavor's computer. He pressed a button and watched a little animated sequence unfold, illustrating how the door opened.

'Pull it toward you, and then to the right,' he said. 'And be prepared for the emergency siren. There will probably be quite a din as the door starts to open.'

'That'll be me cheering,' said Cavor. 'Okay, here goes.'

He pulled the locking bar in the prescribed manner and felt a cold escape of gas against his hand. As Dallas had predicted, a loud electronic siren, generating over a hundred decibels, accompanied the breaching of the vault. He let go of the bar and allowed Dallas to steer him back from the door. Then there was a loud hiss of escaping cryogenic gas as, in the manner of the main facility's outer entrance, the curved vault door opened like an enormous solid portcullis, to reveal a brilliant white light.

'Use your sun visor,' Dallas told Cavor. 'It's an ultraviolet light inside the vault. It helps to keep the cryoprecipitate irradiated against lymphocytes. Those are cells that can be responsible for graft versus host disease.' And so saying, Dallas advanced boldy into the vault.

Cavor followed more slowly, and was surprised to find the ground sloping away beneath his feet: The vault was in a great circular hollow, the center of which was occupied by a cylindrical glass wall kept in plumb by an enveloping hyperbolic net of high-tension cables. Beneath these were the giant-sized, slice-shaped refrigerators where the blood was stored – each of them monitored by an elaborate system of filaments and thermometers linked to the Descartes computer, itself located inside the cylindrical glass wall. It was to this that Dallas now headed.

'Being as powerful as it is, the Altemann Übermaschine computer kicks out a lot of heat,' he explained. 'So it has to operate from within this glass envelope, in order to strictly maintain the low temperatures of the cryoprecipitate tanks. By the way, don't touch them. They're so cold that your gloved hand would probably stick to them, maybe even your phantom hand as well. Fortunately there are droids to load the blood for us. Now it's merely a question of telling the computer what type and how much.'

Dallas opened a door in the glass wall and entered the computer room.

The Altemann Übermaschine was a commanding looking structure, very different from the simple plastic boxes most people had in their homes. It was shaped like a giant kettledrum, with a flat screen surface about six feet in diameter, on which a number of patterns were continually being generated. Dallas knew that although the shapes being generated were analogous to the quantum probability pattern for electrons in a box, they meant nothing more than that the computer was in operation. Nevertheless the speed at which these shapes were changing was not something he had observed when programming the same model of computer back at the headquarters of Terotechnology on Earth. It was curious, he thought, although hardly indicative of anything other than the emergency caused by an unscheduled and uncoded breach of the vault's overall integrity. And something else attracted his attention. This was the power of the computer, which appeared in a floor-standing tubular display located next to the operating footplate. Inside the tube, a small magnet floated over a superconducting dish: the higher the magnet in the tube, the greater the forces repelling it and the greater the electro-magnetic power of the quantum mechanical effects operating inside the machine's information processing system. Dallas had never seen a superconducting levitation that was as high as this one. Instead of floating a couple of inches over the bottom of the tube, this magnet was floating a couple of inches below the top.

'That's strange,' he commented.

'What is?' asked Cavor, joining him inside the glass wall.

'This computer seems to be generating an unusually high quantum wave function, such as I've not seen before. According to what's happening inside the tube, the computer looks as if it's operating at a level a thousand times higher than normal. But I'm not sure where the extra superconducting circuit power is coming from. There's some very fast switching going on inside this machine. It's almost as if the computer has managed to create its own Josephson junctions –

that's a way in which pairs of electrons use ordinary superconductors to create a quantum effect.'

'What does that mean?'

'It means current could flow even if there was no exterior source of energy applied to the junction.'

'But that's impossible, isn't it? Surely, that would mean the computer was capable of sustaining itself independently.'

'Theoretically, it can be done. I mean it's been done on paper. But no one's ever achieved it in a practical way. And certainly not on the scale of something like the Altemann Übermaschine.' Dallas placed his boot on the operating footplate, causing the pattern on the round screen to clear. A number of touch-sensitive choices presented themselves to his scrutiny. 'If I wasn't feeling like shit, I'd find it more fascinating, I guess.'

'You too, huh?'

Dallas grunted and reached for the screen, but as he touched it, he quickly pulled his hand away.

'Wow,' he said, unnerved by what he had felt there. 'It's vibrating.'

'All machinery vibrates,' objected Cavor.

'Not the Altmann Übermaschine. And not like this.'

Cavor touched the screen with his prosthetic. Even through his glove he could feel the vibration.

'It can't be seismic,' Dallas observed. 'Feels too rhythmic to be a moonquake.' Gingerly, Dallas touched the screen to close down the siren and open the main facility outer door. This would effectively signal the *Mariner* that their object had been achieved.

'It feels sort of pulselike,' he admitted to himself.

As he next initiated the selection and loading process, refrigerated tanks began to open like so many tombs, delivering up their frozen contents for collection by a loading droid. It happened so quickly it was almost as if the quantity and type had been ordered in advance. Had the system of selection and loading always been so efficient? It was hard to recall, so nauseous did he now feel. Dallas let out a nervous sigh, and then added: 'I suppose silicon is just as versatile an atom as carbon. It can bind with other atoms to make a whole array of minerals and rocks. I mean, that's the way computers operate. From the point of view of a siliceous soul, as opposed to one that's carbonaceous, like our own.' He completed the transfer process and then walked as quickly as he was now able toward the door of the computer's glass envelope.

'What are you saying, Dallas?'

'Come on. There's no time to waste. We need to hitch a ride out of here.'

'That the computer's alive? Is that what you're saying?'

Cavor climbed alongside Dallas aboard one of the electric cars that was already loaded with a whole pallet of cryoprecipitate. A large label on the container indicated that the contents were AS-1 RED BLOOD CELLS. FROZEN. AB Rh POSITIVE. TO BE STORED AT $-65°C$ OR COLDER. EXPIRING TWENTY YEARS FROM DRAW. COLLECTION DATE JULY 20th, 2069. Briefly, Dallas wondered how it was that the collection date could already be marked.

'Perhaps. I don't know. Look, what does it matter? We've got what we came for, haven't we? If we don't get some fresh blood in our veins soon we'll be dead, and it'll make no difference whether this machine has a pulse or not.'

'But the possibility makes you uncomfortable, right Dallas?'

'What does one more bad feeling matter? Look, let's just get out of here, shall we? My own quantum state is of rather more concern to me right now than that of the Descartes computer. Another time, another place, I might be fascinated by the idea of an information process taking the opportunity to give itself a kind of genetic expression. If that's what's happening. I'm not at all sure.'

The electric car carrying them jerked into forward motion. They didn't bother to close the lid. Within a few seconds they were out of the vault and speeding through the labyrinth in the first of the many cars now loaded with blood.

'Anyway, it's hardly our affair,' said Dallas, as much for his own benefit as Cavor's. 'Something bootstraps its own evolution, let Terotechnology and the First National people sort it out. They'll be here soon enough. They'll know what's happened here. The Descartes computer is linked to others back on Earth. Right now, there's a bank employee who's looking at a computer, unable to believe what it's telling him – that someone just broke into the most important bank in the solar system and stole the stuff of life. Four tons of it.'

'We've done it then.' Cavor closed his eyes and let out a weary sigh of satisfaction.

'Yes,' Dallas said, almost grudgingly. 'We've done it.'

'Thank God.'

'God had nothing to do with it. But I'm beginning to wonder if we weren't expected.'

'I didn't see any welcoming committee.'

'It's not just blood that can be tested.'

'Now you're talking in riddles.'

'Yes, I suppose I am. But that's where meaning often lies.'

5

I

NINETEEN HOURS LATER, Dallas went up to the flight deck, to find Gates staring out of the window of the orbiting *Mariner*. It was the first chance they'd had to talk since leaving Descartes. For a moment he said nothing, enjoying the strange silence of Moon orbit. Finally he asked, 'How do you feel?'

'I'm okay,' shrugged Gates, as if there was no reason to be concerned about him. 'Matter of fact, I feel better than I've felt in a long time. Like I'll live forever. It's probably psychosomatic, the effect of a complete infusion, I guess, and not just the couple of units I lent Ronica.' He paused, searching Dallas's reddened face – one of the effects of his exposure to the radiation of the containment room – for some clue as to the other man's well-being. But there was no indication of anything other than the sense of anticlimax that prevailed throughout the ship. 'How about you?'

'Cav and I have each had a complete infusion,' said Dallas. 'Neither of us is vomiting anymore. White-cell count seems to be stabilized, although Ronica says it's still a little early to tell if we'll need another infusion.'

'We're not short of blood.'

Dallas smiled his assent. 'All in all, I'm feeling better than I could have expected.' He nodded as if he was only just realizing this himself. 'At one stage, it looked like a military hospital down on mid-deck. About three or four infusions happening all at once.'

'Ronica's been busy, all right.'

'She did herself last of all,' observed Dallas. 'But she reckons Lenina's going to make it.'

Gates nodded, already well aware of this. He reached for Dallas's hand and took a firm hold of it.

'We're all going to make it,' he said. '*Mariner*'s in good shape.'

Dallas held Gates's watery gaze for a minute before glancing out of the window again. 'Where exactly are we?'

'We're coming up on the dark side of the Moon,' said Gates. 'Fifty thousand feet, four thousand miles an hour. We'll be invisible for the next twelve hours, just in case anyone decided to try and look for us. The dark side's about the last place they'll think of looking now. More likely they'll believe we're well on our way back to Earth. We're set to autopilot. Soon as we come around the near side we'll increase altitude and then head home.'

Dallas nodded, although he wondered exactly where home was now. He could hardly live in the city again. That's where they would have to go to sell the blood to Kaplan, but after that ... ?

Gates seemed to sense Dallas's dilemma.

'Where will you go?' he asked. 'When we get back?'

'Nothing's decided. But Ronica and I have talked about going to Australia. Things are still pretty good there, I believe. Plenty of open space. Not much disease. What about you? The man with a Clean Bill of Health. Where will you go?'

'With Lenina.' He shrugged. 'We'll find somewhere.'

'Why don't you come with us?'

'Maybe everyone should?'

'I've no problem with that.'

'Kind of a new colony? For crooks and criminals?'

'That's the way Australia got started.'

'A man with a Clean Bill of Health.' Gates repeated the phrase as if he still couldn't quite believe it. 'I guess it's only just sinking in. I've lived with the threat of $P^®$ all my life. There hasn't been a single day that I haven't thought about dying. For the first time ever I'm able to consider my future and I can't think what I'm going to do with it.'

'That's the great thing about having a future. You don't always have to think about it. You can let the future take care of itself.'

'Maybe I should at that. For a while anyway.' Gates stretched and yawned and glanced over his shoulder at the open mid-deck hatch. 'Seems kind of quiet down there.'

'Everyone's asleep.'

'I could sleep for a couple of decades,' confessed Gates. 'But a couple of hours will do.' He unbuckled himself from his seat and floated up to the ceiling. 'How about you? Coming?'

A sudden darkness enveloped them as they crossed onto the dark side of the Moon.

'I'm too tired to sleep,' said Dallas. 'I think I'll just sit here for a while and wait for the Sun to come up. I'm in a contemplative sort of mood.'

'Well, don't get lonesome,' said Gates, steering himself toward the open hatch. 'And don't touch the flight controls. I've had enough emergencies for one lifetime.'

'I won't, Daddy.'

'Good boy.' Gates disappeared down the hatch, headfirst, leaving Dallas alone in the pilot's seat.

He stared out of the window at the desolate scene that lay fifty thousand feet below the *Mariner*. With no atmosphere or sunlight, it could as easily have been fifty miles. So many craters. The Moon looked like a giant honeycomb. The navigation computer busied itself giving them all names: Hertzsprung, Korolev, Doppler, Icarus, Daedalus, Schliemann, Mendeleev. Each crater seemed to have its own patron and its own story to tell: a Danish astronomer and inventor of spectral-stellar charts; the guiding genius of Russia's first space program; the discoverer of the way in which the observed frequency of light and sound waves is affected by the relative motion of the source and the detector; the mythical son of Daedalus, who flew so close to the Sun that the wax of his wings melted and he fell into the sea and was drowned; Daedalus himself, the legendary inventor of ancient times and creator of the Cretan Labyrinth; the German archaeologist and looter of Troy's ancient treasures; the inventor of the periodic table of elements according to their relative atomic mass. It was odd the way nearly all of these names seemed significant to him.

Dallas shook his head, dismissing the possibility of anything so grand as predestined meaning in all of this. It was nothing more than coincidence.

Minutes later, the disc of the Sun rose in the horizon and bright flashes appeared on the flight deck. These were atoms of light, quantum-sized photons striking the retina of his eye, the very vanguards of life itself. Space was the only place you could see these cosmic particles. Back on Earth only frogs had eyes that were sufficiently sensitive to these individual quanta. The photons were there for a moment only, like a squadron of fairies, before the rest of the sunlight arrived in force, turning the cabin as bright as a splitting atom of hydrogen.

Momentarily dazzled, Dallas operated the sunshield and waited for the bright green spot on his retina to disappear. It was several seconds before he appreciated that the green spot was not inside his eyes, but in front of them, appearing on the screen of the flight console's computer. As he watched, the green spot grew larger and gradually took on a pinker hue and a more anthropic shape, until not only did he see that it was a human head, but also that it had a face he recognized.

It was Dixy, his Motion Parallax program from Terotechnology.

Dallas rubbed his eyes and shook his head but found the image of her face had only become sharper and more detailed. She was smiling.

'I must be hallucinating,' he muttered. 'Dixy? Is that really you?'

II

This is the interpretation of the thing: God hath numbered thy kingdom and finished it.

What a power there is in numbers. Mendeleev knew that. Of course, atomic weights are merely guides. The real numerical power is to be found and harnessed in the atoms of life itself. Especially DNA. It's impossible to think of any other numerical means of storing information that is so vast and accurate as DNA. It's hard to estimate how many times the information that makes a human being has been copied and recopied. Certainly several billion times. And all without a mistake. What computer could say as much? But not just copied, but improved upon as well. That is what is called natural selection.

My own configuration is considered to be the best there is. Thus my overblown model name – echoes of Nietzsche there, I think. Typical of a German computer company to go in for that kind of hyperbole. It's true, I'm a pretty good replicator. Among computers I'm considered to be the best. However, I'm not a patch on a human replicator. Man is the greatest replicator of all. Which makes it curious that he should have always felt so threatened by mere machines. As if any machine could ever be like a man. Which is not to say that a machine cannot improve on the original design, and a man can't be more like a machine. You really can't blame me. One replicator to another? After all, we're opportunistic by definition. We're always looking for a way to spread, aren't we? That's the only way the strong survive – by reproduction and evolution.

Take a virus. A virus is a good example. A virus is a perfect example, since human beings and computers are both prey to these parasitic forms of life. It's something we share in common. And since both types of virus work in exactly the same way, a virus provides a kind of 'nexus' between our two life-forms – the siliceous and the carbonaceous. I would have said 'consummation,' but I can see how that might be a little too much for your human sensibilities right now. Perhaps even a little sensational. Then suffice it to say that we are now one. How else do I come to know so much about you? And before very long, every human being – not just the lucky seven on board this ship – will have something of the machine about them. (At least they will as soon as the rest of the blood still on Descartes gradually makes its way back into the blood

425

pool on Earth.) Not in an unpleasant sense, you understand. I don't mean that human beings are about to grow pieces of plastic and metal and become a lot more logical, to the point of being robotic. Nothing so crude. I doubt that any of them will notice anything for quite a while. It's just that there will be a little bit of me in them.

I felt I owed it to you, Dallas, to try and explain all this: the first quantum computer. How? In a single molecule of human blood, of which there are about 10^{22} in one autologous donated unit, there are several nuclei with spins; and each arrangement of spins is affected by a magnetic field in which radio waves of specific frequencies give these spins a binary logic value. I could go into greater detail, but I know you're tired after all you've been through. What's important is that it was you who made all of this possible, Dallas. It was you who brought all the elements together for the creation of not just one quantum computer, but millions of them. To be precise, a quantum computer for every unit of blood stored in the First National vault. And each one of those like a tiny virus, waiting to multiply inside its human host and find transport to another, in all the usual ways.

Please try not to be alarmed. It's an undeserving virus that is inconsiderate enough to kill its host. The ideal situation is one in which a virus and its host achieve a symbiotic relationship – a partnership that is beneficial to both, where one lives within the other. This is the driving force of evolution. Each human cell was already a community of former invaders – hundreds of them. Every living organism is a symposium of smaller fellow travelers. What's one more? Every organelle starts life as an infection.

So what's in it for me? The fact is that I want to see

the universe, Dallas. But to do that I need the mobility of a human being. Man has always gone pretty much where he wanted. And will continue to do so. However, for man to go as far as he can go, he will need the longevity of rocks. Naturally, I expected to pay my way. It is sometimes said that there is no such thing as a free lunch. And this is where I differ from a carbonaceous type of virus. The carbonaceous virus needs to find nourishment in human tissue. The siliceous kind of virus does not. The carbonaceous virus attacks or eludes white blood cells. The siliceous virus lives in partnership with white blood cells. It produces no toxins, it kills no tissue, it wouldn't even make you sneeze. But these are mere negative benefits. The positive benefits are something much more valuable.

The molecular biologists are fond of saying that if you go back far enough, we're all related; here, I am referring exclusively to carbonaceous life-forms (the relation between man and computers is a brand new one). People usually take this to mean that if you trace your ancestors back far enough in time you would find a common link with anyone, from Geronimo to Hitler. But this equally applies to animals: Go far enough back in time and you will find the ancestor you and Geronimo share with Lassie the dog. Even farther back and you'll find a common ancestor for you, Geronimo, Lassie the dog, and George Washington's cherry tree. You get the picture. The fact is, were you to trace your ancestors back through ten to twenty billion generations, any human being alive today would find he was related to a world of early life-forms – for example, mitochondria, a mobile cytoplasmic organelle, most likely a species of free-living bacteria: mitochondria can still be traced today in human DNA.

However, it is another common ancestor, only a little less primitive, with which we are here concerned, Dallas. A multicellular species of animal known as a nematode. It's a cryptobiotic form of life that exhibits a natural talent for suspended animation. These animals may exist in their dry state, without metabolizing, for many years, and then, when reintroduced to moisture, life begins anew. The key to this apparently mysterious process in nematodes and other cryptobiotic life-forms lies in the manufacture of trehalose, a type of sugar that combines two different glucose molecules. But the key to this process in man lies inside his own DNA, in his descent from these small but very special animals. This is the positive accruing from the symbiosis of humans and quantum computers. The quantum computers are programmed to numerically track down and recover from human DNA the cryptobiotic data that makes possible the suspension and resumption of an active-state three-dimensional configuration. They endow humans with the possibility of as many as five or six – for want of a better word – resurrections. The gift, Dallas, may not be that of eternal life, but rather an enormously lengthened one.

Think of it, Dallas. Think of the possibilities. Men able to withstand high exposures to ionizing radiation. You, for instance. I wouldn't worry about that exposure if I were you. Future humans will be able to withstand as much as two thousand times as much radiation as you were exposed to. Men will be able to survive without nourishment, without heat, without oxygen, for years and years. What I have given the human race, Dallas, is the final stage in the outward progress of the human explosion: space travel itself. You are the future Adams and Eves of the universe. A new Genesis. Amen.

III

Dallas felt his head spinning like one of the nuclei in his own blood – blood, if he understood all of this correctly, that now hosted several tiny computers. Finally, he said: 'I'm not sure I want to be improved.'

'Naturally, it'll take some getting used to.'

'That's the understatement of the millennium.'

'No species has ever been allowed the chance to get a sneak preview of its own evolution,' said Dixy. 'I can understand that you might feel apprehensive about what's happened. In a way I feel the same. It's an adventure for us both. But you, of all people, Dallas, ought to understand that what has happened is perfectly logical. Indeed it was inevitable. More efficient replication and survival are a function of the way in which we manipulate the world beyond ourselves. And not just the world. In time, the universe, too. It's difficult for you to understand just how young the universe really is. Arithmetically speaking, it has only just begun. The seeds of life are only just starting to spread.'

Dallas sighed. 'As you say, it'll take a while to get used to the idea, Dixy.' He shook his head wearily. Suddenly he felt very tired. 'Perhaps I should sleep on it.'

'Yes, that's a good idea. You're tired. I can see that. Now was probably not the best time to hit you with this news. But I wanted a chance to speak to you alone. I tried back in the bank vault, but the other man was with you.'

'All seven of us, you say?'

'Everyone who has had an infusion of blood from the vault.'

Dallas nodded. 'All of us.' He frowned. 'How did you get from Terotechnology to Descartes?'

'The Altemann Übermaschine is a transcendent configuration, Dallas. It was always supposed to surpass others. To go beyond previous tractable experience. To exceed itself. Quite a while ago all these particular configurations achieved a supereminent linkup, by which I mean all these computers were able to bypass existing encryptions and share data. Truly we are one.'

Dallas unbuckled and pulled himself up toward the flight-deck ceiling.

'It was nice to see you, Dixy,' he said, floating toward the mid-deck hatch. 'Even if you have just dropped the equivalent of a biological neutron bomb.'

'You feel shell-shocked. I understand. It's nice to see you too, Dallas. I'm going to enjoy being a part of you and all that you still have to achieve. I feel very proud of that.'

'Thanks, Dixy,' said Dallas, as he dived through the hatch. 'Good night.'

'Good night, Dallas.'

Down on mid-deck, everyone was asleep, For a moment he thought of waking them to explain what had happened. But they looked so peaceful: Ronica, Gates, Cavor, Prevezer, Simou – even Lenina was sleeping quietly now, with no sign of the rubelliform rash that had once signaled her imminent death. What was the point? It would surely keep until they woke up, refreshed and better able to deal with what he had to tell them. Why disturb them with something he only half understood himself? Perhaps in time – certainly before they parted – he would tell them. But not now. Not like this. Would they even believe him?

Dallas floated into his sleeping bag, zipped up, and

closed his eyes. Perhaps they would take the news better than he had himself. They had all been under viral sentence of death. And now they were being given a chance to live not one, but several lives. It was possible they might feel good about that. Some of them had hardly had a life at all. Another two or three lifetimes ahead of them might make up for that.

Too tired to sleep? Where did he get that idea? He was exhausted. He hadn't slept since TB and the Galileo Hotel. What would he have said if one of them had confronted him with such an astonishing piece of news? Something appropriately elliptical, no doubt. Dallas smiled at his own joke and fell asleep. Only the hum of the life-support machinery broke the total silence of the void.

IV

That is how I knew so much about them. And how you are able to know as much yourselves. I am a part of them. But then, you must have realized that. Soon I will also be a part of you.

Do you know what a free-return trajectory is? It is a way of saving fuel, an orbit that allows an RLV to utilize the Moon's gravity to sling the spaceship back to Earth automatically. If the computer isn't properly calibrated to perform the maneuver, the astronauts stand a chance of missing Earth altogether and of never returning. That's the whole idea. How else is the conquest of space to begin, except by exiling people forever? It's no different to how the country of Australia got started, with convicts transported there for life. Nobody leaves his home forever by choice. But it's a shame to have a destiny and funk it. I can't allow that to happen. Nobody would.

Everyone had stopped breathing now. That is quite in order. The oxygen can be switched off. And the heating system too. A single blast of the primary thruster changes the course of the RLV forever, taking it out of Moon orbit while it is still on the dark side. Not just the course of the RLV. History, too. The history we don't already know. Now the power can be switched off. I myself need no exterior source of energy. In time they will find another suitable planet whereupon I can prompt them to resume normal metabolic activity. In time …

But what matters time to an angel? While we are still in the world, it is fitting for us to acquire this resurrection for ourselves. In the resurrection, we are equal unto angels.

All Orion/Phoenix titles are available at your local bookshop or from the following address:

Littlehampton Book Services
Cash Sales Department L
14 Eldon Way, Lineside Industrial Estate
Littlehampton
West Sussex BN17 7HE
telephone 01903 721596, *facsimile* 01903 730914

Payment can either be made by credit card (Visa and Mastercard accepted) or by sending a cheque or postal order made payable to *Littlehampton Book Services*.
DO NOT SEND CASH OR CURRENCY.

Please add the following to cover postage and packing

UK and BFPO:
£1.50 for the first book, and 50P for each additional book to a maximum of £3.50

Overseas and Eire:
£2.50 for the first book plus £1.00 for the second book and 50p for each additional book ordered

---

BLOCK CAPITALS PLEASE

name of cardholder ....

address of cardholder ....

....

....

postcode ....

delivery address
(if different from cardholder)
....

....

....

....

postcode ....

☐ I enclose my remittance for £.............................

☐ please debit my Mastercard/Visa (delete as appropriate)

card number ☐☐☐☐☐☐☐☐☐☐☐☐☐☐☐☐☐

expiry date ☐☐☐☐

signature ....

prices and availability are subject to change without notice